םּבּלאֿרֿבֿוֿרּֿי

THE BRAZEN WOMAN
A NOVEL
BY ANNE GROSS

טֿ ֹ;צֿלֿתֿיֿצ

THE BRAZEN WOMAN

A NOVEL

BY ANNE GROSS

BEAUFORT
BOOKS

Library of Congress Cataloging-in-Publication Data available upon request

For inquiries about orders, please contact:
Beaufort Books
27 West 20th Street, 11th Floor
New York, NY 10011

Published in the United States by Beaufort Books
www.beaufortbooks.com

Distributed by Midpoint Trade Books
www.midpointtrade.com

Printed in the United States of America

Gross, Anne
The Brazen Woman
ISBN:
Paperback: 9780825308802
eBook: 9780825307683

Design by Michael Short

TABLE OF CONTENTS

I   THE BEST *SAUCISSON* IN PARIS   I

II   SINK OR SWIM 22

III   ADELAIDE IS HUNGRY 34

IV   THOMAS NEEDS A TOKE 51

V   ON YOUR MARKS 69

VI   PUKING 90

VII   ENGLISH LESSONS 109

VIII   BROADSIDES 129

IX   WATCH OUT FOR VAPORS 147

X   A MAN'S A MAN 162

XI   PEOPLE CAN'T FLY 182

XII   ENDLESS PILES OF LAUNDRY 197

XIII   CALÓ FLAMENCO 213

XIV   THE ARMY MARCHES 227

XV   ROLIÇA 247

XVI   HIDING IN THE BUSHES 264

XVII   THE NEW MOON 279

THE BEST
SAUCISSON
IN PARIS

Adelaide Lenormand winced at the mangled vowels of her native French that came from the older English woman's mouth. It was impossible to look Mrs. Southill in the eyes as she spoke, since her lips worked in curious contortions around the words—extending from the toothless gums, puckering and wrinkling under the nose, and spreading her mouth wide at the corners. Again, Adelaide wished she'd had the foresight to learn English. It would be much more tolerable for her to speak English than to have to listen to the destruction of the delicate tones of her own language.

It was nearly one full week since she'd set out to retrieve the golem from the Quiet Woman, a public house in one of the seedier corners of London. If all had gone as planned, she and the golem would, just now, be stepping over the threshold of her beloved home in Paris, the emerald scarab would be in the Emperor Napoleon's hands, and all would have been set to rights. Alas, nothing happened as anticipated, despite having consulted the cards and studied the stars. There is no accounting for the whims of the young no matter what the spread of the cards tells you, and the golem was young, not quite three months old, manifested by Adelaide's own conjuring.

A pang of worry overtook her as she thought of the golem all alone in the world, confused and likely terrified. The young should be sheltered and directed, not left to their own devices. And yet, the golem had not exhibited any signs of youthful innocence upon entering the world to stand as Napoleon's metaphysical assistant in all matters. On the contrary, the first thing it had done was steal the emperor's emerald and disappear in a cloud of profanity.

No one but a mother would understand the pain of discovering the squandered talents of a promising child. Adelaide had been languishing in a women's prison in Paris when she'd learned that the creature was emptying chamber pots and sweeping floors in a pub, and the agony of this information had compelled her to break free and travel to London.

But instead of finding her progeny, it was her former mentor, Dodeauvie, whom she found waiting for her in the Quiet Woman's dining hall. She and Dodo had only time for one single dinner—a meal of questionable quality, it should be mentioned—before they were attacked.

For Adelaide, the bruises she'd received from the filthy ruffians in the pub were few: a black eye from the back of a hand, a ring of blue and green around her upper arm where someone had twisted it, a deep violet and yellow spot on her hip from a swift kick. All of these marks were slowly fading away. But Dodeauvie, poor Dodo, had been beaten unmercifully. He wasn't recovering as she'd like. Something was wrong, and she hoped Mrs. Southill would be able to help. The old woman might even be able to direct her to the golem, if only Adelaide could understand the woman's brutally masticated French.

Yes, the French word for "time" had a "p" on the end of it, but that didn't give one the right to pronounce it. Having to hear Mrs. Southill's dreadful hissing with every plural noun made her stop listening altogether. "*Pardon?*" asked Adelaide.

"What?"

"What did you say?"

"When?"

"Never mind."

Mrs. Southill gave Adelaide an exasperated look and waddled away to a small campfire to give her steaming cauldron, hung on an iron tripod, a quick stir. The smell from whatever was inside the brew combined with the smell of the suspiciously smoking fire. Adelaide tried not to breathe it in as the fumes swirled around the forest clearing that served as Mrs. Southill's yard. London's fetid vapors filtered in through thickly interlaced branches, weakening the sunlight. The old woman had enchanted the forest to keep out the population spread of London, but whatever magic was strengthening the trees could not keep out the stench of the nearby city. To compensate, a low wall of stones encircling the clearing constricted like an overly protective embrace. The entire effect made Adelaide nervous. Sweat beaded between her breasts and dampened the divination cards she kept under her corset.

She imagined Mrs. Southill spending all her time picking tree bark off sticks, gathering grubs, frogs, and shriveled mushrooms. What an existence. What a travesty. She wished she hadn't needed to pay the woman a visit. "I trust you've been well?" Adelaide politely called across the clearing. Mrs. Southill grunted in response, like the toad she resembled.

Adelaide tried again. "Have you had any news from *la Société*?"

"*Non. Pas de nouvelles.*" No news. This time Adelaide didn't have to see the woman's mouth to visualize her long tongue distastefully rolling over the double "ell"s. The "ess" sound slid into the steam as Mrs. Southill leaned over her cauldron.

Every topic of conversation Adelaide could think of that was polite and neutral had been broached, although with Mrs. Southill, the list wasn't long. After enquiring about the health of mutual acquaintances and mentioning the beautiful weather (at which point the old woman looked sardonically at a particularly grim cloud that curled like a veil into the clearing), Adelaide was left with nothing more to talk about. She followed Mrs. Southill as she went about her business of sweeping the hard-packed earth in front of her hovel, gathering herbs into small bundles to hang to dry, and stirring whatever monstrous concoction that was bubbling. For an old crone, the woman moved fast, and Adelaide had to walk lively to keep up. Her prattle took on a breathless quality, as a result, that sounded annoying even to herself. "Please forgive my intrusion. I can see that you're very busy arranging those rodent bones, so I'll get straight to my point."

"The sooner the better," said Mrs. Southill as she carefully placed hunks of quartz in the eye sockets of three rat skulls. She then snatched at the air, slowly opened her hand, and shook her head in disappointment.

"It's about Dodeauvie, you see. Do you remember my old mentor? He's been hurt." Adelaide pictured Dodo lying broken in his room back at the Dancing Bear, and took a bracing breath. She was here for him. She would see this through. "I've reason to believe he may have suffered internal damage. I'm not sure he can survive much longer if you do not help me."

"I cannot help him if I cannot see him, and I won't see him if he doesn't come to me. And if he's too weak to walk, he's too weak to be helped. So, my advice is to say your goodbyes."

"Have you any woundwort? Perhaps a little valerian root and willow bark?"

"It's all right there! Go get it yourself." Mrs. Southill gestured towards the forest. "You didn't have to come all the way here for your poor mentor. Those plants are common enough anywhere along the Thames. Or is it that you do not deign to pick weeds by the roadside, so you leave it to someone like me?"

"You know as well as I that one must prepare the herbs before applying them. I've no time and none of the equipment to prepare them. You must have tinctures, salves. I'm afraid I cannot pay, but—"

"*La Société* was wrong to raise you in its ranks," Mrs. Southill scoffed. "You have gifts, that is true, but wisdom is not one of them."

"Do not talk to me of *la Société*. You have all underestimated me. Worse. *La Société* has abandoned me." Adelaide tried not to glare as the tiny, bent woman smiled derisively. "I've begged for their help, but they remain silent. Now I no longer care. I no longer need them. I did their dirty work and they do nothing but sit back and watch. You know, not just anyone can call forth a golem," she said haughtily. "They would do well to show more appreciation."

The old woman's smile grew broader. "Appreciation? You do not feel *la Société* has enough regard for your skills?" She moved to a rickety trestle table, grunting again and clutching her wide hip as she bent to sit. The campfire flared up and her stirring stick, of its own accord, rolled around the lip of the iron cauldron before sliding deeper inside, out of view. "Come," she said, "come and sit with me. Let me show you the extent of my regard."

Adelaide sat, but didn't take her eyes from the woman's hands— hands that could easily stir up trouble. "Now," Mrs. Southill said, pushing aside a large basket of acorns waiting to be hulled, "tell me: why do you think *la Société* doesn't wish your continued success?"

"Is it not obvious? They've withdrawn their support. I've not heard a single thing from them since the conjuring."

"The conjuring? What conjuring?"

"The golem!" Adelaide said, her annoyance increasing.

"Oh yes. That."

Adelaide bristled. "Yes, that. *That!* It is no small feat to bring forth such a creature. My entire life has been a preparation for such an accomplishment. And you, *you* have the gall to dismiss this? To wave your hand in the air as though it was nothing? What have you ever done but collect weeds?"

Mrs. Southill suddenly clapped her hands in the air. "What do you think I've caught?" she asked breathlessly.

"Caught? I have no idea. A fly?" Adelaide felt the skin under her left eye twitch. She hadn't the time for games.

Slowly Mrs. Southill opened her hands. "No. There's nothing. I just don't understand why it can't be caught," she mused sadly.

"What was it you were hoping for?"

"I was hoping to catch light."

"Light?" Adelaide put up her hand to stop the old woman before she could explain. "Please, Madame. Have you what I've asked for? I would like to return to Dodeauvie before nightfall. He is in great need."

"What was it he needed? I've already forgotten."

"Woundwort, and willow bark," Adelaide said coldly, "and valerian, if you have it."

"Right. Herbs then. From a collector of weeds." The woman's eyes narrowed, but the smile remained on her face. She made no move to retrieve the tinctures Adelaide asked for.

"Please, Madame." Adelaide sighed.

"Please what?"

"The herbs."

"I've told you already, they're just there in the forest. You are welcome to them, as is everyone in England." Mrs. Southill leaned towards Adelaide, her stooped shoulders straightened intimidatingly. "Or is it that you value my knowledge far more than you are willing to admit? You're hoping I might suggest a cure, are you not? Oh, I like *that*: call me a weed collector one minute, then hold your hand out for a gift the next." Mrs. Southill took Adelaide's hands into her own. Her skin was cool and roughened from years of plucking the tough stems of English country flowers. "The very fact that you denigrate my skills says much about the company you keep. You've traded your womanhood for a power of a different sort—one that doesn't suit you very well. Dodeauville, Zenours, these men gave you nothing but the tools to manipulate others. Remember your roots. Take up your creative handiwork again. You used to make such beautiful lace. That is where your power lies."

"Lace?" Adelaide drew her shoulders back and sat up tall on the uncomfortable wooden bench, pulling her hands out of Mrs. Southill's grip. "You must be joking. My power, my knowledge goes beyond embroidering lace violets or assembling a *bouquet garni* for the soup. How can you ask me to return to lacemaking? It's absurd."

"If you say so," sighed the crone. She pushed herself up off the bench and winced when her joints audibly popped back into alignment.

"The golem was here, as your guest. You said so yourself in your letter. Please explain to me why you didn't capture the golem while you had the chance?"

"That was not the plan. Miss Elsie Duboysie was doing quite well where she was."

"Whose plan?"

"Whose do you think?"

"*La Société*? Then why was I not told?" Adelaide exploded.

Mrs. Southill smiled sympathetically and changed the subject. "I have no cures for those who may be slowly bleeding to death on the inside. Perhaps the woundwort will help. I'll get it for you, but only if you'll have a cup of tea with me. It is not every day that I see an esteemed member of *la Société* in the flesh." She shuffled back to the little campfire and ladled the contents of the iron cauldron into two pewter mugs. "I'm dreadfully sorry," she said, returning to the table. "I've no sugar to sweeten the brew."

Despite the warm weather, Adelaide wrapped both her hands around her mug, which she recognized as a mug from the Quiet Woman. The steam smelled pleasantly spiced yet she peered into the swirling liquid with suspicion. In her letter, Mrs. Southill had mentioned that the golem had been brought to her by a dangerous young man. Could it be that the shriveled Mrs. Southill was friendly with the same barman who had so unmercifully attacked Dodo? She must patronize the pub if she kept the mugs, Adelaide reasoned. She stole a glance at the crone and saw that the silly woman was enraptured by her own brew, licking the corners of her wide mouth. No, it seemed unlikely that the man with the blue wolf-eyes and terrifying scars would align himself with such a toad.

The scented steam that rose made Adelaide think of grain mash in ale and the sour flavor of yeast, of root cellars, and the black loam of a freshly tilled field. Hints of anise and lavender caused her to sigh and sink her shoulders. The pain of the difficult summer began to melt away with the aromatic odor. "Thank you," she said for the first time since entering Mrs. Southill's clearing.

They sat in silence while they sipped the brew. Adelaide had to admit, tea was one thing she could appreciate about the English. It wasn't bracing, like coffee. It was cleansing. She closed her eyes and began to feel her anxieties melt away. As the hot brew cooled, the sensitive areas of her tongue, behind her molars and down the length of her throat, long unused to that particular herbal tang, were suddenly aroused. Adelaide looked up in surprise as her ears warmed and her eyesight narrowed. "Valerian? So you *do* have valerian root?"

"Of course I do. I added only a little to your tea. You seem so anxious."

"And wormwood? Did you put wormwood in my tea?"

"A little more," she smiled devilishly. "It's a mere weed collector's concoction. There's no need for alarm." She fixed Adelaide with her gaze, and her pruned gray eyes began to grow larger while her irises grew wider and blacker. Slowly, the crone's orbs merged into one great eye which loomed over her greasy nose. Adelaide, knowing what was about to come next, consciously slowed her breathing, in through her nose, out through pursed lips, feeling the air as it entered and exited, attempting to control the visions. Valerian, wormwood, and, quite likely, ergot—she didn't have time for this, she thought irritably.

"Don't fight it; enjoy it," Mrs. Southill said. Her one eye blinked. "Come now, when was the last time you've danced with the stars?"

It had been a long time, thought Adelaide. In the days before the Revolution in the small French town of Alençon where she'd been apprenticed to a milliner, everything had been different. The world had been simpler. In the evenings when the town quieted after dinner and curtains were drawn, the women gathered, daughters and mothers, sisters all, would set aside their needlework to brew the tea. She thought wistfully of her old friends. They'd become her family when the convent school turned her out.

She'd been forced to leave Alençon when the fever of the Revolution spread through town. Many of the artisans who made their living making and selling lace had been guillotined for their part in elevating the noble classes with the finery, and she herself had barely escaped the slaughter. Adelaide had left with nothing but the clothes on her back, and a letter of introduction tucked within the pages of her grimoire. In Paris, she'd offered the letter to Zenours with youthful confidence. It had been Zenours who had introduced her to Dodo, and all the other adepts in his circle of influence at his *atelier*. Zenours educated her, honed her skills, but he never believed in the power of a skillfully prepared herbal brew. He preferred to fill her head with books rather than fill her stomach with potions.

"I find it is so much easier to slip sideways out of my old body with a little tea," Mrs. Southill was saying with a faraway smile. "Let us go speak with the others, shall we? Take my hand."

"I won't."

"Why ever not?" Mrs. Southill rose from the table and hovered, waiting.

"What have I to say to any of them? I've no time for this. I must return to Dodo." Despite her misgivings, Adelaide felt her spirit slide from its encasing flesh.

There, see? Mrs. Southill clapped her hands like an excited schoolgirl. *You're much more amusing when you stop grinding your teeth. Let's go.* She grasped Adelaide's hand and together they left the clearing to the black void where time was suspended and souls were indistinguishable from thoughts.

It didn't take long for the others to join them. Adelaide hadn't planned on the meeting, but apparently the meeting of *la Société* had been planned all the same. She didn't wonder how the women knew she'd be seeking the help of Mrs. Southill at that exact time. Why wouldn't they know? Once again she was given a stark reminder of the feminine well of power that could slake her thirst should she deign to drink from it, and was chastened by the realization of how much she still had to learn.

The inevitable tut-tutting from the older women made Adelaide grit her teeth again. *Oh, my poor dear,* cried Madame Griffe. *Your aura is the most putrid color. You are not well. Does she not look unwell?*

It's the dreadful English weather, grumbled Madame Thierreau.

There's nothing wrong with English weather, Mrs. Southill protested.

Then it's the cuisine, Madame Thierreau insisted.

I've found a tea made from the flowers of fennel; taken every day will keep a woman strong, said Mademoiselle Hachette.

No, she needs not tea, countered Madame Thierreau. *She must return to Paris at once, for her health.*

I cannot return, Adelaide said. *I would be arrested the second I set foot on French soil.*

More and more women were arriving and the tittering grew ever louder as the state of Adelaide's health was debated. They came from all over the continent and Great Britain, until nearly fifty sorceress spirits were floating about in the black void, representing the most powerful Western women. The women of France, with the most radical minds and libertine notions, and from whom the movement started, were most numerous among them and took the leading roles.

Mademoiselle Lenormand speaks the truth, a loud voice said imperiously. All activity stopped as Mademoiselle DuBette raised her arms to silence the crowd, her shade shimmering in a call for attention. *She cannot return to Paris. Napoleon is furious. He is redoubling his efforts to find her and his lost gemstone.*

Adelaide felt anger bubbling up inside her. For weeks she'd been chasing the golem, first on the astral plane where they were now meeting, reaching towards the creature who was tied to her through the thin line that attached creator to created, then later, by land and over sea, and all the while knowing she herself was being chased by the Emperor's *Ministre de la police,* Fouché. She was so, so tired of all the running. Now the witches gather? Now was too late. The golem had set sail for America and, as a result, Adelaide would never be able to return to Paris without risking imprisonment. *Where was all this concern for me when I first begged for support?* she cried. *Your concern no longer matters. The golem is gone.*

You don't honestly believe that we've been sitting back doing nothing, do you? Mlle DuBette asked. *I suppose you think you've been doing all the heavy lifting while we've been exchanging the latest recipes?*

Then give me some news I can use. Tell me la Société's *plan for retrieving the golem.* It was hard not to cringe when fifty witches brought together from all over Europe smiled smugly.

The golem? No, the golem is in play. It is the emerald scarab we want. The scarab is the key.

In play? Adelaide shook her head, not understanding.

Yes, dear. The golem is everything Napoleon deserves, and he will have her, in one way or another. But only after you've taken possession of the scarab. He must not take the scarab.

I don't understand, you wished me to bring forth the golem to remain at the emperor's side, did you not? If I can secure the golem, and return the stolen scarab, all will be set to rights. I have spent some time with Bonaparte and he is not the enemy we once thought him to be, Adelaide said. She didn't like to think of her short-lived tryst with Napoleon while she stayed at *Malmaison* in the employ of his wife. However, her skills had been useful in gathering information. *He truly wishes all people to regard each other as equals. His push into Spain was necessary to quell the unrest.*

The black void flared red with outrage, and the eerie sound of a rolled minor chord from a distant guitar was heard. *Afrancesados!* cried a voice from somewhere in the middle of the crowd. *We will remember* Dos de Mayo. *It is burned onto the hearts of all Spaniards.*

Bonaparte has easily taken Portugal. Adelaide argued. *The Portuguese themselves wish for French occupation. Spain, too, will thank Bonaparte for saving them from Bourbon rule. He is, at heart, an egalitarian.*

Mademoiselle DuBette sucked in a breath as though a stiff breeze had blown up her skirts. *Egalitarian? Truly? The man who crowned himself Emperor is an egalitarian?* DuBette laughed. *No, you are wrong. He is a despot. Have you forgotten how he removed Olympe de Gouges's head from her neck for daring to ask that the rights of women be included in the Declaration? Egalitarian indeed!*

Bonaparte had nothing to do with the death of Olympe, cried Adelaide. *She was a Royalist! A* Girondin*! It was the revolution that killed her.*

And what has he done to right that wrong? Nothing. He's done nothing but spit in the eye of Woman since he dared to place the crown upon his own brow. Have you not had enough of this, Adelaide? Have you not had enough? They will never accept us into their ranks. They will never extend a hand to pull you up to sit at their sides, no matter how you strive for your voice to be heard. It will not happen until we force it to happen.

The use of her Christian name was a deliberate breach of formality made to draw her back into the fold. Adelaide knew this to be an attempt to manipulate her, but was no less taken by the tactic. She felt like crumpling into the woman's arms and allowing herself the mothering she knew she'd receive. She was so tired, so disappointed in having lost the golem, so worried about the continued deterioration of Dodo's battered body. But she dared not give in to her fears and exhaustion. She did not doubt that, should she allow them to minister to her, the women's attentions would be genuinely given. However, any show of weakness would remove her from ever being seriously considered for any roles of import. So instead, she set her teeth and questioned further. *If the scarab is central to the cause, why did not Mrs. Southill take it when she had the golem in her hands?* Adelaide glared at the old English crone.

Miss Elsie Duboysie didn't have the emerald. Mrs. Southill said simply.

Mrs. Southill's task was to assess the golem—Miss Elise Dubois, as it prefers to call itself—and set it on its path, which she did, Mademoiselle DuBette said. *Your task has always been to create the golem and retrieve the emerald, which you haven't done. This was a task you might have completed had you not let Dodeauvie back into your life. No, no,* DuBette put up a hand when Adelaide filled her lungs to protest. *You needn't deny it. Your mentor yearned to own the power of the emerald for himself, and your misguided desire for acceptance would have let him have it. I say once again: leave the golem be. Your concern is now with the emerald scarab.*

Yes, but the emerald is with the golem, Adelaide said with a stamp of her foot. *And anyway, it is too late. How am I to retrieve the emerald when it's already half-way to America? You must send me money—I've run out. All of you send money and I can buy passage to follow the golem.*

There's no time to waste. You cannot wait for money to arrive or you'll never find the golem again. You should have taken the emerald while the golem was still here, but it's useless to cry over spilled milk. You'll just have to retrieve the emerald elsewhere.

Don't look at me, snorted Mrs. Southill when Adelaide turned to her beseechingly. *Do I look like I have money to give you?*

I don't understand. How can anyone expect me to get to America without money?

Use your wits, Woman, cried Mrs. Southill. *You're the youngest amongst us. How do young women get anything these days? Wiles and wits!*

But what about Dodo? He's in no condition to travel.

Mademoiselle DuBette took a breath and again her aura flickered red before fading back to her lovely, normal azure. The wrinkles around her mouth deepened as she paused to consider her words. *Dodeauvie has, as you well know, a modest amount of power, and a slightly larger amount of esoteric education; however. . .and I hesitate to say this considering your attachment. . .he has more ambition than talent. In the normal world, ambition is the worthier trait, but in the world in which you and I live, the world of magic, ambition without talent merely makes one a charlatan. It would be entirely different if he were a charlatan and sympathetic to our cause. However, he is a charlatan and antagonistic. Thus. . .* She waved her hand in dismissive circles, letting her sentence trail off. *At any rate, I do not foresee you traveling with Dodeauvie. He has not the strength for it, so you will go alone. We will try to protect the outcome of your quest.*

The outcome of the quest. Adelaide repeated wryly. *What about Dodo's outcome? What about my outcome?*

Your path lies directly within your own control. You may, of course, decide to forget about all this entirely. In which case, I suggest you study the English language and return to learning your herbs. I am sure there is plenty of room in the London outskirts for you to have your very own forest clearing. Mrs. Southill has been satisfied with her own position.

Adelaide looked sidelong at Mrs. Southill, who nodded and winked at her with her one twinkling eye. They all knew there was no chance she'd ever accept a fate less than what she once had in Paris. It was fine for Southill—retreating to solitude had been her choice—but Adelaide could never retreat. France was her body and Paris was her soul. She belonged there, and would do whatever it took to return.

Good, Mademoiselle DuBette nodded when she saw Adelaide straighten her shoulders in resolve. *I know you worry for the safety of your progeny, but rest assured the golem has a protector.*

Oh yes. He's a sweet boy, said Mrs. Southill. *Quite loyal.*

Do you mean Mr. Ferrington? Adelaide thought of the frightful day when the golem's marriage had taken place, the same day as the beating she and Dodo had received at the hands of the men in Mr. Ferrington's pub. She'd learned of the union only after they'd been ousted from the Quiet Woman.

Ferrington? DuBette frowned in confusion. *I thought the lad's name had been changed to MacEwan?*

No, no. I'm quite sure the husband's name is Richard Ferrington, corrected Adelaide.

Husband? DuBette's mouth dropped open in surprise. She looked sharply at Mrs. Southill who hummed nervously to herself.

I'm surprised you haven't heard. Everyone was talking about the wealthy publican who married his chambermaid. Adelaide paused and frowned. *He is to be the golem's protector? He didn't seem like the protective type,* she mused.

The situation is not as dire as it sounds, Mrs. Southill soothed as DuBette's aura flared.

Not dire? How can the golem act independently when she's married? This is most distressing. She cannot be the foil we had hoped for if she's tied to another in matrimony. You have mismanaged this, madame. I am disappointed.

You underestimate the power we created, Mrs. Southill said, eye flashing. *This golem is exactly what we'd hoped for and more. Let the situation play out. My Tommy is with her. He'll do his part, bless him. I sense that a rift between them has occurred, but he's still lurking about like the black wolf that he is. The powers of Isis have their own ways of ensuring success—who are we to question?*

I have never been the type to sit back and let things happen without direction. I am not a fatalist. None of us are—we have all learned to draw down the powers to control them ourselves. The other sorceresses made noises in solidarity with DuBette.

Excuse me? Wolf? The word caused Adelaide to recall the man with a snarling mouth and eyes that pierced. *Then, you are referring to the barman at the Quiet Woman Pub, are you not? He is the one who beat Dodo to within an inch of his life. That beast is to be the golem's protector?*

That beast is Olympe's son. He was chosen long ago, replied Mrs. Southill. *I did warn you in my letter to be wary. The fault is your own if you tested him.*

Olympe's son? Olympe de Gouges? Adelaide was floored. *I know of no son but Pierre, and he lives in Paris. I heard he is the proprietor of a* charcuterie *near the Pont Neuf.*

Yes, yes. Monsieur Pierre de Gouges is a fine man, Madame Thierreau trilled. *Have you been to his shop? His* saucissons secs *are quite delicious— he makes one with hazelnuts which adds a surprisingly wonderful crunch to the pork mixture. Next time you are in Paris you must go see him. Ask for the* saucisson *with the hazelnuts."*

I'm sure it is not he who created that recipe, another sorceress interrupted. *He married the daughter of Madame Gaurant, who, as you'll surely remember, is a very clever kitchen witch.*

Madame Gaurant is an idiot, cried Madame Griffe. *Hazelnuts in* saucisson? *Can you imagine? Any child of Olympe de Gouges would never put hazelnuts in a* saucisson, *Olympe would have found it below her, common. Pierre was always such a disappointment.*

Common? Mrs. Southill cried. *You fool! You snob! If we discount the validity of plants because of their common nature we remove the majority of our tools.*

Madame Southill thinks curing sausage can cure people, laughed Madame Thierreau.

Why not? spat Mrs. Southill. *A good healer uses anything at her disposal. Madame Gaurant is wise enough to know this, even if she is a mere kitchen witch. I'm surprised you don't.*

Please, calmed DuBette. *Please stop your squabble. Many of us have made sacrifices to assemble today. I've had enough talk of* saucisson. *Monsieur de Gouges is a good man, and a wonderful assembler of sausages. However, he is not the man we chose to protect the golem. Olympe de Gouges had another son after her marriage failed. This boy, likely due to a superior sire, had the gifts that his older brother failed to inherit. When Olympe began to beat her drum for the equality of women, she asked that her youngest son be sent away in order for her to put all the strength of her concentration to the task. Young Thomas was sent to London to be raised by our Mrs. Southill. It was a fortuitous decision as he needed the protection of anonymity after*

Olympe was beheaded. Not even he knows his true parentage. He is indeed the young wolf you encountered at the Quiet Woman. We placed the golem near him in the hopes he would pull her into his pack and look over her. He did not disappoint.

Adelaide thought of the barman's hands. His fists had glowed each time they'd landed, like cool breath on red embers. Olympe de Gouges's son had indeed inherited her strength, but a tamed wolf was not a dog. A tamed wolf was still a wolf. The thought made her uneasy. Without realizing she was doing so, she reached out for the golem on the edge of her consciousness, but felt nothing but the faintest flutter of a presence. *I don't understand. Why did you not tell me all this before? You could have saved me much trouble.*

Your dalliance with Zenours's atelier as well as your attachment to Dodeauvie places you in an awkward position with regards to the bylaws and mission of la Société, said DuBette. *We did not know how far we could trust you. You are being tested, young Adelaide. Your position in Paris as the city's premier fortune-teller is compromised, however you may be able to return to prominence should we find you worthy.*

Zenours is dead, she continued. *Dodeauvie, if he survives, will never be the man he once was. The magicians with whom you've aligned yourself are falling away. It is time to return to your real family. It is time to return to the women who first placed your feet upon the Path. We will be watching to see that you do.*

I must protest! I have never strayed from the Path. I've given up my entire life to study it! cried Adelaide.

You veered towards the masculine, thinking it was worthier. You deny your femininity in order to receive a nod from men who spend their time with their noses in books. Studying it isn't enough. Our strength comes from doing, touching, creating. It doesn't come from gathering knowledge for the sake of knowledge, as though knowledge was gold. Anyone can read books and pontificate. We create the books. We go beyond books.

Zenours was a powerful alchemist, Adelaide insisted.

No, he wasn't. He was merely a gatherer of knowledge. He wasn't a creator.

You cannot create unless you understand what it is you're creating.

DuBette's lips became pinched as she paused to consider Adelaide's words. *You hold the man in high esteem, and I am sorry for his loss in your life. He may have taught you much that you would not have learned had you stayed on the more traditional path for our sex in Alençon. However, your pride blinds you to the vast gaps in your knowledge. You are like a book with no binding in a strong wind. Why do you think we convene? What do you think is our purpose? Have you not been listening? Have you not been paying attention? Alchemy is a practical art. The texts show us how it is done.*

Practical? It is a language of symbols, a philosophy. No one has ever made gold from lead, scoffed Adelaide. *Certainly not one of you.*

What do you mean, 'certainly?' You say that as if we women would be the last people to do so. Aren't you ashamed? Let me ask you something, Adelaide. What is it that gives a man power?

Strength, Adelaide replied without hesitation.

No. You are wrong. Wealth gives men power. The weakest worm will have all the power if given enough wealth. Men control nations because men control the coffers. Not armies, and not intelligence, but wealth and commerce. The world revolves around the economy and the economy revolves around gold. Control the gold and you control the world. It's really quite simple.

Yes, but we have no gold.

Really, Adelaide. Try to follow along. What is alchemy but a collection of recipes? Did Zenours tell you of the Book of Thoth?

Of course. It was the greatest alchemical treatise known to mankind, carved on tablets of pure emerald. They've been lost to us for generations.

True. DuBette *nodded. The tablets themselves are gone, but before they were lost two copies had been made in hopes that future generations would decipher the Egyptian hieroglyphs and reveal the alchemical recipes.* La Société *has one copy and Bonaparte has the other.*

The hieroglyphs are indecipherable, scoffed Adelaide. *Everyone knows that.*

To be honest, we thought much the same. Our efforts to translate the Book had been a mere academic exercise, an amusing trifle to occupy us on those rare days when spare time was found. Then we heard that the scarab had been found.

The Emperor's scarab? What does the emerald scarab have to do with any of this?

It is said that one of the great tablets had a large missing piece. A corner had been deliberately chipped off to obscure the most important of all Thoth's recipes. It was carved into a cabochon to be set into a pair of golden wings.

Oh, breathed Adelaide, suddenly understanding. *The Philosopher's Stone. The emerald scarab is the Philosopher's Stone!*

Dubette made an irritated gesture downplaying Adelaide's revelation. *Yes, well, in a sense I suppose it is. In any case, as you might imagine, everyone has redoubled their efforts to learn the meanings of the Egyptian hieroglyphs. But that isn't enough. We must also have the scarab.*

Rest assured, Bonaparte, too, wants his jewel. He knows full well its importance. So you must find it, Adelaide, before the Emperor does. If you fail, you will never be able to return to your beloved city of Paris. You will never be able to rise to the full height of your power and the voices of women will fall upon deaf ears for generations.

Why me?

Aren't you the smartest one of us? Mrs. Southill teased.

We're just silly healers with our silly, stupid weeds! laughed Madame Griffe. *We couldn't possibly take on such responsibility.*

Of course we couldn't, cried another witch. *We need a* philosopher *for the job.*

Enough! Madame DuBette snapped. *This conference is over. Let us remember to light candles for our Spanish and Portuguese sisters before we leave. They have endured much, and I am afraid the bloodshed in their countries will not soon be over.*

There was a flare of sympathizing warm colors in the midst of the crowd. Then, one by one, the women followed the draw of their flesh.

When Adelaide returned to her body, her mood was not buoyed by her sore left cheek where her hipbone pinched her flesh against the hard wooden bench. Peevishly she looked across the table at Mrs. Southill, whose one great eye gazed at nothing at all in front of her. Adelaide reached over and tapped her face. "Come back, you old bat."

The eye blinked in surprise, then narrowed as slowly Mrs. Southill returned from between the folds of the universes. Adelaide jumped in alarm when the old woman snatched at the air between them. Peering between her fingers into her cupped hands, Mrs. Southill sighed in disappointment. "Still nothing," she said. "It's all so elusive."

Sink or Swim

Mrs. Richard Ferrington, *née* Elise Dubois, leaned against the rail of the ship and stared out across the cold, gray water towards the cold, gray shore lined with cold, gray rocks. She shivered and pulled her husband's army issued wool blanket tighter around her shoulders. She'd heard that they'd ship out just as soon as the weather changed and could safely leave Ireland, but it didn't seem as though the weather would change any time soon. HMS *Valiant* had been anchored for weeks in the harbor. Elise shook her head in disbelief: could it really have been weeks? Maybe it was just days. It was hard to keep track.

Every day was the same. In the mornings, the fog crept out over the water, dragging its skirts over the green hills of Ireland's Cork; in the evenings, it slowly returned to the sea. In between morning and evening was nothing more than a long slog of dreary, wet boredom. She'd been told it would be much worse out in the Celtic Sea, but it was hard to imagine anything more awful than being stuck on a ship—essentially an overcrowded island. Despite nearly a thousand soldiers, officers and sailors on the *Valiant,* one ship in an entire fleet of troopships carrying similar numbers of souls, Elise felt thoroughly alone. The sea itself was her companion. Its lap, lap, lapping on the hull was like the sound of a chatty friend helpfully carrying the conversation.

Once, after a long sleepless night, she'd stumbled up on deck just before dawn. Nature's anticipatory hush before daylight didn't last long—honking geese passing low over the water, the tips of their wings slapping the surface as they rose to follow the fog in "v" formation, shattered the peace—but for five eternal seconds Elise felt her entire body had been hollowed out by silence. As the world woke, the low tide whispered in the roundest tones. The slanted light, muted by the ever present Irish clouds, bounced off the still water, creating a checkerboard of gray and grayer squares delineated by crossing lines of foam. The lines stretched from one end of the horizon to the other, trapping floating vegetation. It made her almost believe there was enough magic in the world to find a way back through time to her home in the twenty-first century.

During the day, no one was allowed to disembark except for the 95th Rifle Regiment. She could hear the crack of their guns across the harbor as they practiced skirmishing in the grassy hills. Every day they were rowed ashore, and every evening they'd come back with the fog, stars in their eyes and grins on their faces. Only the riflemen were allowed to fill their lungs with the air of exertion, stretch their legs, parade, joust, and imagine themselves as heroes of war. The resentment Elise felt towards them made her gut hurt.

The regular infantrymen were forced to stay onboard. They lounged in boredom, played cards, and drank with the local women who rowed to the ship and were hauled over the rail. Harbor discipline was lax. Most of the officers had taken rooms in Cork, and the ones left onboard turned a blind eye to the shenanigans happening in the deeper decks of the ship. There was a "don't ask; don't tell; don't even trip over it" policy that everyone profited from.

Most of the men had been pressed into service under disturbing circumstances, but for this small moment of time their bodies and souls had been returned to them. They used the freedom to dance to the beat of drums and fifes. What thoughts they had of the future were for the glory of battle which, naturally, led to thoughts of their death and served only to fuel their desire to drink as much as they could while they were still breathing. As a result, the only sober ones on board were the sailors on watch, forced into mental clarity by the threat of the lash, and Thomas, who lurked nearby.

Elise had grown used to smelling Thomas's pipe at odd times during the day. Even as her own nicotine addiction welcomed the spicy odor, the unwelcome reminder of him made her stomach clench with anger. No one at the Quiet Woman public house had said anything about the split lip he'd given her. They'd looked past the bruise like it didn't exist. For Elise, however, the shame of Thomas's backhand lingered, like an unearned intimacy. Just the thought of it burned, even though the actual wound was healed. They had barely spoken two words to each other in the weeks after that horrible night when she told him she was from the future, so she was surprised when he'd vouched for her nursing skills by displaying the long line of neat sutures she'd sewn in his side, winning her a place in the ranks and a chance to get back to the States.

Except, despite marrying Thomas's employer for the privilege, they weren't going to the States. She was convinced that if she could just stand in the exact spot in Tucson, Arizona where she fell through time, she'd find a way to return to the 21st Century. But apparently Napoleon

Bonaparte caused everything to change. Now she was going on a long trip to a war in Portugal she hadn't signed up for, with a husband she didn't want, and a strong regret that she hadn't paid attention in her high school history class.

She took a deep breath of the sweet smoke of burning tobacco as it wafted across the deck. Her eyes closed involuntarily as her stomach flared with heat. Thomas was somewhere close. The smell of his pipe seemed to follow her everywhere and snatch at her thoughts. He usually kept himself out of sight, but on a crowded ship it was hard to ignore his presence. She hated that all the little reminders of him made her palms itch and her throat catch.

Yesterday she'd run into him sitting with a trio of grizzled sailors. They all had their pipes clenched in their teeth while they knotted lengths of cord into satchels. Out of sheer boredom, she'd paused to watch as Thomas was again shown how the rabbit circles his hole twice before jumping in. He was determined to learn, despite being all thumbs. As his satchel grew into a tangled mess, she breathed in as much of his second hand smoke as she could suck down. She was about to ask if she could join, maybe share a bowl, when one of the sailors noticed her and snarled. "You lost, lass?"

All four looked up. Thomas's lips moved in what could have been either a smile or a sneer—it was hard to tell since one corner of his mouth was disfigured by a long white scar that crossed his cheek, and the other corner was wrapped around his pipe. His blue eyes would have given her more information, but she deliberately avoided looking into them, knowing how his gaze affected her.

"Never mind her, Patrick. She's touched," Thomas grumbled.

"Oh hell, that's just what this ship needs," Patrick said, "another woman as not right in the head. The bloody army has no business allowing camp followers. It's not good for morale."

"Right, and what would morale be like if no one gets their laundry done or their meals cooked?" snapped Elise.

"So the Queen'll be boiling laundry then?" Thomas asked. His voice was gentle, teasing. "Since when?"

"If you're so against women on board, why are you making dainty bonnets for the ladies?" Elise waved her finger at the complicated macramé in Patrick's hands. "Try it on. I bet it really adds a flair to your ugly mug." She'd wanted to walk away with dignity, but when he rose, indignant and puffed to intimidate, her flat feet had churned her legs into a ridiculous sprint across the slippery deck.

The memory of the men's mocking laughter echoed in her brain, and she seethed at all of them—the sailors, the infantrymen, the riflemen, the wives, the officers, everyone. They were all horrible, especially Thomas. They were all ignorant and backward. Not one of them would survive five minutes in the 21st Century. Elise furiously ground a corner of her husband's blanket against her eyes.

Her salty tears were lost in the already damp blanket. Everything she owned, which was nothing much to speak of, was soaked with a mist of salt brine that never dried. Ireland was the pits, Elise thought gloomily, having never actually stepped on the country's soil. She had briefly considered escaping her current situation and swimming to shore, but what was there for her? Nothing but little huts with thatched roofs. Sheep. Rocks. More sheep. She'd heard the town of Cork was more urban, but that couldn't mean much in 1808. London had been urban—about as urban as it gets—and she'd hated it. And anyway, wasn't Ireland all about the sweaters? She didn't look good in lumpy cable-knit sweaters, she reasoned. Elise shivered under the wool blanket around her shoulders, an ironic fashion accessory given her thoughts, as yet another spray of mist passed across the deck. Sure, the humidity was doing wonders for her skin, but a ruddy complexion didn't mean much if your bones hurt from the damp cold. Sinking lower into her black mood, she pictured herself back in Tucson, Arizona.

August in Tucson, when the stifling heat of the day was dramatically broken each evening with monsoon rains, was her favorite month. Cactus grew fat between the wood of their ribs like lungs filling for a long sigh of relief. The spiny ocotillo, normally just a cluster of tall sticks jutting into the sky, dressed itself with green leaves and a corsage of red flowers. The scent of creosote bushes painted the air in freshness. The streets were washed clean of an entire year of desert dust. It had been the start of monsoon season when Elise was stolen from her home and dropped into damp and dreary London by God-knows what forces, losing 200 some-odd years and a few months. All her friends were now gone, her nursing career, her entire way of life and any hope for blissful sun-soaked heat. London had been cold, but at least there were cheery fireplaces at the Quiet Woman. On the *Valiant*, if you were cold, you just put on more wet layers of wool, assuming you had more layers.

As she often did when she was alone, Elise dug between her breasts and pulled out a filthy handkerchief, dislodging stray crumbs of the rationed ship's biscuit that she ate for most of her meals. In the center of the square of linen, hidden and protected, was the emerald scarab. How it could be so warm when she herself was so cold, was only one of its mysteries. Elise wanted to shrink herself to the size of the emerald and tuck herself into the warmth between her own breasts, a feat of magic about as likely as being able to return to Tucson. That and the rest of the irritating thoughts rolling in her brain—the corset that was a thousand times more uncomfortable than a bra with a popped wire, the weather, the wafts of Thomas's pipe smoke, the riflemen's freedom, Ireland, cable knit sweaters—made her want to scream in frustration. Instead she took a bracing breath to concentrate.

Something told Elise that the emerald scarab was the key to her fate. Whether from her own body heat or from something more mystical, there was a power being radiated that she couldn't even begin to understand. On one side, it was nothing more than a large cabochon carved to look like a beetle. Flipped to the backside, however, the emerald was dusty and unpolished with etchings of tiny hieroglyphs like the inverse of braille. For the hundredth time, Elise drew her finger over the writing and wondered what the symbols meant.

It was Richard who had presented her the scarab as a gift to his new wife. But the gift hadn't been an act of generosity; the emerald hadn't been his to give. He'd taken it from Elise months earlier when he'd discovered her unconscious in the street the night she'd fallen through time. He gambled that returning the jewel would trigger in his new wife memories of an auspicious past full of wealth and high standing. It stood to reason that an amnesiac woman found with such an enormous gemstone would be a member of the British noble class, and he'd held on to it without her knowledge until he could secure her in matrimony.

His plan had worked. Her memories began the instant the emerald was pressed into Elise's open palm. "What's yours is now mine," Richard said, with complete belief in the inevitability of civil law.

Fuck inevitable, thought Elise as she squeezed the jewel in her fist and glared towards the misty horizon. She was tired of inevitable. She ached to take charge of her own life again and the emerald was the first scrap of self-determination she'd felt in weeks. She gripped it in her fist, holding on for dear life. With the emerald scarab back in her possession, she remembered everything:

It had started like any other day. . .

No, that wasn't right, Elise shook her head, not any other day.

It'd started in Tucson, in Emmet's bed. She'd awakened with dry-mouth, a churning stomach, and the feeling of her heart pounding against her skull. It was the kind of morning that made Elise consider setting fire to all the trees in the neighborhood because that's where the cicadas hid, and their shrill song was like a power drill into her brain. Quietly, heels in hand and half-dressed, she'd slipped away from the sleeping mass of twitching muscle that was her previous night's conquest and headed out to meet her friend and coworker Anita, who was fresh off a nursing shift at the hospital. On mornings like that, hair of the dog was her first priority. Her second was Ibuprofen.

There's something about a hard hangover that filters an entire day like a sticky film you can't rub off your corneas. No matter what you do—shower, hydrate, exercise, medicate—there's nothing that adequately removes the fragility created by a bender. That evening after a long nap, Elise was still feeling the after-effects, so she'd decided to head to the foothills to run the trails and sweat out the last of the poison.

For Elise, running was as self-indulgent as drinking. Pounding the dusty mountain paths was her joy. Her blood perfused. Her lungs opened. Her skin filtered. Trail running was more about the feeling it created than it was about health. But this time, no amount of churning blood could erase the buzzing in her head. She'd felt like there was a neon light in there behind her eyes, illuminating the desert in front of her with a pulsating sound, but she chalked the sensation up to the impending torrential rains that were sweeping across the valley.

The monsoon arrived faster than anticipated. Having lived in Tucson for almost ten years, she was used to the dangers of the late August rains, but never had she seen anything like the wall of water that had rushed down the trail. Now she wondered if what she'd been feeling that morning wasn't a hangover, but overlapping fault lines of time quivering against an intense pressure, a kind of metaphysical earthquake. Had she been frothed between two separately moving currents of time and thrown to the surface like sea foam? That could explain the sudden appearance of a tsunami in the middle of the desert. It caught her up in muddy water and churning stones and spit her out, a masticated mess, into the nineteenth century.

She'd been pulled from a sunbaked desert landscape to a cold and crappy London pub via, what? Death by drowning in mud? Was she dead? Elise carefully wrapped the scarab back in the handkerchief and returned it to her bosom. The feel of it sliding along her skin sent a shiver down her spine. A strange warmth pressed against her sternum as it settled heavily.

Gazing at the ship's inky shadow on the churning waves, she narrowed her eyes at the sea. She could be in hell, she thought, a colorless and cold hell. A gull landed gracefully on the water, making her smile wryly. Even the birds were gray in hell. She pressed the scarab hard against her flesh to reassure herself that the pain she caused herself meant she was very much alive. She couldn't help wondering, though, what alive meant. If time had no fixed point any longer, why should life?

A familiar thought occurred to her: perhaps death was the pathway back to Tucson. Each time she mulled this question, she felt a little less scared. Now after weeks of consideration, she found she could justify thoughts of suicide.

It was possible that the shock of the cold water would stop her heart, but that was an outcome she doubted. Her heart was strong, despite her nicotine habit. Years of distance running had given her an enviable cardio system.

She was a strong swimmer, so there was a possibility that she would freeze to death before drowning. Despite it being August, the weather was cold, and the water, she guessed, was even colder. Considering how much she was shivering, it was likely she was already suffering from the first stages of hypothermia. This worried Elise since, for all she knew, dying from hypothermia could send her straight to the Paleolithic Age and she'd rather not tangle with mammoths.

Drowning was the only way to return to exactly the same place and time. She was becoming convinced she had to bookend her time travel with similar occurrences—something about the symmetry of it struck her as essential. She hoped the shock of the frigid sea would cause her to gasp and inhale water, then all she'd have to do was fight to keep her body submerged for longer than three minutes. She could do this, she thought. She could force herself to drown.

Elise let the blanket slip from her shoulders and gripped the rail hard with both hands. She could feel her pulse increase through her palms, but it wasn't her death that scared her. It was the terrifying sensory deprivation she remembered from her first trip through time. It had been a swift slide, dark as the night sky, and empty of everything. She had no idea how long it had taken her to fall through, but then again, time isn't an issue when it's suspended.

As she leaned over the churning sea, she thought of the black-haired woman. In her recurring nightmare, the woman played the main part as a glossy black beetle drifting weightlessly in a black void. She made overtures to start a friendship, clacking her mandibles and waving her antennae; she made Elise want to pick up a shoe and stand on a chair.

There was also a feeling of connection, of familiarity. The black-haired woman had been there when Elise first landed in that candle-lit room where people screamed in French and scattered like shadows. The woman intervened when a man bared his small, sharp teeth and took Elise by the throat.

Did it even happen, or was it her mind trying to rationalize how a flash flood could have overtaken her from the heights of the Catalina foothills, where there was no wash?

No. It happened. Elise had the emerald to prove it. Like a gift from fate, the emerald scarab had dropped forward from behind the man's cravat. It revealed itself by dangling on its chain in front of her eyes like a lifeline. She caught the jewel, twisting the chain until it broke. She held it locked in her fist as the floor opened up and she fell again, this time sideways, landing in the muddy lane in front of the seedy, and not so quiet, Quiet Woman.

Elise balanced her waist precariously on the edge of the ship's rail with the weight of her legs being the only thing keeping her from flipping over the side. She didn't have to do this, she thought. She could go look for the black-haired woman and demand answers, beat them out of her if she had to.

For a moment, Elise wondered how she might find a nameless woman without the help of the internet, a photograph, or the ability to speak French. The impossibility of the task almost made her laugh. She leaned further forward. Her toes left the deck.

The cold shock of water as it rushed over her head removed any desire to gloat over how right she was—she did indeed gasp when her body hit the salty sea and it burned in her lungs as momentum took her deep under. She was now a gherkin in a jar of brine, a flesh-lodged splinter in a salt bath, a pickled egg. She was decidedly not a mermaid.

What she hadn't anticipated, however, was the intensity of her body's need to pull her back towards the sky. She may have wanted to die. She may even had had good reason to die, but her body wanted nothing more than another breath of life. She struggled against her instinct for survival as her desperation increased with every second. Luckily, the sheer volume of clothing that tangled around her legs worked well in countermanding her body's orders to surface. She opened her mouth to scream, but had no breath to exhale. Fighting panic, she waited for the black portal to open up with Tucson, Arizona a bright dot on the other end.

Hadn't it already been three minutes? Why hadn't the vortex opened? It felt like eternity. She tried to concentrate on the ship's massive hull, roughed over with barnacles, and was only barely aware of her hands working feverishly to free her legs. Maybe she hadn't drowned in Tucson during that flash flood. Maybe the flood was an independent occurrence, a coincidence. Maybe she should have looked for the black-haired woman after all.

Tunnel vision was not what she'd wanted. It wasn't the same as slipping through an opened tunnel. Five more seconds. Ten more. Thirty more seconds and her vision narrowed into complete darkness.

Adelaide is Hungry

"America?" Adelaide called to a sailor who was coiling rope at the end of the quay at the London Docks. The crowd on the narrow platform surged in and out like the lapping tide against the ships that loomed on either side. Half the workmen were carrying bulky loads on their shoulders. The other half had just offloaded their burdens and were headed to get more. Adelaide was the stone disturbing the flow.

"Your pardon, madam?" he shouted over the noise and commotion, craning his head around two men hauling a large wooden crate to look at her.

"America?" She jabbed her index finger at the two-masted brig on her left. She tried to get closer to the man, but the crowd made it too difficult. Instead she asked another man carrying a stack of wooden planks on his shoulder. "America?"

"Portsmouth," he barked without stopping.

Adelaide sighed and turned to let the flow of traffic take her back towards the warehouses lining the Thames. Although she understood little English, she was becoming fairly familiar with the rhythm of the Docks. The people who made their living on the Thames were a rough bunch, but manageable, and for the most part, much too busy to be dangerous. It reminded her of her own beginnings along the Seine River in Paris. She had started her business small, telling the fortunes of river workers using an overturned crate for a table and a three-card spread. Slowly word of her skill got out. Her crate earned a tablecloth and the attention of chambermaids. Then the tablecloth earned a table and the maids came from wealthier houses. She expanded her spread to five cards and charged more for the merchants' wives, then ten cards. She moved from the Seine to a café, then finally she earned her own apartment. It could be a reproducible business plan if she spoke English. If only English wasn't such a clumsy language.

It had been two days since her visit with Mrs. Southill, and she still had found no passage to America. Her anxiety made it difficult to read her own future with any clarity. Each time she consulted the cards, they revealed too many possibilities. The one thing she knew with certainty was that the possibility of retrieving the emerald grew less likely with every passing minute. The longer it took her to find passage, the more painfully stretched the connection she had with the golem became, making the task laid before her by *la Société* all the more difficult.

Tired of seeing men shake their heads no, Adelaide decided it was time to return to the inn where Dodo convalesced. He would be hungry, poor man, and might actually be happy to see her for at least the fifteen minutes it took for him to eat his dinner. She reached into her apron pocket and jangled the few coins she had left. The deposit they had placed on the room at the Dancing Bear had been enough to silence the proprietor for a while, but they would have to disappear before he began making demands of a full payment. She considered transferring Dodo to the abandoned shack they found when they'd fled the Quiet Woman. It would not be very comfortable, but at least it would be dry, and free.

The scents of meat roasting on rotisseries, baked breads, and sweet fruit, all being sold by shouting vendors along the street made her stomach rumble. Gone were the clever meals she'd had in Paris. *Saucisson sec* was a wistful memory and had been a cruel topic of conversation amongst the women of *la Société*. Now, if she wanted sausage, it would likely be stuffed with ground offal mixed with sawdust. It was never a good idea to save money with cheap sausage.

The cook at the Dancing Bear did not have the same gift for blending flavors as did the fat woman in the kitchen of the Quiet Woman. The faces poor Dodo made while eating the inn's bland and stringy stews and gelatinous puddings would have been hilarious had she not shared his fate. The meals did not improve the character of the Dancing Bear, nor did it improve the moods of the clients who slunk around the dining hall. Dodo, with his bruised and fractured body, was especially sensitive. His teeth might have been dislodged and his jaw broken, but there was nothing wrong with his tongue, unfortunately.

Four coins left. Not nearly enough, but perhaps she could make Dodo's evening more comfortable if she smiled sweetly to a vendor. She stopped a baker who carried a large basket of meat pies that trailed a particularly complex scent and held up four fingers. "Four coins; four *tartes*," she said in her thick, French accent. She tried to communicate friendliness with her eyes and smile, and cocked her head coquettishly.

The baker didn't bite. "Your ha' farthings will get you nothing from my basket. I'm not dispensing charity, madam."

Adelaide pointed to a single, large pie and held up one finger.

When the baker turned to walk away, she stepped in front of him and raised her voice in the way that only a French woman haggling in a country market could, using a piercing combination of stubborn righteousness and sarcastic indifference. Unfortunately, even the cleverest arguments, if presented in the wrong language, were useless. The only thing Adelaide succeeded in doing was to cause the baker to take a step back in alarm, allowing him the space to fill his lungs to maximum capacity.

Most of the English expelled from the man's bellows was not anything Adelaide could understand, with the exception of "frog" which, much to her outrage, was a word that kept getting repeated. The more clearly she made her anger known, through wild gesticulations and puffed declarations of protest, the louder the baker became. Just as she was about to knock the basket of meatpies out of his hands, another man appeared as though conjured. "*Je vous en prie,*" he said gallantly, pressing a large coin into Adelaide's hand. "Pray, take it."

She gaped at the new arrival, startled by his perfect French. "It is too much," she protested. "I cannot accept your gift."

"You must. I insist. It is a pleasure for me to meet a compatriot. If I had flowers, I'd give you flowers. But I see no florists, so I must give you meatpies."

Adelaide smiled and blushed at the compliment. "Then, I accept your gift with pleasure."

After the mollified baker packaged up four pies in brown paper, the mysterious Frenchman introduced himself as Jacques Noisette, a sailor on a nearby ship. "And you are Madame. . .?"

"Mademoiselle," corrected Adelaide. "Mademoiselle Bonnediseuse." She tried not to smile at the obvious pleasure it gave Mr. Noisette to hear the title of an unmarried woman. Carrying her package for her, he drew her away from the road to find a less crowded area squeezed between two warehouses. He offered her a seat on an overturned crate with a sweeping arm and a deep bow. As gracefully as she could, she lowered her broad bottom and balanced her package on her knees.

"I hope you don't mind my asking, but those meatpies—they are not *all* for you, are they?"

"No, no." Adelaide looked at the bulky package, knowing it wouldn't be difficult to eat them all herself. Their scent tantalized. "I've a friend who will share them with me tonight. He's awaiting my return."

"A friend?" The look he gave her was significant. He'd taken note of the pronoun she'd used.

"A friend."

Mr. Noisette nodded and pursed his lips thoughtfully. "Is this friend of yours another of our compatriots?"

Adelaide paused, knowing she shouldn't reveal too much. Dodeauvie was supposed to be under house arrest in Lille for the crime of disseminating Royalist propaganda. It had been a stupid thing to do, but he hadn't been able to help himself as his hatred of Napoleon and the Jacobins was stronger than his sense of self-preservation. It was likely that officials had already noticed Dodo's absence, but if they hadn't, Adelaide didn't want to be the one to reveal his secret. "It is a long story," she said simply, "and perhaps not very unique. My friend came to offer his aid, but now it is I who must aid him. He's fallen sick, you see. And now we are both stranded in this unfriendly place.

"But enough about my own troubles. I am tired of thinking of them—bored by my own story. Tell me yours so that I may forget mine. Why are you wearing the uniform of the Royal Navy? If you are a spy, you should take care. You are very loose with your confidences!"

"I'm no spy," laughed Mr. Noisette. "Though I'm proud to say I can speak both languages with very little accent. I'll allow that has been helpful, especially in these times of war.

"When I was just a boy, I begged my father to allow me to join the French navy. You know, *La Royale* is quite a dream for boys.

'*Honeur, patrie, valeur, discipline*'—few boys were not swept away by the romance."

"I once knew a boy who wished to join," Adelaide admitted with a smile, thinking of her brother. He had not approved of her own career choice, and made very little effort to correspond. "Instead he was apprenticed to a foundry. I wouldn't be surprised if he was now making cannonballs for Napoleon's army."

"He was lucky. I would have been better off working iron. My income would have been sure. I could have had a wife, a family. . ." his voice wistfully trailed off. "In any case, my parents were more than happy to see me in the navy. It was one less mouth to feed in a large family. I was just a small boy, you see, and my father couldn't afford to give me much. The navy promised to educate me. It seemed like a good idea. Perhaps it was, but I wasn't in *La Royale* for long—just long enough for me to recover from seasickness and gain my legs. In our very first battle, our ship was pitted against an English schooner. It was not anything unusual. I've seen much worse since then. But the first battle a man sees is always the worst. It's always the one you think of when you wake in the middle of the night," he paused, as though remembering some horror. "In any case, we were outgunned. Our ship was lost and I was pressed into service for the English."

"How horrible," Adelaide cried.

"It was indeed horrible at first—you imagine? I was only a boy, not much more than ten years old. I couldn't speak English and was beaten when I didn't understand the commands. I didn't have a friend in the world. Every day I waited to see the sails of a French ship on the horizon, but a rescue never came. Eventually I learned the language and made friends. My loyalties changed. It was the English who taught me to sail, and on the seas, one is first loyal to one's ship." He laughed at Adelaide's expression. "You think me a traitor."

"On the contrary, I'm shocked to hear how barbarously you were torn from your country. Your family…I cannot imagine what they must think." Adelaide's eyes welled with tears. "It has been so long since I've seen my own family. When I was torn from France, the members of my family were scattered to the wind."

"Ah." Jacques nodded sagely. "Might I assume Bonnediseuse is not your real surname?"

"You may assume whatever you wish." Adelaide took a deep breath and assumed her role, rolling her eyes and wringing her hands in agony. "I beseech you, Monsieur Noisettte. Help me return to my family. Please, you must help me. My friend was to take me to my mother in America, but he was beaten unmercifully by bandits. They took all his money, all the funds given to him by my family to return me to them. Now neither of us can buy passage and he—oh dear God, poor, sweet man—he is at death's door. And the ship that was to take us both to America has already left." Adelaide wiped tears from her eyes and clasped the old tar's hands. "You can speak English. Perhaps you can find another ship for us. Which one of these is headed to America? Please tell me," she begged, "I must see my mother! My friend tells me her heart is breaking and she hasn't much time left. Every day that I am apart from her is agony!" Adelaide made a big show of looking around for eavesdroppers and lowered her voice conspiratorially, "Perhaps," she whispered, "when my family is all together, we can help restore the Bourbons to their rightful place."

"Hush!" Mr. Noisette ordered, alarmed. "You must take care with whom you speak so openly about returning the King to the throne. Here in London one might think to be safe, but Napoleon's spies are everywhere," he cautioned.

"Oh, I am lost," Adelaide cried out, and exploded into hot tears. "My mother needs me and I'll never see her again."

"Have courage," Jacques said, clumsily patting her hand and offering his handkerchief. "I will help you. I promise."

As he walked Adelaide back towards the throng, he explained that Spain had finally asked England for aid against Napoleon's continued aggression. England, always happy to do battle, was now mustering her troops to send men to the Peninsula. The entire Royal Navy would be needed. Even merchant ships were being pressed into use for transporting supplies and munitions to Portugal. As a result, precious few ships were left to travel to America. "It may take some time to find a ship headed west, but remain hopeful, Mademoiselle. I will find you tomorrow and give you what news I discover. In the meantime, enjoy your meal this evening. *Bon appétit*."

As Adelaide walked up through the narrow, damp streets of London, back towards the inn, she smiled. Jacques Noisette was the first bit of luck she'd had in a long time, and she hoped it was the beginning of a new trend. She had taken a small gamble in playing the role of the exiled Royalist noble, but even if the old sailor had been a secret sympathizer for the Republic, he couldn't very well fault her, considering his own traitorous path. Adelaide shook her head. What contortions for a mere line in the sand between nations.

The proprietor of the Dancing Bear looked at her suspiciously from behind his desk as she walked into the gloomy foyer. She tried not to make eye contact and forced herself to give a cheerful "Good evening" before racing up the back stairs. The inn wasn't located far from the Quiet Woman, and was its nearest competitor. Adelaide was sure there was some overlap between the clientele, and that worried her. She did not want to be recognized. She had been relieved to hear that the wolfish man from the other pub was no longer in London, but his customers were loyal to the man, if not the business, and she risked being beaten a second time should they see her and remember.

If the proprietor of the Dancing Bear knew she was not welcome at the Quiet Woman, he did not say. Thus far he'd kept his mouth shut, even when they'd first arrived with Dodo bleeding and wrecked. He merely held out his hand for payment, and that suited everyone.

"Dodo?" she called into the bedroom as she pushed open the door. "I've brought you a gift," she sang. She tugged at the curtain to let in more light. She'd forgotten to bring up a candle, which would have been an extra expense in any case. She tore her package open and Dodo grunted as the smell of hot meatpies wafted into the room. "There'll be none of that dreadful stew tonight. Aren't you pleased?"

Another grunt.

Adelaide pulled a chair up to his bedside and helped her friend to sit up. The movement caused a fit of weak coughing that brought tears to his eyes. When he finally settled, she gave him the meatpie and then rummaged in her carpetbag for the decoction of pain medicine Mrs. Southill had given her. When she turned back she gasped at the mess Dodo had so quickly created. In attempting to push the pie into his mouth without actually lowering his swollen jaw, he'd released the juices and they ran in rivulets down his chin and onto his shirt. Adelaide gently wiped his mouth with a corner of the sheet and began pressing crumbs between his lips. Almost as many crumbs were blown out as were swallowed. "No more," he lisped after having eaten a mouse's portion.

"Have more, Dodo. You need to regain your strength."

"Don't call me that," he responded weakly.

Deftly, Adelaide pushed a spoonful of pain medicine between his lips before he could make any further protests. "Perhaps you'll be more interested in food when your pain eases a bit," she said pragmatically, wiping his chin again.

Adelaide ate her own dinner as she watched the decoction take hold of her friend. She could see the pain leave him. His forehead smoothed first, then his shoulders lowered and he loosened his grip on the edge of the blanket he'd balled in his fist. Slowly Dodeauvie's eyes closed just as she finished her second pie. Adelaide cast a glance to the third pie, still sitting on the brown paper within Dodo's reach. It would be such a shame to let it go to waste.

She was lifting it up to her mouth when she heard a characteristically derisive snort from Dodo. Guiltily, she looked up and met his open eyes. A self-righteous gleam came from them. "Greedy, greedy. You never change," he whispered hoarsely.

"I didn't think you were hungry." Adelaide hastily wrapped the pie back up, thus removing the temptation. "Since you refuse to sleep, you must have reserves to spare. Lend me your energy." Adelaide bent her head as though in prayer. "Let us seek the creature on the astral plane. Together we can reach farther than I can alone."

"Not this again," Dodo whined, pulling his hands out of her grip. "You must give up the chase. It's over. The jewel is gone."

"I must try. My life depends upon it."

"Don't be ridiculous. You will live. Only I may kill you myself if you persist in this folly."

"But if I don't try to find the emerald, I can never return to Paris. *La Société* made that quite clear. You don't mean to suggest I remain here in this *pissoire* of a city?"

"Oh, *la Société, la Société, toujours la Société...*" Dodo rolled his eyes. "Why do you worry about them? They're kitchen witches! They know nothing!"

Adelaide sighed. Dodo too easily dismissed the reach and the strength of the women. While it might have been true that the women knew nothing of the hermetic philosopy that Dodo revered, they did understand the consequences of crossing the emperor. This was a lesson Dodo had not himself learned, despite having been censured and eventually placed on house arrest for distributing Royalist pamphlets. Adelaide was sure that even though she herself had not stolen the diamond, a judge would never listen to arguments for her innocence if the argument included magic and conjured golems. Her own sentence would not be as easy as that visited upon Dodo's head. Those "kitchen witches" were no fools. "Speaking of fools, did I tell you Madame Southill was attempting to catch light?"

"Catch light?" Dodo looked surprised. "In her hands? How very interesting. I wonder what she plans to do with it if she succeeds."

"Do? What on earth would she do with light? It's just light," Adelaide laughed. "You should have seen her! She looked ridiculous."

Early the next morning while Dodo still slept, Adelaide breakfasted on the third meatpie and left the inn more confident that a solution would reveal itself. As she strolled back towards the London Docks, the gentle lap of the river against the stones on the shore calmed her. For a while, she stopped to watch four young boys slowly wading out into the water. They were filtering sand through their toes as they walked, and occasionally one or another of them would reach down and pull up what their toes had discovered. Bones, scraps of cloth, shards of porcelain, bent lengths of wire all had their buyers. Anything could be sold if there was enough of it. Adelaide admired their fortitude. She too was a scavenger, only her treasures were the hopes people discarded along the path of life. She'd pick them up and present them like lost handkerchiefs. "Did you drop this? Is this yours?" Nothing makes a person happier than being reunited with an abandoned dream.

She stopped before reaching the busy harbor to gather a small bouquet of wildflowers and tied it with a scrap of ribbon she found caught in the reeds. After shaking off the aphids, she tucked the bouquet into her bodice and inhaled the aromatic nosegay. It smelled more herbal than floral, and that made her think of lunch. Her breakfast would sustain her for a few more hours, but occupying her mind with fantasies of her next meal seemed like a harmless diversion as she walked.

Magret de canard, was the first dish she thought of, a plate full of fat duck breast, seared and rare, with a side of little roasted potatoes drizzled in a lovely wine sauce made from the deglazed juices of the bird. *Un joli boudin noir*, blood sausage with baked apples, tart and buttery, would be a delicious meal for a colder day than today. Adelaide could almost hear the sausages sizzling in the frying pan over the hot kitchen fire and nearly wished for fall weather to arrive. Even *cassoulet*, France's equivalent to England's boiled beef, sounded delightful.

The street Adelaide traveled down opened up and the crowd thickened. She barely noticed. She had thought of ten more dishes she found irresistible and now she ached for a familiar meal. Perhaps she could make a life for herself with a new name in France somewhere other than Paris—Marseilles, for instance. Unfortunately, she was not overly fond of *bouillabaisse*, the fish stew that was Marseilles' specialty, and stuffed tripe stewed with mutton's feet was dreadful. She felt a rush when the town of Lyon entered her thoughts. The people of Lyon loved food nearly as much as she did. Then her heart sank when she remembered it was the Lyonnaise Mothers that caused the town's culinary reputation to soar. Those witches would certainly recognize her, and one of them would surely give her up to the ministry of police.

She stopped to stare at a ship. She knew they were all different— first class, fourth class, sloops, schooners—but to her they were merely a means to an end. She stood before a gargantuan naval vessel, prickly as a hedgehog with cannon, and longed to board just to go somewhere, anywhere.

She was imagining how she might survive as a stowaway when an urgent voice cut through her reverie. "Mademoiselle? Mademoiselle Bonnediseuse? Where have you been?"

"Monsieur Noisette," cried Adelaide happily, seeing the old tar pushing towards her past the usual crowd on the London Docks. "I'm pleased to see you." Pleased indeed. Her fantasy had taken a turn and she was starting to become frightened.

"I expected you much earlier this morning," Jacques looked slightly annoyed. "I only have a moment—I'm late to board my ship. There's a Captain Charles Briggs, of the merchant ship *Sea Otter* who is heading for the Azores Islands."

"Azores? I told you, I need to go to America," Adelaide scolded.

"You'll not find direct passage there from here, of that I am sure. All of England looks to Spain. The only ships heading to America's coastline are those who wish to claim American ships for Britain's gain and I can tell you right now you'll not be allowed on one of those frigates. Those privateers will take no passengers, and certainly a woman such as yourself would not want to keep company with the likes of them."

"Whatever shall I do?" wailed Adelaide. This was bad news indeed.

"Listen to me. Ask Captain Briggs for passage to the Azores Islands. From the islands, you have a much better chance of finding another ship that is continuing west. Furthermore," Jacques started walking backwards, drawing Adelaide along with him deeper into the Docks, "the captain speaks French."

"You must introduce me!"

"Unfortunately I cannot. I do not know him personally. I only heard from another sailor that his ship sails soon." Jacques was now rushing her down the street at an uncomfortable pace. Any previous thoughts Adelaide might have had regarding his gentlemanly nature were forgotten as she struggled to keep up.

"But I can't just throw myself at his mercy," she huffed. "What would he think? I need an introduction."

"An introduction from me is meaningless. Neither my accent nor my position ingratiates me to others who do not know me. Besides,

I'm in quite a rush," Jacques stopped suddenly. "The *Sea Otter* is being loaded today—you're in luck. The captain will be nearby, overseeing the storage of his wares." Jacques bowed and pointed to a large three-masted ship that creaked and pinged loudly against its moorings. "Here's where I'll leave you. Best of luck, Mademoiselle," and he turned and ran off.

Adelaide took a deep breath and tried to calm her zinging nerves as she walked towards the end of the quay. Having to make a stop in the Azores Islands seemed like a huge risk for getting stranded, but what choice did she have? She stepped into the flow of the dock workers who were busy preparing the *Sea Otter* for sail, and was drawn along as though pulled by a rope. Despite feeling as though she'd lost control of her own fate, there was something about the ship that soothed her. The *Sea Otter* was broad, with plenty of room for cargo in her hips. As crate after crate was hauled on board, she sank deeper into the water, but no one seemed concerned. A large man on board, as broad around the middle as his ship was about the bottom, was overseeing all the activity. Given how he was pointing and shouting orders, Adelaide felt she could confidently assume he was the captain.

"Sir," Adelaide called out, "*Excuses-moi de vous déranger! Capitaine Briggs. Je vous en prie.*" The man turned and acknowledged her with a bow, a look of curiosity on his face. Adelaide dove in, speaking French rapidly. "I'm so glad I have found you. A mutual friend sent me to speak with you. He said you were a gentleman, and would not hesitate to help a woman in distress, such as myself."

"A mutual friend?" He turned back to his men and shouted curses, distracted by his duty. "Name him," he demanded, turning back to her. He spoke with a thick English accent, but thankfully, he was understandable.

"I know how this must seem, but the present political situation calls for discretion. I would not give our friend away, so indiscriminately, in this day and age."

Briggs leaned over the ship's rail to try to study her more closely, then pushed past his own men to descend to the dock. "You have reason to worry, considering our nations are now at war," he said when he reached Adelaide's side. His smile reassured her. "I think I know who sent you, but I'll remain mum on the matter."

"You may name the man if you wish, but I'll not confirm or deny. I'll not risk his position."

"Surely you know that if our mutual acquaintance is here in England, then there is no shame in being a Royalist. England welcomes you."

Adelaide burst into crocodile tears. "I cannot see that it is anything but dangerous to use that word around me. It has brought such sorrow to my life, and yet my heart swells at the title. Yes, I am a Royalist. My family has been destroyed by the Revolution, destroyed by the Empire. I cannot go back."

"Napoleon has forgiven the noble families of France. You may indeed go back, should you wish it."

"To what?" Adelaide demanded. "My family's estate is no longer in our possession, but in the possession of the people," she spat. "The people! As if they had toiled as long and for as many generations as we did. As if they deserved it!" Great, fat tears rolled from Adelaide's eyes, rimming them in red and blotching her cheeks. Her passion was quite stimulating, especially when she took great, heaving breaths of air that caused her flesh to shudder. "No. I will not reveal the name of our friend who pointed me in your direction. The repercussions, should they fall on his head, would be too horrible. And he was so kind as to suggest you could take me to my family."

"Mademoiselle," the captain said gently, offering his handkerchief, "please do not be so distraught. Where is your family?"

"America," sniffed Adelaide.

"America? But our friend is mistaken. I'm not going to America."

"Our friend said you were going to the Azores Islands, and from there I might be able to find a means for continuing my journey."

"That may be true, but what if you cannot?"

"I've no other choice than to place my fate into the hands of God." Adelaide wiped her eyes and daintily dabbed her nose. "I'm afraid I cannot pay you," she said in a near whisper. "My family has no knowledge of where I am. They don't know where to send money. I've only just learned of their whereabouts, but I've been so afraid any *communiqués* from me would be apprehended and used against me." Adelaide bent forward, placing her head in her hands, "I've been so afraid," she said again, with a hoarse cry.

"Oh my dear, my dear," the captain soothed. "Think nothing of payments. After all you must have gone through, it would be monstrous of me to demand it."

Hidden behind the captain's borrowed handkerchief, Adelaide smiled.

"But," the captain continued, "I'm afraid it would be just as monstrous if, due to my generous soul, I was unable to pay my sailors for their work."

Adelaide's smile froze.

"I'm certain your family, once you are reunited, would be amenable to forwarding payment for your safe passage? Do you not think so?"

"Oh yes. Yes," cried Adelaide, "I know they would be most grateful to you and would shower you with their gratitude."

The captain smiled. "I hope their gratitude would not be extravagant, only enough to share their token of appreciation with my men. It's most difficult to be captain of a merchant ship these days and keep a good crew, what with the confounded frogs, begging your pardon, lying in wait to do us harm, and those Barbary bastards too, begging your pardon. These are truly hard times indeed." The captain sadly shook his head and his graying blond curls bounced at his shoulders. "Hard times, very expensive risks," he repeated, glancing quickly at Adelaide to assure himself she understood.

"Surely you realize that I myself am not responsible for any seafaring hardships." Adelaide caught the elderly gentleman's gaze, opened her eyes as wide as she could in an expression of earnest innocence, and then fluttered her lashes casting her gaze downwards in a show of humility and submission.

"Naturally, my dear," he blustered. "Naturally you would have nothing to do with this dreadful state of affairs. It is for me to worry about. I beg your pardon for burdening you with my worries. Such talk does not befit a woman of your sensibilities. Please," he waved his hand in an invitation, "you must dine with me this evening aboard my ship. Perhaps that would be enough to convince you not to embark with us tomorrow morning. Perhaps by then I'll have discovered a more sensible solution for you."

"I would gladly share your table. You honor me, *capitaine*." Adelaide plucked the nosegay of flowers from her bosom and offered them as a gift. "Please accept these as a token of my gratitude." She looked up through her lashes and smiled shyly. The captain, despite his solid stance, was entirely thrown off balance by Adelaide's performance, an unusual state for an old seaman accustomed to rolling waves.

Thomas Needs a Toke

The coughing started as soon as her head cleared the water and didn't stop even as the rope tightened under her arms. The force of her body expelling seawater was so strong that Elise was sure she'd tear her stomach muscles and break her own ribs. She wasn't dead, but a deep aching cold, the kind of cold that felt like needles in your creaking joints, made her wish she was. She kicked out against the waves and thrashed her arms against the unkindness of life. Suspended in the air alongside the ship, she was a soaked and choking worm on the end of a fishing line slowly rising from the sea. "Pull!" called a familiar deep voice from below and her ears rang with the shout.

Up she went, rising past the hold, the orlop, past the lower and upper gun decks. Without ceremony or finesse, she was hauled over the rail. Hands grabbed her shoulders, then they grabbed her ass to pull her in like a marlin, flopping her onto the deck head first in front of a small crowd of sailors and soldiers. The rope was wrested from under her arms and thrown back over the rail. Then, as Elise continued to cough and choke, another was hauled up from out of the sea. He gracefully climbed on board, taking the helping hands of his comrades as he swung his long legs over the rail. In an instant, he was kneeling at Elise's side. Gently cupping her chin, he lifted her face and Elise was drawn to look into Thomas's blue eyes. The cold water turned his cheeks rosy pink in stark contrast to the three lurid white scars that crossed his features at odd angles. The sudden eye-contact was startling; the tenderness of his touch too much to take when she wanted so much to remain angry with him.

"Damn it, Thomas. I thought I told you," Elise rasped, pulling her face out of his grip and touching her corset to assure herself that the emerald was still there, "I don't need your help."

Quickly Thomas stood and took two steps backwards and glared. Despite the crowd surrounding them, the only sound came from the seawater dripping from their clothes and puddling around their feet. Finally, he shook the water out of his thick black hair, and Elise blinked her eyes against the spray. "Well," he said, pushing his mane away from his face. "Back you go, then."

"No!" Elise screamed as he hauled her up and over his shoulder. She clutched his back desperately as he leaned her over the rail.

"No?" he asked. "Are you sure? Far be it from me to help you live if you wish to die." The crowd pushed at them, encouraging Thomas to drop her overboard.

It was the same sea, but this time it terrified Elise. She did want to live. She did. "Please," she begged. "Put me down."

Thomas stepped away from the rail and let her slide through his arms, setting her feet gently on the deck. "Don't you ever—" His voice broke. Dipping his head towards her, his warm breath tickled the skin on her neck. "Never try that again." He looked at her with an intensity that made her body feel cored. Elise gulped. That was all the agreement he seemed to need.

"Get back, you buggers." Thomas turned to push a path through the crowd. "Someone send for Mrs. Gillihan," he ordered as he stalked away.

Despite being entirely surrounded, Elise felt suddenly alone. Her teeth clattered. One thoughtful infantryman draped a blanket around her shoulders, probably the same blanket she'd dropped earlier.

Only in her mid-thirties, but still the senior woman on board, Mrs. Gillihan played the role of the nurturing, wise elder with aplomb. She arrived on the scene as if by magic. "Oh my dear, my dear," clucked Mrs. Gillihan with her arms spread wide in consternation. Elise was only too happy to lean into them. "Let's get you dry before you catch your death."

Seeing that Elise was now in the capable hands of another female, the men began to drift away. "Where is Private Ferrington?" Mrs. Gillihan called. "Someone tell him we'll be in the galley."

"Don't bother. I'm okay," Elise said as she convulsed in shivers. "It's all good." Richard was the last person she wanted to see.

"Don't be daft. Good? It isn't good. Bad, I should say. 'Tis quite bad. You've nearly drowned! Your Richard will be soon on his way, you'll see. He'll warm you right up."

Thankfully, the woman wasn't about to wait on Richard for bestowing warmth. She draped a second blanket around Elise's shoulders and hugged her to her side as they walked across the deck towards a hatch that led to the only place on board with fire—the normally off-limits galley kitchen. "Move away," Mrs. Gillihan snapped at the gawkers who clogged the narrow steps. "Get on with ye. Leave us."

"Did she fall?" slurred a woman who was practically swinging from the steps. She slapped at her own bonnet ribbons that whipped against her cheek from the wind tunnel created between the lower and upper decks.

"Of course she fell. How else do you think she'd be soaked through?"

"The poor girl needs a good slug of this to warm her up," said the woman. She thrust a flask of something at Elise. "Drink this, there's a dear." Before Elise could accept the offer, the woman pulled the flask back and shook it. "One moment. Let me see if there's any left." She tipped the contents down her own gullet. "Bad luck. None left."

"Be gone, you slattern!" cried Mrs. Gillihan.

Elise sighed heavily. The Slattern made a rude gesture and disappeared back into the murk where surging shadows partied with abandon.

"The indecency of those dreadful women! The very last thing you need is their rum. I pray every day that they will come to recognize their transgressions against God and society. Filthy creatures!" she spat. "Filthy. There's nought but disease between their legs."

Elise thought about the truth of that statement as Mrs. Gillihan ushered her into the warm galley, easily banishing the guard that had been set to keep away the riffraff, and began tugging at the strings of her soaked dress. While it was true she didn't need liquor for its warmth, its comfort sure would have been nice. She lifted her arms and allowed the woman to peel her dress off over her head. The situation made her think of Mrs. Postlethwaite who'd been there for her after the first time she'd nearly drowned. Elise was sure Mrs. P. would have poured her a little glass of brandy. There was always plenty of brandy in the kitchen at the Quiet Woman, Elise recalled. She missed the old gal. She missed her rejuvenating beef stews, the black porter, the nearly feral cats. She even missed Mary.

Elise jumped when Mrs. Gillihan began tugging the strings of her corset. "No need to be shy," the woman said, "I'll not let any men in here but your husband."

Mrs. Gillihan was no Mrs. Postlethwaite, and there was no way Elise would allow her to discover the scarab. "Thank you, I'll take it from here."

"You're a modest thing, aren't you? Suit yourself," she said, turning to the oven to stir up the flames, an unnecessary task, but one which gave Elise the privacy to pop the emerald into her mouth and remove the rest of her clothes. "You should have seen Private MacEwan run after you," Mrs. Gilliham said into the flames. "He didn't even think to spit out his pipe before he leapt overboard."

Elise smiled at the idea of Thomas in a swan dive with his pipe dangling from his lips. Everyone has their treasures, she thought as she tongued the scarab into the pocket of her cheek and wrapped the blanket around her nakedness.

Thomas was hunkered, stark naked, hidden in the dark shadows of the ship's hull. The noise of near one-thousand soldiers, sailors and countless whores echoed against the curved walls and pounded his hot ears, making it difficult to organize his thoughts. He needed dry clothes and a mouthful of rum. "Stanton!" he yelled. "Bill Stanton!"

"Let him be. I've got what you're looking for." Patrick emerged from the dark with enough liquor for a few long swallows, and a dry pair of trousers.

"Bill doesn't know his arse from his elbow," Thomas said, his mood making him incapable of a civilized thank you. "Where is that lad? When I was Stanton's age I made it a point to know when I'd be needed."

"Bill's climbed to the fighting top with young Master Donegal. There's no better place for the two of them, seeing as this ship's been overrun with molls. And anyway, he doesn't answer to you."

Thomas threw back the rum. It burned in the bottom of his empty stomach as he tried on Patrick's trousers. They were tight around his thighs and ended well above his ankles, but fit perfectly around his waist. He rolled them up to his knees.

"There's a devil in you, Tom. Don't look at me like that. I know these things. You'd best sit and smoke it out with me."

Reflexively, Thomas slapped at his bare waist where he normally hid his pipe in his pocket. The memory of tearing his shirt off as he swam down towards Elise made him freeze. He had an extra shirt in his kitbag, but his waistcoat was gone forever. "Bloody hell. I dropped my tobacco in the drink." He tore at his forelock in frustration then put his hand out to steady himself against the stacked crates as the vision of Elise's limp, floating body crashed over him again and again. She'd almost died, he thought. She'd nearly died. "That damned woman!" he muttered.

"No matter, no matter," soothed Patrick. "I've got some."

"Don't bother yourself. I'll not smoke all your leaf. I've got a plan to get more."

Patrick gave Thomas a wary look. "A plan? Private O'Brian, d'you mean? Don't do it, Tom. There's no guarantee you'll win that fight."

"I always win," Thomas snapped. His fists felt like glowing coals. He'd been putting O'Brian off for a while, but now the timing felt right. If O'Brian thought he could best him, then he'd take that bet. Besides, he had expenses. He needed a new second shirt, waistcoat, pipe, and a pouch of good tobacco. A win off O'Brian could make him flush enough to get it all. "Have you seen him?"

"I thought you wanted me to fetch young Stanton. Now you want me to fetch O'Brian? What's gotten into you? You leave O'Brian be.

You oughtn't chase down trouble when you're in a fix."

Thomas shrugged off the old sailor's steadying hand. He was in no mood to indulge his warning. His blood was up. His guard was down. And he desperately needed a smoke. "I'll find him myself," he said, stalking off.

If old Patrick did have one thing right, it was that the members of each company mostly kept tight. His own, including Richard, Bill Stanton, O'Brian and others, all slept together near where the *Valiant's* mainmast speared the lower gun deck—a choice spot. Everyone in his company always knew everyone else's business, which was mostly why Thomas spent his time with the sailors, but it made it easy to find people when he needed them. Richard, he knew, was with Elise in the Galley. Bill, it seemed, was on the fighting top. He lifted a blanket that had been hung for privacy and found Peter Collins nuzzling his young wife. Collins pointed him in the direction of Hobert, who sent him forward.

Thomas finally found Private Benedict O'Brian towards the bow of the ship where the walls began to come together to chase out the light. Peering around a short stack of crates he found O'Brian humping a folded-over girl who was making quiet rhythmic squeaks, like an exhausted and tortured mouse.

"Ahem," said Thomas.

"Bloody hell!" O'Brian, straightening up quickly in surprise. "MacEwan, you bastard. What the devil do you want?" The moll dropped her skirt and took the opportunity to escape.

"If you still think you can best me, let's have the match, then."

O'Brian's sly smile was slow to bloom, and fast in getting under Thomas's skin.

It used to be that old Cooper would organize all the boxing matches and keep the books, which was fine by Thomas. Someone had to do it, and it wasn't seemly for him to do it himself, as he was usually the one fighting. The matches were, generally speaking, clean events—a fighter won, a fighter lost, money exchanged hands, beer was bought for those that lost their bets. The Quiet Woman would also make a bit of money from hosting the event while the magistrate, being Cooper himself, would look the other way at the legality of a public house holding fights.

"Form a queue, men," shouted Private Benedict O'Brian. He waved a small ledger book in the air. "Easy now, no pushing. You'll all get your chance to make your bet."

Thomas sniffed, and narrowed his eyes. The man hadn't lost a minute of time to spread the word, once he'd agreed to the match. No doubt O'Brian would be skimming from the top. Likely skimming from the middle and bottom too, lousy cheat.

No, Thomas didn't have any regrets about accepting the challenge. His knuckles itched with a heat he couldn't dispel. He'd be glad to let them collide with O'Brian's fat mouth, sure enough. "I can best him," Thomas said to Patrick, who was shoving back the curious men and women who reached past him to pinch Thomas's arms in order to make an educated bet. They knew O'Brian already—he was a loud, blustering man, a compact stack of muscles with thighs like logs of hardwood, chest like a lady's traveling trunk, and arms that swung like bullwhips—but Thomas they weren't sure about. Thomas kept to himself.

"Maybe you can, maybe you can't," Patrick replied. "Best not even try. Isn't he in your own Company? Why would you fight your own man?"

"My own man?" Thomas asked with outrage. "I suppose you think I enlisted the bastard? He's not my own. I've nothing to do with O'Brian."

"You do now, like it or not."

Patrick had a point. There was nothing personal about fighting a man in a match, but you did learn a great many things about him while doing it. Thomas had fought many who he'd never see again, but he always remembered. All his fights stuck with him.

He watched as the crowd pushed and shoved towards a happy O'Brian. When he saw Richard line up with the rest to place his bet, he scowled—and him with a wife as just jumped into the drink. Elise was on her own with that one, he thought. Can't say he didn't warn her.

Against his better judgement, Thomas glanced over to the pile of barrels and crates where he knew Elise liked to perch. It'd only been an hour since he'd made yet another resolution to wash his hands of the strange woman, but his eyes couldn't break the habit of seeking out her location. She was there, alright. With her dress having been hung to dry, she sat with her knees pulled up to her chest wearing nought but Richard's shirt. She'd pulled the shirt over her knees to cover as much of her body as possible, but a lamp that hung behind her shone through the taut white fabric, outlining her slender legs. Her auburn hair, full of curls after her dip in the sea, shone like a wild halo around her narrow face.

"Are you even fit enough to fight?" Patrick asked, jerking Thomas's attention back to the situation at hand. He looked significantly at Thomas's stomach where a long red line in his flesh was hidden behind the right panel of his open shirt.

"This? This is nothing. It's an old wound."

"Let me see."

"Stop," Thomas slapped away Patrick's hands. "Stop being such an old Nana. It's nothing, I tell you. Just a scratch."

"And will you be fighting with your shirt on, then? You'd best let the men see – if you lose and that gash is found out, there'll be hell to pay."

"No, of course I'll take the shirt off. It's the only one I've got left."
Thomas reluctantly shrugged off his shirt and a few of the whores
gasped. The stitches Elise had tied had helped the top part of the knife
wound heal, but the bottom was red, and still open. He thought maybe
he'd cut the stitches out too soon, but the damn thing had felt like he'd
wandered into a patch of nettles, and was pulling and itching. Now,
looking at it carefully, he saw he was slowly growing his flesh back
from the center out. "See? It's fine."

There was a sudden flurry of activity as those nearest Thomas
rushed to spread the word of his handicap. A clamor arose around
O'Brian, who was scowling and madly scribbling in his ledger. The
odds had just changed. That suited Thomas just fine. Since he was
betting on himself, he stood to win more.

Pulling out an old fishing net, seemingly from thin air, Patrick
set to repairing it, signaling the conversation was over. All attempts
to convince Thomas to drop the fight had been made, and this was
Patrick's way of washing his hands of the matter.

To clear his mind, Thomas watched as the old sailor deftly shuttled
the needle from loop to loop. Logically, the turns of twine made sense:
cross over, form a loop, bring the end up under itself, now thrice more.
He could follow the motions, he could memorize the pattern, but to
his great irritation, his hands refused to cooperate when given a length
of twine.

He should have known it would be that way. It had been the same
with music. Old Mr. Ferrington had wanted him to play the fiddle, but
Thomas couldn't even finger the holes on a penny whistle and against
all expectations, Richard had been the one to show a talent. Thomas
could easily sing melody, or drop instantly into the background with
a harmonic support should a more delicate voice take the lead. Music
made sense, but his hands were clubs. About all he could do with his
hands was pour a beer, scrawl figures into the old ledger behind the
bar, and fill a pipe.

He could fight. That's what he did best with his hands. He'd always been able to fight. Fighting made sense to him too: cross over, form a loop, bring the end up under itself. The only difference between the twists of a sailor's knot and the twists of a fight was he never got tangled in a fight.

"The scratch line's been drawn," Richard said, pushing people out of his way to reach him. "You ready, Tom?"

"Aye, I'm ready." His hands felt warm and heavy. They itched. He didn't know what to do with them, so he crossed his arms and tucked them into his armpits. "Pat? You coming? I'll need you to be my second."

Patrick scowled and remained silent. His hands flew faster over the net.

"I'll be your second, Tom," Richard said. "It'll be like old times."

Thomas sighed. "Old times, then." He clasped Richard's elbow in affection, then rose on steady feet. He'd thought he was done with the old times.

The crowd surrounding Thomas pulsed close, making him sweat from the heat of everyone's blood-lust. The fight had not yet begun, and already excitement was reaching a pitch near madness. "Get them back," he hissed to Richard. "Get them away from me."

"Don't be daft. They love you," Richard laughed. Half-heartedly, he turned to the crowd and waved his arms at the nearest people like they were squawking hens to be herded into the roost. No one budged.

Toeing the line in front of Thomas, O'Brian narrowed his eyes in a combined expression of concentration and amusement. "The crowd's too much for you?" he sneered.

"Who's refereeing this match? Everyone needs to get back."

Thomas demanded. There was barely enough room to breathe, much less swing a punch.

"Referee?" O'Brian laughed. "Who told you this would be refereed?"

"Broughton's Rules state—"

"Broughton's Rules? Here? We're anchored off Ireland, man. If you thought we'd be using Broughton's Rules, you're a bigger fool than I took you for."

Thomas frowned. Without the rules, a fight would be just out-and-out eye-gouging, hair pulling, kicks to the groin street fighting. It took only a moment to adjust to the new information, the equivalent of a mental shrug. So, he wouldn't be shaking O'Brian's hand or wishing him luck. If that's the way the man wanted it, so be-it; that suited Thomas just fine. No rules, no false formalities.

His vision narrowed as his breathing deepened. The noise from the crowd faded from his consciousness as he found his balance and rolled his shoulders. He lifted fists that filled with an energy he'd taken for granted most of his life.

"Unhand me, vile woman!" cried a voice. "Get back!"

A scuffle, loud and heated, broke out in the audience. Thomas sucked in a breath. He would not allow himself to be distracted this time. She would not break his concentration. He took a wide step to the side—scratch lines were meaningless without the Rules. But she remained a blur in his peripheral vision.

O'Brian's smile was smug and enraging. His eyes darted to the audience to assess the situation, then locked on Thomas as the scuffle broadened to involve more people.

Again, Thomas was forced to step to the side as a man was pushed into the middle of the ring. He heard Elise yelp in pain, and quickly scanned the crowd to find her. She was using her elbows to maintain her position in the front row. Richard's white shirt slipped over her rounded shoulder and down her arm, revealing the corset she wore underneath. Through its tight laces, Thomas imagined he could see the glow of the strange jewel he knew she kept hidden between her breasts. The vision flooded him with an uncomfortable heat.

Circling to the right, Thomas put O'Brian directly between himself and Elise to block his view. Yet over O'Brian's shoulder, he was drawn to look at her hair churning like a dark storm around her determined face. If he had been thinking clearly, he would have known that it was O'Brian's view of Elise he was blocking, and not his own.

Someone pushed her to the floor. Recovering instantly, she slammed her slight body back against the crowd and the circle of men stretched like a knitted stocking to accommodate her. She crouched, elbows out, head down, ready for a second challenge, but none came. A smug, victorious smile played across her lips. She looked up with her green glittering eyes and met Thomas's gaze.

Suddenly his vision exploded in stars. O'Brian's well-aimed left hook threw him sideways into three men who went down with him. The crowd jeered. They were churned up by bad rum and first blood, and gave him only seconds to clear his head before catapulting him back into the fight. *That damned woman*, Thomas thought as he was launched through the air, the image of her sharp features seared in his mind. Like a bull, he put his head down and caught O'Brian under his ribcage with his shoulder and flipped him up over his back. He turned in time to see his opponent land with a heavy thud.

"Get up, you bugger!" Thomas ordered. O'Brian was struggling to regain the breath that had been knocked out of him. He grabbed O'Brian by the collar and lifted him to his feet. "Stand and fight! You'll not get off that easy."

Still gasping, O'Brian managed to stand and lift his hands, but the audience didn't appreciate that Thomas gave him time to recover. He was shoved, called names, spit upon, anything to get him to stop circling and start swinging. Finally, Thomas feinted left, and swung right. O'Brian ducked away, but ever the Irishman, he came back with a straight jab, fast and hard. It connected.

Again Thomas skittered back into the crowd, this time caught by Richard. "What the hell is wrong with you, Tom?" Richard muttered into his ear. "Pay attention. He's swinging with his left." He gave him a slug of rum from his canteen before pushing him back out into the ring.

Thomas heard Elise's voice rising above the cheers of the crowd, but this time he didn't look up. He needed both eyes on the grinning O'Brian, but now one of them was swelling shut.

He watched for his opportunity. A calm settled upon him as he kept himself out of the way of a third jab. Thomas had learned long ago that wild punches were effective only if you were lucky. He wasn't in the habit of trusting luck. He needed to learn O'Brian's style, and quickly, to use it against him. Keeping his hands raised, he watched his opponent's chest as it rose and fell. The moment when that one breath was caught, lungs filling for the effort of throwing another fist, would be the moment O'Brian would be finished.

The sensation of heat rose from his fists up through his arms and into his shoulders and chest. The crowd faded away from his thoughts. Now there was only O'Brian. Thomas felt his muscles prickle with a flush of blood under his skin, hot and engaged. The deck floor rocked gently with the waves in the protected harbor and Thomas's knees bent with the changes in the floor's incline. Forward, back, forward, back, they rocked.

In the end, it wasn't any one thing that finally launched Thomas and Ben O'Brian against each other. It was the irritating creak of the anchor chain; it was the bead of sweat that pooled in an ear; it was a small bubble of intestinal gas, unconsciously released. It was any and none of these things. Instinct took over, and Thomas was no longer the man he wanted to be. He was, once again, the man he was accustomed to being.

As a child at the Quiet Woman, it had been his job to punch down the dough after it rose. Growing up, he'd helped to bake countless loaves of bread in the warm kitchen behind the bar. He'd learned that to create a sustenance, a violence occurred. The transition from kneading bread to kneading patrons to persuade them to pay outstanding bills hadn't been too difficult. The concept was the same, in practice as well as principle.

Every time his scarred knuckles connected with O'Brian's face, Thomas was making bread in that wooden bowl. There was a fairness to it, a practicality. Unlike the last time when he'd lost control and beat that Frenchman to within an inch of his life, this fight was well considered. Three swings and a pause for a breath. Three more swings. Three more. They didn't all land and they weren't too hard. After all, O'Brian sparred better than most, and he was, as Patrick had reminded him, a member of his company. Their lives together were just beginning. Today they fought each other, tomorrow they'd fight side by side against a common enemy.

O'Brian stumbled and went down on one knee. It was already nearly over.

There was no hitch to the Irishman's breath or flicker in his eyes. Nothing to warn Thomas that O'Brian would kick his feet out from under him. By the time he realized what happened, he was already staring at the ceiling. A second kick to his ribs knocked the air out of him and caused him to curl. He threw his arms over his head, insulating him from O'Brian's vicious left foot.

Thomas had also done his fair share of grinding meat in the Quiet Woman's kitchen. This now seemed more appropriate. When he was ready, he turned and took O'Brian's right ankle into his hands and pulled hard. In the space of a breath, he was astride the downed man.

The swing that Thomas landed was a full-out, shoulder driven, cross from the right. It should have knocked the bastard out cold. Instead, it opened Thomas up for a counter that sent white-hot pain through his gut. The knife wound that hadn't quite healed completely was slammed by a deliberately aimed blow. Again he was on the floor with his knees pulled up, this time because his abdomen wouldn't uncurl. Thomas felt peeled open and turned out. He heard, rather than saw O'Brian struggle to pull himself on his feet. Then the man's face, pulped and swollen, loomed over him. His teeth were red with blood when he grinned and cocked his fist. Everyone on deck hushed.

"Move one muscle and you'll be skewered," growled a strange voice. The sound of steel sliding from a scabbard made both fighters freeze. Despite the fact that Lieutenant James Mason was half his age and forty pounds lighter, Thomas didn't doubt his warning. Beyond the sword that was pointed at his neck, Thomas could see a group of well-heeled gentlemen surveying the situation with stern faces as the scruffy crowd of infantry and whores began to slink away. The officers had returned to the ship.

Elise, however, remained in the front row. Her feet were solidly planted. Her eyes were wide and alarmed. Richard dropped his red coat over her shoulders and tried to pull her away.

"What in the name of God is happening here?" demanded Major Letchfeld. His long sideburns trembled with outrage over his round jowls. His tight waistcoat stretched dangerously as he took an affronted breath.

As the lieutenant lifted his sword to allow Thomas the space to stand, Sergeant Taylor stepped in. "Get up, you damned bastards," he shouted unnecessarily. Both men were scrambling to their feet already. Sergeant Taylor had been whoring with the rest of the infantry while the officers were gone, but now he was wearing his jacket as though it'd never left his body. The brass buttons gleamed with hypocrisy.

"Come, come, men. Stand up, show some spirit," Major Letchfeld barked. "You'd no trouble fighting like cockerels five minutes ago, let's see you stand now."

Thomas smoothed his black hair away from his face and came to attention. The wound in his side burned as he stretched his torso to its complete height.

The major's eyes widened in surprise. "Well, aren't you a craven looking beast? Look at this man, James," he said to his lieutenant, pointing a plump finger. Mason sheathed his sword and peered curiously at Thomas.

"Eyes down!" screamed Sergeant Taylor. "Keep your bloody insolent eyes down!"

"Do you see? On view here," continued the major in a conversational tone, "is an extraordinary example of the moral degradation in our rank and file. They can't help it, you know, it's the low breeding." He brought his face inches away from Thomas to study him. "Tell me, Private. . .?"

"Private MacEwan, sir!"

"Tell me, Private MacEwan: what was your crime ere you took the king's shilling? Were you a thief? No? A rapist, perhaps? Had you murdered? Ah, yes. Murderer." The major made a satisfied cluck, having perceived some kind of twitch, some indication in Thomas's face that he'd found the correct crime. "One can always tell these things, James. You'll learn. You'll learn, given enough time. You see, faces never lie, and this brute wears the marks of an illustrious life on his face."

"So you say, sir," Lieutenant Mason diplomatically replied. Thomas kept his chin up and his eyes glazed. "Shall I have these men flogged, sir?"

Thomas felt rather than saw O'Brian stiffen next to him, a surprising feat given their already rigidly at-attention bodies. A flogging would mean only a dozen more scars if he was lucky, fifty if he was not. He wondered what kind of man the major was—a cruel man or a fair man.

"What a devil of a thing to have to do, just as we leave for battle. No, James. I think not. There's no time. Too much to do before we can get under weigh. But, by God, Sergeant Taylor, I order you to watch this sly dog. Do you hear, Private MacEwan? You will be carefully watched."

"Yes, sir!" shouted Thomas.

The major was a lazy man, thought Thomas, the very worst kind of leader.

ON YOUR MARKS

"This is unacceptable!"

The scholars looked at the floor, they looked at the ceiling, they looked anywhere but at Napoleon Bonaparte, who was imperiously waving one finger in the air. All eight of them, to a man, were thankful not to have to speak directly to the Emperor—that exalted task being the responsibility of their project leader, the famous alchemist Heinrich von Flugelderhorn, brought all the way from his country estate outside of Vienna.

"You promised a formula. I see none before me. Where is my formula?" Bonaparte demanded, his finger now jabbing the blank scroll on the massive marble table in front of him.

The sound of air being sucked slowly through the emperor's flared nostrils momentarily masked the sound of the dripping and bubbling solutions contained in a jungle of pipes and beakers assembled between the alchemists and their employer. With Napoleon's captured breath, the noises returned, loud and unbearable like the squeaks of a trephine slowly working against the skull.

"To create a working formula," von Flugelderhorn explained, "one must first have all the data, know all the variables." In a gesture common to all professors of philosophy, he pulled his monocle away from his face with a patronizing smile, pausing to allow Napoleon the time to catch up with his reasoning. Then, placing his monocle back in his ocular orbit, he tapped a sheet of paper he didn't need and wasn't reading, and continued. "You see, we have only a small portion of the information nee—"

"I do not accept this!" Napoleon shouted. "You've had days. Weeks. And I see no progress. If you need further data, then get the data. Get it!"

Von Flugelderhorn nodded and smiled a conciliatory smile. Then he gestured to bring to Napoleon's attention all the various scattered papers filled with lists of numbers and markings from languages long dead, and followed this with an almost imperceptible bow, nearly a shrug, indicating an inability to fight fate. He adjusted his monocle and cleared his throat. "Ahem. One cannot, you know, rush these kinds of investigations, your highness. These things take—"

"Time? I have no time! There is no time! Do not ask for time!"

With a great sweep of his arm, Napoleon cleared the table of everything in front of him. Glass exploded against the wall and on the floor. Chemical reactions began happening at random, fizzing and sparking in puddles that spread dangerously across the table. A cloud of noxious green steam hung over the mess causing handkerchiefs to appear at everyone's noses. "England has the Stone, you idiot," screamed Napoleon. 'England has the Stone! How is it that you can speak twelve languages and yet understand nothing? Nothing!"

"Your highness," started von Flugelderhorn as he slid shards of glass from the top of a particularly important sheaf of papers that was in danger of melting. "Please don't misunderstand. Concurrent to these experiments, we are decoding the copies of the Rosetta Stone. And anyway, England is at least two years behind us and not aware that they're engaged in a race. Even if they were to decipher it first, it would only be to our advantage. After all, should they make an important discovery, do you not think they'd share the information? Of course they would. They would trumpet their findings all over the globe just to embarrass France. England may laugh, but ours will be the last laugh."

"YOUR EMPEROR WILL NOT LAUGH!" Napoleon's shout rang out like a sledgehammer against the stone walls of the laboratory. Von Flugelderhorn had to concede the truth in that point.

He tried another tack: "I should say, despite difficulties deciphering the Rosetta Stone and the resultant delay in our ability to translate the Thoth tablets, we've been making headway with Nicolas Flamel's notes." He pushed an enormous tome along the table, a manuscript illuminated in brilliant inks of all colors on delicate vellum, and swung it around for Napoleon to read. "You see these scribbles in the margins of the text, here, and here?" He pointed to barely legible notes that surrounded Flamel's text and lowered a magnifying glass for the emperor to see. Napoleon pulled it closer to himself to study the script. "Do you see? There. No, not there. There, where I'm pointing. We missed it initially, thinking it was merely the annotations of an uneducated monk, but luckily young Mougandmot here has excellent eyes. He saw that our good monk added quite a bit to Flamel's text. Given this new information, we're now able to theorize that what Flamel called the 'breath of the dragon' is—"

"So then you *did* find the formula!" Napoleon's narrow eyes grew less narrow with excitement.

"Well. . . no."

"No?"

"No. But we were able to theorize that the 'breath of the dragon' is—"

Von Flugelderhorn gasped in horror as the precious, handwritten fourteenth century book was hurled against the wall. Miraculously, the ancient leather binding held, although interior pages were unforgivably crimped.

"I'll hear no more of your theories and postulations! I want only results! Results!" cried Napoleon. "Do I make myself clear?"

The silence in the room was thick. Everyone nodded. The emperor glared at each scholar in turn and no one met his eyes. He straightened his waistcoat with a sharp downward yank in the kind of gesture that ends conversations. "Decode the Stone and translate the Thoth tablets. Forget Flamel. Forget these ridiculous experiments here. Flamel's text is merely a shadow of what the tablets will reveal. Stop toying with your endless recipes like women and concentrate on the Stone. Europe can become united in only two ways: through war, or through Thoth. The sons of our Empire depend upon you. They tire of war."

It was hard not to feel the truth of Napoleon's barb—they did, all of them, so enjoy the hopeful promise of an alchemical recipe. Iterating each formula, in a controlled and slightly tweaked manner between each experiment, was the kind of work that made one breathless with wonder. Every alteration to the recipe held possibility. Each chemical reaction was met with excitement. Indeed, every single one of the men in that laboratory, at one time or another, wondered, red-faced, if they truly differed from a coven of witches hovering over a kettle.

The thought reminded von Flugelderhorn of something else. "Speaking of war, perhaps we may have solved a problem of an entirely different nature?" He waited for Napoleon to nod before charging ahead. "Jean-Claude, quickly! Show the emperor what you've discovered."

A young alchemist, surprised at suddenly being singled out, dropped a pair of beaker tongs and they clattered loudly on the floor. "No, leave that. Leave the tongs, Jean-Claude. Go get the pot." The young man nodded and ran out of the room.

"I think you'll like what you see," von Flugelderhorn said as they waited. They could hear Jean-Claude's running footfalls on the marble floor, then a scrape of the soles of his feet as he slid into a turn at the end of the corridor. The sound of running grew distant.

A scholar in the back of the room coughed. Napoleon looked at the ceiling, then began flicking glass shards across the table towards a surviving experiment still bubbling over the heat of a candle. Von Flugelderhorn wiped a bead of sweat from his temple.

The sound of foot falls returned, distant at first. Then came the scrape of shoes as the young man slid into the turn. Finally, Jean-Claude burst back into the laboratory. "I have it!" he shouted with an optimistic smile. He held aloft a ceramic pot which he then presented to the emperor with a flourish. The pot was covered with what looked like a sheet of wax.

"What's this?" Napoleon asked.

"Open it," said Jean-Claude with a grin. "Open it, your highness."

Napoleon turned to look at von Flugelderhorn for confirmation before peeling off the wax layer, revealing a cork stopper. He tried to lift the cork from the jar, but it was wedged tight.

"Twist it open," said Jean-Claude. "Twist it, your highness."

Napoleon twisted and the cork came off with a loud pop. All eight men in the room politely applauded. "I don't understand," Napoleon said taking the spoon helpfully offered to him and dipping it in for a mouthful of jam.

"That jam is eight months old," Jean-Claude hooted.

Seeing the emperor suddenly balk at taking a second spoonful, von Flugelderhorn jumped in to explain. "The jam may be old, but I assure you it is perfectly safe to eat. Jean-Claude has discovered that if you put a sealed jar in a bath of boiling water, the air within is removed. With no vapors inside the container, the food takes much longer to spoil. Unfortunately, this vaporless state does not last forever. We've discovered that a jar which does not pop upon removal of its lid has contents which are spoiled."

"Poor Hervé," came a sad whisper from the end of the table.

Von Flugelderhorn nodded sympathetically. "Indeed. Alchemy is not without its tragedies. More research needs to be done, but I thought you'd be interested in our progression towards preserving food for the army."

"You thought of this?" Napoleon asked the young man.

"Well, to be honest, I'd watched my *mémé* doing something similar last summer."

"Your *mémé?*"

"Yes, my grandmother."

"Your grandmother," Napoleon repeated, and shook his head sadly, taking another spoonful of the sweet jam. "I ask for gold, and they give me *grandmère's* strawberry compote."

Adelaide's spirits were high as she approached the inn where she and Dodo were staying. The invitation to dine with Captain Briggs on board the *Sea Otter* was a huge turn of luck. She'd spent the entire trek back from the London Docks trying to imagine what she might be served. It almost didn't matter at this point. Any dish would be welcome, as long as it wasn't the watery stew of turnips and slippery meat she'd grown accustomed to eating.

The mental image of the captain gazing down at her from the height of the his ship was almost as enticing as the offer of a meal. He was a handsome man, that *Capitaine* Briggs. Stout, but muscular, tall, but not towering. He exuded strength and leadership without the overt trappings of power. Adelaide blushed just thinking about the way he'd accepted her little bouquet, with a bow and a flourish of his hat, revealing blond curls that were beginning to silver at his temples. Even the accent with which he spoke French was charming. Her luck was turning, most definitely.

There would not be enough time to ensure Dodo recovered from his wounds before she embarked on the *Sea Otter*. Of course, he would have to be left behind. She felt a stab of regret. Or, at least, she thought she did. It might better be described as a poke, or a glancing blow of regret. Or it could have been hunger pains. Adelaide decided she would send word to Mrs. Southill asking for her to look in on Dodo, forgetting that she had no money to pay a messenger and no friend to do it for free. But she refused to let thoughts of her mentor's physical condition dampen her spirits. Dodo was a strong man, a sorcerer of high repute, and would pull through.

Adelaide stepped into the Dancing Bear and felt the delicate hairs in her nostrils curl. The ever present odor of boiled offal and rancid smoke from a chimney that wouldn't draw was apparently an attraction, considering the number of men who patronized the bar, night after night. The humidity kept the smell suspended like herbs in oil. Three mouse-like sneezes and a lace-edged handkerchief to her face dulled the vile experience.

When Adelaide had left that morning, the proprietor's narrow bottom had been planted on the stool behind the reception desk. She wondered that it wasn't sore, as he was there still, scribbling columns of numbers into an enormous ledger. He paused in his work to insert the sharp end of his quill under his powdered wig—a wig he undoubtably wore as a trapping of respectability—to scratch the inevitable itch. Adelaide curled her lip. In France, such a hot monstrosity was certainly not *au courant,* at least not since the Bourbons lost their wigs in the same basket as their heads.

"Mam'selle Bonnediseuse, a man is here to see you," he said without looking up.

"A man?" Adelaide's blood ran cold. Her thoughts went straight to Dodo's wolfish attacker. "For *moi?*" Mademoiselle DuBette had said the man from the Quiet Woman had left with the golem, but he could have sent a member of his pack.

"That's right, mam'selle, a frog. . .er. . .Frenchie. I sent him up to see your husband."

"Frenchie?" Damn the English and their awful language. What was the man saying? Had a man from France arrived? "'Ere?"

"Not here, lass. Frog's up there." The proprietor stopped scratching his head to give a meaningful jab at the ceiling before waving the quill at the back stairs. Then he went back to his ledger book, information imparted, conversation over.

Adelaide looked towards the stairs with a lump in her throat. Napoleon's head of police had found her. As Dodo had warned would happen, *Ministre* Fouché must have read the letter from Mrs. Southill and discovered the whereabouts of the golem. Dodo, oh poor Dodeauvie. Her mentor was likely already dead, Fouché would see to that. Adelaide felt her eyes well up with tears as she backed away from the reception desk. At any moment, the minister could descend and find her. Every second she remained in the Dancing Bear was a gamble, both to her own life, and to the lives of the women in *la Société* who were now depending upon her.

With a jolt, she remembered her grimoire—her cherished book of spells. Dodo was using it behind his pillow to prop himself up. She took two steps towards the stairs, drawn towards her life's work.

Indecision and fear surged through her. Her mind raced to come up with some solution, some machination for retrieving her belongings. If she'd had more time, perhaps she could have considered climbing in through the window in the dead of night. The thought made her wince, remembering that the last time she'd climbed to escape a tight spot, Dodo had found her frozen in fear along the top of a high wall.

She would never fool herself a second time into climbing through windows, but she couldn't leave her grimoire without knowing with certainty that it was irretrievable. She would have to ascend in the normal way, using the stairs. She mustered a brave smile for the proprietor, who didn't notice, and walked towards the stairs as though headed to meet death himself. She held her head high as she passed near a table of men, suddenly feeling very self-conscious of the way her skirt swished around her ankles. "Good evening," she said. One had the good decency to at least nod acknowledgement, but the other four lifted their mugs of rank, black porter to hide their faces while their eyes continued to follow her.

The staircase banister felt solid as she began her ascent. Enough hands had slid along its surface, either going up or coming down, to have imparted a golden gloss to the wood. It was the kind of banister that invited a person to lean, to trust. Adelaide used it to pull herself up each reluctant step.

She sharply sucked in her breath at the first sounding creak of her weight on the stairs. She then strained her ears to hear any corresponding shifting of weight from the ceiling above, the sound of someone entering the hallway, footfalls descending the stairs from around the blind corner.

Nothing.

She released her breath in a long, pursed-lip blow and moved towards the wall where a line was painted with the sweat of countless others who had used one hand for stabilization as they traversed the stairs. Adelaide's fear abated for just a second, long enough to take note of the trail of filth and yank her hand away. The creaks weren't as loud near the wall, yet she still went slowly, trying to be as light-footed as possible while silently cursing all the *saucisson* makers in Paris.

At the top of the stairs she paused to let her heart settle, concerned it might be heard beating like a drum, before approaching the door to the room she and Dodo had been sharing. The door was pulled all the way closed. She tiptoed forward and put her hand on the doorknob.

What if it was a colleague of Dodo's? What if Jacques Noisette had found her to give her a last minute message? It didn't have to be Fouché, she reasoned. There were so many possibilities in life, all of them viable. She was a purveyor of these possibilities—each card she turned, each colorful image translated was a seed of action deposited in the fertile minds of her clients. She ached to know what her own future was, right at that moment, but her cards, fanned against her chest, had been silent for what felt like weeks.

Tonight she would just have to draw her clues from the life around her, like everyone else. She squatted and peered through the keyhole.

Just as her eye came level with the opening, a loud voice punctured the silence of the hallway. "Oh hooo. . .what have we here? A peeping Thomasina?"

Adelaide straightened instantly, barely stifling a startled screech by merely emitting a gasp, and turned towards the man who had just caught her *in flagrante delicto.*

Adelaide had no idea what he was saying. She watched as his tongue flicked words behind his gray teeth. She heard "spanking" and "naughty" and, based upon his lecherous grin and his wiggling eyebrows, assumed his intentions weren't good. His thin arms came towards her, sticky, like the legs of a spider about to draw in prey.

"Don't be shy," he whispered.

The sound of chair legs scraping on the wood floor came from

Dodo's room. It might as well have been the sound of a heralding trumpet. Adelaide didn't wait to see if friend or foe would walk through the door. She pushed the man aside and ran.

To hell with Dodo and his interminable death. To hell with her heavy grimoire and the spells that didn't work. To hell with possibilities and probabilities—Fouché had been behind the door. She knew it. She knew it in her gut. She ran past the four men drinking at the table. She ran past the proprietor who yelled for his back pay. She ran until her lungs burned and her legs ached, two entire London blocks. Then she walked. Swiftly.

That night would be spent on the *Sea Otter,* and the next morning she would set sail with Captain Briggs. Perhaps she'd find the emerald. Perhaps, she thought hopefully, the handsome captain would help her forget the damned rock entirely.

Mrs. Southill eyed the small group that waited patiently in front of the grand doors to the British Museum, once the Montagu house. It had taken her some time to walk from her clearing in the woods, but the exercise had felt good. Every so often it was nice to spend time in London so that she could, upon returning to her woods, feel confident in her decision to hate it. For her journey, she had brought a drawstring pouch, the same pouch she'd given the golem, and filled it full with the tools of her trade. There was always a need for a healing woman's touch. In the East End of London you couldn't walk three steps without hearing someone with a wet cough—and no wonder, the very air smelled like death. She stopped to give a child with a festering wound a fresh plaster. Willow bark was given to a young man who'd been living with an old man's back for nearly four days, keeping him from work. A bit of tincture of clove was given to a woman with a bad tooth, but Mrs. Southill had advised the moll to see a barber. Even with the soothing tincture, she would suffer for days with throbbing pain that slowly increased into blinding agony if she didn't see a barber. Alternatively, if the woman was brave and took Mrs. Southill's advice, she'd suffer the blinding agony of a barber's forceps that would slowly resolve into occasional throbbing pain. A toothache was a terrible thing.

Mrs. Southill had promised to tend to the child again the next morning on her way home. She wasn't entirely certain where she'd spend the night. She had the vague idea she'd stop by the Quiet Woman to see Mrs. Postlethwaite after completing her errand, but that was something she'd worry about later. At that moment, she was more interested in solving the problem of maneuvering around the crowd that had arrived at the museum before her.

At the top of the steps, two young ladies chirped to each other in familiar tones. They seemed the type to be entirely bored of London, but too headstrong to want to return to their family's estates after the end of the season. Likely tired of having to make that dreaded call at Mrs. So-and-so's estate, or yet another staid dinner at the parsonage, a pass through the halls of the museum, while not entirely a thrilling afternoon for young ladies so full of repressed energy, would be a welcome change.

The ladies' chaperone stood slightly to the side. She was still a young woman herself, perhaps the poor cousin of their mother's youngest brother, or a newly widowed sister of their father's closest friend. In any case, she'd taken on her role of interloper with ease, foiling the eager looking suitor, who stood two marble steps below the women, from all his attempts at making himself the most clever man imaginable. Each time he opened his mouth to relay his opinion on the current gossip, the chaperone heaved a sigh and rolled her eyes. Any smiles the ladies turned upon their handsome friend lost the power of innocence in the face of such exasperated derision from their older companion.

Three other men stood on separate steps, entirely oblivious of the women. Their eyes were glazed with deep thoughts; their satchels overflowing with books and documents. They were the typical academic types—ill fed, all arms and legs, with necks that were stuck in a position horizontal to the ground.

These were the elite few that had arrived prior to the museum's opening and had grouped themselves at the top of the stairs. Every one of them had noted Mrs. Southill below, not by directly turning their heads towards her with nods, but with sidelong glances and a couple wary twitches. Still more people were approaching across the courtyard of the once stately estate.

Mrs. Southill would take a case of gout or an outbreak of pustules any day over the anxiety inducing social trivialities required to mix politely amongst the London well-to-do. As the crowd gathered, her anxiety caused her to squeeze her hand around the long scroll she carried, forgetting that she would need the paper to be without a crease for her plan to work. She told herself that she was only imagining people were looking at her and that, anyway, the opinions of others did not matter, but the side-long glances were very real and made her think again of haughty Adelaide Lenormand.

That witch was a trouble-maker, thought Mrs. Southill. She'd shown no sense of creativity, no sense of wonder when she'd explained her project of capturing light. She shook her head, still amazed that a witch with Mlle Lenormand's talent wouldn't be interested in harnessing a power like that. Mrs. Southill was convinced that if she were to succeed, it would be a feat of magical ingenuity seconded only to Merlin's putting Arthur on the throne.

But no, Mlle Lenormand was only interested in serving her mentor Dodeauvie and had been irritated by the delay in her afternoon. The young witch's behavior had been shocking. How could she have acted so put-upon by the Society's request for her help—help they wouldn't have needed had she completed her task instead of making a mess of it? It wasn't as though she was the only one being asked to make sacrifices. Mrs. Southill's own task was as odious as any, given her predilection for solitude.

She attempted an ingratiating smile at the youngest of the women at the top of the stairs, who flushed and quickly looked away from her toothless grimace. The reaction caused her to give the paper scroll another couple squeezes. It hurt to not have her smile returned. She looked down at her best apron, which she'd tied over her tattered dress that morning in the hopes that the worst of the moth holes would be hidden, but now Mrs. Southill realized that even her best apron was dreadfully stained. To feel shame about her attire at her age was worse than feeling it as a young woman. London society was a cold and unforgiving mirror, and Mrs. Southill would have rather not seen herself reflected so starkly.

Suddenly the doors to the museum were thrown open and a strange breeze cooled her cheeks, as though the art and history within the hallowed halls had sighed. A well-heeled scholar stood in the doorway and peered at the small crowd over his precariously set spectacles. He bowed at the young ladies and beckoned everyone to enter. The invitation erased all the unease that Mrs. Southill had been feeling. Excited to see the collection of curiosities that were being hoarded inside, she hurried up the steps after the group.

Her old knees creaked. It had been a long walk, after all, and she was tired. She pressed on her thighs with each step, giving herself a little aid, only completing the last three steps by making loud grunts. Once at the top, with her heart beating in her throat from the effort, she rushed towards the door.

Who cared if the fancy ladies sneered at her lack of fashion?

The treasures of the Acropolis and the Parthenon were behind those doors! The art and antiquities alone were fascinating enough, but then there was the natural science—bugs on pins, stuffed birds in drawers, bones of all sorts—which drew her like a moth to flame. And a library. A library that could possibly compete with that which was lost in Alexandria. What were a few derisive looks when access to all these things were held in the balance?

"Not you," the imperious scholar said, holding up a hand.

Mrs. Southill glanced behind her. Perhaps he was talking to someone else? "I beg your pardon?"

"Did you not hear me? Not! You!"

"There's nothing wrong with my ears. I was under the impression that the British Museum is open to all curious and studious persons?"

"Curious you may be, but studious?" his mustache wagged derisively. "Hardly. You've not even the sense to studiously attend to your *toilet* before exiting your home. Leave, harpy, or I shall have you hoisted away." He made a face as if the very idea of touching her was distasteful.

Mrs. Southill battled to keep her outrage hidden, but she could feel the steam building. She wasn't less than anyone else. She was, in fact, worth more than most. She didn't need anyone else's approval—until, of course, that disapproval kept her from entering into society's most interesting places. She opened her mouth to make further protest but found she couldn't form any words. So she did the only thing she could do and brought the tightly rolled scroll of paper down hard over the man's head. The violence felt so satisfying that she did it three more times before she left. She might even have gotten in six thumps, altogether.

Late that night, Mrs. Southill blinked in the dark chamber of the British Museum, waiting for her old eyes to adjust to the light. Hulking figures of stone statues, an audience of standing gods, loomed along either side of her, eerily lit from below by the lantern she held. Unable to see their expressions, she imagined the statues to have affronted looks, as though listening to a speech that had suddenly taken a controversial turn.

She approached one of the stone figures and squinted at it from top to bottom: massive headdress, broad shoulders, narrow waist, loincloth, muscular legs. Then back to loincloth. Then back to massive headdress. Then back to loincloth. The Egyptians must have been quite large, she thought with some admiration.

It hadn't been difficult to get access inside after closing. Once the museum closed, the housemaids entered with their brooms, pails, and dust cloths. Mrs. Southill knew many of these laborers. They came to her all the time, thinking nothing of traveling the narrow path through her protective forest. They came wanting to be pregnant, wanting not to be pregnant, terrified for their first birthing. They came concerned about the stinging urine, the hacking cough, the twisted ankle. They brought her their babies to cure croup, diarrhea, fever. They brought her their burns when their skirts caught fire in the kitchen, or after they'd been scalded in the laundry. Mrs. Southill knew a maid or two, that was sure. And she'd merely had to ask one that worked in the British Museum to open the door.

She'd waited until very late to enter, in order to make sure there would be no one to bother her. There was still no guarantee that there wasn't someone still lingering over some old manuscript somewhere in a dark corner, but she had a plan should she encounter the lone academic. She'd just start scrubbing something with a corner of her apron.

In fact, Mrs. Southill felt quite relaxed about having illicitly gained entrance to the museum. She'd be quite comfortable spending the entire night in this scholar's palace, multiple nights even. It had the same quality of solitude, the same feeling of safety, as her forest clearing. Here, after hours, when the crowds of tourists had left with just as little in their heads as they'd had when they'd arrived, the building could breathe again.

Unfortunately, a full night was not possible. There were only a few hours in which Mrs. Southill could linger as dawn was nearing quickly. She turned from the handsome statues and walked right past a wrapped mummy, despite the allure of the mysterious symbols on the coffin in which it slept. She didn't bother to stop and look at a collection of painted amphorae resting on a table. She did, however, hesitate over cuneiform on unrolled papyrus, but then shook herself out of it. Mrs. Southill had a job to do. She singlemindedly headed towards her true goal, paper scroll in hand.

The scientists and scholars Napoleon sent with his army couldn't resist stealing the art from out of the sacred temples of Egypt, chipping them from the walls and changing the very nature of architecture thousands of years old. It had been part of the emperor's grand plan to bring science and modernity to Egypt, but the opposite had occurred. Instead of studying Egypt within the country of Egypt, French academia dictated that Egypt be plunged in alcohol and taken away in jars. Then, when the English defeated the French in the Battle of the Nile, the plunder changed hands and England took Egypt away from France. And here it was now, spread before her.

But it wasn't statues of Isis or the gold of buried kings that Mrs. Southill was after, it was a simple hunk of black granite. The rock had once been nothing more than a brick in a wall at Fort Julien, recycled from another building in another location, pulled down by time, or war, or both. It had been discovered, not by one of Napoleon's 151 men in the Commission of Sciences and Arts, but by a mere soldier, who recognized its potential significance immediately. This brick, however mundane, was actually a miracle of lost information. *La Pierre de Rosette*, the French called it. The Rosetta Stone.

Mrs. Southill stood before the hulking stone, breathless with wonder. It was more like a large boulder than a brick, nearly four feet tall. Its low pedestal gave it a few more inches, making it nearly as tall as the witch herself. On the bottom, carved lightly in its polished surface, was Ancient Greek writing. Translated, it revealed itself to be a decree announcing a new ruler, and how he should be worshiped. Above the Greek, two other sections were inscribed, each with its own language and system of writing, one being the strange pictographs of the ancient Egyptians. It was presumed that the top two sections were translations of the Greek decree, so that all persons in the land of Egypt, no matter their language, would understand the same new law. If this truly were the case, then the words in Greek would be the key to unlocking the meaning of each Egyptian hieroglyphic. This rock, this miracle of linguistics was about to release the tale of Ancient Greece's sister in significance—just as soon as someone could figure out the code.

Mrs. Southill could feel her heart pounding in her neck. Egypt was the seat of all Western culture. The thought of how much human knowledge had been lost because no one had been able to decipher hieroglyphics was more than a tragedy. It was unconscionable. The Rosetta Stone would remedy the loss. There was the Greek, right there at the bottom. Up above was the Egyptian. The one mirrored the other. It should have been simple enough to break the code.

Yet it was clearly a problem. The Rosetta Stone had been in England's possession for six years, and still no one had figured it out.

Mrs. Southill drew her roughened fingertips over the smooth surface of the Stone and was surprised at how delicate the engravings were. It certainly looked curious: falcons, seated figures, and eyes were aligned as though each picture was a word, scythes over jagged lines. It was hard to believe the key to reading the ancient formulas in the Book of Thoth were right here, under her very nose.

But it wasn't for her to unlock this mystery. She'd let the other women worry about deciphering the hieroglyphics.

Carefully, she unrolled the large scroll of paper and smoothed it up against the surface of the Stone. With a wide piece of graphite, she rubbed the paper vigorously, with the expectation that the graphite would transfer all the Stone's engravings onto the paper. Mrs. Southill filled an entire corner of the page with gray, but the hieroglyphics weren't copied. She peeled the paper away from the stone and ran her fingers over the engravings. They were too finely done. She'd have to think of another way.

"Meg?" Mrs. Southill called out into the hallway. "Meggie? Are you about?"

There was a splashing noise, the sound of a wooden scrub brush being dropped back into a bucket. "Coming Mother Southill," Meg yelled back. The glow of a second lantern revealed her approach, a gray maid in a yellow light.

"Look at this," Mrs. Southill said, "the rubbing doesn't work."

"Did you try rubbing the paper harder?" Meg asked, setting down her lantern to push a damp curl out of her eyes. She was sweaty from the effort of scrubbing floors.

"Doesn't matter how hard or soft I rub. It doesn't work. Do you think there'd be any pots of ink about?"

Meg thought for a minute, then nodded. "How many will you be needing?"

After five pots of ink, forty-five minutes later, Mrs. Southill found herself scratching her head again and staring at the Rosetta Stone. "That didn't work either."

"It's a right fine mess you've made for me," Meg tutted.

The two of them had painted the entire engraved surface of the stone in a thick layer of ink. Then Mrs. Southill had done her best to press the paper on the stone as quickly and carefully as she could, as one might do in a printing press, but the stone hadn't taken the ink very well. It rolled off its surface as fast as they brushed it on, and pooled upon the parquet floor before she could get an imprint.

Now the expensive scroll of paper was ruined, smeared all over with black blots and hand prints. Meg had a long ink smudge on her forehead where she'd pushed her hair out of her eyes and Mrs. Southill knew she likely had it worse. "I'll clean it," Mrs. Southill said. "It's not right to make you do it for me." She felt deflated. "I'll just have to draw the entire thing. Might you let me back in again tomorrow night?"

Her fingers felt cramped just thinking about the chore. She'd have to come back every night for the rest of the week. *La Société* wouldn't be pleased by the delay—they were already six years behind. Six years of letters demanding the right to a *facsimilé* in order to study the hieroglyphics; six years of being pushed aside by all the scholars, English and French, who were themselves working on the translations. A society of old women who dared to think they could do what the men hadn't yet accomplished? The notion seemed to be absurd to the academics in charge.

Meg, already scrubbing on her hands and knees, didn't look pleased. "I don't understand why you're wanting to make your own paper."

"Thousands of years ago, Mankind forgot how to read this language. Wouldn't it be nice to learn how to do that again?"

"I can't even read English, and I've done just fine."

Mrs. Southill sighed. She had no salve for the poverty of mind. "I know dear, but do you not enjoy being told stories? Think of this as unlocking the door to a lost library of stories."

The maid shrugged. She didn't have time for stories. "I still don't understand why you're marking your own paper. I can get you a paper."

"None as has this stone on it."

"Indeed, you are wrong. Mr. Smith and Mr. Babbins both have a sheet of paper like yours, big as the stone, with all its markings clear as day."

Mrs. Southill stared at the maid in surprise. "Here? They have it here?"

"Well, not here. Not in this here hall. Those two have desks in the library, three halls over."

PUKING

They hoisted anchor early that morning as the fog drifted in. Elise couldn't figure out how the captain had decided the weather had changed and the sailing would be smooth. Had the moon been veiled by a thin cloud at midnight? Did a bird crap on the left shoulder of the first mate? Perhaps the captain had licked two fingers and raised them to the wind—at least that would have had a smidge of science involved. Whichever method used to figure out when to leave Cork's protected harbor didn't matter now. It was obvious to all that the oracle he consulted for weather information had been as drunk as the rest of the crew on board *HMS Valiant*.

For two days the army had been confined below the gun decks in dank and crowded quarters as the ship heaved through stormy seas. No one wanted to be washed overboard in the storm, so no one complained. As the hours rolled by, the air, confined as they were, became thin on oxygen and thick on odors. The officers wouldn't let them light candles, and lanterns were only lit as-needed, so everyone mostly stayed in one place instead of stumbling around in the dark.

Elise was parked on a pile of crates under a grate in the low ceiling where a very thin light shone from the gun deck above. Once again she was alone with only the bad companionship of her thoughts to keep her company as she fought the swelling seasickness to keep down her meager dinner. At least now she could notch suicide off her list of possible methods for returning to Tucson. Drowning hadn't worked and her one moment of courage was a moral outrage to just about everyone else. Those who hadn't seen her suicide rescue, heard about it as word raced from stern to bow. The act was one more reason for Richard to feel humiliated by her, and he gratefully accepted the others' silent condolences and looks of sympathy. No one had any sympathy for her, Elise noted wryly.

It had been a stupid decision to marry Richard, but Elise hadn't had any other ideas. She couldn't bring herself to sell the emerald, and she didn't have any other money, so as far as she could see, marrying Richard and becoming an army camp follower was the only way she could get to America. And now she was stuck.

As the ship heaved over the sea, Elise tried to forget where she was by thinking of where she wanted to be. Nostalgia and wishful thinking helped her cope. Shivering in the cold, she wistfully recalled experiencing the opposite misery of too much heat. How many times had she heard, "but it's a dry heat" when she'd been suffering through temperatures over 100 degrees? She thought of better days, when a drive across Tucson towards the Catalina Mountains was considered a desperate act in self-preservation.

Considering the way Anita drove her Jeep, desperate wasn't too far from the truth. Elise lit the end of her cigarette and rolled down the window.

"Do you have to do that now?" Anita flapped one hand in the air to clear the smoke. "You're letting all the AC out."

"You should leave the doors off this baby. It'd be more fun. You know, treat it more like a Wrangler and less like a fashion accessory. Have you even taken this thing off-roading?" Elise caught the dirty side-eye Anita shot her. "Fine, fine. I'll just smoke half," Elise consoled. "Hey! Keep both hands on the wheel, please." Anita had reached under her seat for an abandoned mailer and was using it to vigorously fan the smoke out the window. "Okay! I'll put it out." Elise grabbed the dashboard as the Wrangler wove in its lane.

"Damn it, Elise. Not in my ashtray. You'll stink up my car!"

"Do you really want me to throw it out the window and start a grassfire?" Elise slammed the tray back into the dashboard. "I didn't think so."

All three smoldered angrily as they headed up Catalina Highway— the two friends, and the cigarette still smoking under the dash.

Elise missed Anita with a full-body ache.

As the ship pitched over the waves, her stomach surged with it. She breathed with pursed lips, in through the nose, out through the mouth, concentrated, steady. Sweat beaded on her forehead. The waves broke against the side of the *Valiant* with sickening regularity. A cigarette would be a terrible idea, considering she was hugging a bucket, but she wanted one so badly. Just a single puff.

There was a rush of feet in the gun deck above as sailors moved quickly to answer sudden orders. Their dark shadows thrown through the grate in the ceiling flitted like ghosts. Their footfalls were thunderous in comparison to the silence of the seasick infantrymen. When the sailors had gone, presumably to the weather deck, the eerie sounds of stretching rope, creaking wood, and rattling chains resumed, harmonizing with the storm raging beyond the walls of the ship's hull.

In this grim atmosphere, Elise heard someone yelp in pain, far aft of where she was sitting. "Get off me you fiddle-scraping blockhead! Watch where you're going!"

It was too dark to see who was approaching, but Elise knew all the same. "Begging your pardon," came the obscenely cheerful reply.

Then, closer, "Look out! Damn your eyes—you've trod on my foot."

"Your pardon. . ." The sound of protests from various soldiers got louder as the man eliciting the ugly curses made his way up the center of the narrow corridor and was tossed about by the pitching floor. Elise sighed resignedly.

"What are you doing up there?" Richard asked when he finally reached the stack of crates where she perched. His face twisted into a look of annoyance. "Come down from there. It isn't seemly to have you crawling all over the cargo. You'll hurt yourself."

Elise ignored him and looked across to the starboard side of the deck. The shadow of O'Brian's hunched back loomed against a wall of stacked crates. He was retching into a bucket. After the fight, she'd given him a poultice for his black eyes and he tried to return the favor with a kiss. Instead he got a mouthful of hair and a hard shove. It wasn't the first time some idiot mistook the use of her nursing skills with making a pass. It was nice to have O'Brian occupied with nausea, since that effectively stopped him from leering at her. The sexual vacuum created by the loss of the Irish women was felt by everyone, especially the remaining women who were only about six percent of the population on board. It didn't even seem to matter that they were all married. To the women's delight, they were still petted and flirted with. All but Elise.

Richard gripped her ankle as the floor dropped out from under them. The ship was falling into a deep trough in the waves. She clung to the chains that anchored the crates in their stack against the curved wall and held on tight as Richard pulled. "Get down here at once," he ordered. "This entire nightmare is your fault."

Elise weakly kicked her leg to dislodge Richard's hand while her mind floated back to Tucson.

"Slow down," she had said to Anita. "If I get sick in your car it'll be your own fault."

"Seriously?" Anita protested. "I'm not going all that fast."

"Just slow down around the curves." G-forces slammed Elise's stomach against her ribs.

The way to the top of Mount Lemmon was normally a pleasant drive on a twisting two-lane road. The air cooled as the miles melted away. Elise rolled the window down again and felt the wind slip under the sleeve of her shirt when she hung her arm out of the car. It raised goosebumps on her skin, smoothed away the sweat, and brought her the sharp smell of piñon pine as they moved out of the low desert and into the coniferous forest.

This time, however, Elise leaned out of the window for a purpose other than to enjoy the view into the deep canyon. Instead, she stared at the horizon to steady herself and hoped the wind would slap her back to normal. "Oh God," she moaned. "For fuck's sake, Anita. Slow down." Her words were blown away, unheard. Her stomach surged again as her friend whipped around yet another hairpin. The tires of the bouncing Jeep were barely clinging to the asphalt.

Elise would have given anything to be back in Anita's tidy silver Wrangler. It was cruel irony that Richard blamed her for the present situation.

"None of this is my fault," she said around the angry tears that were forming. "None of it."

She kicked one more time and his hand was finally jerked from her ankle. The slick decking was disgusting—there was no way she'd get down there in her bare feet, no matter how much it embarrassed

Richard. Everything was battened down but the people on board, and their buckets. The rule was to do your business at the ship's head, but in weather like this, the rule didn't apply. Careless missteps in the dark or a sudden buck of the ship would send a bucket rolling. Elise had gotten used to the stench, but there was no getting used to the feel of something questionable under your feet.

She compulsively touched her dress where her emerald was tucked under her corset. The action helped recalibrate her. "Did you lose again?" Elise asked Richard. He shrugged and shuffled around in the shadows of the crates to find a dry spot to spread his blanket.

Elise sighed. She wouldn't have cared much one way or the other, except now that she was his wife, her fortune was tied to his, and Richard's bad luck was hurting her effort to stay hydrated. As a camp follower "on the strength," she was entitled to one half of the rations of a soldier and none of the liquor. This meant either she drank the foul water stored on board in barrels, or she shared Richard's beer. Given what she knew about water-borne diseases, she selected choice number two. Unfortunately, Richard was constantly gambling away his beer rations.

On the other hand, beer wasn't going to help an already churning stomach.

A moan rose in the damp air. The sound, a waveringly long note, came from behind a blanket that had been hung to allow privacy for another married couple—a convenience Elise and Richard hadn't felt necessary, given their marital circumstances. Despite her own misery, Elise still had enough strength to roll her eyes. The couple had no business being that happy.

"It *is* your fault," Richard pouted. "Our being here is entirely your fault. You should have let me sell that jewel."

"Shhhhh!" Elise looked around to see if anyone had heard Richard. No one was paying attention to them.

"We could be tucked safe in the Quiet Woman had you done so. Look at you—you're pitiful," Richard sneered up at Elise and she felt her self-confidence weaken. She ran a hand through her greasy hair and pulled down the shapeless dress she had currently hitched over her hairy knees. "You are content to remain slattern and unpleasant when wealth could have given you the veneer of social respectability. It was most definitely you who brought me into this position. I blame you."

"Go ahead. Blame me then. I don't care."

When they'd first boarded the ship they hissed their arguments at each other, but now they no longer bothered to keep their voices down. The tight quarters made it difficult for others to politely move away when they started bickering, although most still tried. A positive result of their spats was acquiring more space than the others were afforded.

"It's not just me you damned to this fate. Tom blames you too. He told me so himself."

Thomas. The name was like a hammer on Elise's chest. She'd tried to give him medical care too after the fight, but he told her he didn't want her damned poultices.

She felt her mouth fill with a swell of saliva and she swallowed hard. The memory of her drive into the mountains of Tucson flooded her.

"Oh my God, Anita. Pull over."

"Hang on for just another minute. We're almost there."

"PULL OVER."

Elise had the door open before the Jeep even stopped. Her lunch of a strawberry and mango smoothie created a vibrant orange line against the roadside sage. Anita stepped out of the car and came around while looking at her watch impatiently. "We're going to be late," she said.

"Late? Late for what? We're *camping!*"

"Everyone's waiting for us at the trailhead." Anita sighed when Elise bent over a second time. "Okay. Get it all out." She caught up Elise's hair.

"I'm not getting back in there." Elise pointed weakly at the Jeep and wiped her mouth with the back of her hand.

"Walk to that tree and back. Then you drive."

"No way."

"It'll make you feel better. You can't get carsick when you're in the driver's seat."

You can't get seasick when you're unfurling the sails. Elise imagined sailors, three decks above, happily stomping their feet in the puddles while the captain pumped a jig from a squeeze-box. It was a pretty fantasy. They weren't seasick, thought Elise. They were driving. Her stomach muscles rippled nauseatingly.

Another moan from behind the curtain cut through the gloom. Richard gave up his seat on the floor and climbed the crates to sit next to Elise. She scooted over to give him space. They were comfortable enough together, despite their constant bickering, but there was little chance Elise would be emitting her own full-throated moans any time soon.

She wasn't averse to the idea, just indifferent, even though he was unnaturally good looking. While the entire regiment was soaked in the sweat of nausea, Richard's skin took on a healthy sheen from the humidity and his cheeks remained rosy. When everyone else had turned inward in their misery, Richard thought nothing of pulling out a deck of cards from his pack to seek out the ship's carpenter and purser for a game and a conversation. It didn't seem fair. His beauty was wasted, Elise thought as she surveyed his profile. Richard was attractive without any attraction.

She clenched her fists as another high pitched moan emanated from behind the blanket.

"Shouldn't you look in on Mrs. Collins?" he asked.

"What for? She sounds a little busy right now." In the weeks that they'd been on board, she'd exchanged very few words with Amanda

Collins. There were only about five other women in Richard's company, including Mrs. Gillihan and Mrs. Collins had the least amount of personality of any of them. Anyway, she hardly ever came out from behind the curtain.

Richard shrugged. "You know your own business."

He reached down to his knapsack and pulled out his fiddle. The squeaking sounds his instrument made as he rotated the tuning pegs and plucked the strings were a welcome distraction. When he drew out a long note with his bow, the other soldiers, suffering as they were, heaved a sigh of relief. It didn't matter what decade it was, music was eternally a balm. Elise took her bucket and climbed to the top of the stack to avoid Richard's sharp elbows and settled back against the curved wall.

The melodies Richard pulled from his fiddle meandered without pause from one song to another. Elise was beginning to recognize the more common refrains that circled back around in various keys and rhythms. The way people would join in making music without any kind of showmanship was one aspect of her new world that she truly appreciated, and she loved it when someone was moved to stand and sing. Only once had Thomas emerged from the shadows to join in with his earthy baritone, and there was barely a man in the company that hadn't wiped tears from his eyes when he sang, "*Man to man, the world o'er, shall brother's be for a' that,*" except for Sergeant Taylor, who had threatened to break Richard's fiddle in two for daring such a "republican" song.

A sudden choked, gasping sound burst from behind the blanket curtain, causing Richard to play four atonal notes in rapid succession as his bow fell off the fiddle.

"I can't think why you shouldn't be calling upon Mrs. Collins," he insisted.

"Why are you so concerned about her" Elise felt her stomach

clench again, but this time it wasn't from nausea. It was caused by sudden fear. She sat up straight. "She's not pregnant, is she?"

"Good God, woman. Didn't you know?"

Private Collins poked his head from behind the curtain. Even in the gloom Elise was able to detect his wild-eyed look. He walked towards her like a drunk man, careening from side to side. Other soldiers caught him as he passed, thumping him on his back, giving words of encouragement, and keeping him on his feet.

"Some nurse you're turning out to be," Richard laughed ruefully. "You can't even tell when a fellow female is nearing her time of confinement."

"How am I supposed to tell? I can't exactly ask. I mean, I thought she was just fat." She reached for Mrs. Southill's medical kitbag. "How'd she get on board? I thought pregnant women weren't allowed?"

"Quite right," Richard nodded, "but no one could bear to see the couple torn asunder. She was weeping so prettily." He attempted to take her elbow to steady her as she descended to the floor, but Elise shook off his hand and leapt into the air like a cat.

The ship began rising up a swell which created a slick ramp for Elise to surf down with one bare foot in front of the other. Private Collins caught her mid-way. "How far apart are her contractions?" she asked as they made their way towards the curtained corner. Collins shook his head, not understanding. "Her pains! How many minutes between her pains?"

"She's in a great deal of pain," he agreed. "It's her first."

Elise ducked behind the curtain. Mrs. Collins, while holding her stomach in the eternal gesture of all pregnant women who loved their unborn babies, was puking into a bucket. She looked up at Elise with glazed eyes and lowered herself into a squat, bracing herself against two crates on either side of her. Her face, pale as a boiled turnip, was streaming in sweat.

Elise felt her own stomach heave in a sympathetic reaction and gagged on the scent.

"Will you be all right?" Collins asked, concerned. "Shall I fetch Mrs. Gillihan to help? Perhaps Private Hobert? He's birthed plenty of lambs."

"Hobert? No. God, no," Elise said in horror. Hobert, formerly a shepherd, was so used to having only his sheep as company that he felt no compunction in sending snot-rockets in all directions whenever his sinuses clogged, which was all the time. Elise considered any area within a ten-foot radius of the man a biohazard zone. "I've got this."

Amanda Collins's thighs trembled as she let out another moan. The cries must have alerted the entire deck to the imminent birth and Mrs. Gillihan, unable to resist the call for her opinion, whether or not it was asked for, poked her round head under the dividing blanket. "Is it happening? Oh! It is!"

"Looks like it," Elise offered a shoulder to support her young patient, who was trying to find a comfortable position.

"I'm so thirsty," Amanda whispered to Elise. Her words were a kick in the gut. Here was a woman who clearly had more need for hydration than anyone else on board, and yet Elise's hands were tied. "Aren't you sharing your beer rations?" she asked Amanda's husband.

"Beer?" Mrs. Gillihan questioned. "Mrs. Collins drinks water, surely."

"My wife doesn't care for ale," Collins agreed.

"You're not letting her drink that shitty water, are you?" Elise watched in horror as Peter Collins lifted a canteen to his wife's lips. Mrs. Gillihan recoiled at Elise's choice of words.

"If you've a better idea, speak up."

Better ideas whirled like spun gold in her brain: carbonated water with a hint of lemon, spicy iced cola, coconut water. She'd give her left lung to walk into Eegee's off Speedway and order a Frozen Strawberry

Fizz, but she'd settle for lukewarm water from the tap and be grateful for the hint of chlorine. "You should at least boil the water first."

"Boil it? Whatever for? And how are we to boil water here?" He waved his arms to take in the entire belly of the ship.

"I don't know, can't we get boiled water from the ship's galley?"

"So all of us in the army can take our tea? Do you suppose the cook will supply us with crumpets as well? You must be joking," Collins laughed.

"You run along," Mrs. Gillihan dismissed Elise. "Go on. I can stay and help Mrs. Collins."

"You've helped other women before, right?" Elise didn't trust the woman's confident self-assessment.

"I've been present for a few births and had four of my own."

"You've got four kids?"

"No, the good Lord saw fit to call three of my precious angels to his bosom, but I've a daughter in London." The woman smiled happily, unaware she'd caused Elise even more unease.

"I'm sorry." Elise wasn't sure what more to say. Her offer of sympathy didn't seem fitting to the situation, somehow. "So, you're trained?"

"Trained?"

"Yeah, trained. You know, to help in deliveries. Midwifery."

"Are you?" Collins asked Elise.

"Well, not midwifery, but nursing. I did study labor and delivery— all nurses have to." She eased her shoulder under Amanda's armpit, hoping to steady them both. "But whatever, if you want Mrs. Gillihan's help, looks like she's got everything under control here. I'll just. . . whoops. . .here, take her. . ." Elise shifted Amanda's weight to her husband and stepped away. "We all good? Yes?" She lifted the curtain and made to duck out.

"Good? No! Wait!" Peter Collins stammered, his arms full with his wife. "Amanda needs you!"

"Certainly she does not," Mrs. Gillihan clucked disapprovingly. "I'm sure Mrs. Ferrington has better things to do. She had quite a spill the other day and a birthing can be quite taxing, you know. Mrs. Ferrington should rest." Her eyebrows nearly reached her hairline with meaning.

Elise sighed. "Look, this is stupid. If you want me to leave, I'll leave. But if you want me to stay, then you have to trust me to call the shots, not Mrs. Gillihan. So, decide."

The Collinses looked at each other. They didn't look confident about their choices.

"Mrs. Gillihan can sit here and stroke your hair and coo," Elise tried to reassure them. "That's cool with me. But cooing isn't going to get the baby out. Just so we're clear."

"Please," Amanda said between huffs. "Please stay. Get the baby out."

"Dear," objected Mrs. Gillihan.

"She will stay," Private Collins insisted, immediately taking his wife's side.

Elise took a deep breath, knowing her next statement wasn't going to go over well. "So, where I'm from, midwives get paid." The indignation that followed her statement nearly blew the blanket off the wall.

"We've nothing! How do you expect—"

"Beer. Richard's gambled his away and I won't drink the water. Pay me half your beer ration for the next two weeks."

Collins's mouth dropped open. "My beer? Half?" he stuttered.

"I can call in Hobert if you prefer?" Elise put her hands on Amanda's abdomen and pressed deep to feel for the baby's heartbeat and position, knowing she'd already won. "Hobert probably won't ask for payment, except for maybe, here and there, when he feels a need for a sweet favor from your wife. . .after she's recovered, of course." Elise wiggled her eyebrows.

Amanda's wail took on an edge of panic. "Give it to her! Give her your beer!"

"I think your missus would like for me to have your beer," Elise said wryly.

Collins grumbled and accepted the terms.

As Elise continued to probe Amanda's belly, her concern grew. "How far along are you? How many weeks?"

"Weeks?"

Elise sighed again. Poor nutrition, bad water, sea sickness—all these things could cause a premature birth, but there was no way to know if the baby was term if Amanda hadn't been keeping track of the weeks. She was having contractions, so early or not didn't matter at this point. The baby would come if positioned correctly. "I need hot water, towels, and soap," she said to Collins.

"I haven't got any."

Elise turned to Mrs. Gillihan. "Please. This is the perfect way for you to be helpful. We need this area to be as clean as possible. Cleaner than clean."

Doubt played across the woman's features as she weighed the consequences of getting supplies versus leaving Amanda in the care of a woman with questionable morals. "Right," she said finally, and disappeared. On the other side of the curtain, Mrs. Gillihan could be heard barking orders.

Time seemed to crawl. Elise distracted Amanda with meaningless chit-chat and rubbed her back as they waited for hot water. Just as she decided to douse her hands in rum and hope for the best, a triumphant Mrs. Gillihan returned with young Bill Stanton behind her holding two buckets of hot water, mostly full, and a lump of lye soap. Mrs. Gillihan held a stack of clean linens cradled in her elbow.

Setting to work immediately, the two women worked in tandem, the elder using one bucket to scrub the deck, the younger using the other bucket to wash her hands and her patient. Mopping the sweat from Amanda's brow, Elise tried to gather her thoughts. Despite her bravado, she hadn't had that many opportunities to help deliver babies as an ER nurse. The pregnant women who burst through the double doors at the hospital were almost always shuttled straight to the labor and delivery ward where an entire crew of medical workers specializing in childbirth waited. Now Amanda only had Elise to rely on, and Elise had no one but herself. She explained what she was about to do and waited for Amanda to nod before reaching between her legs.

She was barely dilated. Elise looked at her medical kitbag and wished it contained a magic wand. "The baby's not in position," she said to Mrs. Gillihan.

"Breech?"

"No, sideways." She tried to hide her worry. She would have given up five years' worth of beer rations for a simple stethoscope and a watch. She pressed her ear to Amanda's stomach to listen for the baby's heart beat and heard gurgling intestinal noises instead. "I'm going to get the doctor," she announced. Why hadn't she thought of that before? Everyone had been sick for days, but not once had there been any sign of the doctor. She'd almost forgotten he existed.

"The doctor? Do you mean the army surgeon? Why? Is Amy in any danger?" Collins asked.

"Are you not calling for the surgeon a little prematurely?" Mrs. Gillihan asked.

"Amanda's fine. I just want the doctor." Suddenly, there wasn't anything Elise wanted more than to put the responsibility of mother and baby into more capable hands. She felt like a rookie nurse with a raw deal. It was hard not to think about all the things that could go wrong, and all the equipment she was missing. Giving birth was something a woman's body was built to do, but that didn't mean much. After all, human bodies are built to do a lot of things, like breathing, yet people died all the time from lung related illnesses. She'd rather deal with a gaping wound or a broken bone any day. At least you could splint a bone or sew a wound. "Um. I'll be right back." Elise darted away before anyone could ask more questions.

At the bottom of the ladder to the upper decks, a dark silhouette stepped in front of her, blocking her path. She didn't have to see Thomas's face to recognize him. His broad shoulders, slightly hunched by a lifetime of leaning over people to intimidate them, gave him away. "What do you want?" Elise asked. "I'm in a hurry."

"How is she?" Thomas's legs were spread and steady against the pitching floor.

"Fine. Why do you care?"

"Why should I not care?"

Elise shrugged. Thomas loomed. The ship lurched. In tandem, they both took a wider stance for balance and Thomas grabbed Elise's arm to steady her.

"You going to get out of my way?" she asked, pulling away from his helping hand. "I need to get the doctor."

"Do you mean the surgeon? Is Mrs. Collins in any danger?"

"Why is everyone asking me that? I don't know, probably not. Maybe." His warmth remained on her arm, her skin sensitized to the roughness of his hand. "I'll feel better with the doctor around."

"He's a surgeon, not a doctor."

"Aren't surgeons also doctors?"

"Entirely different fields of study. Mr. Russell is quartered in the ship's storeroom. You'll likely find him there." Without another word, Thomas stepped aside to let her pass.

The air grew slightly more breathable as she climbed her way to the upper decks, and the sound of the raging storm grew louder. She gripped the rail, white-knuckled, as the ship plunged in and out of the waves. Even with the ship battened down, everything was wet. Fleetingly, she thought of Tucson, of the broad desert and endless sky, warm and dry—the kind of warm that crackled in your hair and smelled sharp, like the acrid smell a line of fire ants leaves behind.

It seemed strange to house a doctor in a storeroom. The sailors all had fourteen inches of space to swing in their hammocks when they were off shift for the four hours at a time they were allowed to sleep. The army men had the floor. She supposed sleeping in a storeroom was a great privilege. Elise assumed the storeroom had to be closer to the weather deck, but hadn't a clue beyond that. After two men had given her incomprehensible directions laden with nautical slang, Elise pounded on a door that looked promising. The answering groan gave her hope that she'd finally found the right place. She pushed open the door and was slapped with an eye-watering scent of sweat and vomit.

It was less storeroom and more broom closet. On the floor was a small pile of leather trunks of all sizes. One was open, revealing an impressive collection of books. Under the trunks were three layers of crates. And shoved whereever there was space left in the small room, were cages of live chickens. Suspended from hooks in opposite walls was a hammock, the bottom of which barely grazed the home of a skinny hen who had lost most of her feathers. A lump of blankets in the hammock moved and a pair of bloodshot eyes peered out.

"I'm looking for Doctor Russell," she said. The eyes blinked. "Wait. Are you?" Elise had a sinking feeling. "Doctor Russell?"

"I am the army's surgeon, George Russell. Who the bloody hell are you?" The man's head stretched out of the blanket like a turtle coming out of its shell. His orange hair was plastered to his forehead with sweat. His mustache, such as it was, lay limp over his upper lip. The youthful freckles that dotted his nose were the only indication of a healthy past spent outdoors.

He reached under his hammock and drew a sloshing pail closer towards him and dry heaved over it. "Yes? Yes?" he asked impatiently when he managed to look up again. "State your business."

"I'm Elise Du--, er, Mrs. Richard Ferrington. Your nurse?"

"My nurse? Who sent you to nurse me? I've no need of a nurse."

"No, I'm on your staff."

"My staff?"

"Um. Yeah. I'm an army nurse."

"Army nurse?"

Elise took a steadying breath. So many of her conversations consisted of her saying things and people repeating whatever she said in incredulous tones. "Amanda Collins is in labor. We need you downstairs right now."

Russell smacked his lips together unpleasantly. "Ah yes, now I remember Corporal Whiffle said you'd called yourself the best nurse in the entire British Army," he laughed weakly. "I suppose that means you're nearly as helpful as a loblolly boy."

Elise narrowed her eyes, suspecting that Russell had just insulted her. "Mrs. Collins is having her baby right now."

"Who is Mrs. Collins?"

"Private Collins's wife."

"Private?"

Elise took the man's coat off the top of a barrel and held it up for him. When he made no effort to move, Elise grabbed the corner of his blanket and tugged.

Russell pulled back. "Just one moment. Why would you need me? Is the baby breech?" he asked.

"Transverse."

"Transverse?" He peeled Elise's hand from the blanket. "Is the mother in any danger?"

Elise felt herself flush. Normally she'd have data to give, mother's vitals, baby's heart rate. Approaching a doctor without having a complete report on the status of the patient was inexcusable under normal circumstances, but she didn't even have a watch to time the contractions. "No, I don't think so. I mean, not yet. I'm just worried that her labor won't progress without the baby's head engaged. I think the baby is premature, but Amanda doesn't know her due date."

"Bloody hell, are you a nurse or not? You've been caught in your lie, madam."

"No, I *am* a nurse, but—"

"Unhand me you hag," Russell shouted while trying to roll himself tighter into the blanket that Elise had been trying to pull away. "I am unwell. A real nurse would see that instantly. How dare you attempt to rouse me from my deathbed for a transverse presentation." To more colorfully illustrate his condition, he swung his bucket at Elise. She jumped back to avoid wearing its contents and felt a light sprinkle of backsplash on the tops of her feet. "Mrs. Amanda Collins," he said, gasping and coughing through heaves, "can go to hell. And God help her whelp if you don't know enough to turn the bugger. Nurse indeed! Go do your job, madam."

English Lessons

Adelaide sailed the ocean like an old hand. The ship called upon the forces of all four of nature's elements in a manner remarkably similar to casting a spell—wind was captured and harnessed by white sails so large they swallowed the sky, water was cut by the keel like the sharp blade of a sleigh, and flames had steamed the wood into the shape of the *Sea Otter's* curved hull. The ship herself was like the great mother earth, her rounded belly protecting all within. The ship's crew was like a large coven who lent their collective power to the captain so that he might conduct them all from one place to another at speeds that took Adelaide's breath away. She stood on the lower deck of the *Sea Otter* and rode the bucking ocean. Under the open hatch, she took great gulps of salt air and felt nourished.

Accustomed to placing candles at the four cardinal directions as a calming meditation, Adelaide could easily take her bearings, even when the ocean looked equally roiled by weather in every direction. In this small way, she and the good Captain Briggs were alike. He was always aware of where his ship was in relation to the rest of the world. The crew's confidence in their leader's navigation skills was a basic trust, and yet to Adelaide, this skill was unremarkable. Although unable to light candles on board, Adelaide set her own personal compass every morning with a drawn card and a nod to the cardinal points.

The weather had been violent in the North Sea. Rain, and wave after pounding wave, had soaked everything and tossed the ship like a leaf in the breeze. But now that they'd left Britain behind, there began a nearly imperceptible lifting of the weather. Adelaide felt nothing but relief. Not just relief from the incessant darkness of her cabin, but also relief from the responsibilities that *la Société* had placed upon her. So much time in her cabin had purged her of any fears of the task set before her. Now it seemed like nothing more than a triviality. Should she actually find the emerald, which she deemed unlikely, it would be nothing more than a happy surprise, like having *un joli bonbon* offered to mask the flavor of a spoonful of medicine.

Standing on deck in the heavy drizzle, she gazed out at the *Sea Otter's* wake. Above, the white sails sliced though the dark sky. Sailors were out on the yardarms, dropping the reefs in the abating wind. Normally Adelaide ignored them all as she took in the air, but as she promenaded along the perimeter of the ship—which wasn't much of a walk given the many obstacles of sailing tack in her path—one grizzled sailor caught her eye. He was sitting on the lee side of the purser's cabin, hunched against the wall. In his lap, a ball of thick worsted wool danced as the front panel of a guernsey sweater fell from the knitting needles that flashed in the sun. He was working a complicated pattern of knots, a spell the likes of which she'd never seen. "Making wind?"

Adelaide asked in her simple English.

The sailor gave her a slow grin revealing a mouth full of broken teeth and swollen gums. "*Passing* wind d'you mean? Oh aye. I'm passing it. I've been farting away my whole life on this bitch of a ship." Then he leaned aft and bore down, squeezing his eyes closed with the effort. "Thank ye for asking."

The captain and his officers on board had made it their project to help Adelaide learn English. Dictionaries and grammar books had been lent to her, and every evening over dinner, she practiced speaking with the gentlemen. Being immersed in the language on a small merchant ship helped, but it turned out that she didn't have much of a head for English. Adelaide was hardly surprised by her difficulty. Germanic languages were entirely without poetry.

She made a second attempt at communicating with the strange sailor, her curiosity overriding his insulting response. "*Tricotage. . .* knitting," Adelaide insisted, calling up the obscure word from the depths of her recent memory and pointing to the bearded man's handiwork. "Knitting wind."

He stopped laughing. Adelaide felt his gaze take in her simply cut dress, the Alençon lace that edged her sleeves and petticoats, her shawl that warmed her shoulders with its complicated twists of yarn. His eyes pierced her so that she could almost be certain he saw the divination cards that she kept pressed against the soft skin of her bosom. "You think I can knit the wind, do you?" He crossed himself in an act of protection. "It's bad enough having women on board, but now we've a witch. And I suppose you want me to show you all my tricks?"

"Knitting," Adelaide said again, not understanding his meaning. She dearly missed having her own needles. There was something about feeling the wool thread through her fingers, pulled by the slowly winding pattern. The repetitive motion calmed. The smell of the wool healed.

The sailor took up his project again and shook his head. "I'll not put this power in your hands. This is a man's job. Always has been, always will be." The creamy wool snagged on his rough, weather-worn hands leaving tufts of fiber in the cracks of his fingers. He slipped five stitches onto a third needle, and bypassed them only to turn back to knit them three stitches later. Adelaide gasped. She'd never seen such audacious patterning. "Show," she demanded, "show!"

"No. I will not," the man said primly, balling up his work and turning his back with his beard in the air.

She sighed. Of course he wouldn't share his spell. What was she thinking? But the strength of her desire to knit didn't allow her to give up. "I touch?" She breathed the question hesitantly, and was rewarded with a leering grin.

"Mademoiselle Bonnediseuse, I must say I'm surprised to see you out in this rain. Is Nigel bothering you?"

Adelaide turned quickly, startled, and then struggled to keep her face neutral at the sight of Mrs. Briggs. The blue-eyed blond stood ramrod straight under her umbrella, showing no discomfort from the rolling waves. Her knees, spread apart for balance, puffed out the skirt of her immaculate white dress as they bent in rhythm with the rising and falling deck. Jacques Noisette had failed to mention that the handsome captain traveled with a young wife. The flirtation Adelaide had looked forward to was now more difficult to achieve. Worse, Mrs. Briggs' French was intolerable. Captain Briggs had a charming lilt to his accent, but his wife merely drawled, as though her tongue was too meaty for her lower jaw to support the weight of it.

"I must apologize for the crew," Mrs. Briggs said, drawing Adelaide away from Nigel, who had submissively bent his head over his knitting again. "With the war resuming, it was nearly impossible for my Howard to find any sailors worth their salt. The Navy is in constant need of able seamen, and the very few who haven't volunteered are forced to join by press gangs, leaving no one to crew England's merchant ships. Nigel here is one of the best men we've got, but a bit strange. I'd stay away from him if I were you."

"I was admiring his knitting needles," Adelaide said. "They're beautifully fashioned. I wish I had my own again."

"Knitting needles?" Mrs. Briggs laughed in surprise. "You've barely a stitch of clothing to call your own, and that is what you miss? I must say, my dear, you do surprise me at every turn. I'll put the ship's carpenter to work for you. He'll turn you a pair of needles in no time, and when we reach the Azores Islands, I'll have the captain buy all the wool your heart desires. Nothing makes Howard happier than to buy me gifts and I'll tell him what I want most is for you to have yarn."

Mrs. Briggs affectionately threaded her arm into Adelaide's elbow, inviting her to share her umbrella. "Personally I prefer needlework to knitting," Mrs. Briggs continued as they walked together. "There's something so satisfying about stitching a spray of violets or a bouquet of garden roses. No matter how far out to sea I find myself, I'll always wear flowers stitched in the softest silk. Isn't that wonderful? But you are correct to think so pragmatically. Embroidered flowers are absolutely absurd. Just think, a woman such as myself living out here on the ocean and embroidering roses! I should heed your better judgement and spend my time knitting Howard a guernsey." Her laugh tinkled pleasantly.

"Have you ever embroidered lace?" asked Adelaide hesitantly. She wasn't sure how far she should go down this path, but it was difficult not to encourage Mrs. Briggs's interest in textiles, despite the woman's atrociously accented French.

"Embroidered lace? I thought lace was knotted."

"Not all of it," Adelaide lifted her sleeve to show the hidden lace at her wrists. "See how the threads of this lace make a mesh? How the stuffed cordage lines each rose pedal? This detail is not possible with common bobbin lace."

Mrs. Briggs hesitantly reached out a tiny hand, reddened from the weather, to touch Adelaide's wrist. "It's beautiful." Her smile was soft and her blue eyes sparked with imagination. "How wonderful would it be if the bouquets I love so much to embroider could become lace."

"If you are interested, I could show you a bit of the art."

It took ten years of apprenticeship, countless hours of building trust, and a sacred initiation for Adelaide to achieve mastery of the embroidered lace. The guilt she felt for suggesting to pass along a few tricks to her hostess was considerable, but one evening's worth of embroidery lessons wouldn't reveal too many secrets, she reasoned. She was surprised how it made her long for her old hometown of Alençon. The world had been simpler in those years she'd spent in that sleepy village in Normandy.

"That would be a delightful way to pass the time," Mrs. Briggs said. "I'm so glad you're here. I must say you've been a delightful surprise. Although, I'm sure you are most anxious to return to your family and all the rich comforts you surely miss.

"Indeed," Adelaide said quietly. She hadn't yet grown accustomed to her adopted identity of a French royal exile in disguise as a commoner.

"It's been wonderful to have another woman aboard! I know it is selfish of me to think such a thing, but I do hope you soon grow tired of your family and come back to me. Life on the ocean has a strong appeal, and I can tell it calls to you." Her smile was infectious.

Adelaide patted the younger woman's hand that rested on the crook of her arm and looked at the subtle pattern of entwined white silk rosebuds adorning her gown. White on white. It was a ridiculous garment for a woman living on board a ship, but she understood the desire to wear beautiful things, despite the circumstances. She couldn't help but think wistfully of her own gowns, left behind in Paris. Once home, she was sure it would be a long time before she would yearn for adventure as Mrs. Briggs predicted.

Perhaps Mrs. Southill was right when she had counseled her to return to lace making. There was indeed an allure to the adornments of fashion. She hadn't felt its pull in years, turning to rough knitting when she most needed extra power in a cast spell. There was nothing about magic that forced her to use wool, it was just easier to work with. Mademoiselle DuBette had accused her of throwing away a powerful talent for the more elusive draw of masculine success. But then, one could question why some activities were labeled as masculine and some feminine. The sailor Nigel's insistence that the knitting he was completing was not for a woman's hands seemed to challenge the idea of what was women's work.

They stopped their promenade near the bow of the ship and stood silently, sharing the exhilaration of the ocean spray. Then they returned to their walk.

"Your husband has been very kind to me. I'm not sure I deserve such charitable treatment," Adelaide said.

"Yes, yes," Mrs. Briggs assured her impatiently, her countenance suddenly changing. "His generosity knows no bounds, especially when it comes to the fairer sex. But I do not believe him to be offering charity. I understand an agreement of exchange was made? That you would petition your family to pay for passage once you were returned to them?"

"Yes, of course. I merely meant that he has a charitable heart, and a large capacity for trust."

Mrs. Briggs smiled at the compliment and excused herself to attend to the cook, who, she said, was sure to burn the roast should she not intervene.

The reminder of the upcoming dinner caused Adelaide's stomach to rumble. The previous evening's repast had been a delicious pairing of leg of lamb, the fat crisped on the outside, the flesh pale pink and tender on the inside, and sliced potatoes drenched in a white sauce of clarified butter and egg yolk, the whole thing seasoned with shallots and tarragon. The night before that had been lamprey boiled in its own blood followed by three roast chickens stuffed with crushed hard tack, chopped onion, celery root, and egg, seasoned with rosemary and sage. Despite Mrs. Briggs' deprecating tone, her cook had admirable skills.

Adelaide watched, deep in thought, as Mrs. Briggs headed to the galley. The captain was a resolutely loyal husband, much to her annoyance, and what man wouldn't be with such a pleasant slip of a woman? But his eyes did wander. She'd felt them on her many times. But even if he did stay constant, at least his countenance gave her the compliment of suffering from suppressed desire. Adelaide noticed how his clear brow had broken out with the worst kind of pustules since the beginning of their voyage, evidence that his beautiful wife wasn't giving him any aid. It was obvious to Adelaide that any woman who embroiders with white silk thread on white cloth would not be the kind of woman who could satiate great passion.

She looked down at her own functional, brown travel dress and sighed again. "The man wears the jewel; the jewel does not wear the man," she recalled Napoleon saying about the dazzling emerald. She wondered if the brown frock wears the woman? If that was the case, it would explain why her clothes made her feel tiresome and colorless.

Back in her cabin, Adelaide peered into the tiny mirror nailed to the wall. Here was her silk, she thought, running a hand over her rich dark hair. Who needs white roses embroidered onto white dresses when one's hair has luster, when one's eyes convey heat? Who needs jewels when one's conversation sparkled? The thought made her feel better as she ruthlessly pinched her cheekbones to give them a youthful pink hue.

Out of habit, she closed her eyes and reached for the golem, having done so every day since she'd first called the creature into existence. She felt her mind push against the confines of the small cabin in which she sat, probing every square inch. Then she pushed out further, in concentric rings of awareness, penetrating other cabins, the stateroom, the entire deck, then farther, pressing, pressing. Now she was passing above the waves, breaching the ocean like a dolphin, striving to swim faster than the forward thrust of the ship's bowsprit. Then out, out until there was nothing but the black void.

The golem wasn't there.

Every day that passed with no contact released some of the pressure. Adelaide blinked into the mirror. What if she was sailing in the wrong direction? The idea both horrified and pleased her.

The dinner bell tolled. The smell of a lovely roast cut through the sharp sea air. She tucked an errant curl of hair under her bonnet and headed out, all anxiety forgotten for the moment.

"My dear Mademoiselle Bonnediseuse," cried Captain Briggs, standing up from his chair as she swept into the dining room. She regarded him with a raised brow and a smile. With the exception of those unpleasant first few days when she'd been indisposed, she'd had every meal with the captain and his greetings had never lessened in their effusiveness. He pulled out a chair and helped her to her seat. Seating himself directly opposite, he looked at her appraisingly. "Wonderful to see you and Gertie taking in the air this afternoon. I apologize I could not join you, as my duties were elsewhere. Perhaps when we reach the Azores, Gertie and I might have the honor of taking in a little concert with you? There's a Miss Rutherford who plays the piano exceedingly well. Her dinners are most enchanting."

"Oh Howard," exclaimed Mrs. Briggs. "Perhaps Mlle Bonnediseuse has previous commitments? We shouldn't impose! Although," she smiled at Adelaide, "it would be delightful to continue our friendship. Do excuse my husband. He can be overly direct—a result of too many days at sea and not enough in society."

The captain patted Adelaide's arm affectionately. "I am every bit the barbarian my wife accuses me of being." He turned to his other guests and explained in English, "I saw this lovely woman promenading on deck with my wife in the *rain*, of all things! I assure you they were quite oblivious to the weather! We have a lover of the sea in Mlle Bonnediseuse, that much is apparent. Had she been born a man, she would have been an Admiral in *La Royale*, I'm sure of it. Some are not meant for life on land, and grow old and die without ever knowing it." He turned to Adelaide, who was quite befuddled by the captain's English. "Land, dear. Land. *Le terrior*. Dreadful stuff. Fortunately, it'll still take a while to reach the Azores."

"Zat eez wonderful," Adelaide gushed, without understanding. A particularly scraggly looking sailor leaned over her shoulder to ladle a lovely potage into the bowl in front of her. He took the liberty of his position to peer down her dress. Adelaide discretely whipped his shins with her napkin and he moved on to serve the captain's wife where he had better luck, but unfortunately for him, a lesser view. A basket of ship's biscuit, wrapped elegantly with a linen napkin as though it was cut bread, was passed to her. It'd been such a long time since she'd eaten a good *baguette*.

"Gertie tells me you've read her palm," the captain said, switching back to French.

"It's nothing, a parlor trick. Just a distraction from the tedium." Adelaide smiled. "I thought I might show her how to make lace as well."

"What fun to have such a talent as palm reading. Perhaps you might look at my hand tonight? No?"

"I could not possibly bother you with such trivialities. It is a meaningless parlor trick. My nurse showed me the art when I was quite young. But really, one shouldn't take stock in these things." Adelaide was alarmed. She hadn't meant for anyone but Mrs. Briggs to know her talent, as the mere suggestion of a French prophetess could point a finger towards her real identity.

"At the very least, show me where my love line is. You must indulge me." He offered his hand across the table for Adelaide to see. "Our lovely Mademoiselle Bonnediseuse is a palm reader," he said to the other guests in English.

"This one." She reluctantly pointed to a line that cut across his palm.

"Isn't that interesting?" He snatched his wife's hand. "That's just what Gertie told me. Then she changed her tune when I noticed hers was much shorter than mine. How can it be that my wife's love line is shorter than mine?" Captain Briggs roared in English to his guests. His wife blushed, although it was hard to tell whether from anger or from embarrassment. "Which one of you rakes is taking advantage of my Mrs. Briggs in these close quarters?"

"Give me your hand, Mademoiselle Bonnediseuse," the captain demanded, "I too have talents. You will be amazed." He snatched Adelaide's hand and held it tight, locking his eyes to hers. "See here? This line? This is your line of vitality—" His whisper-light touch on her open palm sent a chill through her arm and down her spine.

"My dear husband," interjected Mrs. Briggs, "If you continue to stroke our guest's hand, I shall become very angry."

"If I were to point from this height, would that put your mind at ease?" He lifted his finger six inches from Adelaide's palm. "But now there's no point in pointing at all. From this height I could be speaking of any number of lines." Adelaide tried to withdraw her hand altogether, but it was held tight. "Oh look. Isn't this interesting? Mademoiselle Bonnediseuse's love line matches my own, long and *true*."

"And you persist in ravishing her palm!"

"Ravishing? I'm merely stroking it."

"I assure you this talk of lines and fortunes is meaningless." Adelaide waved dismissively with her other hand while the dinner guests loudly sucked soup from their spoons and pretended nothing was happening.

"It's not meaningless. It explains everything." The captain finally dropped Adelaide's hand.

Adelaide looked back and forth between the stern faces of her host and hostess, then gazed sadly at the congealing potage of white beans, salted pork and onions in front of her. She had so looked forward to dinner, and there was still the roast to come.

"If you're suggesting that my love has ended while yours carries on," started Mrs. Briggs, swelling with indignation, "I cannot imagine how blind, how self-righteous, how unfeeling, how—"

A sailor suddenly threw open the door and ducked inside. "Captain! Masthead's sighted sails."

"The first of many, I'm sure," the captain said to his dinner guests, who shifted nervously in their chairs, "all looking to catch the same trade wind." Nevertheless, he nodded at his first mate, who excused himself and pushed past the sailor to investigate.

"She's making for us with all sails set," the sailor continued, "she's faster than we are, Captain."

"Has she shown her colors?"

"Not yet, sir."

This finally got his attention. He pushed his chair from the table and stood. "No, please," he protested as his guests rose with him. "Do everyone sit and eat. I'm sure it's nothing. I shall return presently."

The emotion showing on Mrs. Briggs' pretty face revealed her to be torn between her duty to her husband and her duty to play hostess to her invited guests. Finally, she too excused herself. That gave leave for everyone else to follow their curiosity and head out to see the oncoming ship for themselves. Adelaide stayed. At least now she could eat in peace.

Five minutes later, she dropped her spoon, startled by a sudden bellowed order of "all hands" and the insistent clanging of the bell. The rushing sound of the second watch of sailors pouring up from below alarmed her. Self-preservation being a stronger instinct than her predilection for gourmet dinners, she finally left the table to see what she might be missing.

It wasn't entirely chaos on deck, not quite. The men seemed to know where they were supposed to be, and what they were supposed to be doing, but getting there, and doing it seemed problematic. Some were moving quickly to obey orders, and once finishing their tasks, waited for more direction, which didn't come from officers fast enough. Sailors stood about in the soaking rain, unable to move under their own initiative. Others moved languidly until the bosun's baton was felt on their shoulders, only to return to their slow pace once the bosun had moved on.

The officers who had been guests at the captain's dinner table had all returned to duty, and were relaying orders across the length of the ship. The passengers, unwilling to stand in the rain, had returned to their cabins. Adelaide joined Captain Briggs and his wife at the rail and squinted into the distance. She wiped the rain from her eyelashes to better see, far out on the horizon, a ship that rose and fell with the churning ocean waves. It was an ominous vision, despite its distance.

"Couldn't it just be another merchant ship?" Mrs. Briggs asked her husband.

"There's no escort," replied the captain.

"But this is a merchant ship and we don't have an escort," said Adelaide.

The captain smiled wryly. "You speak the truth."

Adelaide looked at Mrs. Briggs, feeling her alarm grow. "Why doesn't the *Sea Otter* have an escort?"

The captain ignored Adelaide. Instead, he slapped his spyglass shut and squinted up at his sails. "Mr. Hadley, the sails are luffing just a bit, wouldn't you say?"

The first mate flushed instantly with shame. He puffed out his chest and bellowed more orders and the bosun sent men to ascend both masts to tighten the canvas as Nigel, who was manning the helm, turned the wheel to bring the ship into a full run.

Suddenly the wind picked up and the deck pitched under her feet. Adelaide shrieked in surprise and grabbed the rail to keep herself from sliding down the incline to the larboard side of the ship.

Mrs. Briggs, with the barest of adjustments, remained steady on her feet. "They'll overtake us," she said softly to the captain.

"First let us see if they give chase." He handed his wife the spyglass when she held out her hand.

With brass and glass pressed to her eye, she stood there, frozen, watching the horizon. The ocean rose and fell, rose and fell, but she kept the telescope steady.

Watching her watch the horizon made Adelaide queasy. Her scalp itched. Her left eyelid twitched twice. That was no merchant ship on the horizon, she was sure of it. She tried to remember what it was the *Sea Otter* was carrying. Had she ever been told? She pictured the wooden crates she saw being loaded aboard the day she'd fled her room at the Dancing Bear. They had been long and narrow, and took two men to carry each one. "Surely they've no use for a merchant ship."

"Only if that brig is English," Mrs. Briggs said. "Don't forget, Napoleon decreed all trade with England to be illegal. I would not be surprised if the French were patrolling." She looked up at the sails and shook her head. "There's too much slack. We should be traveling faster. Damn this crew."

"But the French fleet is so diminished. How—"

"Privateers, that's how."

The word sent a chill of fear through Adelaide: Privateers. "Then we're doomed. They'll murder us all," she said quietly.

The ocean rose and fell a few more times before Mrs. Briggs turned to look at her. "Not necessarily," she said. "Should we fight, they'll be unmerciful. Should we surrender, they'll merely take us into their custody."

"And should we run?"

"Our little *Otter* is weighed down; she's a pack mule in a thoroughbred's contest. We cannot outrace them. But if we manage to keep them off until after dark, we stand a chance to lose them in the night." She wiped the rain off the lens of the telescope before placing the glass back up to her eye and locking her gaze on the horizon. There would be no sunset. In this weather, the world would go from pale gray to grayer to black as night descended upon them. All lights on board would be extinguished. All voices hushed. Yet, Adelaide knew the strange ship would stubbornly hold a course straight for them as though drawn magically.

"Report." The captain returned to issue the order to his wife.

"They're gaining," she said with the glass pressed to her eye. "We must prepare the guns."

"Prepare the guns?" Adelaide gasped. "Whatever for? You just said we might hide from them after dark. Cannon fire will only serve to make them unmerciful—you said so yourself. Just give them the cargo."

"One needs to prepare for the worst, and hope for the best," Mrs. Briggs said. Her tone was exaggeratedly solicitous, verging on insulting. A change had come over her—not fear, but solidity. She seemed to take up more space. "Do not ask my husband to lay himself out without allowing him the dignity of drawing his sword."

"We should have been given an escort," Adelaide whispered.

"Perhaps you are right," Captain Briggs said. "It was a risk either way, to draw attention to ourselves with an accompanying ship from the Royal Navy, or to slip across the ocean without escort and risk attack. We chose a middle ground. The *Sea Otter* is well armed and we shall put up a grand fight if called upon to do so. We cannot allow France to take our cargo. In any case, we still don't know if that ship is French."

Captain Briggs's eyes told a deeper story, and suddenly Adelaide knew she was on no ordinary merchant ship. "Oh," was all she could think to reply.

"Try to be brave, there's a dear. We'll need you and Gertie to run the powder. I can't spare a single man here on deck."

"Run powder? Oh dear God," Adelaide whispered as Mrs. Briggs drew her away.

She followed the young woman away from the rail and across the deck as though following an executioner to the guillotine. In the captain's chambers, Adelaide sat despondently on the narrow cot and watched Mrs. Briggs rummaging through trunks. If the French were to capture the ship, she thought to herself, it would only be a matter of time before the minister of police discovered her and returned her to prison. She could be sure that Fouché would not show her any kindness—especially after having embarrassed him by escaping his grasp.

"I cannot be taken," Adelaide breathed.

Mrs. Briggs pulled out two pistols and handed one to Adelaide. "Should it come to that, you can negotiate the terms with this to protect your maidenhood. Do you know how to use it?"

"Of course not," Adelaide snapped. "Who do you think I am?"

Mrs. Briggs rolled her eyes and snatched the pistol back from Adelaide. "I'm offering you teeth and claws to fight, but if you prefer to use the charms of your sex for protection, you can stand in front of me. I'll try to shoot around you."

"What a thing to say," said Adelaide, shocked. "Fine. I'll take the pistol."

"Too late, I've changed my mind. I'll keep both." Mrs. Briggs carefully poured powder from a horn into both pistols and rammed the shot with authority. Then she tucked the pistols under a belt she cinched around her waist, fore and aft of her body. "Let's go," she said, pulling Adelaide back onto her feet.

She led Adelaide down a narrow ladder to the lower deck where the sailors slept. The second watch had left their beds so quickly that they hadn't had the time to take the hammocks down and they swung eerily as though filled with reclining ghosts. Adelaide pressed a handkerchief to her nose. The smell of one single unwashed Englishman was bad enough, but an entire crew of them left an overwhelming lingering odor.

Suddenly the ship shifted to lean on its opposite side. Both women stumbled and clutched each other to keep their feet. The cargo leaned against ropes that moaned and creaked under the stress of added weight. Above them, cannon carriages rumbled loudly across the deck as the men used the ship's incline to maneuver the heavy guns into a ready and secured position. "Oh, for pity's sake," cried Mrs. Briggs. "Can they not simply pull harder? The fools! We'll lose speed!"

They moved farther aft and descended to another deck. The air grew still, the corridors dark. When Mrs. Briggs finally stopped, Adelaide nearly walked right into her. "It's so dark in here," she said. "I'll go get the lamp."

"No!" cried Mrs. Briggs. She snatched Adelaide's arm and pulled her back. "You cannot bring a lamp into the powder magazine!"

"But I can barely see my hand in front of my face."

"We'll just keep the door open and do the best we can. Powder monkeys don't need eyes. They merely need swift feet."

Adelaide peered into the darkness, letting her eyes adjust. Oddly, it was reassuring to know that she was in the company of a woman who embroidered white violets and hung pistols from her waist. Mrs.

Briggs's white muslin looked like the gray ashes of a dead fire, second in brightness only to the lamp that swung from the beams well down the corridor, away from the stores of gunpowder. Only an hour ago Mrs. Briggs was helpless in a lovers' quarrel. Now she was the angel in white descending into battle.

"So, we move all the cartridges now," Adelaide suggested, beginning to fill her arms with the little felt pillows of powder, "and stack them near each cannon. Let's get it done before the fighting starts."

"I think," Mrs. Briggs said in a diplomatic tone, "that would be unwise. Should one of those musket balls hit a pile of cartridges, it would spell disaster for the gun crew. Either that, or the powder could get too wet in the rain to discharge the cannon."

"Yes, but should a musket ball hit the cartridge while I'm carrying it, it would spell disaster for *me*," replied Adelaide sharply.

Mrs. Briggs shook her head and pushed Adelaide back out of the room. "We will wait until the very moment we're needed. Sit."

Unused to taking orders, Adelaide suspiciously eyed the corner under the lamp where she had been directed to sit, sure there would be rats.

"Oh for heaven's sake. Must you curl your lip at everything I say like a French poodle?"

Adelaide sat. "Tell me again what we are waiting for? Is it for cannon balls to rip through the hull?"

"They need the *Sea Otter* whole. They won't incapacitate her."

"But what if they do? What if they board?"

"If it comes to that, the enemy will have their blood up." Mrs. Briggs looked meaningfully at Adelaide. "They'll not be wanting to hold your hand."

"I can handle any man."

Mrs. Briggs sniffed. "I am quite positive that you can."

They sat in tense silence, listening to the sounds of the sailors as they ran back and forth across the deck above them. Adelaide touched her chest, longing to pull a card and see her future. She thought of her cozy parlor in Paris. Normally at this moment, the fireplace would be warm and cheery. Agnes would be humming to herself as she dusted the room. Adelaide would be preparing for a client's visit, sifting through her notes and drinking sweet Madeira from a delicate crystal glass. She thought of the crystal—Baccarat, a gift from a particularly thankful client—and how its facets perfectly matched the flames in the fireplace as she twirled the red liquid around and around. The drink had been perfect for settling into her thoughts, for stimulating her senses, and she dearly missed the routine. Had it only been a month? Surely it'd been longer since she had been in her own home, but it seemed like a lifetime ago. Where would she be tomorrow, she wondered, since her today was so completely different from her yesterday?

Above her, men did their duty without thought. Adelaide marveled at their selflessness. She knew her duty too, but constantly questioned, constantly chafed. It was exhausting. She clutched reflexively at her chest again. The memory of Mademoiselle DuBette's warning should she fail in her task echoed in her mind. "You will never be able to rise to the full height of your power, and your voice, all our voices will fall upon deaf ears for generations."

Adelaide looked at the slender Mrs. Briggs. She was sitting up straight, alert, her hand casually draped over the handle of her pistol. *There* was a power. *There* was a voice. But a voice unheard, nevertheless. The quest had been given to Adelaide for women like Mrs. Briggs— women who took to the oceans in equal partnership with their husbands, who wrote letters to the government, like Olympe, who healed the downtrodden like Mrs. Southill. Suddenly Adelaide realized the importance of the quest set before her, and trembled.

Could she succeed? It seemed impossible. Waiting for the fates to spin the thread and weave their tapestry was a terrible burden. It was always all about handiwork, always a well tooled textile. Adelaide wished again for her knitting. "Wouldn't it be wonderful if we had our needlework with us to pass the time?" she asked. She couldn't tell if Mrs. Briggs' sigh was an indication of exasperation or wishful thinking.

Adelaide patted her apron pockets, and pulled out a carefully folded packet of papers that the captain had given her. In the dim light, she began to read aloud, "I will go to zee market to buy zee—"

"Oh for heaven's sake," snapped Mrs. Briggs. "Must we do this now?"

"What *else* shall we do? I cannot just sit here, I'll go mad."

"Honestly I don't know why you bother with that. I can speak French perfectly well."

"—to buy zee 'ot bread from zee bakair's boot."

"Baker's booth."

"Bakair's boot."

"Pinch your tongue between your teeth and do this: thhhh thhhh thhhh."

"*zzzz zzzz zzzz*"

"Never mind," sighed Mrs. Briggs. "Continue."

BROADSIDES

The English lesson was a disappointment. Mrs. Briggs had pretended to support Adelaide's efforts, but neither woman could keep up the charade for long. Finally, Adelaide folded up the lesson and placed it back into her apron pocket, agreeing, without actually saying so, that it was better to stare down the black corridor in silence than to continue forcing her tongue into odd contortions.

How long had it been since dinner had been interrupted—an hour? Two? Time crawls when the only directive given is to wait. Adelaide shifted uncomfortably on the pile of ropes and the loops slipped under her thighs, causing her bottom to sink lower inside the large coil.

Why anyone thought she would be a good candidate to run gunpowder was beyond her. Had they even asked? Had she volunteered for the job? No! Adelaide's mood was beginning to reflect the dark and gloomy deck where they waited. She stared at the door to the powder magazine with a strong sense of foreboding.

She wiggled her bottom and pushed against the ropes while her feet swung in the air, unable to find purchase. As a result, the ropes rose further up under her arms. She leaned her head back, finding her new position to be more comfortable, but much less mobile. "Mrs. Briggs?" she whispered into the darkness. "Gertie? Are you awake? I believe I am quite stuck."

A soft sigh was her only answer, followed by steady, deep breathing. The young woman was asleep, Adelaide realized with astonishment. Had she no sense of the gravity of the situation? They were about to be attacked by a privateer. A *privateer.* The thought really hadn't settled into her own mind until noticing that it hadn't *un*settled the mind of her hostess. Now, the longer Mrs. Briggs slept, the more Adelaide began to wiggle restlessly. And the more she wiggled, the more solidly wedged she became in the coiled rope.

She could wake Mrs. Briggs, but it seemed almost cruel. Thus, it fell to Adelaide to find a means for escape, and not just from the ever tightening coils of rope. She, too, closed her eyes, but for a different purpose:

Women of la Société, I call upon your collective spirits to aid me in invoking the power of the Goddess Isis, mother of magic, daughter of Earth and Sky. Help me draw down her strength. Imbue my flesh with the power of creation so that we may place ourselves at the—

There were rustles in the corners of Adelaide's mind, rustles in the corners of the *in-between* place they all identified as the astral plane. The sisters were coming. The sisters were answering her call. Adelaide began again.

Women of la Société, I call upon your collective spirits to aid me in invoking the power of the Goddess Isis, mother of magic, daughter of Earth and Sky. Help me draw—

Madame Thierreau! So good to see you. And how is your sweet daughter?

Fine. She's fine. Oh look, here comes Madame Voix. Bonsoir, Madame!

Adelaide glared at the two women. Their hissed whispers did nothing to conceal their complete lack of respect. *Ahem! Ahem!* She waited until she'd regained their attention before continuing. *Help me draw down her strength. Imbue my flesh with the power of creation so that we may place ourselves at the center of all that is, and will be. Come together in collective purpose. Raise your arms to the Goddess and join me in this prayer.*

A smattering of the women present raised their arms above their heads, with palms extended to the sky to catch the spirit of Isis. Some raised their voices to join the prayer: *All powerful Isis, we ask that you act through these worthy women to imbue me with the strength of your—*

Bonsoir les filles! Who is calling down the Goddess? Mademoiselle Lenormand? Is that you?

—imbue me with the strength of your wisdom that I might—

Shhhhhh!

Sorry I'm late, I had to finish putting down Gaston. He fusses so.

Darling Gaston! He must be cutting his teeth by now.

—That I might—

Yes. Let me tell you! Between Gaston and my snoring husband, I barely get a wink's sleep.

Oh, you poor dear.

Shhhh. . .Mademoiselle Lenormand is drawing down the power.

—that I might use it for the continuation of all feminine—

Mademoiselle Lenormand, dear. Would you mind if we sped things up a bit? I've my husband's parents here for dinner and the roast won't cook itself.

Adelaide paused her incantation and watched as, one by one, more women's spirits popped into the void, no doubt arriving after having made sudden excuses of headaches and "women troubles" to separate themselves from their families and chores. They greeted each other, some delightedly, others grumpily, and turned towards Adelaide who stood in their midst. Obviously she'd begun the incantations too early, since many were still arriving. She sighed and began again: *Women of la Société, I call upon your—*

We've heard that part already.

Really, Madame Gillet, your roast can wait, snapped a red-haired witch standing nearby.

Why should Mademoiselle Lenormand have to repeat the prayer simply because some *of you cannot be bothered to arrive on time? My arms are growing tired. I shouldn't have to stand here like this forever.*

You're not in your body. How could holding up your arms be tiresome?

My spirit tires at the thought of exercise? retorted Madame Gillet.

Might I have everyone's attention, please? Adelaide begged.

There was a sudden glow, a golden flash of light that dazzled as it flooded the black void and sparkled through the shimmering shades of the gathered witches. Mademoiselle DuBette had finally arrived. Adelaide felt the odd sensation of simultaneous relief and dread.

Why? asked DuBette.

Why? Adelaide echoed back stupidly. It was difficult to stay concentrated on any train of thought in the presence of DuBette, as seeing her kept one's mind occupied on the splendor of the vision, forcing whatever issue was at hand into the shadows. She was an elderly witch, dressed fashionably in gauzy light blue silk that revealed a still youthful body. A necklace of cut crystals sparked light around her face and bosom. Or maybe it was her long waves of gray hair that loosely floated about her head that dazzled.

Why do you call us together? DuBette clarified. *You have never been given the authority to do so. Do you have the emerald?*

No, Mademoiselle. Not as of yet.

Then why?

My ship, the Sea Otter, *this grand vessel whose true course lies secret to those seamen who capture the wind in her sails, a true course that is charted not upon maps but upon the fabric of time and known only to the witches who set it upon its path. A voyage that will no doubt become legendary, heralded by those that—*

Oh for heaven's sake, just tell us what you need.

The ship's about to be boarded by privateers.

I see.

I can hardly retrieve the emerald if I'm captured or killed.

Mademoiselle DuBette sighed. The other women shifted their feet uncomfortably and looked at each other.

Please hurry. Those monsters will be here any moment now.

Adelaide, dear, your training with the sisterhood in Alençon was cut short by the Revolution. As a result, you never learned how to be truly independent. You went from answering the demands of the nuns at the convent—a masculine school under masculine rule, despite being entirely run by women—to answering the demands of the men at Zenours's atelier.

I don't understand. What has that to do with privateers raping and murdering me?

Too many men have opened doors for you.

So you would then have them ravish me?

When men open doors for you, you forget how to insert your own key into the lock. At first they do it to be deferential and gallant, then they do it because you become incapable of doing it for yourself. When women open doors for you, it is because they find you interesting, and would like to invite you into the room. Right now, you do not think you can open your own door. You expect deferential help, and you do not trust that we welcome you.

I expect help, yes. Why should you not help? And in any case, you don't make it easy to trust. The entire reason I'm in this situation is because you sent me away with no resources.

No. You are in your current situation because as the golem's creator, you are the most likely of all of us to find it. Generations of women are counting upon you to use your maternal ties to this creature and retrieve the emerald. Please, Adelaide. Do not give up. You are stronger than you believe and have plenty of resources at your disposal, you just have yet to learn to find them within yourself. How will you know the full extent of your own powers if you always ask for help? You will only know your depth when you've seen the bottom of your well. Those who have helped you haven't done you any favors.

So, to drain my well I must be raped and beaten?

Oh, stop being so dramatic.

These men are pirates!

Hardly. They're privateers.

Mademoiselle DuBette, please—

I've said my piece. Do not call upon us again until you've the emerald scarab in hand.

Those witches won't help me because they cannot, thought Adelaide uncharitably as her spirit settled back into flesh. As usual, returning to her body was uncomfortable. Her feet tingled because the ropes pinched her legs at her knees. Her shoulders ached where she had been leaning on the coil. It was never a good idea to leave one's body without first settling it on cushions. That horrible DuBette has organized a society of charlatans. They've placed all their hopes on me because they are powerless. I should be leading them, not DuBette.

The sudden slap stung, causing Adelaide to cry out in surprise and pain. The second slap was harder. "Stop! *Nom de Dieu!*"

"Thank God you're back," said Mrs. Briggs. She dropped her open palm. "You'd fainted at the most inopportune time. The call for us has sounded. We're about to be broadsided."

"Pull me out! Hurry!"

Mrs. Briggs grabbed Adelaide's wrists and pulled hard. They fell to the floor when her hips popped from their prison of ropes.

"Take off your shoes." Mrs. Briggs was on her feet again. She'd already been into the magazine. She bent down to gather up the cartridges—pillows of gunpowder the gun crews would push into the barrels of the cannons—that had dropped out of her skirt.

Adelaide reluctantly unlaced her boots, thinking glumly that it would be a quick solution to their problem should a spark from the cobbler's nails hit powder and cause the ship to blow.

"Hurry! And, please be careful," Mrs. Briggs called as Adelaide entered the magazine for her own stash of cartridges.

"Shall I hurry? Or shall I be careful?"

"Do both. For God's sake, do both."

Adelaide took a moment just inside the powder magazine to let her eyes adjust to the diminished light. Slowly the shadows receded from her vision, allowing her to make out the stacked barrels of gunpowder. It seemed a bit much for a simple merchant ship, but then again, there were more cannons on board than she would have expected, and for that she was grateful, given the current circumstances.

Thus burdened with the explosives, the women rushed down the length of the ship, then up the ladders and through the hatches to deliver their gifts to the gun crews.

Out on the weather deck, the crew was slowly organizing for battle. There was a good deal of head scratching as they took up unfamiliar duties. Those that weren't clustered around the cannons were busy jamming rods down the noses of muskets. Captain Briggs stood on the quarterdeck, occasionally yelling orders, but mostly shaking his head sadly while his first mate strode up and down the weather deck, dispensing advice and beatings, the one not necessarily being more useful than the other.

They were a grizzled lot—the leftovers that hadn't been selected to sail on the man-of-wars. Adelaide had heard them all boast of killing frogs when they thought she wasn't within earshot, but however much a man puffs himself up when discussing the theoretical, when faced with real situations with calculably unhappy odds, all bravado disappears. Adelaide didn't have to be a fortune-teller to see what was in store for everyone. The pinched faces of worry that the men wore made it clear.

As luck would have it, just when bad weather would afford some protection, it began to clear. A patch of clouds had parted just enough to shine a sliver of moonlight upon the glistening deck under her feet. The idea that they would slip away undetected was now a pretty fantasy. No longer a mere dot on the horizon, the privateer's full sails loomed like the extended wings of a hawk about to pick off prey. Soon, she would luff her sails and swing alongside the *Sea Otter*.

"They'll sink us," Adelaide muttered in dread. "We're all going to die."

"Their goal is not to sink us," said Mrs. Briggs, "but to render us useless. You don't get paid for a captured ship if it sinks."

"Will they take prisoners?" Adelaide asked. The idea was only slightly more appealing than a watery death, but not by much.

"Prisoners are a risk. Prisoners can rise against captors. Besides, most ships carry only enough to feed their own men."

"That's not very reassuring." Surely the privateers would take her prisoner? They wouldn't slay a woman simply because it was more convenient to do so, would they? And if they took her prisoner, it wouldn't be very genteel if they didn't also feed her. "Let us remember privateers are not the same as pirates and take heart."

"Indeed," said Mrs. Briggs, in a half-hearted tone.

"This is suicide," Adelaide muttered. "Obviously we do not have the advantage here. Surely Captain Briggs sees the futility of a pitched battle? We should surrender!"

"We cannot let the *Otter* fall into French hands."

"Is this ship worth all the lives you risk?" Adelaide searched Mrs. Briggs' profile seeking any sign of indecision, any hope that she might listen to reason. "Madame Briggs...Gertrude, please," Adelaide placed her hand on Mrs. Briggs' arm. "Have a word with your husband on our behalf and on behalf of the men who follow him. Turn him away from this folly. He must surrender."

"Folly?" Mrs. Briggs cast a cool look at Adelaide. "The *Sea Otter* is my home. You would ask me to turn over my home without a fight? Howard and I live and breathe these ocean waters every day of our lives. It has been our choice to do so." She handed a cartridge to a gun captain. "I have no children. *This* is my family." Her gesture encompassed the entire crew. The gun captain blushed and turned back to his job, pretending to have not heard. "No. I will not give France the advantage of my ship. I'll sink the *Otter* myself if I have to," she said.

"Here they come, ma'am!" shouted a sailor. "Take cover!"

Adelaide whipped around. The privateers' ship was slowly erasing the horizon like curtains being drawn across a stage, sliding along their larboard side. The sound of luffing sails was an ominous pause between scenes. She stared in alarm at an enormous painted carving of a woman which was affixed to the prow. From her open dress her bare breasts jutted in an offering to Poseidon. Her black hair, whipped up above her head, gave strength to the ship's bowsprit. Her ruby lips were drawn away from her teeth in a permanently fixed grin. Emblazoned along the bow of the ship was her name: *La Damquiris.* She laughed in the face of danger and her jovial spirit was unquestionably more powerful than the bloated *Otter* on whose back Adelaide stood.

"Fire!" screamed Captain Briggs, and the order was passed along by his officers like a lit fuse. The *Sea Otter's* cannons ripped in sequence from stern to bow, the rearmost guns hitting their marks while the foremost missed, as *La Damquiris* hadn't yet come full up. It was a first strike calculated to take out the opponent's guns, but had limited effect. She continued to slide along the *Sea Otter's* larboard side, slowly, taking care to remain parallel.

"Run!" Mrs. Briggs screamed. "Take these forward." She pushed more cartridges of gunpowder at Adelaide and shoved her towards the gun crews as the order to reload crashed down from the quarterdeck. She herself ran aft, passing the cartridges into waiting hands.

Adelaide choked as the wind blew the acrid smoke into her face. Her eyes stung and her ears rang. Nevertheless, she ran, pressing her burden into eager hands. She skirted a man who was being dragged away and the sight of him caused her to skitter sideways and gasp. As his mates hauled him down a hatch and into the protection of the 'tween decks, he looked at her with an expression of surprise. His round eyes were starkly white against his blackened and bloodied face, a casualty of his own cannon's touch hole. For a woman who had spent her entire career peering into things that didn't concern her, the man was a chilling reminder of the consequences of peeping into the wrong hole at the wrong time.

Suddenly the larboard rail exploded, projecting wooden shards over her head. Adelaide threw herself to the deck. Even with her eyes closed, everything was lit with white and red flares.

Opening her eyes, she blinked and lifted her head to view the carnage. The weather deck was swarming with men. One stumbled backwards and tripped over her prone body. Sprawled on his side, he frantically alternated between cradling his thigh and stretching himself lengthwise across the deck, as though trying to crawl away from his own leg, and the splinter that had speared through his thigh. Adelaide reached towards him, touched him, wanting to give him reassurance despite alarms that told her to run, and he latched on as if she was a line and he was drowning. He squeezed her wrist. He pulled himself towards her, hand over hand, along her arm.

Instantly she regretted her kindness. She shook her arm like he was a nasty thing to flick off and cringed as he sprayed spittle through his screams of pain.

Two men arrived, one man to peel his hands from her arm, the other to jerk out the splinter. Adelaide retched as they dragged the man away. And since retching caused her to turn her head, she was given an entirely new perspective on the ship. It had only taken a single pass of cannon fire from *La Damquiris* for morale to shatter. Men were loading muskets now, not cannons. It wasn't about the crew any longer, it wasn't about the *Sea Otter*, or "family" or even just following orders. It was about survival. One musket, one man, one life. . .

Or so it seemed, until one brave sailor put his own needs aside to mount a rescue of Adelaide. He grabbed her under her arms and grunted loudly as he tried to pull her away from the melee, only managing to slide her bottom four inches along the wet deck.

"*Laissez-moi!* Unhand me!" she cried.

"Heave!" he yelled to another he'd called over to join him. Adelaide slid another four inches.

"Damn your eyes!" Adelaide cried in English, hoping the curse would startle them into dropping her. It felt as though they would tear her arms from their sockets.

Suddenly, the two men flopped on top of her, flattening her against the wooden planks as the world was once again rocked by cannon fire. This time, the enemy had aimed high.

If discipline had been strained before, it was gone now as everyone on board scattered from the mainmast. It had been gouged on one side by a cannon ball, and thus imbalanced, was in a slow motion fall, its fibers stretching and popping like a thousand overbent twigs. The final loud snap was like thunder that shook the very decking and vibrated the hull. Torn rigging whipped men who were unfortunate to be in the way; the sails caught them up and swept them into the ocean.

Some sailors, high up in the fighting top, managed to hold on to the mast until they were shaken off into the water. Others fell directly to the deck like dropped eggs, joining the dead already picked off by the French who crowded the rail on the enemy ship.

It was over. With the mast gone, the *Sea Otter* was now nothing but flotsam. The men from the *Damquiris* would soon board, using cannon smoke and the chaos to their advantage.

It was in this moment that Captain Briggs strode purposefully down the deck, his saber drawn, his eyes flashing. "To me!" he called. "Men, to me!" His chest heaved against the constraints of his linen shirt with the zeal of battle. His long hair, lifted by the wind, was lit from without by the flames of the battle.

No one with any sense moved, much less answered his call to arms.

"Where are my bloody cannons?" screamed Gertrude Briggs.

As one, the men swung their heads to view the captain's wife striding fearlessly over the dead. "Keep firing those cannons!" she yelled. With a musket in each hand and two pistols bouncing against her hips, the sight of her ignited the hearts of the crew—an angel in white come to lead them to victory. The French could have their allegory of liberty, Marianne, with her wild hair, torn dress, and fleshy bosom. The men of the *Sea Otter* had Gertie Briggs. Gertie Briggs would get the job done. Gertie Briggs was courage incarnate. Gertie Briggs was a proper English lady, by God. The men rose up behind their leader.

Adelaide, swallowed hard. It wasn't that she was against rallying cries and inspirational speeches. She wanted to believe Mrs. Briggs could lead a charge. But Adelaide had the power of prophecy, and clear eyes. She could see they would be boarded by an overwhelming number of French criminals with blood in their eyes and hate in their hearts. And being French herself, she knew the power of the contemptuous smile affixed to *La Damquiris*. The privateers' figurehead was simply stronger.

Rising to her feet, but keeping low, Adelaide slunk towards the open hatch with the hope of hiding in a dark corner in the ship's hold. Her ears rang with the combined sounds of the exploding guns and the defiantly screaming crew. These English were crazy, she thought.

She never made it. Two men pushed a crate from the hold out onto the deck and blocked her path. The wooden lid was pried off to reveal a large cache of muskets. The overflowing powder magazine suddenly made sense: the *Sea Otter* was running munitions. Men eagerly swarmed past Adelaide to arm themselves just as the first of the privateers latched their grappling hooks to the rail. The acrid smell of gun smoke tickled the back of Adelaide's throat as the shooting resumed.

Unsure of where to go, she was frozen to the spot as questions rushed through her head. Who were they shipping guns to? What was England scheming? She snapped back when a musket ball flew past her ear. Moving faster than she'd ever moved in her life, she dove under a fallen sail, still flapping in the wind like a fish landed for dinner. A fallen yardarm served to form a tent pole. She hunkered behind it, sheltered from flying projectiles.

It was pitch black, and stifling under the sail. Her sweat tickled as it rolled down her sides, feeling like fingers in the dark. She smelled her own breath. Then she smelled the breath of someone else. Instinctively, she turned towards the warmth and saw a shadowed outline of a man. Adelaide's scream came from her stomach. Her pelvis pushed it out through her throat and her tongue threw it across her lips.

"Bloody hell. Put a cork in it, miss."

"*Qui est là?* Oo eez dere?"

Adelaide squinted into the darkness, but it was what she heard that gave it away—the rhythmic click, click, click of wooden knitting needles. "Mr. Nigel?"

"Oh aye, it's Nigel all right." He flipped up a corner of the sail to let in more light.

"But, you are not fighting?"

"Me? Out there? Oh no, not me. A man such as myself would be dead in five seconds flat. I'll do my fighting from here. There's all kinds of fighting, there is. We all do our part in our own way." The sound of knitting didn't let up as he spoke. Adelaide struggled to understand what he was saying. She heard, "fighting from here" and "all do our part" and slowly the meaning fell into place.

"I 'elp," she said.

Nigel hesitated, then poked around in the large ball of twine he was knitting from until he found the other loose end, which he gave Adelaide, along with a squinty eye and a grunt of professional acknowledgement. After more rustling in the dark, he produced a second pair of needles.

She slid her haunches to a spot near enough to the old sailor so that she could share his ball but far enough away that she wouldn't smell what was coming out of his mouth as he breathed into his ratty beard. She didn't normally object to getting under covers with strange men, but she preferred it when they were a bit younger, and a good deal more *propre*. Adelaide folded back another corner of the canvas sail, partly to release Nigel's trapped odor, and partly to let in more light to see what she was doing. It also afforded her a good view of the battle, and those she would attempt to protect. The pattern she chose to knit would have to be a convoluted lace, with tight stitches in order to keep them all safe. She began casting on, and felt the spell working on her at once. Now she could breathe more deeply. Now she could think more clearly. The hemp twine flew through her fingers and lace fell in a narrow strip into her lap.

Outside of the tent, the screams of battle continued. Perversely, the disadvantage of smaller numbers didn't stop the men of the *Sea*

Otter. If a sailor was still standing after facing off with a privateer, he turned, and quickly found another man to fight, and if he managed to survive again, he soon engaged another, and on and on until he was finally killed. It was systematic, unthinking, and so like the English, who will always have room for another ale if it's set in front of them.

Captain Briggs himself was a striking figure, backlit by the moon as he fired shots into the melee. Each time he got off a round, he passed his musket behind him to his wife, who had a freshly loaded musket to take its place. She would then reload the emptied musket to have it ready for him when he was ready to trade again. Adelaide found their efficiency strangely romantic. She swallowed a pang of jealousy. The captain had never been within her reach. He had merely been toying with her to excite his wife. It had been a ploy for more demonstrative affection. That knowledge didn't stop Adelaide from wishing she, too, had the kind of love that Gertrude and Howard Briggs had for each other. Even so, not for a million emerald scarabs would she ever dream of standing in the midst of a losing battle to load muskets for a man.

No, she wasn't being fair to herself, she thought. She'd done her part. She'd run gunpowder while under fire, and she didn't do it for any one man. She did it for an entire crew. That was more noble, wasn't it? Adelaide wasn't sure. There had been a certain amount of self-preservation involved in passing out gunpowder to outfit the cannons, but that knowledge seemed to diminish her bravery. She wondered if she shouldn't still be running powder.

She looked away from the captain and his wife. Tears, unnoticed, dropped onto the small pile of lace that was growing in her lap. Click, click, click. The knitting needles set a rhythm underlying the screams of the dying, the clash of steel upon steel, the sickeningly wet thuds of musket stocks against skulls. It was a devil's orchestra. These men weren't noble. They weren't brave. These were useless deaths of ignorant men who were fighting for a ship they had already lost.

Even a spider has the sense to give up and hide when her web is being destroyed by a broom. A dog will cower and lick your hand when all is lost. But these men were more unthinking than animals. Their continued resistance to inevitable loss was causing the destruction of everything.

Adelaide knew these thoughts weren't helping her cast the protection spell she knitted, so she tried to close her ears while opening her heart.

It is an age-old contradiction—an open heart creates a vulnerability, but a closed heart is powerless. One may attempt a balance, but the heart isn't a door that can be simply left ajar. There is no keyhole, no crack beneath the door. You either feel, or you don't feel. You either hear the pain of others and react with strength or cowardice, or you close your heart and don't react at all. It was a lesson Adelaide had to learn over and over again. She desperately wanted to block the battle from her entire consciousness, and had, in fact, successfully blocked herself from the sight of it, but her hands wouldn't allow her to close her heart. Each knot she created in the lace was a crewman, and as she twisted and lifted the stitches, the men twisted and lifted in her thoughts.

A scream, long and piercing, caused her to drop three stitches and tangle an especially tricky yarn over. Adelaide looked up from her work. In the dark, she could see Nigel genuflecting. Instinctively, Adelaide mumbled a prayer to the Holy Mother for a blessing—Isis, Mary, Gaia, all the faces and names of the same deity, all responsible for drawing the grief-stricken to their breast for comfort. The *Sea Otter* was gone. The scream from Gertie Briggs announced that her captain was gone.

Reluctantly, Adelaide peered outside again. A large circle of strange men stood on the forecastle, hats in hand, weapons down. With the exception of the moans for mercy from the dying men, all was quiet.

The fighting had stopped. All over the ship, bodies were strewn about in careless poses, arms and legs at awkward angles.

A tall man in a stiff uniform doffed his tricorn hat as he approached the cluster of men. An opening was made to accommodate the man, giving Adelaide clear view of the scene at the center of the circle. A gasp of pity caught in her throat as Mrs. Briggs, crumpled and diminished, was revealed. She cradled the head of her husband; his blond curls pooled in her lap. Draped about her were the ruined folds of her gown, stained red as she pressed the cloth against her captain's chest to staunch his draining blood. Her wails made the men shift, embarrassed and uncomfortable in their sympathy. Few could lift their heads to look at her, yet none of them could turn away.

"Madame," said the man with the tricorne hat. "My deepest condolences. I salute the courage and strength of your husband. . ." he trailed off. Mrs. Briggs didn't seem to notice. He waited for a moment, perhaps hoping she'd stop weeping, then turned to another at his side—a young lieutenant, based on his epaulette. "Take her below. Make sure she's given every courtesy."

The lieutenant reached down to lay a hand on Mrs. Briggs's shoulder. Under his touch, she revived. She puffed large, in fact. Outrage twisted the features of her face and straightened her body. Her muscles tensed and her shoulders rolled back. All eyes lifted to rest on her bosom, swollen with breathless anger. "Your touch is a violation," she hissed, and slapped away the young officer's hand.

"Your pardon, madame." He bowed deeply and stepped backwards with a glance at his captain. His derisive shrug was almost imperceptible.

"Madame, I am *Capitaine* Oscar de la Soie, of *La Damquiris*. Your husband's ship is now under my—"

"No! Never!!" cried Mrs. Briggs. "I'll never let you take the *Otter*!"

"Please, madame, it is inevitable that you submit—"

Mrs. Briggs was suddenly on her feet with a pistol in her right hand leveled squarely at de la Soie's chest. "Take your men and leave this ship, or I'll kill you where you stand."

No one moved.

"Leave!" screamed Mrs. Briggs. She reached around with her left hand to force back the pistol's heavy hammer, but de la Soie drew his own firearm, and cocked it easily with his thumb.

The crack of the pistol caused Adelaide to let out a startled scream.

As one, the captain, his lieutenant, and the crew of *La Damquiris* swung their heads from Mrs. Briggs's crumpled body to look at the sail under which Adelaide was hidden.

"Well, now you've gone and done it," Nigel said. He threw his knitting down and folded his arms across his chest in disgust.

WATCH OUT FOR VAPORS

Three hours after Mr. George Russell's total rejection of Elise's plea for assistance, Amanda Collins's baby still hadn't turned. Elise had taken a wait-and-see approach to the delivery, but with the baby's head not engaged in the birth canal, Amanda's cervix wasn't dilating fast enough. It wasn't a stretch to think it would be another day for labor to progress. But given the conditions on board the *Valiant* and the weeks of poor nutrition Amanda had endured, waiting was no longer an option. The kid had to come out. "Hey, buddy," Elise whispered to the rippling muscles of Amanda's contracting stomach, "time to get off your back and do a headstand." The baby wasn't going to do it on its own, however. She'd need some muscle, and some support for the young mother.

Thankfully, even if the baby hadn't turned, the weather had. The waves were still choppy, and the rain was still pouring, but the ship was no longer pitching over giant swells. Elise finally felt confident that the vomit bucket was no longer needed, and happily passed it to the other side of the curtain where Bill Stanton took it away (after being encouraged to do so with a slap to the back of the head delivered by Private Cox).

"Where's Peter Collins?" she asked stepping to the other side of the blanket while being careful to maintain Amanda's privacy. The entire company was seated near the Collins's corner. The vigil caught Elise off guard. She hadn't expected to feel included by the ranks, but the show of solidarity was heartening. She told herself that it had nothing to do with her, and everything to do with Amanda. Her husband was a well-liked member of the company unlike Richard, who turned his nose up at the "rabble." Still, she felt like an essential member of a team again, and that felt good.

To pass the time, Hobart, Cox, Ben O'Brian, and Richard were all holding fanned cards close to their face in the dim light, while the others huddled around them. "Playing whist again?" Elise piped. She was thankful for a break and a little fresh air while Amanda rested with her head in Mrs. Gillihan's lap. "Who's winning?"

"Shhhhhh!" Richard hissed. "For God's sake, you're louder than that whelping bird of the Collins's. Haven't I told you no one speaks whilst whist is being played? It's just not done! Do excuse my wife's exuberance, gentlemen."

"How is she?" Peter suddenly appeared at her elbow, hissing his question so as to not disturb the game. Elise could smell the alcohol on his breath, which made sense. If you're already helpless to control a situation, might as well go all the way and get drunk.

"She needs you."

"Me? Now? Why me? *Really?*"

"Just give me a few minutes, but yeah." She sat on an upended bucket and bent her head, propping it up in her hands. "Just give me a few, okay?" She hadn't realized how exhausted she was.

"A few what? I don't take your meaning. What is an 'oh-kay?'" Eyes wide as saucers, Peter stared at Elise, waiting for clarification.

"Shhhh!!" said Richard, taking a trick of cards.

"She's asking for a few minutes' rest," Thomas grumbled from the shadows.

"Ding ding ding ding," Elise said, without looking up, garnering more puzzled looks.

"Of course—take all the time that you need," Collins whispered.

It did feel good, Elise decided, to be needed. She sighed, feeling the loss of her previous life. Being a nurse wasn't glamorous, but at least she knew what her purpose was. She woke up each evening knowing she'd be spending the night managing lines and saving lives, going home in the morning tired and satisfied. She hoped that if she could pull Amanda through the birth of her first child, then she might gain, at the very least, a friend. Amanda was young and naive, but Elise had to hand it to her—she was teeth-clenchingly tough. She took a deep breath. "Okay, Collins. Let's do this."

"For God's sake, must I?" He turned pale. He could volunteer to go to war, but apparently helping his wife give birth was too much to ask. "What can *I* do? If you wish to be paid in ale, then it should be you to do the job, not me." A thin wail came from behind the curtain.

"A woman needs a woman, not a man," Hobert said, sniffing. A murmur of assent rolled through the company. "It's not right for a man to see his wife in that condition."

"Is that what you said when your sheep were squeezing out lambs?" Elise countered. "I suppose you just stood aside and shielded your virgin eyes while your flock managed by itself? An ewe needs an ewe, right?"

"That's not the same thing, is it? An ewe ain't a woman." There was an uncomfortable silence amongst the men as everyone considered how Hobert might have come to that conclusion.

"Hobert's point is sound," Collins said. "It's not my place. It's not right."

"None of this is right," Elise swept her arms out to include the entire ship. "If it was right, your wife would be in a clean bed and her mom would be holding her hand." The audience made an assenting hum at her line of reasoning. Everyone was enjoying the distraction from their boredom and had to agree the ship wasn't an ideal place to give birth. "Look, you don't have to do anything you haven't already done before. I'll take care of the messy end. You just need to take care of the front end. Talk to her. Hold her. She's terrified." Elise grabbed a beam in the ceiling as the floor rolled. "Please," she begged, "Amanda doesn't know me. She needs a friend with her. She needs the man she loves encouraging her. Be her husband, Collins. Be her friend." Elise looked at Thomas who was standing slightly apart from the others. "He'll listen to you, Thomas. Tell him he needs to be with his wife."

Everyone turned to look at Thomas and he lifted his hands helplessly. "It's not for me or you to say how a man treats his wife."

"Oh, bullshit. Come on! You know Mrs. Postlethwaite would be on my side." Elise hoped that invoking the old beloved cook at the Quiet Woman would persuade Thomas.

"Hobert is right. A woman needs a woman."

"There now, that's settled," said Richard, "Tom agrees with Hobert. Shall we finish the game, gentlemen?"

Thomas's hand shot up. He wasn't finished. "A woman also knows what a woman needs. Collins, if Elise says your wife needs you, then she needs you."

"Don't listen to MacEwan," O'Brian slapped a card onto the small pile that was growing between the men's knees. "I must'a hit him too hard—he's gone soft in the head. Why should you follow the advice of a woman as threw herself into the ocean? Bloody foolish, if you ask me, following any slag's advice, but that one?" He shrugged, washing his hands of the entire situation.

Elise felt heat rushing to her cheeks. Thomas quickly moved to place himself between her and the card game, casting a sharp eye at Elise's balled fists. "O'Brian's still sore that I beat him," he said. "There's not a thing I could say that he wouldn't say the opposite."

"Fight didn't end proper. You didn't beat me."

"Seem to recall it was you on your back when it was called, not me."

"It wasn't called."

"Oh, who cares!" Elise snapped, stepping around Thomas. "What are you going to do, Collins?"

The young man hesitated. "She really wants me?"

"Yes! How many times do I have to tell you?" Elise couldn't explain why it meant so much to her to have Amanda be with the man she loved, but something told her that the baby's outcome would be better if the experience was shared between both parents. Amanda needed all the small advantages she could scrape together, and it wasn't much.

"All right then, if she needs me."

Elise was overjoyed at the small victory and ducked back under the curtain with renewed confidence. "Look who's here, Amanda!" she chirped happily as Collins shyly followed behind her. "I brought him back with me."

Amanda's eyes were clear as she turned. She was on her hands and knees—a stable position in an unstable environment. The frightened smile she tried to give Elise melted into horror as she recognized her husband standing backlit in the opened curtain. "Nooooooo!!!" cried Amanda.

"For heaven's sake, Mrs. Ferrington," barked Mrs. Gillihan. "Why would you bring him in here? Leave us at once, Mr. Collins. At once."

Collins's mouth rounded in a surprised pucker, mirroring his wife's mouth as she wailed, and he turned to bolt. Elise grabbed his forearm and meaningfully dug in her fingers. "Shut up, Mrs. Gillihan! Collins, tell Amanda how much you love her."

"Make him leave! He can't see me like this," Amanda wailed.

Despite the cold, sweat rolled down the back of Elise's neck. Once again, despite all her good intentions, her modern values were colliding with the values of the nineteenth century. She was positive she was witnessing a crossroads in Amanda and Peter's marriage. After this day, the couple's union would be forever changed. But Thomas was right—it wasn't for her to decide after all, and she would always advocate for her patient. "You heard her," she said to Collins, who was gaping stupidly at his wife. "Out!"

The directive was more than he could bear. Peter Collins fell to his knees and reached for his wife. "Oh my darling Amy," he cried, his cheeks wet, his face twisted ugly by emotion. "Let me help. Let me lift your burden."

Amanda recoiled from him, and the rejection caused him to melt into a nearly incomprehensible stream of pet names and cooing. In normal circumstances, any woman would have relented under this barrage of tenderness, but a sudden contraction turned Amanda inward so that she seemed to barely hear her husband. What did entreaties like "my sweet pickle-bottom" matter when, outside of her own control, powerful biological mechanisms were underway to create a hole the size of a honeydew melon between her legs? Luckily for Collins, his two long, bony thighs pressed together provided an alternative cushion from Mrs. Gillihan's lap, and she pragmatically accepted his questionable comfort and rested her head. He bent over her, cooing and murmuring in her ear while gently stroking her hair.

When the contraction ended, Amanda breathed out a long exhale of relief and curled her arms around her husband's waist.

Gently, Elise eased her patient back onto her hands and knees and pressed against her swaying belly, feeling for the baby's head and shoulders. She had a few minutes before the next contraction took over, just enough time to quickly explain what she needed to do to push the baby's head into position. Even after she heard the muffled "yes" of understanding from Amanda, she hesitated before beginning the cephalic version. She knew there was a possibility the baby wasn't in position because it was caught up by the umbilical cord, or cordoned off by a placenta that had attached at the wrong place on the uterine wall. Forcing the baby to move into position could potentially create a situation that might strangle it, or cause Amanda to bleed to death. Then there was the possibility that the baby would swing into breach position if Elise mistook its head for its butt.

Swallowing her nerves and wishing with all her might for a sonogram machine, Elise gently prodded Amanda's pendulous stomach to find the lumps of baby on either side. She pressed her fingers harder into flesh and felt for thighs, for the solidity of skull, for width, and then she took a deep breath. "This might hurt," Elise said, wishing it wouldn't.

"Hold her," she ordered Collins, and motioned a very disapproving Mrs. Gillihan back to Amanda's side with a thrust of her head. To Collins's credit, he gripped his wife solidly by the shoulders and nodded his readiness with a steely grimace. Elise braced herself against Amanda, hugging her from behind. She pressed deeply into Amanda's stomach with the heels of her hands, kneading, removing space, cornering the baby against her fists and giving it no choice but to swim against the pressure.

Eight hours later, Edwina was born. After having been pushed, squeezed, and otherwise mauled by Elise and Amanda, she flopped onto the deck with a gush of blood and howl that matched the weather. Elise's chest swelled with joy and relief as she and Mrs. Gillihan cleaned the red faced cherub and swaddled her for her parents. Little Edwina was met by all with the love and awe due to a miracle of biology. Only months earlier in Amanda's womb, she'd had pharyngeal slits and a post-anal tail, but now she was a fully-fledged bobble-headed, frog-limbed, pee-producer.

Elise's head was a jumble of conflicting thoughts and emotions as she helped make the new family as comfortable as possible. As the storm eased into a light rain, she staggered sleepily to her own corner of the ship and climbed back up onto the pile of crates. Although dawn was undetectable, as deep as she was in the bowels of the *Valiant*, Elise knew she'd worked an entire shift.

Up above her, the sailors changed their watch, just as they had the morning before, and the morning before that, and the morning before that. It was the same world, just another day in a long string of days, another long trudge through the past, and yet, for Elise, everything felt different somehow. Already men were climbing out along the yard arms to remove the reef in the sails. The deck was being scrubbed clean of the refuge the sea had tossed aboard. The wheel was being unleashed and a new course was laid.

Richard, asleep with his heavy great-coat under his head as a pillow, lifted the blanket and made room for Elise to curl up under it. She tucked her spine against the warmth of his body and nearly didn't notice when he pulled her in closer. It was just another day, but now with new life in it. A squirmy baby, with the nub of a pointy carrot for a nose and a conical head, was fiercely nursing a few yards away. Elise smiled, closed her eyes, and fell instantly asleep.

Even though it was late afternoon when Elise finally woke up, the whole world seemed inexplicably lighter after her long sleep. Elise was vaguely aware that Richard had slipped away not long after she'd gone to bed to do whatever it was that Richard did—gamble, trade for favors, polish the buttons of his waistcoat—but she hadn't been aware that the other infantrymen walked on their tip-toes and spoke in hushed voices when passing the stack of crates where she slept. All Elise knew was that when she woke she found a breakfast of salt pork and hard tack artfully arranged near her head. The offering was a sign of gratitude from the company, and although it softened her towards the men, it didn't move her as much as the small effort Collins was making to hold a conversation.

"I trust you've slept well?"

"Like a log."

"Ah, ahem, I am gladdened. . .uh, that is to say, I believe I'm not mistaken in taking your meaning—"

"I slept well."

Conversation with Collins was a stuttered and uncomfortable effort of two people with nothing in common. However, spending hours together encouraging Amanda had created a guarded friendship between them. Collins handed his porter to Elise with a companionable smile and she tipped the skunky-smelling stuff back without thanks, secure in the knowledge that she'd earned every last drop. Weeks in a cask at sea did nothing to improve the flavor of the beer, but Elise swallowed it on ceremony, cementing the relationship.

"Well. . ." Elise said, wiping her mouth with the back of her hand.

"Yes." He nodded decisively.

"I'll just go check on Amanda."

"Right."

"Catch you later."

"Err?"

"I mean, 'bye.'"

Elise ducked away, rubbing the sleep from her eyes. It wasn't the first time she'd ever had beer for breakfast, but she would have preferred a cup of coffee. It would have helped to prepare her for Amanda's worried whine when she entered the Collins' corner.

"Edwina is off her feeeeeed."

It took Elise a few breaths before she was able to translate the new mother's concern. "Maybe she's not hungry?" Elise swore under her breath. This was moving well beyond her expertise. Amanda needed a lactation specialist.

"No, she's hungry alright. She's just too weak—can't suck hard enough, poor sweet girl." Amanda nuzzled her daughter, who emitted a strange, lengthy drone that wavered as she bounced in her mother's arms. Then Amanda mashed her heavy breast against Edwina's face in an effort to tempt her to eat. "See? She won't eat. It's been nearly five hours. That's too long, isn't it?" Edwina continued her drone, muffled, but determined.

"Let me have her a minute." Elise said, and carefully took the bundle from her mother's arms. Edwina's little belly was round and soft; her skin was pink. All good. Her grip reflex wasn't very strong, however. Elise pressed her ear to the soft baby's chest to listen for breathing and heart rate. With her nose so near to Edwina's head, she caught an unwelcome scent. "Is that alcohol? I do NOT smell alcohol, do I? Why is there alcohol on your baby's breath?"

Amanda's laugh tinkled. "Oh, Lady Letchfeld was here and brought me a little bottle of the major's brandy. Wasn't that kind? She suggested I give Edwina a thimble full. She said it's the best tonic for a newborn. Can you imagine? I never in my wildest dreams thought anyone like the major's wife would pay me a visit, much less bring me a gift. Wasn't that kind of her?"

"Mystery solved," Elise drawled. "Your kid's too drunk to suck."

"Don't be ridiculous. It was just a little nip from the bottle. Nothing more than a thimble-full, a mere tonic. Lady Letchfeld would never suggest Edwina get cut and fuddled. It's only for quieting her."

"What does she know? Does Lady Letchfeld have a baby?"

"You've no baby neither," Amanda's bottom lip jutted stubbornly, "and she's a Lady."

"Just because the woman is richer than me, doesn't make her smarter than me. I swear if I catch you giving that baby any more liquor I will hurt you," Elise said, looking directly into Amanda's eyes. "How's that for the voice of authority? I. Will. Hurt. You. You know what? Just give it to me. Give me the brandy."

Amanda's eyes welled with tears. "No! Lady Letchfeld gave it to me as a gift."

"And my gift to you is taking it away. You'll kill Edwina with this shit." Elise held the baby like a football in one arm and used her free hand to work the bottle out of Amanda's grip. With the bottle safely in Elise's apron pocket, she gave Amanda an awkward side-hug, which wasn't well received.

A fat tear dropped onto the baby's head. "Oh God, don't do that." Elise hugged Amanda again, tighter. "Look, nobody cares if Edwina fusses. Everyone on this ship expects it. Babies are supposed to cry."

Amanda wiped her arm across her eyes.

"And anyway," Elise continued, "it's not like you have an instruction manual. You'll make lots of mistakes, and get a lot of bad advice. That's ok. I'll help as much as I can. Has Mrs. Gillihan been around to see you yet?"

Amanda nodded. "She's been very helpful. She shared her rations with me this morning. She said I have to feed myself to feed the baby."

"Ok. Good." Elise nodded, thinking guiltily of the breakfast she'd gobbled down. "Mrs. Gillihan's had babies. Listen to her, not Lady Letchfeld. She knows what she's talking about."

"Is anyone there?" came a loud voice from behind the curtain. "I say, knock, knock."

From the floor where she was seated, Elise lifted one corner of the brown wool blanket and found herself face to knee with a pair of muscular legs encased in white stockings. Looking up, she saw a red-haired man with a pathetically thin mustache. George Russell was now the picture of health, with pink cheeks instead of green ones and a brocade waistcoat covering most of the vomit stains on his linen shirt. He smiled broadly. "Ah. Mrs. Ferrington, is it not? Your servant, madam." He bowed formally. "I'm jolly glad to see you here—I was concerned you might have lost your nerve."

"Nope, I'm here. Still have my nerve," Elise smiled. "What's up?"

Russell's eyes widened and in the ensuing silence, he made a big show of clearing his voice while Amanda elbowed Elise hard.

"Mrs. Peter Collins, I presume?" Russell finally said, giving Elise a meaningful look.

Elise blushed, realizing her mistake. Hastily, and somewhat awkwardly, she made a formal introduction.

"And may I present Mr. Andrew Jenkins, my assistant." A thin man behind Russell loomed, a consequence of being too tall under the low ceiling. Jenkins barely nodded. "Your servant," he muttered insincerely before turning to stare blankly at something on the leeward side of the deck.

"And how is the new mother then?" Russell asked.

"Doing well," Elise announced. "Baby's heart and bowel sounds are within normal limits. No abdominal distention, feeding well, neural reflexes—"

"The patient is not bound, sir," Jenkins interrupted as he peered over the surgeon's shoulder into the enclosure.

"Not bound? Good God! Jenkins, you are correct! My dear Mrs. Collins, why are you not bound?" Russell looked accusingly at Elise.

"Why on Earth is she not bound?"

"Bound?" Elise couldn't imagine what he was talking about.

"Yes. Bound. *Bound.*" He glared, waiting for the word to explain itself. Finally, when Elise showed no understanding, he explained in a sarcastically slow and steady tone, "One cannot allow bad air to enter the womb, can one?"

"Bad air?"

"Think, Mrs. Ferrington. Think! Details such as these are important. Noting details can make the difference between those that live and those that die."

"Die?" Amanda sniffed once, quietly, then a second time with more conviction, as if she'd made the decision that yes, an emotional reaction to the situation was indeed warranted. Elise shot a glance at her and narrowed her eyes, waiting. Amanda's chin trembled hard enough to turn her lower lip into a soft pucker of unhappiness. "Why didn't you bind me?" The tears finally spilled as she slapped her thighs together. "I am lost. LOST. The vapors will be the death of me."

"The what?"

Russell shook his head. "I must say, Mrs. Ferrington, I'm quite disappointed in your performance thus far. I was led to believe you were an experienced nurse. I am one assistant short and hoped, despite the obvious disadvantage of your being a member of the fairer sex, you'd be able to aid us. But I see now," continued Russell, "that Jenkins and I will have to bear the burden ourselves." His lips were pressed thin as he quickly tied Amanda's thighs together with a muslin bandage. Then he reached into the cross-body bag he was wearing and handed Jenkins a brass bowl. "There's nothing for it, I'll have to bleed her. Let's hope this will be enough to keep away puerperal fever." He rummaged again in his bag for a lancet while Amanda compliantly held out her arm.

"Are you nuts?" Elise exploded. "Bleed her? How can that possibly be a good idea?"

Russell froze. His two brows melded into one over his hazel eyes and his mustache twitched. "Might I have a word, Mrs. Ferrington? In private." He held the corner of the blanket up, indicating that Elise should exit with him.

"My dear Mrs. Ferrington," he began, stepping well away from the Collins's corner. "I will not have you questioning my orders. This is very bad business, very bad indeed. Should you do so again in such a shocking manner I will have you flogged and sent back home on the first returning ship."

"Promise? No really, I'm scared."

The surgeon's eyes widened in surprise.

"How old are you anyway, Doc? You seem pretty young to be so dismissive. You think binding her thighs is going to keep away puerperal fever? Show me the clinical research that backs up that idea. No? No research? Is all you have anecdotal evidence?" Elise watched the surgeon's chest expand as he filled his lungs and opened his mouth to object. Then he seemed to change his mind and the objection never came. Instead he cocked his head, puzzled. He wasn't very tall, nor was he muscular, but he had nice wide shoulders that widened further when he was mad.

"Save it," she said as he opened his mouth again. "Bleed her if you want. Tie her up. What do I care? It won't make any difference. She's fine, no thanks to you. She's fine because of me. Because I brought her through the birth. *I* did. *Me.*"

"Now see here, madam. I have been in the surgical theatre since I was sixteen years old and never in all my years—"

"All eighteen of them?"

"How dare you."

"Whatever, kid," Elise walked away. "Have at it."

The air grew lighter as she climbed from the dank deck where the army was quartered to the first gun deck, as though she was rising from thick valley smog into clear mountain air. Elise noted bleakly how the presence of weaponry required a high level of cleanliness, whereas no effort had been made to clean the deck for the foot soldiers. The black cannons with their noses up against closed ports were ready to spit iron out into the ocean. Elise empathized. She seethed over the conversation she'd had with George Russell. How could he possibly believe puerperal fever was due to bad air entering a patient's uterus? She couldn't quite believe she'd just been dressed down for not having tied Amanda's thighs together. The surgeon's pairing of the words, "fairer" and "sex" did nothing to soothe her rage, either.

Elise ran down the length of the second gun deck, past resting sailors on the first watch who looked up at her in surprise. "Get out of my way," Elise yelled at a man who happened to be walking towards a coil of rope at the same time she leaped over it. Hitching her skirt above her knees, she rushed to get ahead of a large group of men who were making their way up to the weather deck.

"Oy! What's the rush? No need for pushing," the men protested.

She pushed anyway and emerged into the world sucking in sharp ocean air like a drowning woman. Tears began flowing down her cheeks. Everything smelled clean and expansive, like possibility and self-actualization—two things that were now out of reach.

She didn't bother to drop her skirts as she ran towards the mainmast, loving the way her legs felt as the sun and air hit them for the first time in weeks. Her bare feet slapped against the wet decking and left dirty footprints in her wake.

On the forecastle, two officers on watch pointed towards her when she grabbed the ratlines to stand on the ship's rail. A wave hit the side of the ship and she held on against the force of the spray, squeezing her eyes shut against the stinging saltwater, curling her toes. Then she began to climb.

"You there! Get down this instant," called a sailor. She climbed faster. This time, she would climb her way out of the nightmare she'd fallen into.

A Man's A Man

"Prime and load!" shouted Sergeant Taylor.

Thomas pulled a cartridge out of the cartridge box slung over his shoulder and tore the paper cylinder open with his teeth, poured gun powder into the pan of his musket, then dropped the ball and paper into the muzzle. The movements were second nature, given all the mind-numbing, earsplitting drills he'd had to do since joining up. All the men were bored with tossing off musket balls. They could fire three rounds a minute with their eyes closed. But now that the weather was finally clearing, he had to admit it was a nice diversion. He was mostly curious to see if Sergeant Taylor would give the order to fire at an inopportune moment. It was one thing to lob musket balls when the ship was directed down into the trough of a wave, but entirely different when the ship's bow heaved. He half hoped Taylor would get it wrong.

The strategy of drilling the buggered enlisted men until they all stood on the edge of madness was an ancient gift passed down from his Lordship to his damned Lordship, Thomas was sure of it. How else do you get men to kill each other without provocation? Drill them every day while filling the empty halls of their heads with thoughts of duty and honor. Every day was nothing but endless horizons on the ocean, endless jacket buttons that needed polishing for inspection, endless lines for rations, endless drilling, endless waiting, endless waiting, endless waiting.

The landed classes in England were scared of what had happened in France. They were scared of the ideals of France, of commonality between men, of minds meeting minds without thought of stature or birth. So what to do? It was brilliant, really. Send the common rabble to war against the very nation that rose against hierarchy so none would get any inkling of what the French were actually up to. None would feel the draw of the Revolution if they were too busy spilling revolutionaries' blood. But I know, Thomas thought. They couldn't fool him.

Anyway, it was all unnecessary effort. England would never rise up against her King. England wasn't France. In England, a man like him, a jumped-up street urchin turned barman with no known family, could read a thousand books, entire libraries even, and still not have an opinion that mattered to anyone. In England, only gentlemen were allowed to have opinions, and grown orphans, men from the gutters, kept their heads down. In France, a man was a man, equal, as God intended. But Thomas was an Englishman through and through, so it didn't matter that France had a new constitution that extolled brotherhood. Just because he didn't keep Rousseau in his pack didn't mean he hadn't read and reread the philosopher by candlelight after closing time at the Quiet Woman. But no one needed to know about it. Ideas could get you killed. Ideas were strange that way.

The salty gunpowder dried Thomas's mouth as he rammed another musket ball home.

The problem with boredom is it gave a man plenty of time to think. The problem with thinking is that without books, his mind always wandered back to Elise. Elise, who never seemed to know her place. Elise, who looked everyone in the eyes and spoke her mind like her opinion should be counted.

He squeezed the trigger and a spark from the flint hit the pan. The resulting explosion made his ears ring.

"Reload!" shouted Sergeant Taylor, and Thomas tore into another cartridge.

Again and again he replayed the conversation he'd had with Elise that night in the yard of the Quiet Woman, turning over every word, every action, growing by turns angry and regretful with each remembered phrase until it finally ended in the vision of her sprawled on the ground with her mouth bleeding and her eyes wild. Why had he thought hitting her would convince her to stay behind in London? "If you can't take a slap like that," he'd told her, "you won't last two seconds in the army." What a fool he'd been. You can't tame a beast with blows. Again and again, night after night he agonized over the miscalculation. Hit a woman once and she'll come back with soft tears, soft words, and even softer hands. Hit Elise once and you'll never forget it. You'll relive it every day of your miserable life.

Maybe she wasn't a real woman. Maybe she was something else. A man-girl. The memory of that first night, when he'd picked her up out of the mud wearing next to nothing was burned into his mind. He'd brought her into Mrs. P.'s kitchen and helped bathe her on the hearth like she was just another of old Mrs. P's stray kittens—tiny waist, round breasts, and hard thighs. He'd had no doubts she was all woman then, no doubts at all. His spark hit the pan again.

"Reload!"

He almost believed her story of being a traveler from the future. There did seem to be something otherworldly about Elise. Her strange words and sloppy broad mannerisms should have repulsed him, but instead Thomas found himself transfixed by her legs. He'd seen the way she'd jumped from the packing crate to help Mrs. Collins at childbirth. Thomas had caught a glimpse of her legs before her skirt floated back to the floor—tight calves, fading tan, delicately boned ankles. She was nimble and unafraid to display her strength. She refused help because she didn't need help. She didn't mince about in order to garner advantage. She thudded to the floor, loudly, in a way that was both entirely unbecoming and entirely enchanting, like watching a cat leap from an overhead shelf to land hard on the kitchen table before walking away—one paw crossing neatly in front of the other, as though the jam jar hadn't been knocked to the floor. And it didn't hurt that her large green eyes, when they weren't rolling with derision, flashed with intelligence and spirit.

"Reload!"

At this rate they were going to run out of powder before they even got to Portugal, thought Thomas as he reached for another cartridge. He felt something hit the stiff leather stock that encircled his neck as he primed his musket. Without turning, he knew O'Brian had spat his cartridge paper at him. He rammed his musket. That was no accident of proximity. The damned bastard spat on him.

Their fight may have ended, but it hadn't been settled, and Thomas knew that until he put O'Brian down and in his place, he'd be putting up with no end of slights. There would have to be a reckoning soon. The last thing he needed was to worry if he'd be killed by the enemy line, or by a musket ball in his back.

He discharged his weapon. The sound of it was a final salute to his foul mood.

"Attention!"

Thomas drew his body taught while his mind flexed over a lifetime of slights. The back of his neck burned from the insult of O'Brian's paper cartridge.

Lieutenant Mason and Major Letchfeld walked the line, while Sergeant Taylor glared at his men with steely eyes. "Oh dear, oh dear," tsked the major. He stopped to place the handle of his riding crop underneath the chin of a private. Why he was carrying a riding crop on board a ship in the middle of the ocean was beyond Thomas. "Do you see this man's cheek, James?"

"Powder burns, sir," replied Mason. "Probably a hang fire." He stepped in towards the hapless soldier. "Name."

"Cox, sir."

"Show me your weapon, Private Cox." Mason snatched the musket out of the private's hands when it was hesitantly offered and handed it to the older officer.

"Oh, I see now," Major Letchfeld said, squinting at the brown bess. "Private Cox's touchhole is clogged."

All the way down at the other end of the line, someone sniggered.

"What's so funny?" Sergeant Taylor demanded angrily, stepping forward. "Who thinks Cox's dirty touchhole is funny?"

The loud explosion of air escaping someone's pinched lips was barely masked by the sound of Bill Stanton's drum rolling aft along the deck. "Sorry, sirs," he called as he tripped over himself to recapture the rolling snare. "Won't happen again, sirs."

Major Letchfeld sighed as the sergeant rushed to beat Billy back into line, "It's a good thing that boy wasn't holding a musket."

"That's quite enough, Sergeant," Lieutenant Mason called. The boy's cries were making the men restless. "Private Cox, you will clean and present your weapon for inspection to Sergeant Taylor during second watch for the next five days. During first watch, you're to guard the ship's bell. If, in that time, I hear of any transgressions in your ability to maintain your firearm, you will be flogged."

A fair punishment, Thomas thought. A misfire from an ill-kept weapon was certainly no laughing matter and the carelessness had to be checked. It was likely that Taylor would find some reason to force Cox to clean his musket multiple times a night before passing inspection, which meant that between caring for his weapon and standing guard, Cox would only be able to snatch a few hours' sleep at a time. Despite this, Cox got off easy, and everyone knew it.

"Hum, hum. I must say," Major Letchfeld said. His disapproving huffing sounds made his round belly bounce on top of his stout thighs. He paused, as though trying to decide what exactly must be said. "I say," he tried again, and tut-tutted. Then he continued down the line, studying each man for irregularities. Finally, he reached Thomas. "Oh hooo!" he exclaimed, standing in front of him. "Isn't this the man we caught in the brawl? Yes, I believe he is. Him and that other fellow behind him. The French will piss themselves just looking at him. A rare specimen—a true veteran. Ah, the battles you must have seen, Private. . ."

"Private MacEwan, sir."

"Where did you get those honorable scars, Private MacEwan? Buenos Aires?" He pointed to Thomas's face.

"The streets of London, sir," replied Thomas. The major looked confused.

"Begging your pardon, sir," Sergeant Taylor piped in. "That one there's a new recruit."

"Streets of London. . .?" Letchfeld backed away from Thomas to get a better look at him, from his polished shoes to the top of his feathered shako. "It's easy to forget, isn't it, James?" he addressed Lieutenant Mason, but couldn't take his eyes off Thomas. "They look so damn sharp in their uniforms, it's easy to forget they're all criminals. I don't doubt this one's murdered a few men."

"So you say, sir. I believe that was your assessment after we caught him brawling. He's the one I told you about. Private Thomas MacEwan: the singer."

"Singer? This ruffian?" Now he stepped in close, so that Thomas felt the need to straighten himself taller just to make more space between them. "Tell me, Private MacEwan, do you like singing?"

"Yes, sir! Been singing all my life—it goes with the job."

"A singing murderer," the major laughed. "How poetic."

"Publican, sir," Thomas corrected, "I was a barman before I took the king's shilling. A drink always goes best with a song, sir."

"I was under the impression that Ferrington there, our fine fiddler, was the publican."

"My former employer, sir."

Major Letchfeld's eyes shifted from Thomas's scarred face to Richard's smooth skin and handsome features, then back to Thomas again. It was obvious to Thomas that the major was weaving a story about his past. "My wife's been telling me all about the tall blond private who plays the violin. These are hard times indeed when such talent languishes amongst this lot." He waved derisively towards the rest of the soldiers. "Private Ferrington, you must put on a concert for us at dinner tonight. Betsy would be charmed."

"Delighted, sir. Delighted." Richard grinned.

Major Letchfeld clucked happily, then turned back to Thomas, and his expression quickly changed back to severe disapproval. "Tell me, Private: do you like your tongue?"

"I find it very useful, sir."

"Then I'd better not hear you've been singing that traitorous song again or I'll cut it out. Am I understood?"

The major's tall hat reached the tip of Thomas's nose. It was disconcerting to be threatened by a man so short you could see over the top of his head. "Begging your pardon, sir. Which song would that be? I sing many."

"What was the song, James?" Letchfeld demanded. "Something written by that dreadful Scotch rhymer?"

"'A Man's a Man,' sir?" Richard piped in.

Thomas had to stop himself from heaving an exasperated sigh. Always ebullient, never helpful: that would be Richard.

"That's the one." Major Letchfeld smiled delightedly. "Let us never hear that song again, shall we? Shall we Private MacEwan?"

Thomas leaned forward slightly and turned his ear towards the major. "Which song, sir? I didn't hear, sir. My ears are still ringing." He wanted Letchfeld say the words.

"'A Man's a Man, for A'That!'" shouted the major.

"Yes, sir! He is indeed, sir," shouted Thomas back. Despite Lieutenant Mason's scowl, promising further uncomfortable interactions, his mood lifted slightly as the major turned his attention back to Richard.

"Good. Good. Well, I've seen enough. Fine looking lads. Keep them sharp, Sergeant Taylor, and watch out for that MacEwan. He's a sullen one. Ever plotting, that one, up to no good." The major ambled off towards the cabins where cool wine and his warm young wife awaited.

The second after the men were dismissed, their spines collapsed back into normal alignments, causing all their gear to clang. With the officers gone, Hobert felt free to clap Cox on his head, knocking off his shako. "Don't worry," he wheezed loudly. "With all this hard tack we've been eatin' we're *all* a little clogged in our touchholes."

"That scamp," Richard laughed at Billy, who was clutching his drum protectively as he was pushed and shoved good-naturedly between the older soldiers. "Reminds me of our own Johnny, doesn't he?" Thomas allowed that he did, and swallowed a pang of homesickness.

Much like Johnny, the boy was carefree to the point of being slippery—that's what these boys were these days. No sense of responsibility; no sense of shame. Thomas strode away from Richard mid-prattle and grabbed Bill by the arm. "Listen to me," he growled. The boy's eyes opened wide in alarm. "You watch yourself. You won't be everyone's darling for long. Soon enough you'll be everyone's fool and when that happens it won't be a gentle swat you'll be getting like today, you'll be feeling the licking end of the lash. Keep your head down, boy, and just beat your damn drum, or it'll be me as beats you."

Bill twirled and twisted to escape Thomas's tight grip. "Let him be, MacEwan," laughed Collins. He was standing with Richard, and the two of them were smiling sardonically, likely at his expense. "It was a harmless jest."

Thomas opened his hand, and the boy ran off to scamper up the mainmast where his new friend, the tiny Midshipman Donegal, was on watch. "You know I'm right, Peter," Thomas said. He pulled his shako off his head and pushed his fingers through his dark hair. He hated his hat.

"If Bill needs a wet nurse, my wife could help him better than you. Lay off the poor lad. You'd do better to look to your own problems. You think you're making a grand example of keeping your head low?" Peter Collins didn't bother to wipe the grin from his face when Thomas glowered and took two steps at him. "What's that bit about a man being a man? I'm not looking for trouble from you, Tom. Just giving a bit of friendly advice."

Thomas blew out the puffed up breath he'd been unconsciously holding and pushed his hand through his hair again, standing down. He didn't want trouble either, that was sure. Not while in the army. He was fairly certain he wouldn't get trouble from the sergeant, who knew better than to follow Letchfeld's orders to keep an eye on him.

Like Thomas, Taylor was from the gutter, and knew when there was a better man about. But Collins was different, a family man, a man Thomas wanted to keep at his side, close. "How's your babe faring? Your missus?"

Thomas didn't hear Collins's reply. Richard was heading down between decks and he had a bone to pick. "Richard! A word, please."

"Oh for pity's sake, Tom," Richard cried out. "What now?" The other soldiers filed past as the next company emerged into the light to take their place in the drill line.

"Have you gone entirely mad? They," Thomas waved in the general direction of the forecastle where the officers kept apart from the enlisted men, "are just as dangerous as the French. And here you go making plans to dine with them."

"Dine? Oh no, I'm not dining with them. I wasn't given that honor. I'm merely providing them with entertainment while they work their jaws." Richard leaned forward conspiratorially. "Did you hear? The lovely Mrs. Letchfeld is interested in music and likes my fiddle." He wagged his eyebrows. "Isn't that wonderful?"

"Richard, stay away from the major's wife."

"How you *do* worry—" Richard's thought was cut short by a vision at the corner of his eye. "Oh hell, there she is. What's that woman up to now?"

"Who? Lady Letchfeld?"

"God grant it were so. My wife."

Thomas turned in time to see Elise's scruffy head rising from below deck, pushing men aside to force her way up against the flow. Just as soon as she had both of her big feet on the deck, she took off running with her skirts clutched above her knees and her loose auburn hair streaming behind her like a glorious banner in battle. The sight of her long legs knocked Thomas back two steps. The sight of her tears made him step forward.

"For pity's sake," Richard cried. "She's going to climb the mast. She'll ruin everything! Letchfeld will surely retract his invitation. I swear to you, Tom, that woman is not natural. You know it to be true— have you ever seen a woman climb like that? It's simply not natural. She's entirely immodest."

"You've nought to complain about, Ferrington," scoffed Collins. "If you don't like it, correct it. You've only yourself to blame if she's too frisky for your tastes."

Since Richard was, himself, calling attention to his own wife, it didn't seem untoward to Thomas to take another eyeful of Elise's strong calves when the Atlantic wind blew up her skirt.

"Are you suggesting I beat her?"

"I'm suggesting you keep your piehole shut. Your wife gave me my daughter."

"I'd find another way of putting that, if I were you."

"Perhaps old Mr. Tilsdale was right," Thomas said, thinking of a man he'd served regularly at the Quiet Woman. "Perhaps she is a bit of a lunatic. She's certainly high-spirited."

"Are those men gambling on my wife?" A group of sailors had stopped to watch Elise scale the ratlines. "They are! Those bastards are gambling on my wife!" Richard's outrage seemed a little hypocritical to Thomas. "I'd wager the damned woman will go all the way to the top. In fact, I've no doubt in my mind. A sure bet."

It was the one sure thing Richard would never deign to gamble on. The sad irony wasn't lost on Thomas.

Elise barely noticed how the rope chafed against her palms. She was fixated on a platform above her, midway up the mast. A hole had been cut to allow access to the platform from below, and she imagined herself emerging through into a sanctuary. Seated on that platform, she would have nothing but the freedom of the open sky. She would fly back to her own time. She would soar upwards, leap from the platform and be sucked up towards heaven and carried home.

Suspended high over the rail as she clung to the ratlines, it soon became impossible to know if she was still crying, or if the water streaking her cheeks was just ocean spray. Were her eyes burning from hot tears or the brisk wind? She blinked hard and squinted down at the deck, far below, swaying in a direction sickeningly at odds with her own motion. When the ship slipped over a rise in the waves and fell into the trough, Elise's weight fell forward against the net while the deck rose up behind her. Just as disconcertingly, when ship rose with the swell and heeled starboard, her weight fell away from the lines and over the water, causing her to grip the net with desperation while the fore deck rose up in front of her. She swallowed hard to quell the vertigo that caused her stomach to surge.

She was just ten feet from reaching her goal when Bill Stanton's round face appeared, framed by the hole in the platform. For a moment she considered climbing back down. Even the sky was full of people, she thought bitterly.

"I've won; she's made it." The wind carried the young drummer's voice to her. "I'll give you my stockings this evening, and you're not to darn them slap-dash. I expect neat stitches."

"No! Look, she's stopped. It's not settled." The authority of a second boy's opinion was undermined when his youthful voice cracked. "The bet was that she climb all the way onto the platform. That was the agreement."

They were questioning her ability, not her desire to climb. Elise tore the rest of the way up the ratlines. George Russell's words were still echoing in her head, and if she heard the words "fairer" and "sex" she knew she'd get violent, especially if it was from a pair of dumb-assed teens.

When she stuck her head through the lubber hole, Bill hooted his pleasure. On the platform next to him, with knees slightly bent to accommodate the rocking floor beneath, was another youth Elise recognized as belonging to the sailors—a midshipman and mini mascot in full naval regalia. Both boys clung to ropes that continued further up the mast.

"Begging your pardon, madam," said the small officer, "if you could be so kind as to complete your ascent on your own. I'm afraid neither Bill nor I can come to your aid as it would undermine any conclusions as to the winner of our bet."

Elise pulled herself through the hole, but vertigo and the swaying boards kept her from standing. "What if it's just my ass on the platform?" she asked. "Who wins then?"

The two boys looked at each other. Plainly, they hadn't thought of that scenario.

"If she hasn't the courage to stand, I don't see that—"

"The wager was whether she had enough courage to reach the platform, not to stand upon it."

"Please stop talking like I'm not here."

"Your pardon, madam. We do not mean any disrespect," said the smaller boy.

"You're plenty disrespectful all the same," Elise drawled. "Don't worry, I'm getting used to it."

The midshipman suddenly found his manners and bowed formally with one foot in front of the other while keeping one steadying hand still on the lines. "Welcome," he said, "I believe you are the first lady ever to have graced the *Valiant's* fighting top. Given that there have been plenty of lubbers who couldn't find the courage to climb, you have my utmost respect."

"I just wanted to look at the view." She was sure the view would have been a better experience seen alone.

"Then you're a woman after my own heart, Mrs. Ferrington," Bill said with a sigh. "I'm not sure how anyone can live without having ever seen the sea from a ship's masthead. But the fighting top is more comfortable, I suppose." He settled down on the edge of the platform to swing his legs into the air, wrapping himself in the protection of the netting. "Come join me. You can see the edge of the world from here."

"I am Gerald Donegal, at your service," said the younger boy, realizing he would never be introduced by his rude friend. "Let it be known that, although I did bet against you, I have never been more pleased to be wrong."

"Don't be fooled by his uniform or his manner, Mrs. Ferrington," Bill drawled. "Gerry may have a tidier coat than mine, but his stockings are still riddled with holes. Mine, on the other hand, will soon be as good as new."

It felt strange and unfamiliar to have the corners of her mouth curl into a smile. When Bill made room for Elise to sit down next to him, she gladly accepted his invitation. Six legs in a row swung casually over a long drop to the deck below. "What are you boys doing up here?" Elise asked.

"I'm on watch," Gerry responded, "but I've no idea why Bill is here."

"I'm here for the peace and quiet," Bill said. The left side of his face was red and beginning to bruise. Elise felt a flare of anger at the evidence of a beating, then swallowed hard and tried push her anger away.

"Shouldn't you be down there with those guys?" Elise pointed to a small crowd of men that were trying to form two rows around coiled ropes and open hatches near the bow of the ship. Sailors cut through the line of infantrymen as they tugged a sheet to tighten a sail, heaving in tandem on the rope. Finally, the sergeant whipped his soldiers into forming rank.

"Those lads?" Bill derided. "Those are fine lads, to be sure, but not sharp like the men in our own company." He puffed himself up a little with pride. "Our Sergeant Taylor would have us shooting three rounds a minute.

Our own—the words sounded hollow in Elise's head. She wished she could feel as possessive as Bill about the men whose wounds she knew she'd soon be patching. Her company was tied to the Forty-Fifth Regiment of Foot, but that knowledge didn't inspire any feelings of pride. When you don't know the players, or the rules, there wasn't much point in picking sides.

"I still think it's odd that after spending so long fighting the Spanish in America, the 45th is now asked to save the Spanish from the French," Bill mused.

"These guys were in America?" Elise asked with a twitch. She gazed out at the horizon, across the sails of two other ships in the fleet and tried not to feel cheated, once again, by time.

"Not all of them," Bill said. "Not me. Not your husband. Many of us were just recently recruited. But a good number were indeed in Buenos Aires." He shook his head in wonder. "It's a soldier's life to see the world. I don't envy the lads that stayed home."

Buenos Aires. Elise's eyes bugged at the information. She had wanted desperately to get to America, but *Buenos Aires*? Wasn't that in Brazil? No, wait, Argentina. She frowned, positive that wherever it was in South America, it would have taken forever to get from there to Tucson, Arizona. Why had she assumed any ship going to America would land someplace like Boston or Virginia?

"I don't envy those who fought in America," Gerry responded. "They're a sad lot, they are. No one's shown any regard for their efforts."

"Useless efforts," agreed Bill. "Oh look. They're going at it again."

From Elise's height, the men below looked like toy soldiers

come to life, each movement choreographed for an audience of three sitting up in the nosebleed section. But when the kneeling rank fired, followed by the standing rank, there was no mistaking the reality of the company's deadly purpose. Smoke obscured the faces of the men for a just a moment before the ocean breeze swept it away.

Elise wasn't the only one affected by the display. Bill was leaning over the edge of the platform to such a degree that her alarm bells went off. Gently, she touched his elbow to pull his attention back to his surroundings. She was just beginning to like the kid, and he wouldn't be nearly as much fun with his brains spread all over the deck.

The thought gave her a headache. Elise put a hand to her temple as pressure behind her right eye increased.

"Mrs. Ferrington? Are you quite alright?" asked Bill.

"Yeah, just the change in the weather I guess."

Suddenly, Gerry shot to his feet and pointed out onto the horizon. "Sail," Gerry cried. "Sail ho!" He was practically swinging over thin air. "Sail ho," he called again.

"Jesus! Be careful!" Elise clutched the ropes as the platform bounced under Gerry's shifting weight. The space behind both her eyes were now throbbing in a dull pain.

"Is it one of ours?" cried a voice from below.

Gerry gathered his feet under him, pulled a brass telescope from his breast pocket, and trained it on the horizon. Bill had climbed to his feet as well and was shading his eyes with one hand and squinting, ready to take the spyglass the second it was offered. "Can you make her out?" asked Bill. "Is she French?"

"No colors, sir!" Gerry hollered down to the officer below who was waiting impatiently.

"A merchant ship?" Bill suggested

"A single merchant ship with no convoy? Unlikely. Not in these seas."

"Then a French ship?"

"Possibly," Gerry said, "but the French have been tied to their shores by English naval barricades. Perhaps she's a privateer."

"What's a privateer?" asked Elise, rubbing her temples.

"May I see?" Despite the fact that Bill shook his hand next to Gerry's head to get his attention, it was still the politest "my turn" whine Elise had ever heard.

"She's sailing away," Gerry mumbled to himself. Then stepping back to the edge, he called down, "she's sailing away!" Elise grabbed the back of his jacket just as Bill grabbed the glass.

A sloop in their fleet veered towards the marauding vessel. "The *Staghorn* is turning. She's going to give chase!" said Bill excitedly.

In the far, dark reaches of her mind, Elise felt the lightest touch, a familiar feather stroke. She raised her hand over her chest and felt the scarab where it lay hidden. A rush of heat made her dizzy, almost as though the scarab had ignited her brain like a spark. Then her headache eased. Elise stared out towards the quickly retreating ship and felt a disconcerting sense of familiarity that she couldn't place.

"The privateer is too far away," Bill said. "I'd wager she came upon us by accident. Why else would she run? The *Staghorn* will never catch her."

"The *Staghorn* will catch her. You'll see." Gerry's eyes shone bright with enthusiasm. "I wish we were there instead of here. They're going to have all the fun."

Below at the foot of the mast, a small crowd had gathered. The men looked stiff, ready. Soldiers were fingering their muskets. Sailors were facing the forecastle, waiting for orders. A few were hanging on the rail looking out towards the horizon where the ship had been sighted. They all had become so bored with the drudgery of ocean life that they welcomed a fight, hoped for it. Minutes rolled by without a command. "The privateer's gone," Gerry announced to no one. He'd retrieved his spyglass and now it was so tight against his face that Elise wondered if he'd give himself a black eye.

The *Staghorn*, however, was still in plain view, although a slowly diminishing presence on the horizon. If the two ships did battle each other, Elise imagined it would be boring. To call all the ships traveling together a "fleet" was misleading. Sure, the water slipped past their hull with a certain degree of efficiency and left a pretty wake, but they weren't anywhere near fast or fleet.

"I hope there'll be some cannons fired tonight. Perhaps we'll even see the glow of guns!" Gerry sighed wistfully at the thought. "I do so wish I was on the *Staghorn*. There aren't that many chances to engage the enemy on a troopship."

Gerry just confirmed Elise's thought. The chase, such as it was, would probably last all day and into the night.

"Our navy guns are fearsome enough," said Bill, "but we also have the British Army at our disposal. A privateer would be sorry indeed to engage a ship with the 45th on board.

"The Royal Navy doesn't need the army to win a battle. We can best any fleet in the world. Admiral Nelson proved that during the Battle of Trafalgar."

The sun slowly emerged from behind a long smear of clouds as the boys' discussion got heated over the merits of army versus navy. Elise leaned back to lie flat on the wooden planks. Despite the fact that the three of them were crowded on a platform that was barely larger than a dining room table, she felt she had, finally, enough space to breathe. She reached her hands back behind her head towards the mast and uncurled her vertebrae, nubby bone by popping nubby bone, along the boards. Seen through the mesh of ropes, the sky above was even more vivid than a Tucson sky, more clearly blue, entirely free from smog and dust. Elise squinted into the sun and smiled for the second time since she'd been married. It had been so long, so damn long, since she'd felt the warm sun.

Chère Mademoiselle DuBette,

I am gladdened to hear how much progress has been made with the Rosetta Stone. At this rate, I would not be surprised if we were able to begin the translation of the Thoth tablets by next year's end. That I had even a small part to play in this fills my heart with pride.

In answer to your question, I have not had a letter from Mademoiselle Lenormand and am, as you are, disturbed by her silence. Concern, at this point, seems well merited given the circumstances of her last communique. It would surprise me to learn that she blocked herself from contact on the astral plane. I do not think this to be the case. I, too, find myself growing more and more concerned about the possibility that we have over-estimated her abilities, or perhaps under-estimated the threats against her.

It is with these thoughts in mind that I applaud your decision to ask for help in finding the emerald from those of our gender who may have a more questionable bent to their magical practices. In light of this decision, I agree that letter writing is preferable. It would not do to have our conversations overheard in the void by dark forces now alerted to the presence of the scarab. It should, however, be mentioned that if we succeed in translating the Thoth tablets before Napoleon's alchemists do so, all women shall benefit, even those of us with questionable proclivities. If, Goddess willing, such a thing were to occur, I hope you'll agree that we must be more inclusive. In any case, I am not displeased to have the excuse to receive such lovely letters from you.

I do hope Mlle Lenormand took our words to heart and is handling herself with the intelligence and substance of character we know to be her style, and will recover the jewel quite on her own. I'll admit to being troubled by her silence. But perhaps it is mere petulance on her part to be silent—a behaviour which should come as no surprise to any of us—and not an indication of anything dire.

Thank you for informing me of your decision. I'm sure I need not call to your attention the coming of the new moon. I shall remain extra vigilant as the Goddess leaves our night sky, and look forward to her return. For no reason that I can articulate, my heart quails this cycle of the moon.

I remain your Sister in heart and mind,

Mrs. Ursula Southill

PEOPLE CAN'T FLY

The days were finally what summer should be—warm and full of sunshine, lazy, languid. A cool breeze lifted everyone's spirits and filled the canvas sails, pushing the *Valiant* onto her side so that she cut through the ocean at a neat clip. Elise, bored but content, ended up spending her days with Amanda, taking her turn with baby Edwina when the young mother needed a break, and hiding whenever Doctor Russell approached.

Babysitting wasn't her first choice for stimulating activity, but it was better than spending the day polishing the buttons on Richard's waistcoat and jacket, a chore he was dead set on her performing, as was, he said, her duty as wife. Their arguments had calmed a bit now that she was spending more time with Amanda, but that wasn't to say Richard wasn't finding ways Elise could improve upon herself. Sometimes his suggestions were oblique, sometimes bold, but they were always coupled with beseeching eyelash batting and sad looks that got him nowhere.

Every evening since Elise first climbed up the mast, she returned to the fighting top while Richard, released from his own duties, reluctantly polished his own buttons and fiddled his fiddle. Elise cherished her time under the open sky where the sun's slanting rays would warm her bones without crisping her skin. The boys, Gerry and Bill, had grown accustomed to her presence and either ignored her altogether, or brought her into their discussions. Her opinions were totally dismissible or blew their minds. For her part, the youth of her companions was a relief—Elise felt relaxed enough around them to be herself, knowing that they hadn't lived long enough to have solidified into jerks. She liked them enough to drop seeds of modern thought into their still-forming brains and felt smug when they ascribed her ideas to being radically "American" instead. An easy friendship developed between the three of them.

It was the last day of their journey. Elise had heard that hopeful rumor many times before, but this time Gerry assured them it was true. He'd looked at the charts and done the math during his navigation lessons and could say with conviction that they'd rounded the corner. As far as Elise could tell there were no corners in the ocean, but she took his word for it. If they were approaching shore, that would explain why they were seeing more birds in the sky.

The wheeling of the gulls had sparked a lively debate about flight that Elise was mostly ignoring. Bill was of the opinion that the ostrich had the best feathers for creating a set of wings, but Gerry thought peacock feathers were a better choice. It was, apparently, not enough for the two of them to spend all their waking hours as high as possible on the ship, they wanted wings to fly. Both thought that the bigger the feather, the better the possibility. After twenty minutes of argument, Bill turned the question over to Elise.

"What do you think, Mrs. Ferrington? Ostrich or peacock? Mrs. Ferrington? Are you listening?"

Elise, flat on her back, pushed herself up onto her elbows and squinted at the boys. "It's the shape of the wing, not the length of the feather," she responded authoritatively, then laid back down, hiding her face from the sun in the crook of her elbow.

"That cannot be right," Gerry shook his head. "Have you never eaten the wing of a bird? It is a measly meal, all gristle, a mere sliver of skin and bones. So it must, by logical reasoning, be the feathers that lift the animal as the flesh is so obviously lacking."

Elise sighed and pushed herself back up onto her elbows. Both boys were looking at her seriously. "Have you ever seen peacocks or ostriches fly? No? That's right, because they don't," Elise shot back, "so how would those feathers get a man off the ground if they can't do it for the bird? Huh? How? They wouldn't. Those feathers are like Mrs. Letchfeld—they're good for decoration only."

Bill hooted with delight, but Gerry was less amused. "You shouldn't speak of your betters that way."

"She's not better than me. She's just richer."

"Really, Mrs. Ferrington, must you pull your skirts up that high? It's quite shocking." Gerry's eyes were fixed at a spot on the mast as she hoisted her dress up her thighs. His sunburned face couldn't get any redder, however.

"I like to feel the sun on my legs."

"It's terrible for your complexion. You're already turning quite brown."

"Good."

"Is that a knife? Have you tied a knife to your thigh?" Gerry's shock made his voice crack.

"Leave her be, Gerry." Bill defended. "Her knife is none of your business."

"I dare say it is my business when she insists on pulling her skirt so high."

"They're *legs*." Elise said. "You have a pair of them too. What's the big deal?"

Both boys stared in surprise, then doubled over in laughter. "You are entirely cracked!" laughed Gerry. "What's the big *deeeaaallll*," he mimicked. Bill was laughing so hard he had to sit down to keep from falling off the platform as they traded choice Eliseisms in exaggerated American accents.

Elise closed her eyes, hiding her smile behind the arm she once again slung over her face. Lying there, soaking up the sun, she could almost make herself believe she was on some kind of exotic vacation. Vaguely she thought of how much a long vacation on a tall ship would cost in the twenty-first century. The thought made her feel somewhat better as slowly she fell into a drowsy nap.

When she woke, the boys were arguing again.

"You didn't guess correctly, Bill. You've not won."

"Yes, I did. I guessed King George."

"But I wasn't thinking of him."

"You're thinking of him right now. I could have said, 'the moon' or 'Sergeant Taylor' and I'd still win. No matter what I say, that's what you think of."

"Yes, but you're supposed to determine what I was thinking immediately before you make a guess."

"It's called, 'What Am I Thinking?' is it not? No one calls the game, 'What Was I Thinking?' I don't understand how you can be so dense about this."

Elise blinked sleepily and sat up. The sun had moved slightly to her left. Or had the ship moved? She leaned forward over her outstretched legs and peered between her feet at the horizon. As she blinked away the bleary film of her nap, she caught sight of something on the ship directly in front of them. Anyone on the deck of the *Valiant* wouldn't notice, but from her vantage she could see that a large crowd had gathered on the *Galahad's* bow. Faintly, the sound of cheering came across the water. Elise cast her eyes to the horizon in front of the fleet and felt a surge of joy. "Shut up you guys," she said, "I think I see something."

To the boys' credit, they were instantly on the alert. Gerry wound one arm and one leg into the protective ropes and leaned far out over the platform as he opened his glass and placed it to his eye.

"Bless your sweet green eyes, Mrs. Ferrington. Land ho!" he cried to the officers below. "larboard-side bow!"

The hoots and huzzahs that rose into the air made Elise grin. Despite having become somewhat accustomed to Gerry's squirrelly ways, she still felt the need to grab a part of him to prevent him from falling. Far below, men poured out from the hatches to swarm the deck, emerging like so many red ants spilling onto the grass. It had been a long and mostly unpleasant trip. News that it was nearly over was a relief for everyone. Even the officers allowed the good cheer to soar unchecked, while staying well away from the enlisted rabble.

"Look! Is that Private MacEwan?" Bill pointed down into the crowd and rested his arm across Elise's shoulders. "No, cannot be. That ol' bastard's never smiled a day in his life."

Elise looked to where Bill was pointing and sure enough, Thomas, his shirt sleeves rolled well over his elbows and a sailor's kerchief tied around his neck in flagrant disregard for army regulation, stood staring up at her with his scar-twisted smile. He ran his hand through his thick black hair, then gave a shy wave. Elise felt her throat close in response and she gulped hard.

"Well, look at that! The bruiser's waving at me! Ahoy, MacEwan!"

Bill yelled down, waving vigorously back.

That evening, the fleet dropped anchor well outside the mouth of the Mondego River. In the narrow space between sunset and total darkness, the crew of the *Valiant* had neatly furled the sails, coiled and stowed the lines, and otherwise prepared the ship for disembarkation in the morning. Spirits had been high as the work was completed, and they remained high as the men tucked themselves up in their blankets for a few hours before the morning. Few actually slept, however.

Richard, after having exhausted himself playing for the celebrating officers, tossed and turned on the hard packing crate, jarring Elise awake every time he moved. "Please stop kicking me," she begged. "Go to sleep!"

"Oh? You think it's just that easy, do you? Maybe if you'd stop stealing the blanket I might find some peace."

Elise considered pushing him off the crate, then sat up and draped the entire scratchy blanket over him and tucked it around his arms and legs, swaddling him tight just like Amanda's baby.

"I can't move," he said sullenly.

"That's the point. Shut up." She cradled his head in her arms and waited. Slowly he began to relax. His chest rose and fell at a steady rate; his jaw dropped slightly open.

"Richard?"

"Hmm?"

"My hand's gone numb."

He rolled onto his side to use his own arm as a pillow and untucked himself, throwing a corner of the blanket over Elise. "You're not so bad, I suppose," he murmured, and then fell fast asleep.

As Elise massaged the blood back into her arm, she noticed a bulge in Richard's sleeve. Carefully, she dug her index finger inside the cuff and hooked out a handkerchief. Her stomach clenched. The letters E. L. were embroidered in a fanciful script on the corner of the delicate lace kerchief. She pushed it back up his sleeve. Just a snot-rag, she told herself. Whatever, she sniffed.

It was such a familiar feeling for Elise that she almost didn't notice when despair surged again. She shouldn't care, didn't care. Of course Richard would be using every charm in his arsenal to climb the social ladder. Elise had chalked his newly optimistic mood to the return of sunshine, but perhaps it'd been the return of hope in the form of someone else's pretty wife: Lady Elizabeth Letchfeld. It seemed, Elise thought with a rueful smile, that bad boy musicians were just as irresistible to women in the nineteenth century as they were in the twenty-first.

She was still awake when the roll of the drums calling all hands sounded. The roar of sailors' feet rushing over the deck a mere foot above her head caused dust to filter between the joints in the floorboards and into her eyes. Next to her, Richard pulled the blanket over his head with a curse. Aft of where they lay, officers arrived to wake their sergeants, who, in turn, shouted their wake-up alarms at the men in their company, kicking the laggards and complainers. The last thing Elise wanted to see, first thing in the morning, was Sergeant Taylor's wiggling uvula at the back of his throat, so she rolled Richard off the crates with a hard shove. He landed with a satisfying thud. His howl of pain followed by a blue cloud of profanity made Elise smile.

It felt as though they were being roused earlier than usual, although it was impossible to tell. Deep inside the ship, there were no visual clues, no windows or clocks; there were no audible clues, no neighbors starting up their cars for work, no birdsong or cicadas. She guessed that not even Sergeant Taylor knew, and was driven to work by his ranking superior. The major probably had a reliable timepiece, some rust-prone piece of machinery dangling dangerously from a delicate chain—perfect for carrying on an ocean-faring ship.

It had taken Elise a while to adjust to the idea that access to a watch was something reserved for the moneyed classes and even asking for the time was an impertinence. For the enlisted men, their moments were marked not in hours or minutes, but in bugle horns and drum beats. It was never four pm, eight-fifteen am, or even, "when the sun is at its zenith." For the soldiers, it was time for drill, time to eat, time for inspection, time for bed. No one dared to ask for more time; no one pressed the snooze button.

Despite having slept very little (a confident assumption she was willing to make), Elise was more than happy to join the crowd rising towards the weather deck. Three hundred or so sailors and officers, plus the entire army battalion of eight hundred men and their hangers-on of women and children, were all hurrying to see the sun rise behind the golden beaches of Portugal. Also rising from below decks to the surface for disembarkation were the many provisions for the British Army—all the necessities to conduct an extended campaign in a foreign land.

The mood was breathless and bright-eyed. Army and navy officers were cordoning men off into groups and tasking each with specific orders. They were all moving at once and sometimes at odds with each other. The promise of fresh food and water and the chance to stretch their legs on land was enough to force a smile from even the grouchiest pressed sailor or soldier.

Everything, and everyone, would have to be rowed to shore in cutters. The *Valiant* had a limited number of these boats, so multiple trips were needed. Rum rations had been suspended in order for the operation to run smoothly, but many men were still drunk from the bumper rations officers had allowed the previous night. The rest of the men had caught up on their buzz by mid-morning since those in charge of moving the rum barrels were lightening their load by drinking and passing around as much as they could.

"There you are, Mrs. Ferrington!" cried a familiarly unpleasant voice. "I've been looking all over for—I say! Come back here!!"

Elise heaved a deep sigh and turned back around. George Russell and his assistant Jenkins were pulling the medical gear out from the storage closet where he'd been quartered. It lay spread out on the deck in various states of disorder. The stacks of caged chickens that had survived the captain's table—the surgeon's roommates for the duration of the voyage—were clucking loudly in protest at their rough handling. "For the love of God," he cried as he banged on the top of one poor hen's cage, "stop your infernal racket. Mrs. Ferrington, lend us a hand, would you?" The chickens squawked louder in alarm. No one likes to be yelled at, not even chickens. "It seems neither the good captain nor Major Letchfeld can spare a single man," Russell complained.

Reluctantly, Elise stepped forward to gather a set of muslin wrapped surgical tools that had tumbled from a leather case. Each bundle had an ominous wooden handle jutting from the protective cloth, the kind found on handsaws. She shuddered.

"They'll ignore us until the very second they need us the most," continued Russell. "You watch. Then they'll be surprised when we're ill-prepared, and place all the blame squarely on our shoulders. You'll see." To illustrate his vexation, he slammed down a heavy trunk. Jenkins jumped backwards in alarm, barely saving his toes. The deck boards bounced under Elise's bare feet.

"Which boat do we drag this stuff to?" asked Elise, eyeing the growing pile of medical equipment.

"Women and children go first," Russell sniffed. "It is difficult to understand why the army would allow such useless baggage to join their ranks. Women and children indeed."

"Oh!" Elise smiled happily. "That's me. I'm a woman. See you later."

"No you are not," snapped Russell, grabbing her arm as she

turned to walk away. "You are an attachment to the Army Medical Department. You stay."

"I thought I was useless."

"You deliberately misconstrue my words."

"No, I think I got your meaning just right. Thanks a lot, Doc." Elise started dragging a heavy trunk towards the rail of the ship where it could be easily loaded into a cutter, ignoring the surgeon's continued threats.

The temperature was rising to a level Elise hadn't felt since she'd left Tucson, but the humidity was something she hadn't counted on. She was drenched in sweat by the time she'd hauled the trunk around the crowds. Breathing hard from the effort, she stopped to catch her breath and looked longingly towards a beach already swarming with activity. Although it was hard to tell exactly what was going on so far away, she didn't see any skirts on shore, despite what Russell had said about women and children going first.

Instead, guessing from the uniforms, it had been the officer classes who had taken the first boats over to smooth the path with Portuguese officials in the nearest town. The riflemen, clearly visible in their green jackets, had also landed to secure the area. A small swarm of artillerymen were struggling to move a heavy cannon that had gotten bogged down in the sand. They made angry gestures, pointing up to the sky, pointing out to the grassy field beyond the beach, sometimes pointing back to the ship. It wasn't too hard to figure out their conversation as the cannon was slowly dragged off the beach.

A woman's frightened screams suddenly brought Elise's attention back to the *Valiant*. Farther down the rail, a small crowd had gathered around a rope ladder that descended into a cutter still tied up alongside the ship. Thomas and two other men from her company were in the boat, as were Lady Letchfeld, an enormous pile of wardrobe trunks, and Lady Letchfeld's two maids—all of whom, Elise presumed, had been packed into the cutter while still on board the *Valiant*. Floating nearby, three other cutters had already launched. Sailors, with biceps bulging as they gripped the oars, looked sharp in their worn white trousers and shirts, their faces shaded by straw hats jauntily askew on their sweaty heads. All of them were gazing up at Amanda whose screeching was drowning out the angry howl of her baby.

Elise looked back towards where she'd left Russell and saw that he was busy organizing knives into various leather sleeves. Jenkins was alternating between hovering anxiously over his employer and stacking bedpans. Stealthily, Elise moved towards the commotion, not wanting to be noticed by anyone who might try to give her work to do.

Inside the surging mass of men, the smell of alcohol nearly knocked her over. Sergeant Taylor, surrounded by his company, was red faced, sweaty, and calling for swift action. He'd given Amanda orders to descend into the cutter, but she was frozen in place and he was unused to having his orders called into question. Each time Amanda called up the courage to poke her head over the rail to look at the boat three decks below, the three women in the cutter sent up encouraging kissy noises and words of comfort which only provoked her to shrink away in fear, hugging her baby closer to her chest.

"Come along, love. Don't worry. I wouldn't ever let you fall." Her husband was just over the edge hanging onto the rope ladder, beseeching her to take that first step.

"How can you say that?" Amanda demanded. "There won't be a thing you can do if I fall."

"You shan't fall. I'll be right here," Collins said. "Give me our daughter. We'll go down together."

"We'll drown together, you mean. We'll fall and drown."

"Where is the gamming chair?" Elise couldn't see Mrs. Gillihan in the crowd, but her complaining alto voice was loud and clear. "I'll not climb down a rope—the very *idea*! Mrs. Collins is perfectly correct to be angry! Heavens, what on earth were they *thinking*?"

Elise pushed her way through the throng. "Amanda! What's going on?"

A look of relief washed over the young mother's face at seeing Elise. "I can't do it. It's too far."

"You'll be alright. It's not that far."

"It is! It's far!" Amanda stamped her foot.

"Okay, I'm here, now. I'll talk you down. And your husband will stay right by you, won't you Collins?" Elise gave him a meaningful look and he nodded emphatically and made affirmative noises. "See? He's not going anywhere. He won't let anything happen." She had unconsciously assumed the calm voice she used on panicking patients in the ER. "First, give the baby to me."

Peter Collins nodded again, as though Elise had been talking to him. Amanda looked dubious, but took a hesitant step towards her husband.

Suddenly, Sergeant Taylor grabbed Amanda by the arm. "Look here, either get in the bloody cutter or say goodbye to your husband! I've no time for this nonsense."

Elise threw up her arms in exasperation. Amanda's loud tears resumed.

"Sergeant Taylor, I insist you produce a gamming chair this instant," Mrs. Gillihan shouted from nearby.

"Give me that baby," Sergeant Taylor snapped. He ripped a howling Edwina out of her mother's arms. "The baby stays with me until you're in that boat."

Amanda's rage burst forth in ear-piercing screams. Taylor had found the magic button to get the woman to move, only she didn't move in the direction he'd hoped. "Get this woman off of me," he shouted.

The men were delighted for the excuse to grab any woman in their path, and Elise charged right in, making it easy for them. "Don't touch me!" she shouted, as she was lifted into the air. In front of her, O'Brian and Hobert had Amanda by her hands and feet and were swinging her back and forth like a hammock. "Hooo!" the crowd cheered as she was swung over the rail. "Hooo! Hooo!"

"MacEwan!" O'Brian called down to Thomas. "Look sharp!" He winked at Hobert and they let go.

"Hooooooo!"

Elise saw the young mother twist in the air, arms cranking like a two-tailed cat falling from a third story window, then disappear overboard without even a scream.

Elise's deep gasp of horror pressed the emerald scarab painfully against her sternum. It flamed over her skin, burning neurons straight through her limbic system. Her capillaries flushed. Her vision ringed in red. The heat rushed to her fists, to her feet, to her brain, and curled the hair along her arms. Each defensive movement Elise made to dislodge the hands that gripped her was well calculated. One man fell away with a bloody nose. Teeth marks appeared on another man's wrist while a third got caught in the eye with a fingernail. She ducked and knocked another soldier off balance with a twist of her shoulder, sending him skittering along the deck to tangle with the ankles of his mates. The more she fought, the more the men leapt into the fray, lapping up the bruises she delivered like happy dogs.

A few feet away, Collins swung off the rope ladder to charge O'Brian. The company roared with the pleasure of a fight and tightened their circle. Sergeant Taylor, not wanting to be left on the outside of the action, started swinging indiscriminately at his men with his one free fist while clutching Edwina to his chest with his other. The baby was an inconveniencing burden in a brawl, but not entirely incapacitating.

"No fighting in the ranks! No fighting in the ranks!" the sergeant shouted. The men who saw him coming protected their heads with their hands and backed away. Striking a superior was a serious offense, even if done accidentally. Taylor cut through his men like butter.

The sudden sound of a pistol cracked like thunder. Everyone froze. "Put that woman down at once!" Heads snapped around at the sound of the barked order. "Do as I say. Put Mrs. Ferrington down this instant."

George Russell, his youthful freckles vivid over his pale nose, stood with his smoking firearm in the air. His splayed leg pose was impressive, except that the position shortened him and he didn't have the luxury of inches to spare. His gloomy manservant, Jenkins, lurked behind him with his hand held out to receive the pistol.

The surgeon's authoritative voice, if not stature, caused the men to set Elise back on her feet. "With me, Mrs. Ferrington." He turned sharply, expecting Elise to follow, but instead she rushed to the rail.

"Amanda!" Elise yelled down. Three decks below, Thomas was lying flat on his back in the bottom of the rocking cutter with Amanda tight in his arms. They both looked dazed.

"We're all right," one of Lady Letchfeld's maids called up. She and the other girl were trying to revive their slumped mistress, who seemed to have fainted.

Slowly, Thomas pushed himself up on the bench and pulled Amanda into his lap. Even from Elise's height, she could see something was wrong. He ran his hand through his hair, then gazed at the blood in his palm.

"Thomas!" yelled Elise. "I'm coming down!"

A heavy hand on her shoulder stayed her. "Wait just a minute, if you please." Russell had returned.

"I need to make sure everyone's okay down there," Elise protested. "I think Thomas hit his head, probably on one of Lady Letchfeld's trunks."

The doctor peered over the rail with curiosity, "Thomas, you say? Quite admirable to catch the young woman."

"Yeah. He's a real prince." Elise peered down again. Amanda's face was pale, her expression dazed, as though her brain hadn't quite caught up to the journey her body made. She mouthed something, and Elise knew exactly who Amanda was calling for without having to hear it: Edwina.

"I shall descend and tend to whomever needs help," the surgeon announced. He turned to Jenkins and took his medical kit. "You will stay and help Jenkins pack our supplies."

"Don't go down without the baby."

Russell nodded and smiled. "That's the spirit, Mrs. Ferrington. Excellent suggestion. Ah, here's your husband. Just the man I need to see."

"Where the bloody hell have you been?" Elise was surprised by how genuinely rattled Richard seemed. "I've been looking all over for you. They're sending the women down first."

"About that," started the surgeon. "As you know, I've retained the services of your missus, and thus, I'm afraid she will be unable to accompany you for much of the campaign."

Elise placed a hand against her chest over the now cold emerald. She began to tremble.

"Elise? Don't let's get weak-kneed now." Richard's voice receded. "Swooning doesn't suit you, my dear."

Elise leaned heavily against her husband and felt his arms encircle her waist. He wasn't all bad, she thought as the adrenaline rush wore off.

"Damn it, Elise. This really won't do. You pick the oddest times for feminine foibles—it's quite off-putting."

Behind her, Lieutenant Mason had arrived. She could hear him barking at the sergeant. "Why are you holding that baby—are you now a nursemaid? No, don't bother to answer. Just give the damn child to Mrs. Gillihan."

"There," said Russell with a satisfied smile as the gamming chair was finally sent for. "The lieutenant will set things right."

ENDLESS PILES
OF LAUNDRY

Thousands of men, all dressed in linen shirts and red wool, were sweating like pigs on the Portuguese beach. It had been a long day of getting supplies off the ships and safely organized, and now that evening was coming, no one was anxious to continue the work. Initially, officers had kept their men occupied and out of trouble, but the officers were just as anxious as the soldiers to finally get a bit of space. Most left their lieutenants in charge and went to explore the town further inland. The lieutenants, after giving their superiors enough time to relax in the taverns, soon followed, leaving sergeants to deal with the rabble. The result was an easing of oversight that suited everyone.

Just as the English were anxious to go into town, the town was eager to go to the beach and meet the English. Laden with the early August harvests, the Portuguese trekked the dusty trail to find their new marketplace and traded profitably, even without a common language. Up and down the beach, hands flashed in elaborate attempts at negotiations for all kinds of goods. Fresh fruit, the likes of which many soldiers had never tasted, were quick to sell out. Soap, sewing needles, hair combs—those items used up or accidentally forgotten back home—were sought, with costs rising quickly as supplies dwindled.

Shelter became the second order of business. The officers last to disembark were out of luck since all the extra rooms in town had all been taken by the time they'd been relieved of duties. Not that many would sleep, as the third order of business was women and then liquor, or liquor and then women, or, the best option, liquored women.

Elise, having landed on the beach with the medical division, had been put to the task of boiling laundry almost immediately. Stirring great cauldrons of linens and bandages was not what she had expected to do as a nurse and the higher and hotter the sun moved overhead, the grumpier she became as she sweated over the fire. This was not nursing; she hadn't signed up for this. The other nurses seemed comfortable hauling water, making a large fire and using driftwood as a laundry stir-stick, but Elise wanted to use her own stick over George Russell's head.

Private O'Brian was another person who needed to be brained. Elise was still shocked by what had happened that morning. The vision of the young mother getting tossed overboard played over and over in her mind. The fact that O'Brian hadn't been punished astonished her. It was as though the result justified the action.

George Russell, having spent three weeks swinging in a hammock in the storage closet, had made it clear that it was his intention to spread a blanket on the warm sand for his bed. All of the army's medical officers were clustered in one area of the beach, which was quickly becoming a kind of make-shift hospital, and she was being encouraged to join them. But the master-servant relationship that was unfolding was more than Elise could bear. If she'd been given work to match her ability that might have changed her mind. There were certainly plenty of interesting cases turning up—patients with stomach complaints, strange fevers, heat stroke, and brawl-inflicted open wounds and broken noses. But no one asked a glorified laundress for input. Her own company respected her more than the doctors, and spreading her blanket with them sounded more fun than being at the beck and call of the doctors who thought they were better than her.

The situation gave her insight as to why Richard was having a hard time getting along with everyone. Although Richard wasn't as well educated, she was surprised to realize that he and Russell were in nearly the same social class. Both were business owners without two coins to rub together. Earlier that morning, Elise had watched the surgeon carefully count out money for his breakfast in quiet agony over whether or not he could spare the expense of purchasing half a melon, dripping with sweet nectar. And Russell himself wasn't entirely comfortable amongst his own peers. He clung to the older surgeons for social recognition and approval, and in return they treated him like a cute puppy, petting him for any creative suggestions he came up with, and rewarding him with information when he faltered. He was, Elise realized with a shock, using his tour of war to leverage his civilian career.

One good thing about stirring laundry, Elise decided, was that it was an excellent way to observe things without being, yourself, observed. No one noticed a lone woman poking boiling laundry with a stick. She slipped into the background and tried to learn the limits of the surgeons' medical knowledge as she listened to their conversations. She watched the movements of the officers outside of the makeshift hospital to discover what plans were being hatched. Men were organized into task forces, scouts, lookouts. Caravans of supplies were gathered. Inspections of goods and men were constant. No one bothered to organize the women.

What Elise wanted most was another ship, one that would take her to Boston, or Virginia. Even better would be a French ship that might take her to Louisiana. She tried to remember something she'd learned in high school about the Louisiana Purchase and came up empty. Also empty, was the horizon of French ships, and if Bill and Gerry were correct, there'd be nothing for days but the English fleet that brought them.

Shouts and loud squealing turned Elise's attention down the beach. A small crowd of thirty men were gleefully chasing a terrified pig in the surf, splashing water on each other and falling headlong into the sand with knives and bayonets brandished for slaughter. Elise's eyes narrowed, trying to decide which one of the murderous idiots would be carried away by the undertow, and which would be impaled by his own weapon. She couldn't blame them. She'd happily risk impalement herself if it meant she could take her wool dress off and leap through the surf.

The pig ran out of the ocean and up the beach, past a strange, tall man who stood apart from the rest of the army in demeanor and dress. He held a long staff against his shoulder on which he'd hung strings of beads, tiny cooking pots, wooden spoons, and colorful scarves. He was a walking gift shop of goodies. Elise stopped stirring when she noticed the wide brimmed straw hats that were blowing behind him like kites, caught up by the Atlantic breeze and tied tight to the staff by neck straps. Then she noticed the man himself. His shirt was open nearly to his navel, revealing a torso of stretched sinew and skin over ribs that stuck out like a washboard. Around his neck he wore one of the scarves he was selling, a red and black plaid that offset the dark brown waves of his hair. His pale trousers were barely held up with a long piece of rope that also served to attach bulging pouches to his waist. Elise dropped her stirring stick, mumbled an excuse to the other women, and walked over to him.

His golden eyes followed as she approached, flicking up and down, assessing. He shifted his staff to his other shoulder, puffed out his chest, and flicked his long hair.

"I'd like to see your hats," Elise said.

His smile was slow to grow, revealing a tiny set of gray front teeth embedded deep into red gums. Elise pointed at the hats and he stabbed his staff deep into the sand next to her and made a two handed flourish of invitation. He was surprisingly graceful, almost making up for his dreadful mouth.

"Do you speak English?" Elise asked as she untied a hat from the pole.

He shook his head and said something in what she assumed was Portuguese.

"Nope. That doesn't work either. *Habla Español?*"

The man's smile disappeared and he spat in the sand.

"Oh. Well, that answers that, I guess." Elise had hoped to use some of the Spanish she'd picked up in Tucson, but was unsure if her *barrio* slang would work. She chose another hat to try on. "What do you think?" His golden eyes sparked and he grinned his approval. It really was too bad about his teeth. Elise reached into her apron pocket and pulled out her offering.

The change in his attitude was instantaneous. He snatched the hat from her hand and began to retie it to his staff. "No, wait. You don't know what you're doing." When he didn't respond, she said it in Spanish in desperation.

"My hats are worth at least two of these coins."

"So you *do* speak Spanish."

"Bah."

"You're looking at a six-pence piece. In England, I could get three of those hats for one of those."

He flipped the brass disk in his hand as he thought, his expression unchanging. Then he pulled a hat with an inadequate brim down. "Try this one."

Elise shook her head. "No, it's the other hat I want." Reluctantly, she pulled another coin out of her pocket, but the man curled his lip and sniffed. "I could get ten hats for what I'm offering you," she said.

"I am not as stupid as you think. What's in your pouch? Perhaps we can still negotiate."

"This?" Elise was so used to carrying the kit bag that Mrs. Southill had given her that she usually forgot she had it. She opened it up to show the man, certain none of it would interest him. He pawed through it and pulled out a spool of silk thread and a silver needle. "No, wait! I'm going to need that!"

"I foresee that you'll have this replaced for free." He handed her the hat. "I'll keep your 'six-pence' too."

"Shit," grumbled Elise, feeling cheated. She placed the hat on her head and was rewarded with another gummy grin.

Russell marched past her through the sand, suddenly catching her attention. He was headed towards Major Letchfeld, who was barely visible over the tall beach grass where a rutted cart path curled towards town. Lady Letchfeld's fashionable bonnet bobbed along next to him. "Major!" cried the surgeon. "A word, if you please." Despite Russell's quick steps, his ever present shadow, Mr. Jenkins, kept up at a slow amble—his legs a third as long as his employer's.

Elise left the preening trader to follow discretely behind the duo. There was something about Russell's urgency that gave her the impression she shouldn't miss the conversation.

"Your service," Russell made a hurried, anxious bow to Lady Letchfeld. "How do you do, sir?"

"Yes, yes, Mr. Russell. Fine, fine. What is it?"

"I don't mean to trouble you, so I'll get straight to the point: I've no method for transporting my equipment." Russell stared at Elise for a moment, thrown off by her presence as she skidded to a stop nearby, kicking up sand. "Mrs. Ferrington? Might I be of service?"

"Nope." Elise looked Lady Letchfeld up and down. The pretty woman blushed, suspecting the reason for Elise's insolence.

"I, uh, yes well," Russell said uncomfortably, feeling the chill. "I'm glad you're here. As you can see, Major, I'm already one assistant short and have been forced to accept Mrs. Ferrington as an aide. I cannot ask her to march with a pack laden with surgical equipment, nor can I or Mr. Jenkins here be expected to carry all our equipment on our own backs like the infantrymen do. There's simply too much. It would be quite impossible."

"My dear sir," said Major Letchfeld in surprise. "We all have been affected by the lack of foresight by those planning this war. You, just as I, must find your own methods for transporting the items you will need. It is not for me to supply you."

"Who must I see for a cart?"

"If you'd like a cart, go into town like everyone else, and procure yourself one."

"You misunderstand. I've been into town. There are no carts. There are no mules."

"Well then, I'm not sure what it is that I can do to help. Is this not the commissariat's duty? I cannot give you something that does not exist," the major said. "Since this is your first venture on campaign, you should know that on foreign soil, we all do without the conveniences of our beloved England. We must all make sacrifices."

Russell sucked in a breath and looked pointedly at Lady Letchfeld's luggage. "Yes, I see that sacrifices are inevitable. When I report to General Wellesley, I'll be sure to compliment the ability of your lady to remain as elegant as she was in England, as well as explain your theory of sacrifice. I'm sure he'd be very interested to hear your opinion on the matter of 'making do.'"

"General Wellesley?" Major Letchfeld sputtered. "Why on Earth would you report to Arthur Wellesley? Here," he pulled a small coin purse from his waistcoat, not willing to take a risk on Russell's bluff. "This should help convince a local to give you two sturdy beasts. And I give you leave to find another man within the ranks to help with your burdens."

With all the slavering words of gratitude that the surgeon poured on, the major and his wife were properly washed back into amicable moods, allowing the surgeon to exit semi-gracefully. He motioned for Elise to follow. "Walk with me," he ordered. Mr. Jenkins fell in behind them as they headed back down the beach. "Tell me what you know of Thomas MacEwan. He was once in the employ of your husband, was he not?"

"Thomas? What do you want to know?"

"I've a mind to acquire him as another medical assistant. I spoke with him earlier today. Is he trustworthy?"

"Yeah, he's solid."

"Solid?"

"Um. . .trustworthy."

Without slowing his stride, Doctor Russell turned to Jenkins. "Find Private MacEwan and bring him to me. Mrs. Ferrington, I'm sending you back to the *Valiant*—it's being made over into a hospital and will remain anchored offshore until the army returns. You'll be much safer there. Quite a few men have picked up a fever, and more nurses will soon be needed."

"Needed to do what?" Elise's eyes narrowed.

"Swab brows, empty commodes. Whatever it is that you women do: make patients comfortable."

"Commodes? Seriously? I could have been changing bedpans at the Quiet Woman. I'm an ER nurse, not a chambermaid."

"You'll do as I say, madam." The young surgeon squared his shoulders. His look of determination matched the one etched on Elise's face.

"You're crazy if you put my talents to dumping bedpans."

"You've had multiple opportunities to show me your worth, and from what I can tell, your self-assessment exceeds your true abilities."

"I'm not getting back on that ship. I'm staying with my husband and that's final."

"I've already spoken with your husband. He was quite amenable to the idea of your returning to sea."

Elise's jaw dropped. Damn that Lady Letchfeld. "We'll just see about that," Elise sputtered.

She stepped off the path and attempted to withdraw with a dignified huff, but the burning and shifting sand under her bare feet made her waddle and hop, which wasn't the exit she'd hoped for.

It took awhile to finally find where her company had set up their camp, since the men had abandoned their blankets in the sand near the edge of the beach to continue with their duties. It was Mrs. Gillihan's presence that tipped Elise off that she'd found the right encampment. She was sitting on an enormous log of driftwood and tending a pot full of mysterious ingredients. "Watch your skirts," she said in warning as Elise walked near the campfire.

"There you are!" Richard called out as he stepped from behind a tuft of tall beach grass.

"We need to talk," Elise said, still mad about the disloyalty he'd shown in trying to send her back to the ship.

"Not now." He dropped an armload of firewood near Mrs. Gillihan and started pulling white shirts and stockings out of his pack and piling them in Elise's arms. A sour and musky scent rose from his garments like steam from a tea kettle, mingling with the sweet smell of wood smoke and ocean breezes. "You'll have to hurry. The other women are already down at the river. You can't miss them. I'm sure they'll not fault you for being late, working for the surgeon and all."

Blinking back tears, Elise pulled Richard's clothes against her chest and slumped away, defeated. Laundry. Again.

The laundry party down by the Mondego River was the first time any of the women could get away from their husbands, and they took advantage with gossip and swift trade in goods and services. Elise volunteered to look after some of the children and took five of them wading into the river. In return, two mothers did her laundry for her. By the end of the day she was bathed and refreshed, and had an armload of wet linens. Back at the campsite, she spread them out over the tall grass to dry.

Mrs. Gillihan was throwing some of the fruit she'd purchased into the pot to boil with freshly butchered pork, creating a sweet stew whose scent drew the men back from town with full canteens of liquor. It had been a long day, and everyone was exhausted. The beach was dotted with campfires, each individual company keeping to their own, and each company's handful of women stirring pots in the center of a ring of blankets. The fires were fed to lovely heights as the sun began to set and the Atlantic wind turned cool.

The hollow thumping of a drum announced Bill Stanton's return. He grinned at Elise. "That's a natty hat, Mrs. Ferrington," he said.

Elise had been glad to have it down by the river. The children, scrubbed free from filth, if not lice, came out of the water pink with fresh sunburns, but she'd escaped with nothing more than a refreshed tan on her arms, thanks to her hat's wide brim.

"You get on with you, hobbledehoy," clucked Mrs. Gillihan at Bill. "Leave Mrs. Ferrington be."

"Elise!" Richard came tripping through the sand towards her. Everyone seemed to be returning at the same time. "Have you a clean shirt for me? Damn your eyes! It's still wet!"

"Of course it is! I just washed it, didn't I?" She watched as Richard started flapping a linen shirt over the fire. He was swatted away by Mrs. Gillihan, who guarded the pot of stew with narrowed, steely eyes. "Mr. Ferrington, what shall we sing tonight?" Bill asked with a roll of his drum. "Bring out your fiddle."

"Not tonight, lad. I've been invited into town to play for the officers." Word of Richard and his fiddle was spreading throughout the officer classes. One old colonel took particular interest. He kept his troops meticulously sharp in dress and demeanor, and Richard's handsome face and thick blond hair played right into his idea of fashion. The colonel was weighing the possibility of having a violinist play during troop advancement, believing a violin would add a certain *je ne sais quoi* that a drummer alone couldn't manage. Now Richard was pawing through his things to find the right clothes to wear to present himself in town, ever hopeful of being raised above the rabble. "Where's my waistcoat?"

"It's in there somewhere." Elise quickly walked away, suddenly anxious to be nowhere near her husband. "I'm going to get some more firewood."

Behind her, she heard Bill shout for Cox to take up his pipe and blow. The resultant laughter faded and was replaced by a joyful tin whistle as Cox did as he was told. Elise allowed herself a look back and saw Bill's silhouette against the fire. He held his drum sideways in the crook of his arm and skillfully rolled one drumstick over its head, creating a sound like thunder.

"My BUTTONS!" Richard's bellow was heard clearly over the music. "Which one of you heathens stole the buttons off my waistcoat?" Elise resumed her walk, jangling in her apron pocket a couple brass discs she'd flattened between two rocks.

Thomas slumped across the beach towards the camp, exhausted. His knees felt leaden, too heavy to lift his feet. Even though the day was cooling as the sun began its descent behind the ocean, he still felt its heat radiating through the leather soles of his shoes. Sand was a new experience for him. He was unused to the very ground shifting under his feet and working its way through his shoes and stockings to irritate the skin between his toes.

It'd been a long day of irritations and back-breaking work. It was hard to believe it had only been that morning since he'd caught Mrs. Collins in his arms. He was still shocked that the only outcome had been cracking the back of his head. O'Brian was lucky he'd been too busy to deal with him. Each time he thought of the man's idiotic grin peering over the side of the ship, his knuckles would heat and his hands would curl into fists. O'Brian would get what was coming to him. He'd make sure of that.

On a positive note, the experience had given him an opportunity to meet the army surgeon, the young Mr. George Russell, who had offered him a position as his aide. He'd still have to fight, a soldier is always a soldier, but it balanced things out a bit. He felt confident Mrs. Postlethwaite would approve. She never did like him fighting.

How he missed the Quiet Woman's old cook. He'd never realized how much Mrs. Postlethwaite looked after him and now, without her in his corner, he felt unmoored. He missed her cooking, the large kitchen, the stool near the fireplace, a nice porter, aged and tapped just at the right time. He wondered if he'd ever have any of those comforts again. Mrs. Gillihan had a nice touch with her stews, but even she couldn't hold a candle to Mrs. P., and anyway, she fed her husband first and Thomas was tired of crumbs and hand-outs. Old Mrs. P. never gave him what was left over. She gave him full thought. That was all a man needed: full thought. His chest felt squeezed with homesickness.

Up and down the beach, campfires were being lit, sending up the comforting smell of wood smoke and inviting companionship. Strains of a popular song could be heard at most of the camps: "*For the guns they shall rattle, and the bullets they shall fly, afore they'll drink little England dry. . .*"

"*Aye dry, aye dry me boys, aye dry,*" his baritone rumbled softly. It was impossible not to join in the refrain, even if just singing for himself.

"Hey! How's your head?"

Thomas looked up quickly. He was too surprised to think of anything to say. Elise had come seemingly out of nowhere, from the ocean itself perhaps. Her hair was damp, cheeks rosy and scrubbed. "You've bathed."

"Uh, yeah, Thomas. I did." His observation seemed to have amused her for some reason.

He looked behind her for the trail of her footprints, just to make sure she hadn't come to him through a mystical pathway, and was almost disappointed to see her large feet had made craters in the sand along the edge of the surf all the way back to where their company was gathered.

"*They may come, the frogs of France, but we'll teach them a new-fashioned dance. . .*"

There was something strangely grounding about being near the ocean, despite the shifting sands, rolling waves, and the agonizing days of illness they'd just spent on the ship. The ocean was eternal. Its vast space made him feel as though everything was lengthened and stretched; it made this moment with Elise feel suspended. She turned to look at the last glow of the setting sun and her damp hair was lifted in a sudden breeze to veil her face. Overhead, the evening stars were just beginning to emerge. The moon, a slivered crescent ascending, rested on her shoulder. Soon it would be a new moon—a night without light. Something about that thought made him tremble.

"Then drink, my boys, and ne'er give o'er, drink until you can't drink no more. . ."

"Not a bad idea," Elise said. She took a long drink from her canteen. "You sure your head's okay?"

"I've got a right knot on my head, but it's nothing time will not heal." He took the canteen she offered and tipped it back. "It's water!" Thomas spat, surprised. Then felt embarrassed when she laughed.

"No, it's okay. I boiled it first. I never thought I'd say this, but I'm so glad to be able to drink water."

The woman never made any sense. Why did he care if the water was boiled? She reached a hand to the bandage that wrapped around his head, but then dropped it, thinking better of touching him. "It's strange to see you without all that hair hanging in your face."

"Aye, now you can see I'm a monster."

"I can see your eyes." Her own green eyes were glittering like fresh leaves.

"Aye dry, aye dry me boys, aye dry," they sang the refrain softly together, unable to resist the pull of the music, happy for the distraction.

"Why aren't you with the others?" Elise asked. "Everyone loves your voice."

"I've just come from seeing Mr. Russell. And anyway, no one likes my songs."

"Your songs are all sad."

"Everyone will be wanting to hear the sad ones soon enough, after the killing's done."

Elise's smiling face turned somber at the reminder of the coming battles. "So, you going to help the doc? He asked me about you this afternoon."

"I don't know. Possibly, as long as I can still fight." Thomas rolled his sore shoulders back and then quickly pulled his red jacket closed over his dingy shirt in embarrassment. He hadn't enough money for laundry after paying to replenish his smoking habit. The thought of a fresh bag of tobacco made him pull his new clay pipe from his breast pocket. "Shall we walk back?"

Thomas had expected to share the smoke with her. She looked sorely tempted as he pressed a pinch of the leaf into the bowl. Instead, she turned her gaze further down the beach. "I kind of wanted to be by myself a little," she said. "I think I'll walk a bit longer. Listen to my own voice for a bit."

"That's all you listen to these days." He was surprised at how disappointed he was at her rejection, and instantly regretted the bitterness of his words.

"*You* never hear a thing I say, so if I don't listen, no one else will."

"That's unfair. I hear everything you say. That doesn't mean I believe everything." He started to push his hand through his hair and stopped just short of ripping off his bandage. He didn't want to discuss her strange story. He didn't want to even think about it. Not now. Not with the moon on her shoulder and the sunset in her hair.

"Why not? Why wouldn't you believe me? You saw my running shoe. You said yourself it was the strangest thing you'd ever seen."

"How am I to believe you've traveled through time on the basis of one shoe?"

"What about my accent? Everyone says I have a funny accent. Everyone's always laughing at me."

"You're American! Of course you sound ridiculous."

She stepped backwards. Her face clouded.

"Elise, wait. I did not mean—"

"No, forget it. Forget everything."

"Come back to camp with me." Thomas felt as though he was scrambling to catch a falling knife. "I'll pack my pipe for you. You can hold onto it as long as you'd like. Just, don't wander away. You need to stay close to the others, close to me. If Richard was…" he paused and looked towards the camp, as though Richard would be right there, which, of course, he wasn't. "What I mean is, if Richard were looking after you the way he should, it would be different. I cannot protect you if you wander away."

"I told you I could take care of myself."

"Oh, aye. That's why you're walking straight south towards the French encampment."

"Stop right there. You told me you wouldn't be watching out for me anymore. Let's keep it that way. I'm not sure I can handle your kind of protection—you've got a mean right hook."

Her words nearly knocked the breath out of him. "Hitting you was the only thing I could think of to convince you stay in London. I'm sorry it came to that." There were only three steps between them, but the distance felt immeasurable.

"Real convincing, Thomas. Your fist is full of logic. You going to hit me again? Maybe that'll get me back in line."

"No," he whispered. "I'll not hit you."

She turned and ran. It shocked him how fast her legs could take her. He expected her to run herself out quickly, but instead she dropped her speed to a lope and kept going with her skirts hitched high above her knees. She looked comfortable, like she'd been running her entire life, like she was naturally made for long distances. He watched her until she became just a dot on the beach. And then he kept staring into the distance, hoping she'd come back.

CALÓ FLAMENCO

It felt good to run. Elise quickly fell into a rhythm, forgetting the reason for it. Letting her legs move in total freedom, she filled her lungs to capacity and gloried in her own strength. Unhindered, she ran until her tears disappeared. When she finally slowed, she felt new again. She walked in circles to cool down, her annoying skirts lifted above her waist and tossed over her shoulder. How she missed wicking synthetic fabrics cut into small, skin tight garments.

Her awareness moved from the sound of her breath as it slowed, to the sounds surrounding her. Now a mile down the beach, the cacophony of the English Army had faded to a low hum, masked by the ever present sound of the surf—a steady beat to match her pounding heart. A chorus of insects added a whirring vibrato in a high soprano, shrill and even. Underlying all of it was a single melodic line that rolled like a mournful dirge in the distance. Elise dropped her skirt. Suddenly the stars seemed too bright. The slivered moon was a spotlight. She was not as alone as she'd thought.

Thirty feet or so from the edge of the beach, where the sand hardened over the tough, matted roots of marram grass, came the glow of campfire. She stepped closer. This music was different from the English ballads Elise was accustomed to, with clear periods at the ends of the sentences rather than lilting question marks. This music was declarative, argumentative. It invited a stomped foot and a tossed head.

Staying low under the cover of the arching grass, Elise crept closer to listen while silhouettes passed in front of a great bonfire that burned in the middle of a clearing. A violin—you could never call an instrument that called forth such defiant music a fiddle—shot chills down her back. A guitar rolled chords with all the masculine posturing of a twirled moustache. As quiet as a breeze, she flitted past the horses penned in their corral and crouched in the shadow of a colorfully painted caravan.

The same man who had earlier sold her a straw hat was standing with his arms raised to the sky while a long undulating syllable of pain escaped a mouth so far open that it obscured the rest of his sharp features. He doubled over as he ran out of breath, as though kicked in the stomach. The guitar ran through a scale while he recovered. The small crowd surrounding him murmured encouragements. A log fell on the fire, sending sparks into the sky. Slowly, the man straightened again and the guitarist paused. He squeezed his eyes shut and the silence became as poignant as the music.

The people around the fire took a collective, sympathetic breath. Then one person began an irregular rhythm of clapping that everyone seemed to recognize. It was taken up by four others, each with a new pattern of claps that blended into a heartbeat you could feel in your

neck. A single chord rolled from the guitar, producing a sound so satu-
rated in anxiety that when the singer jerked his arms back in the air,
Elise gasped. The clapping swelled over the song. The guitarist played a
roving scale that tested boundaries. Elise crossed her legs on the dusty
ground, leaned against the wheel of the caravan, and made herself
comfortable. She wasn't going anywhere anytime soon, she decided.

Like a call to prayer, the man's song soared into the sky. His offered
words weren't caught by any god, however, and anguished and angered
by the rejection, he stamped his foot and covered his face with his
hands.

A disturbance rippled through the audience. People stood from
their chairs, stepped aside, made way to clear a path. The violin and
guitar were silenced, even as the rhythmic clapping carried on. A
woman, hunched and leaning heavily on a cane, was encouraged to
rise and advance towards the fire. She moved slowly but deliberately,
helped along by extended hands. She shuffled into the center of the
clearing and the clapping suddenly stopped.

The old woman drew up to the man and slowly raised her arms
above her head, elbows first, while rotating her arthritic wrists in circles.
Her shoulders pulled back, her chin lifted, her golden eyes sparked.
She opened like a colorful paper fan. When the castanets clacked and
fluttered against each of her palms, the guitar started again. "*Calma,
Avó. Cuidado,*" the man said. "Gently, Nana. Be careful."

The woman's arms pushed powerfully back down at the earth, in
defiance of her grandson's admonishments. Then she stretched her
arms out to embrace the world as her feet began to thrum a duet with
her clicking castanets. Her tapping feet slowly carried her in a circle as
she flicked her golden eyes over the audience. Elise wouldn't have been
surprised if they were all her children. She seemed to have captivated
their attention. They called out encouragements, laughed, raised their
clapping hands. Then the old woman snapped her head around and

looked behind her, directly into Elise's eyes.

If Elise could have made herself any smaller, she would have. She felt every spoke in the wheel of the caravan against her spine as she shrunk away from the woman's powerful gaze. Her breath was sucked straight from her lungs. Her vision narrowed, edged black. Her body was unresponsive, frozen against her strong desire to run and hide. Elise breathed a sigh of relief when the man stepped between them, blocking the woman's view.

The guitar sounded a trilling sequence of chords. The violin scraped an ascending scale. The woman returned to her dance as though the moment that had locked her to Elise had never happened. She moved as though the strength of her spirit usurped the sapping strength of an extended lifetime, but when the song ended, time was once again a valid force and the woman transformed back into a person sapped of strength, crumpling into her mortal body. The man seemed to anticipate his grandmother's sudden frailty, and put a supportive hand to her humped back. "*Calma, Avó,*" he said again, as the small audience surged forward to surround the woman and draw her back into their midst.

Elise leaned her head back against the wheel and closed her eyes. The world swam behind her lids, an echoed sensation from weeks aboard the *Valiant*, and for once the feeling was comforting, like being rocked in a cradle. The music continued, but now it combined in her consciousness with the sound of the surf, just steps away. She felt her shoulders fall and was surprised that she had been holding them tightly near her ears. Briefly, she considered running back to camp to grab her blanket to spread on the beach somewhere closer to the caravan circle, halfway between where she ought to be and where she wanted to listen, but exhaustion kept her from moving. It had been such a long day.

In the warm light of the campfire, a beetle crawled towards her, threading its way through the grass. Its long legs seemed to struggle with the sand that rolled under its horned feet. It wildly waved navigating antennae, as though using them for balance. If you could call a fat green beetle beautiful, then it was beautiful. Its back reflected the starlight in a metallic sheen. Its wings, shooting out from under their casings every time its legs slipped in the sand, were rainbow-hued like a puddle on an oil soaked driveway. Elise's heart raced. In London, the beetle had been black. She wasn't sure if this was the same one, but hated to think there were now multiple bugs haunting her dreams. "You!" She pointed an accusatory finger at the lumbering beetle. "Send me home right this minute."

Elise nervously pinched her lips between her teeth and waited as it continued towards her. It didn't speak; it didn't transform into the black-haired woman. It behaved like a bug, determinedly crawling over or under any obstacle. Elise scooted sideways out of its path. "Go away," she hissed, suddenly wanting nothing to do with it. "Either send me back or leave me alone."

Infuriatingly, the six legs kept rolling the wide insect forward, undeterred. When it was within arm's reach, Elise leaned forward and flicked it with her thumb and middle finger. The contact made a surprisingly loud cracking noise. Briefly, a pang of guilt passed through Elise as it sailed through the air. It opened its wing casings at the last moment, like a doomed parachutist, and hit the ground heavily, four feet away.

Elise jerked awake with a sharp gasp and painfully hit the back of her head on the wagon wheel. Her entire field of view was taken up by the man who had been singing only moments before. He was leaning over her, his face fixed in a sly smile. "I remember you," he said in Spanish. "You're the woman who tried to give me a button for a hat."

"English?" She was too tired to think in a foreign language.

He motioned for her to get up. "I don't speak English. Why are you here?"

"I just wanted to listen to the music, but I'll go if I'm not welcome."

The man hesitated, eyeing Elise with suspicion. In the light of the fire, the long dark curls that fell to his waist took on an auburn hue. He was thin and wiry, but there was no doubt he could do some damage if provoked. She hadn't liked trying to stiff him, but a girl's got to protect her complexion. "You got a good deal," she reminded him. "Silk rope and a silver needle for a hat. It was a fair trade."

"Thread," he corrected her Spanish. "I took your thread. It was a fair trade, yes." He smiled at her with the same unsettling golden eyes as his grandmother. "My *avó* sent me to bring you to her."

Elise used the caravan to pull herself to her feet and ignored the helping hand he offered. As he led her across the center of the clearing, she knew everyone was looking at her. Conversation stopped. The music faded away, leaving an unpleasant tritone hanging in the air. A tight community was weighing the significance of her presence.

On the other side of the fire, away from the eye-stinging smoke, he gestured for her to draw closer to him. "Please, allow me to present my grandmother, Senhora Ineriqué." The old woman gave a nearly imperceptible nod, just enough acknowledgement for Elise to feel sized up and shaken out. "And, I am *Quidico Laetitia de Laroque*. However, Quidico is sufficient." The man swooped deeply in a formal bow, one foot forward, his right arm twirling as his long hair swept the ground.

Elise bobbed at Quidico in a quick curtsy, hoping it was enough. "I'm Elise Dubois. . .I mean. . .Ferrington." Then she turned and curtsied at the old woman, too.

"*Avó*," croaked the woman, pointing to herself. She was so curled forward with age that it looked as though only one single vertebra touched the wall of the caravan she was leaning against. It was hard to believe this was the same woman who had strutted out such a gracefully postured dance.

Quidico turned to his grandmother and spoke in a language that wasn't quite Portuguese, or quite Spanish. At first it seemed as though they were arguing, but then Avó made a decisive gesture and Quidico snapped his mouth shut mid-sentence.

Avó pointed to Elise, then patted the bench beside her. Elise sat.

The violinist put his instrument back to his shoulder and started to play a modal melody. The guitarist returned to his percussive strumming. Conversations were picked up where they'd been left.

The old woman straightened, each vertebra rolling backwards to return to a stacked column, and fixed her cataract filmed eyes on Elise's green ones. With one arthritic finger she reached towards Elise and touched her bodice right over the emerald, pushing in so that the gem pressed painfully against her flesh. "*Dame*," she hissed. "Give."

"No! You can't have it!" Elise recoiled. She stood to leave, unnerved, but Avó grabbed her wrist and pulled her back down while gesturing with her other hand.

They glared at each other for a moment until the old woman started cackling. "*Calma*, Elise. *Calma*." She turned to her grandson and they spoke briefly together in their strange language.

"My *avó* says you are from a distant land. I told her you were from England, but she thinks you are not English. Is this true?"

"I'm American," Elise said.

Quidico nodded. "So you do not believe in American independence then. Why would you not? The Americans seem like a proud people, like the Romani people."

"What? They're totally proud. Of course I believe in independence. Fuck the British colonialists." Elise couldn't believe the words coming out of her mouth.

"Then why are you here following the English Army?"

The question was a sensible one, and Elise struggled to find a sensible answer. "I got married," she said lamely.

"Avó says you are lying. Avó says if you are here instead of in your husband's bed, your marriage is meaningless."

Elise held up her hand to show her wedding ring, and the old woman guffawed. Quidico leered. "There are many kinds of marriages," he said. "Very few have the weight that deserves a ring and yet I always see one on every woman's finger who calls herself a wife, whether or not she deserves that title. Why is that? I've been married three times. Three times I've had to ask that my ring be returned to me."

"That's a really boring story," Elise yawned.

Quidico frowned. He tried to pierce her with his golden eyes. "The marriages did not deserve—"

Elise interrupted with a deep sigh. "I get it. Three marriages, none of them worthy of a ring. Look: I'm here following the English Army because I'm stuck. That's all."

Grandmother and grandson conferred again. "My *avó* wishes to know if you would like her help to become unstuck."

Elise hesitated. The old woman leaned forward, her hips popped as she bent at the waist. "You want to go home?" she asked hoarsely in English. She flicked her fingers over Elise's shoulder, as though home was just there, back at the beach.

"You sly little lady, you speak Spanish?" Elise grinned. Now she was getting somewhere. "Where did you learn?"

"I learned the language of the stars. That is the first language. All others are easy."

"Language of the stars? What's that? Astrology or something? I'm a Taurus."

Avó made a dismissive gesture. "Astrology is for amateurs. I'm speaking of the language spoken throughout universes and the places between. That's the only language that means anything. Perhaps someday you too will learn. I've a feeling you may."

"Between what?"

"You've been there. Do not tell me you do not understand." She rolled her weight onto her right hip and started untucking her blouse from her skirt and in the process released gas.

"Ugh! Avó!" cried Quidico.

She cackled, revealing the same tiny front teeth as her grandson. "I've something to show you Elise Dubois Ferrington, don't turn away. It is something you did to me in the between space." She lifted her blouse and revealed an enormous red welt on her side, the edges of which were already turning a vibrant shade of purple.

Quidico gasped and reached protectively towards his grandmother. "When did she do this?" He turned to Elise, face blackened by anger. "I'll kill you, you button thief. I'll lay out your intestines for the gulls and your eyes for the ants."

"I didn't do that! I swear I didn't touch her!"

There was a flurry of conversation between grandmother and grandson in their language, and then Quidico turned back to Elise with a grudging bow. Avó smiled. "You do not remember flicking an emerald beetle away? Foolish woman."

"That was you in my dream?" Elise suspected that she was being conned, but she was having a harder time discerning what was real.

She was too tired for this. Suddenly she wished she'd gone back with Thomas. She could be smoking a pipe, listening to the company's music and eating Mrs. Gillihan's familiar food. She tried to stand, but again the old woman grabbed her wrist and pulled her back down onto the bench. She was surprisingly strong.

Avó drew a circle in the air and gave Elise a significant look, completely baffling her. Then she turned back to her grandson and spoke urgently to him. He looked surprised at first, and the rapidity of their conversation increased. The woman's arthritic index finger punctuated the air between them as more circles were drawn. Then Quidico smiled and nodded, finally understanding something.

"Avó says she can help you. She says you're to find your way back."

"That's just where I'd like to go—I'm really tired and I'd love to get back to camp."

"No, you misunderstand me. She wants to help you return to your home." He too drew a circle in the air. "She says that while everyone else rides the waves like driftwood towards shore, you've skipped over the waves like a flat stone thrown into the sea. You've jumped backwards."

Elise felt as though she could barely breathe. How did this strange woman know? "Yes, that's it exactly," she said, burning with hope. "I was cut loose. I bounced once, in Paris, I think, and then I landed in London. I want to ride the waves again. I want to be driftwood."

The woman's smile was slow to develop. She lifted one hand and made a circle with her thumb and index finger. Then with her other hand she pierced the circle rhythmically with a finger before pointing first at her grandson's crotch, then at Elise's stomach.

"My grandmother says—"

Elise stopped him with a hand in the air. "That doesn't need translating."

"With you, a woman who skips the waves, I could sire a powerful future. We would have a beautiful, strong child with fire in his soul. The bloodline would be strong."

"You've got to be kidding." Elise studied his face. He wasn't kidding. "You're barking up the wrong tree, buddy." Again, Elise stood to leave, but the man caught her elbow and held her back. He leaned his head to the side and knitted his dark brows in an attempt to convince her with a soulful look.

It might have been the music, or the firelight in his long, wild hair, but Elise found him to be appealing in his own strange way, notwithstanding the tiny front teeth. The last time she'd had an orgasm was with Richard in front of the door to the Quiet Woman's cesspool. It couldn't possibly get worse than that. Since having a second husband was out of the question, any other proposal could be heard for exactly what it was: a business proposal. The old crone again pointed at Elise's stomach, then pointed at her grandson before pumping her left fist with her index finger. "Please stop doing that, Avó,"

A bark of laughter from the old woman quickly turned into a violent fit of coughing. Elise was all but forgotten as the devoted Quidico knelt by his grandmother's side and took her thin hands into his own strong ones while she struggled to find her breath. Finally, she closed her eyes and nodded. The fit was over and she patted Quidico's cheek affectionately in thanks before turning back to Elise. "You want go home. Home to the future?" Her voice was a strangely coarse accented English. Again she drew a circle in the air.

Grandmother and grandson stared at her as if it was a normal question and they were awaiting a normal answer. "Yes!" Elise cried. "Yes!"

Avó stretched flat all the wrinkles on her lips in a smile. "Your future is already the past," she said. "Do you think time stopped marching forward just because you traveled here? I felt the tear in time two months ago, maybe three. Many of us felt it. But you can't go back. What was once your present is now the past to those you left behind." She drew another circle to illustrate her point.

"There's got to be a work-around. If I was thrown back to a specific day, why can't I go forward to a specific day, my present?"

"There is no such thing as a 'present time.' Not even for me," Avó continued, "there is only ever future, and past. Time is like walking. You may look forward at the path ahead, or look behind you at the root you tripped over. But the ground under and between your feet can never be seen if you're walking—it's always shifting, always moving. There is no 'work-around.'" She flipped her hand in a dismissive gesture.

"But once the present becomes past, then it's there for all eternity. It's etched. Right?" Elise was beginning to feel panicky.

Avó shrugged again. "Why would you think any moment is etched? Moments shift in meaning all the time. Nothing is etched."

"Facts are facts. Things happen in time. You and I: we're talking on a specific date at a specific time. Nothing can change that."

"It all depends upon which layer you reside in. Who is to say you haven't traveled through layers?"

"Layers?" Elise blinked in confusion. "Which is it? Circles or layers?" She didn't know why she bothered to ask, either choice was an equally muddy explanation. She tried another tack. "Just send me back to when I left. How many ways can I say this?"

"You want me to throw you forward at a moving target? It's not possible."

"What if you're wrong? What if the whole universe stopped when I left it?" Elise jumped up off the bench. "That's it! The universe stopped and is waiting for me to return."

"Did it really?"

"You can't say for sure that it didn't. You don't know."

"That's a very self-centered thought. Do you really think you have that much power over the universe?"

"If it didn't stop, then there are two futures, the one I left, and the one I'm about to experience now. That can't be right."

The old woman started chuckling. "Only two futures? You limit yourself, my dear. And how do you know that the future you left is the correct one? Again I must point out your self-centered thoughts. Could it not be that what you think of as your present time is actually someone else's past, like my own present is the far past to you?"

Elise threw up her arms in exasperation. "If you complicate everything, I'll never get back!"

"Precisely."

"Fuck!"

"Of course, there is also the possibility that you are now two people, one here, and one there."

"WHAT?"

"I'm merely making a conjecture. There's no need to yell. Sit down."

Elise sat.

"The future must be a very beautiful place. You seem anxious to return. Tell me, do people still die in war in the future?"

"Yes."

"Yes? Oh, that's too bad. Still fighting over borders, no doubt. The Romani people have no borders." She sat, thoughtful, before continuing. "And tell me, are people still starving in your future?"

Elise didn't like where this was going. "Yes."

"Yes? Oh that's dreadful," she shook her head and clucked disapprovingly. "And what about stealing, do people still steal in your future?"

Elise nodded, feeling uncomfortable under the woman's piercing gaze.

"How far did you travel?"

"About two hundred years or so." Elise thought of her world, so different from where she was now, and began to feel depressed. She came from a place where the most popular novels and TV shows were about apocalyptic end-times, and most of the plotlines were plausible.

"In a few days there will be a new moon," Avó said. "This will be the perfect time for the type of magic that may return you to your home. On that night, you must come and find me. Our caravan will be close—moving armies make good customers so we follow. Come to me on the new moon and make a baby with my grandson, and I will send you forward two hundred years where you will raise my great granddaughter to be a leader of men. In return, you will give me the emerald scarab."

Quidico threw his shoulders back and placed a hand on his hip as Elise flicked her eyes up and down his body, assessing her situation. His posture sagged slightly when he heard Elise's deep sigh of resignation.

"So, what if you accidentally send me to the '80s?"

"The 1880s?"

"The 1980s."

"That is a possibility. In fact, I'm fairly sure the society of women I belong to will not be happy with me for this very reason. It is a dangerous spell. But I do this as a favor to you. I like you. I want you to be happy, and I want my progeny to live into the future."

"Fine. Quidico and I will make a baby on the night of the new moon. But he doesn't get a fourth wife if your spell doesn't work."

"Of course not." The old woman was almost too quick to agree.

Elise thought of her IUD and wondered if a spell would counteract it. There could be some validity to the old gypsy's claims if she could enter her dreams as a bug, but Elise was doubtful. Biology was biology. Magic was magic. "Do we shake on it, or something?"

"And the emerald?"

"I'll be keeping that. A baby's already one hell of an ask."

The Army Marches

It was late when Elise left the Romani caravan. She wandered back to camp by the light of the stars with her head full of hope of returning to Tucson. The next morning however, after being roused early from the hole she'd dug for herself in the sand, her mood was less optimistic. Once she shook the sleep from her brain and figured out where she was, the memory of the strange deal she had made with Avó left her feeling headachy and regretful, like she had a bad hangover.

She missed the days when she could drag herself out of bed with her eyes still in slits and shuffle to the kitchen to make a hot cup of coffee. Now, coffee wasn't even a remote possibility. Tea, a sorry second for any caffeine addict, was available to those few who could find the coin to set aside for it, but rare, and never in the mornings.

With the entire army preparing to march, Elise searched for Amanda, hoping to walk with her and share the burden of carrying Edwina. She felt her heart sink when she couldn't find the young mother with the other women.

"Mrs. Gillihan says you sent Mrs. Collins back to the *Valiant*," Elise said, chasing down the surgeon as he gathered his equipment in the low light of a rising sun. "Why would you do that?"

"Oh good, you're here," George Russell said. "Take up that pack, if you please. I tried not to pack it too heavily for you."

Elise shoved her own little bag of herbs into the top of the pack and swung it onto her back. It wasn't terrible. "Why did you send her back to the ship?"

"I believe I told you there's a fever sweeping through the ranks, did I not?" Russell continued about his business of organizing supplies into wicker panniers to be slung over mules. "Those who have fallen sick and cannot march have been sent back to the *Valiant*. Mrs. Collins volunteered to nurse them to health."

"You confined a new mother and baby on board a ship full of sick and dying people?"

The young surgeon stopped what he was doing and faced Elise. "Why are you so concerned about Mrs. Collins? She didn't want to be with the company any longer. She's frightened of O'Brian, and well she should be after what happened yesterday morning. Her own husband thought she'd be safer back aboard the ship. It's for the best."

"I'll trade. Take her off and put me on. She and Collins could transfer to a different company to get away from O'Brian."

"I don't understand. I thought you did not wish to return to the *Valiant*. I sent her because you insisted on staying here. There's no pleasing you, is there?"

"Amanda is safer on land than she is on that ship. She'll be exposed to contagion."

"You've got it all wrong again, Mrs. Ferrington. It's the miasmas in this dreadful country that are making the men sick. There's nothing on the *Valiant* that's dangerous. I'm doing her a favor, quite likely saving her life."

Elise felt like weeping. She felt like screaming. Instead, she just hung her head and walked away.

For the first mile of the army's march south, the sand massaged the arches of Elise's feet, ground down the hard calluses that had formed from months without shoes, and worked away dirt that had all but tattooed the cracks in her heels. While the other women she marched with complained about the itching sand that got up in their bloomers, Elise reveled in her freedom. After the long confinement on the ship, a stroll on the beach was heaven, at least for the first few miles.

No one had anticipated the long miles the army would be forced to march, especially not the women. None of the wives had seen a map. No one had discussed the game plan with them. They only knew that they were headed south towards the enemy.

The army had insisted that the women who followed be stout and robust, but the ability to endure long distances was much different from the ability to haul water or scrub linen. Slowly, they began to fall behind. They stopped to nurse babies, they took off their shoes to shake out the sand or wandered into the tall beach grass to deal with private matters. Some went to find the supply carts to beg for a lift from the implacable drivers, if not for themselves, then for their weary children. The ever industrious Mrs. Gillihan, however, disappeared into the underbrush to forage for food for the evening camp.

Despite a nicotine habit Elise had never been able to kick, the years of a long-distance running routine made the march more tolerable for her. It wasn't a lack of endurance that made her tired, it was a lack of comfort. While the soldiers slogged through the loose sand, she walked where the waves broke and tamped the ground for more solid footing. That helped, but still her shoulders chafed under the straps of her badly balanced pack of medical supplies. Her tight corset dug into her ribs. Soaked in sweat, everything clung to her skin.

As the morning faded towards noon, the heat began to rise, stirring the insects. Off the beach in the shelter of the reeds, the cicadas trilled. The sound brought back memories of the desert in Tucson, of the arching shade of the palo verde trees, of ice cold margaritas on the back patio. The heat also caused the flies to stir from the line of decomposing ocean debris the waves pushed onto shore. The black flies buzzed around Elise's face and caught rides on her clothing. The brave ones bit her before she could swat them away. Smaller insects, no larger than grains of sand, hovered near the ground and were caught up in the hem of her skirt and trapped around her legs.

It had been smart to start early to get as many miles out of the way as possible before the sun got too hot. Despite the fact that much had been left behind on the ships to supply the men along the way as they marched south down the beach, they were still expected to carry their own food and water. And despite the heat, they were regulated to strap their heavy wool greatcoats and blankets on the top of their packs, which were already full of their gear. Many also carried comfort items, like a straight blade for shaving, soap, extra clothes, pots for cooking, shoe polish and metal polish for keeping their gear looking sharp for inspection, all of which added weight. Their Brown Bess muskets weren't light either—ten pounds of walnut and iron, coupled with iron rounds, cartridge, and a horn full of gunpowder. Elise had even seen a soldier, who had been a cobbler in his former life, pack a heavy iron hammer and a cobblestone in his kitbag in anticipation of needing to mend shoes while on the march.

The men slowed as the day got hotter, plodding forward steadily under their burdens. Elise found herself flanking the column, then passing the overburdened light infantry altogether. To her surprise, as soon as she reached the riflemen in front, an officer on horseback waved her back to the rear. "It isn't safe for you in front!" admonished a rifleman as she turned around.

"Then walk a little faster," she snapped.

It annoyed her that anyone would check her speed or limit her range.

Another rifleman laughed. "Pay her no mind. That's loony Mrs. Ferrington—she'll do as she pleases. Made quite a name for herself on the *Valiant.*"

"She can do as she pleases, as long as it's behind the column. Not in front."

Elise made a face and cut east to leave the beach behind. She found a dusty and rutted path that snaked in the same direction as the marching army, and followed it through mounds of heather, tall grasses, and fragrant wild rosemary. Further out where the sand gave way to loam, row after row of staked grapevines revealed a countryside sparsely inhabited, but well stewed in wine.

The emptiness of the landscape felt alien to Elise who, since entering the nineteenth century, had been in constant contact with other people. She could still hear the movement of the army on the beach—anyone within a mile of the army would hear the squeaking of leather and the clanking of metal on metal as their kits bounced in rhythm to their march. It was a haunting soundtrack to play behind her view of the hills, dotted with lonely vineyards scratched out of the wild and fragrant scrubland. Briefly she thought of Tucson and its rushing traffic, the startling sounds of booming Air Force jets, the scattered conversation of passing strangers on the street. She missed it, but at the same time, it was hard not to overlay what she saw with the knowledge that in two hundred years, the pretty rolling hills would, in all likelihood, be paved over. It reminded her of her conversation with Avó the night before, and of her pointed question: are there still wars in the future?

Elise pulled her knife and cut a sprig of rosemary to lace into the woven straw of her hat. Then she gathered more to give to Mrs. Gillihan to flavor her stews, along with wild thyme that carpeted the edges of the path. As she bundled the stems together, she crushed the leaves and breathed in the summery scent.

Elise scanned the prickly vegetation as she pushed her way through the wilderness, her mind occupied with vague memories of the lesson Mrs. Southill had given her on medicinal plants. She had a small bundle of yarrow in her kitbag, or what the old lady had called "soldier's woundwart," but Elise was on the hunt for more. Luckily the white flowers were fairly easy to recognize. As she bent to gather the feathery leaves, a sudden explosion of noise made her fall back in surprise as a pair of partridges were flushed out of the undergrowth with raucous cries. When the sound of their panicked escape died away, her own pounding heartbeat echoed loudly in her ears. There was no other sound. The soldiers had stopped marching.

Branches tore at Elise's clothing as she bushwhacked back to the beach to see what was happening. She was just a few feet away when a bright streak of green and brown leaped at her from her left side and tackled her to the ground. It happened so fast she didn't even have time to fight. She was steamrolled onto her back and pinned with her wrists caught over her head. "Well hello, love," the man said, grinning under a complicated mustache that curled into his sideburns.

"Get off of me!" Elise bucked her hips to dislodge the man, and he whooped in delight, then flattened himself along the length of her to stop her from fighting. He smelled like the salty flesh of the mussels they'd eaten the afternoon before, fresh from the ocean. Elise went limp, hoping to draw him into a false sense of security. "If you think this is fun," she growled, "you should try it with me on top."

He looked at her in surprise, his smile spreading, but he wasn't about to be tricked into giving her control. "You speak English. You're one of ours, then? What are you doing so far out in front?"

"Let me up, you idiot. My husband's in the Forty-Third Regiment, Second Division." Elise took a breath, suddenly confused. "I mean, 42nd, third division?" She paused, "Wait, 45th. . .I think."

"Oh, you're quite convincing, aren't you?" He slammed her wrists back down above her head as she started struggling again, then leaned his face close to hers and whispered against her cheek. His mustache created tingles down her spine as it grazed her skin. "You've a strange accent. Perhaps you're a spy? Sneaking about in the fields, are you?"

"Private Drake! What the hell are you about?" A commanding voice boomed above them. "Let that woman up at once."

Drake leapt to his feet and stood at attention. "A spy, sir."

"A spy?" the officer's voice dripped in doubt. "Madam, your name please."

"Elise Du. . .I mean, Mrs. Richard Ferrington." She cringed at having erased her own name.

"Richard Ferrington?" the officer looked confused as Elise rose and brushed off her skirt. "You don't mean to say you're married to the Private Ferrington as plays the fiddle? He was playing for us just last night."

"Yeah. That's the one."

"Dick Ferrington is married? Well he's a right scamp, isn't he?" The officer clapped Private Drake on the shoulder, trying to draw him in on the joke. "I'd no idea he was married, what with the way he carries on with Lady Letchfeld." Drake smiled in response, unsure how to respond.

Elise did not smile.

"Escort Mrs. Ferrington to the back of the column. Really, my dear, you shouldn't be this far forward. It's not safe."

"So I've been told."

"At your service, madam," mumbled Private Drake, clearly disappointed to have missed his opportunity to rape a French spy. Elise slapped away his proffered elbow and slipped a couple of brass buttons she'd torn from his jacket into her apron pocket.

It didn't take long to get back to the beach and backtrack to the troops. A rest had been called, hence the silence Elise had noted earlier, and many of the men had simply sat down, still in the column. Those with more energy had dragged themselves away from the incessant flies and tried to hide from the sun in the spare shade of boulders and driftwood logs. Elise left Private Drake to return to his picket duties, or whatever else he was doing back in the weeds all alone.

The distinctive sound of Richard's fiddle rose mournfully over the resting men, and Elise followed it to find her company.

"Brutal weather we're having. Damned brutal," Richard said, lifting his bow from his violin. He scooted over to make room for her under a wool blanket draped between four long sticks shoved deep into the sand. Bill Stanton lay at his feet, his head resting on his drum. "I'm not sure I can take much more of this. I'm sure this heat will make the wood crack."

"All it takes to crack your wood is a couple bottles of wine and a wad of cash." She knew he was referring to his instrument, but she couldn't help herself.

"You wouldn't happen to have a bit of water, would you?" he asked plaintively, ignoring her comment. "I'm clean out."

Elise narrowed her eyes at him. His face was sunburnt, but more than that, his lips were swollen, and his eyes sunken and bloodshot. It wasn't all that hot in comparison to a Tucson summer, but Richard was a man who'd never left the cool, damp streets of London. To him, this had to be hotter than hell. "Didn't you fill your canteen before we left the river?" As the words left Elise's mouth, she realized the futility of the question. Even if he had filled it to capacity, the canteen barely held a liter. She reached up to brush sand from his hair and realized it wasn't sand at all but salt from his sweat. She felt a sudden dread. Richard, at least, was healthy, raised strong on Mrs. Postlethwaite's bread and beef stew. Many of the other men weren't as well off. Slogging through the beach with their heavy packs wasn't going to be easy for them. And she was sure some, the younger ones especially, were dumb enough to have forgotten to refill their canteens before they'd broke camp.

She looked again at Bill. It was amazing how teenagers could fall asleep at the drop of a hat. Ever since he'd left his friend Gerry back on the *Valiant*, he'd been clinging to the men of the company like a security blanket. "How's the kid?"

"Bill's lagging a bit. We've redistributed some of the weight he's carrying between us. Collins's idea."

Elise nodded, happy to hear they were looking out for the youth. Having lived in the Tucson desert for so long, she'd had the foresight to steal a second canteen while packing the surgeon's medical supplies. But her second was only half full. She gently shook Bill and placed it to his lips when he stirred awake. "Easy, there. Just sip it," Elise cautioned. Then she gave the last bit to Richard.

"What about Thomas?" she asked. "How's he holding up?" She glanced around, looking for the barkeep. All the soldiers looked irritatingly similar in their uniforms. "Which way did he go?"

"I think I saw Tom head back into the bushes, so I don't think he'd appreciate being looked for right now."

Elise nodded. If he could still pee, he wouldn't be too dehydrated. She tried to remember if she'd seen any sign of a stream on her earlier foray, any clusters of trees growing in a line or an oasis of bright green in the wide expanse of dusty sage. Nothing stood out in her memory but the drought tolerant grapevines that drooped in the hot sun. She looked at the heaped lumps in the sand that were resting men and felt a moment of panic. "Where's the damn wagon train?" she said suddenly. "Wouldn't the supply carts be carrying water barrels?"

"Perhaps," replied Richard, doubtfully.

"You don't sound convinced."

"Well, it's just that we're bound to come across a river or stream soon enough. Seems like a bloody waste of energy to be hauling barrels of water."

Elise felt her jaw drop. She took a deep breath and swallowed hard. "Where's the doctor?" she asked.

"Doctor? Do you mean Mr. Russell? For God's sake, let me be. Stop asking so many questions. How should I know where our surgeon is?"

Russell, it turned out, wasn't too far away.

"Mrs. Ferrington," the surgeon began, "while I appreciate your concern for the wellbeing of the men, I cannot think how this scene you are creating does anything but stir trouble. You would do better to help the lads think of something other than their thirst."

"Think of something else?" Elise repeated, dumbfounded. "People are going to *die.*"

"You do have a flare for the dramatic. Why should the army carry barrels of water? We just had a grand river full of water."

"That was miles ago!"

"And there's sure to be another river soon. Rivers empty into the ocean. That is what they *do.*"

"Look kiddo, you might not have noticed, but we're not in England anymore. I've been a half mile forward of the column, and there wasn't any water. Don't forget, the human body is about sixty percent water, or should be. If we don't get water soon, everyone's brains are going to shrivel into raisins."

The end to the rest was called. Elise gave Russell a significant look. "No one's going to listen to me. They might listen to you. You need to tell the officers that the men need more water."

The surgeon pinched his mouth into a line and looked away.

"Fine. It's on your head, then," Elise snapped.

Elise left to find where the other women were gathered. It didn't take much to convince them to find some shade and wait out the heat before catching up with the soldiers. No one thought that marching in the heat of the day was a good idea, and Elise was thankful to not have to see the men suffering without having any means for alleviating it.

Four hours later and much refreshed, the women began their own march to find their husbands. The trail the army had left on the beach was easy to follow, and the camp followers hurried along, anxious to return to their loved ones.

The flotsam left behind by the army was small at first, and the women took the time to pick up the items—an iron pan here, a greatcoat there—thinking that the gear had been accidentally lost. But as they continued, the items grew in number until it became a long trail in the sand of abandoned personal goods—items of trivial weight, like combs and polishing cloths, revealing the desperation of the men to lighten their loads.

Elise wept over the first body she found, a young soldier, desiccated and sunburnt, had dragged himself to the tall fescue that lined the beach. She stepped over the next two bodies in her rush to catch up to the column, her heart clenched in fear for the safety of the men she knew.

The army's trail turned east, as though a sudden change of mind had occurred, and followed a dusty and rutted road through alternating pine forests and vineyards. The women lifted their skirts and brushed the sand from their legs, as thankful as the men surely must have been, to leave the ocean behind. It was well after dark when they reached the little town of Lavos. The army had already laid their blankets down in the surrounding fields and dropped, exhausted and thirsty, into fitful sleep.

Elise and Mrs. Gillihan split from the other women and searched together through the mounded blankets looking for familiar faces. They found George Russell first. He was shadowed under the light of the stars and burdened by clattering canteens as he wandered from man to man. He looked at Elise with a hollow expression and nodded before he resumed passing out drinks of water to those too weak to have gone into the village to get it for themselves.

After the shock of the first day's march, the men grew accustomed to the hardships and despite a brutally fast pace, the mood within the ranks was high, excited. No one questioned why they were being pushed so hard. The why of it was obvious to everyone: they were racing towards the enemy and that suited everyone just fine. Now that they'd left the scorching beach behind, all anyone could think about was killing. The anticipation of it had risen to a fevered pitch, and why not? What was the alternative to the infantrymen being rushed to battle? Death. It would soon be kill or die, and the men would rather think about killing.

So when the sound of shots rang out, cutting through the quiet of the called rest, many men jumped to their feet with their weapons in hand. Others, not wanting to end the precious break in the march prematurely, waited for orders. From behind bushes, still others raced to return to the ranks after hastily finishing their business. They looked about anxiously and questioned their mates to find out what they missed, gaining no insight.

Three officers on horses rode by at a canter, heading south towards the front. A heavy silence descended after the beasts passed.

More shots.

"Easy, lads," Sergeant Taylor called out to the company as he walked by, rounding up and counting his men. "This don't concern us.

Just stay together and don't go nowheres."

It was a simple instruction, but somehow comforting and better than silence. It gave the men something to do and reminded them of the value of cohesion. Stay together. Don't go nowheres. "Ferrington, you idiot, put this blanket away. Get ready to go." Taylor ripped the shading blanket down from where it had been pinned to three bushes and threw it at Richard. This was less comforting. "You," he pointed at Elise, "fall back."

"It's the frogs," Bill croaked out excitedly. He blinked away his nap and rubbed his eyes, squinting in the glare of the sun.

"Sounds like skirmishers to me," Thomas appeared out of nowhere, buttoning his trousers. He shrugged on his pack and jammed his shako back on his head.

Now that Thomas had been recruited by the surgeon to be another aide, he spent most of his time marching with the medical supply carts. Whenever he did show up, it was to speak with Richard, or check in on Peter Collins. He didn't speak to Elise. He didn't even look at her. Elise hoped that the combination of his cold shoulder and scarcity would make being angry with him easier. It didn't. Every time she saw him her stomach twisted into knots.

The sound of a braying animal caused all four of them to turn and look. George Russell was pulling at the lead of his mule, trying to encourage the beast to turn its head away from the lovely patch of grass that it had been dining upon. The diminutive surgeon's hat had been knocked to one side and a tuft of his red hair protruded out to the left of his head like the lit end of a firecracker.

"Doesn't he look just like a tinker?" Bill laughed.

"Mind your manners," Thomas admonished.

Jenkins, ever steady in the presence of his employer's fiery temper, thoughtfully slapped the mule on its hindquarters and the beast jumped forward. Equipment in the over-packed wicker panniers jangled as they hurried towards the sound of the shots. Elise watched them pass, then jumped to her feet and pulled on her own pack. There were wounded. If the surgeon was running, there were wounded.

"Where do you think you're going?" Richard asked her.

Elise didn't answer. Richard hadn't earned the right to question her. She looked at Thomas and defiantly lifted her chin, daring him to object. He said nothing. Instead, Thomas stalked away then broke into a run, his pack jangling like the mule. Elise jogged along behind.

With her skirt hitched up in one hand, she jogged easily along with the doctor, but well out of reach of the frightening mule and its big teeth. She was sure the animal would lunge at her the second she let her guard down, and each time it brayed, she blanched in fear, feeling certain it was itching to take a chunk of flesh off the nearest jerk that was forcing it to run in the heat. The fact that Russell held the mule's lead so close to its nose did not reassure her of the gentleness of the animal, but further convinced her that the surgeon was an idiot.

It felt good, running towards danger, purposeful. The whole thing reminded Elise of that shot of adrenaline she used to get when the ER team ran out through double doors to meet whatever was being run in. The hospital she'd worked at in Tucson had its share of victims of violence and she'd seen gunshot wounds before. She tried to review what had happened with each case as she ran along behind the surgeon. In the ER, there were bags of replacement fluid to hang, catheters, suction vacuums, oxygen masks, antibiotics, and anesthesia. There were protocols for the use of each tool, and specialized teams. Now, all she had to help her were two clanking wicker baskets full of torture devices with wooden handles, a couple of thugs to pin patients onto their backs, and a surgeon who didn't understand the basic principles of contagion. She ran faster, suddenly wanting to leave the others behind.

The skirmish was over by the time they'd reached the men at the front. The 95th Rifles looked at them in surprise as the small medical team burst in on them, out of breath, sweaty, and looking very much like the tinkers Bill had compared them to, but once their purpose was explained, they were quickly pointed in the direction of three men who'd been shot.

"It's Mrs. Ferrington," hooted one of the wounded. "Hallo! Remember me? Didn't think I'd be seeing you again—just can't stay in the back, can you?"

Elise recognized him right away. The mustache that reached his ears made it easy. "Drake, isn't it?"

"In the flesh."

"You two have met?" Thomas asked suspiciously.

"We met in the bushes," Elise gave the man a sardonic smile as she felt for his pulse. "Didn't we Drake?"

Private Drake took one look at Thomas and wisely kept his mouth shut.

The man's pulse was hard to feel in his wrist, and he seemed to be getting more pale by the minute. She pressed down on his fingernail and let go, looking for capillary refill. All she saw, however, was that he needed a bath and a large bar of pumice soap to scrub his hands. There was a round circle of blood between his legs. "Shot in the thigh?" Elise was getting a bad feeling.

"Aye. Grazed likely."

"Can you move your leg?"

He nodded. "It hurts, though."

No nerve damage then, that was good. "Let's have a look." She motioned for him to pull his trousers down and caused a small explosion of outrage. "Oh, so *now* your bashful?" Elise said, thinking of how she'd been pinned down by the man. "Fine. Then I'll just cut a hole in your pants." Another wave of loud objections assailed her ears as she pulled her knife from its sheath under her skirt. "Look, they're going to have to come off one way or another."

"Over here, Mrs. Ferrington, if you please," Russell called out.

Elise left Private Drake and rushed to the doctor, thinking his call was due to a more urgent case. Instead, she found a young man excitedly recounting in detail how his small company of riflemen had come across the enemy while the surgeon examined the pathway that a round had taken through the flesh of his deltoid. "We thought the French were still miles ahead. Imagine our surprise when we saw members of their rearguard. It looked like they were set up for teatime, or some such nonsense."

"Mm hmm," Russell said, uninterested. He motioned for Jenkins to swab more blood away.

"Did you need me for something?" Elise asked.

"I believe the others were uncomfortable with your presence, no?" He waved her to move on to the third patient. "See what that man needs."

"Have you looked at him already?"

"No, Mrs. Ferrington," he said, sounding annoyed. "As you can plainly see, I'm busy at the moment."

Elise frowned. Apparently, there was no such thing as triage in nineteenth century medicine. Good to know, she thought.

"So, Drake there wanted to see if he could put a round through their wine sack, just to scare them a bit," continued Russell's patient, "but Drake's not much of a shot, see?"

"Mm hmm," replied the surgeon.

The third patient was sitting on a stump, trembling and pale. He was holding his left wrist while blood dripped onto the ground. A hole had been shot through his palm. "You've got the right idea, sweetie," Elise said to him, "but hold your hand up. Higher. Good." She wasn't sure why everyone's first instinct was to grab the wrist of their injured hand and hold it between their legs.

"I can't be a one-handed farmer. I need to keep my hand," the man said. He looked frightened. "One-handed farmers starve."

"Can I take a look?" Hands were tricky. There was so much going on in a very tiny amount of space: tendons, bones, nerves, vessels, and all of it miniaturized. Hands took specialists to repair. She hoped that the ball had gone through the webbing between his thumb and index finger. It hadn't. This poor guy was sunk.

"Elise?" Thomas called. There was an urgency and helplessness to his tone that made her head snap up. He was standing with Private Drake slouched in a faint in his arms. "Where should I put him?"

"Set him out on the ground," Russell snapped impatiently. "He'll come to in a moment. Can't stand the sight of blood is all."

Thomas looked at Elise for confirmation. She pulled a blanket from Drake's pack and Thomas dragged his charge over to her and laid him down. Elise slit Drake's pant leg from ankle to hip while Thomas kept Drake's torso pinned in case he came back from his faint.

"I can't see what's going on," Elise mumbled. She tried to use the pant leg to wipe up the gore, but that only revealed an entrance and an exit in the man's thigh, not the true source of the bleeding. The flesh was swelling as blood pooled under the skin. "Mr. Russell," Elise called, "this man's femoral artery is cut. He's bleeding out."

Russell turned from his patient, one eyebrow raised in exasperation. "Must I explain everything to you? Put a tourniquet on him. I can't do anything until I'm finished here."

Elise gaped at the surgeon in surprise, then pulled herself together and tied Drake's bloody pant leg tight around his thigh above the entry wound. Her jaw was set. Since Russell's reply was nothing but a brush-off, she would have to deal with the matter herself.

"Get me a clean scalpel, silk thread and a needle," she ordered Thomas.

He didn't move.

"Knife, Thomas. A very, very sharp knife." He pulled his own knife out from a sheath hung at his belt and offered it to her after wiping the blade on the grass. Elise swallowed hard to keep from screaming at him. "Is there a campfire around? Go hold the blade in the fire. Ten seconds in direct flame, then bring the knife here without touching the blade to a single thing." Elise sighed and looked at her filthy hands after Thomas had trotted off. There wasn't much point in trying to keep a sterile field, she thought sadly. Drake was going to have to flip a coin on infection, like everyone else.

When Thomas returned, she carefully took the hot dagger and motioned for him to pin Drake down again. "Make sure you've got his arms. He might wake up swinging and I don't want to get hit." She was trembling as she straddled Drake's thigh to pin that down too.

Just as she brought the knife down, a shadow fell over her. "What in bloody hell are you doing?" The young surgeon's eyes flashed angrily. His freckled hand shot out to snatch her wrist causing the knife to skid dangerously across Private Drake's flesh. "He's bleeding out," Elise repeated angrily, checking to make sure she didn't cut her patient by accident. "We have to do something."

"Did you not place a tourniquet as I asked?" he demanded, imperiously pointing to where Elise had cut off the blood flow over the wound.

"If you stop perfusion for too long, the limb will die. Tourniquets are only fine for the short term—"

"What's this stuff and nonsense about perfusion? Private MacEwan, I'm surprised at you. I'd have thought you'd have more sense than to let this woman practice her witchery on my patient."

"Your pardon, but Mrs. Ferrington has a real talent for healing," Thomas said quietly. "She saved the life of one of my regulars."

"Your what? Your regular? I hope to God you're not speaking of an event that happened at a public house. Put that ghastly knife away. Jenkins, get me my scalpel. Out of my way, Mrs. Ferrington."

The scalpel flashed against Private Drake's flesh, releasing a flood of trapped blood. "So now," he said, turning back to Elise. "Tell me, what should happen after the first incision." His eyebrows arched as he awaited the answer to his pop quiz.

Elise sucked in a breath. The surgeon's slice had been alarmingly swift. "I'd be damn careful not to cut the femoral nerve," she said. A muscle in Russell's jaw twitched—his only acknowledgement to her pointed statement. "And then I'd push my finger inside to look for the artery. Once found, I'd determine where the hole was and sew it up with silk. After that was done, I'd sew the whole thing back up and hope for the best. If you didn't use a tourniquet, then you could find the artery by feeling for its pulse and tie it off above and below the hole before repairing it, keeping perfusion to the rest of the limb."

Russell took a long time to reply, peering closely at the wound he'd opened. Elise pulled the flesh farther apart to give him more room to probe inside, causing Private Drake to scream and buck in pain under Thomas and Jenkins's strong arms. "You've done this before?" he asked.

"Nope." She swabbed away more blood, allowing the surgeon a better view. "I'm not an OR nurse, I'm ER, so I never got many opportunities to watch this kind of thing."

Russell looked up sharply, then returned to the wound.

"I'll admit I would have probably made a mess of it if you hadn't stepped in," Elise continued, knowing she was probably saying too much, but too full of adrenaline to shut up. "I didn't know when you'd be finished with that other guy and I figured if I started there was a chance I could save Drake's leg. He might die anyway, depending on how much blood he's lost."

"Silk." Russell held his hand out and was rewarded with a threaded needle from Jenkins. In short order, the artery was repaired. "Sew him up, if you please, Mrs. Ferrington, and release the tourniquet."

"Who, me?"

"I don't know about this business of tying off the artery above and below the tear, and that bit about an AR or an OE was befuddling, but the rest of your explanation was sound and I'm not in a position to refuse help, even from you."

Roliça

The moon was a pale sliver in the fading light of the evening sky. On its side, it reminded Elise of an irritating smiley-face emoji from an unwanted admirer. And, coincidentally, there directly under the moon on the ridge of the hillside stood her unwanted admirer. Quidico's leering face delivered the message in person.

Looking up at him, Elise's stomach twisted unpleasantly. His long dark hair hung loose over his shoulders, lifting like one of his many scarves in the wind. He stood with his legs splayed, hips thrust forward. His shirt was open to his navel, and he slid one hand slowly up his naked chest as a lascivious smile played at the corners of his mouth in a visual reminder of what she'd promised him. Elise had spent the last few days trying not to think about it, but apparently Quidico had no problem with the idea. Now that the officers had called a halt to the advancing troops, the caravan had finally caught up. Elise hoped that didn't mean she going to get visits like this one every night until the night of the dirty deed.

"Is that bloke bothering you?" Collins's voice made Elise jump.

"No, he's okay. I mean, thank you. He's not bothering me."

"You'll let me know? Me and the lads'll take care of him on the double. Just say the word and we'll teach that tinkerer to know his place." He gave Quidico a two-fingered salute and Quidico retreated, slowly, with a strut. "The man's got no respect. Someone should teach him better manners."

Elise squinted at Peter as he stumbled back to where he'd spread his blanket and sat heavily back down. "You okay, Collins? I mean, are you feeling poorly? You don't look so hot." No one seemed to be rehydrating the way she would have liked. She walked over to him and put a hand on his cheek. It was burning hot and damp with sweat.

He brushed her away. "Don't fuss. Just a long march, is all. Give me a few moments and I'll be right as rain."

"Have you heard? We're to have our first battle with the French tomorrow," he said, changing the subject.

Elise smiled. It was insane how excited everyone was for the next morning's fight. "You're going to make Amanda proud."

"Not just Amy, but little Edwina, and if I'm lucky, Edwina's babies too."

"That's right. You'll be telling your war stories to generations of Collinses."

Elise sighed as she stirred Mrs. Gillihan's stew. The army had been called to a halt after the 95th's exchange of shots, even though it was still early, and was now encamped in the fields outside of the ancient stone walls surrounding the town of Óbidos. The French troops were closer than they had anticipated, only a few miles away near the next town of Roliça. Had the English continued, they would have run up against the French rearguard, resulting in many more casualties than just the three men she'd cared for that afternoon. The British Army would camp, resting overnight while the higher-ups decided what the next step would be.

Only a few more days remained until the new moon. She couldn't wait. Avó's spell had to work. The more she heard people talk about the upcoming bloodshed, the more desperately she wanted to go home. Avó was powerful enough to make it happen—she was the scarab, wasn't she? Elise put a hand to her chest and pressed the emerald into her sternum as she gave the pot another couple of stirs. She couldn't be sure it wasn't her own heart, but she thought she felt the scarab pulse.

She'd taken over the job of cooking when Mrs. Gillihan took a long business trip to a bush after her expression changed in the space of sixty seconds from quiet thoughtfulness, to slow understanding, and settled on the face of a woman who'd be grumpy for the next few days. Elise glanced back at the moon, thankful that her IUD had followed her into the nineteenth century so she didn't have to deal with the mess of menstruation. She gave the willow bark tea she was steeping for Mrs. Gillihan a quick swirl, and set more water to boil for any other women who might need it.

Earlier that day, after sewing up Drake's thigh, Elise had entered Óbidos. She wanted to see it before the main column arrived—the men made it hard to trade for food when they ate everything available. And she needed to buy before the vendors figured out the difference between real currency and flattened buttons.

She'd managed to hustle a loaf of bread in the marketplace, and a wine skin full of wine from a tavern keeper, and spent the rest of the afternoon wandering cobbled streets hemmed in by white-washed homes. Eventually, she found a road that led her high enough to see beyond the orange tiled roofs to the surrounding countryside. She sat on the steps of a church, near the castle that dominated the town, and stared blankly at the charming homes that spilled down the hillside. She barely tasted the wine and crusty bread as she tried to forget that Drake had died.

She was going to be so glad when the nightmare was over, she thought as she stared into Mrs. Gillihan's campfire. Screwing Quidico would be a humiliation, but what was one more humiliation? She shouldn't have let herself be fooled by Drake's chirpy talk, or distracted by the doctor's call for help. She should have put the tourniquet on sooner.

No one blamed her, even though he died as she was sewing the last stitch on his thigh. Russell had coldly checked her work—a cadaver exercise at that point—and commended her on her "neat hand" in stitching. Jenkins had sniffed and given her more equipment to stuff into her pack, which she took to mean he'd finally resigned himself to her presence. And Thomas had awkwardly nodded at her before walking away. He wasn't speaking to her anymore anyway, not since she'd run from him that night on the beach.

Despite the wine that still sloshed in her sour stomach, Elise had been sharp enough to make herself scarce when the town slowly began to fill up with soldiers looking for trouble. In the fields, the women were setting up fire rings, and pulling out provisions. It was a comfort to return and be given practical tasks to do.

She stirred Mrs. Gillihan's pot and wiped her eyes and nose on her sleeve, hoping no one noticed.

They didn't.

"Dick! There you are," Bill called out as Richard approached from the town. He brightened to see his partner in music. "I wasn't sure you'd be joining us this evening."

"The officers've got their heads together, making plans. Best not to distract them."

Elise rolled her eyes. Lady Letchfeld had to attend to her own husband, apparently.

"Tell us what you've learned," Cox said. "You must have heard something we haven't."

"Well, one thing I've learned is there's no love lost between the Portuguese and the French. The reason that the locals have been so welcoming is because the French slaughtered everyone a town over—men, women, and even children."

"Bastards," Collins growled.

"We'll kill those frogs, won't we lads?" Bill said.

"We will, but you won't. You'll be picked off first thing."

"Shut your fat mouth, O'Brian," snapped Collins.

"Everyone knows it's the drummer boys and the color bearers that go first. They do it to lower morale." O'Brian shrugged. "That's just how it is."

"That's not true!" shouted Bill. "Tell him, lads. Tell him that's not true."

"Don't you fret, Billy," Thomas said quietly. "Musket rounds and cannon balls have got no names attached to them. It's any one of us as could die tomorrow."

Thomas had meant to be encouraging, but the silence that met this statement felt awful to Elise. "What else did you hear, Richard?" she asked.

"I heard the man as killed all those people is moving his forces to join that fellow we just ran into today, and sounds like they're close. Our Wellesley doesn't wish that to happen. He himself climbed to the top of a windmill on the other side of town and saw that we outnumber them as long as reinforcements don't arrive. If we put a wedge between the two French generals, they can be defeated separately, and then he'll lead us to Lisbon to roust out Marshal Junot and the rest of the frogs! If all goes well, we'll all be back in England before year's end!"

At the last pronouncement, the men cheered Sir Arthur Wellesley in particular, the British Army in general, and then, of course, each other.

After sharing Mrs. Gillihan's stew of salted beef and root vegetables, they spent their time drinking, gossiping and obsessively polishing their weapons late into the night, despite Richard's insistence on getting a good night's sleep. When everyone had finally settled into their blankets, fear began to well up in the silent spaces of the dwindling conversations. "How about you give us a song, MacEwan?" piped up Bill, a small voice in the dark night.

In the shadows cast by the dying campfire, Elise saw Thomas sit up and draw a hand through his hair. She closed her eyes, waiting for his soft baritone to wash over her.

"*The minstrel boy to the war is gone. In the ranks of death you will find him—*"

"Bloody hell, Tom! Not that one, for pity's sake," cried Collins.

You could hardly call it morning when they were roused off their blankets by Sergeant Taylor. Judging from the stars still wheeling in the heavens, it was night. No man would get up at such an ungodly hour unless the devil himself was coming to get him. Thomas grumpily folded his blanket and tied it to the top of his pack. Then he nudged Bill with the toe of his boot. When the lad stubbornly rolled over, pulling a corner of his blanket around his shoulders, Thomas smacked him with his shako until he finally groaned acceptance. "Up and get your drum," Thomas growled, replacing his hated, and now battered, hat back on his head. On the other side of the cold fire ring, he could see Elise was doing much the same to Richard.

There was no breakfast, and no one expected it, or even thought of it. After a hasty, but thorough inspection, the company fell in with the column to be marched a short distance farther south. By the time they reached their destination at the foot of an embankment of wooded hills, the sun was just beginning to rise. The army was louder now, and felt much more haphazard with the addition of raw Portuguese recruits into the infantry and calvary. Although they didn't mix with the more disciplined English soldiers, their enthusiasm was infectious. They were anxious to send the French packing and regain their country.

Most of the other camp followers—the women, children, and peddlers who floated in the army's wake—had remained behind, but Elise now traveled with Russell and Jenkins. Everyone on the medical team were working hard to turn a nearby farmhouse into a field hospital. Thomas caught glimpses of Elise moving furniture to the lawn, tossing dirty water from a bucket, rolling bandages on the front porch. He'd never seen her work so willingly before. She belonged with the healers, that was sure.

And he belonged with the fighters. Thomas sighed and shuffled his feet. He stood in a long line of men that stretched across a field strewn with boulders and edged by a pine forest. The problem with being a soldier was you fought only when told to fight, and the waiting was endless. He looked over at Richard to see how he was getting on, and snorted in laughter. "Dick, what have you done to your hair?"

"I've powdered it. I think it looks quite sharp, don't you? The Lady Letchfeld," he hissed, looking around to see who was in earshot, "was generous enough to lend me a bit of black ribbon to tie a queue. Luckily my hair has grown just long enough."

"That is lucky, indeed," Thomas said. Richard looked twenty years older with white hair, but perhaps that was what the lady preferred. It would explain her marriage to the elderly major.

"Quiet in the ranks!" snarled Sergeant Taylor. "The officers can't hear themselves think with you hens cackling. Eyes forward."

Thomas sighed. More mindless waiting then. He stared into the woods where they knew the French were gathered to his left. Wellesley's army was grouped in front, with the Portuguese forces under Colonel Trant to his right, and six cannons and a third large force under Ferguson and Bowes. Thomas suddenly realized that the army was positioned to enclose the French and defeat them from all sides. It would be a clever maneuver on Wellesley's part, if they could first get everyone in place—not an easy task when it involved eleven thousand men. Thomas thought of all the drilling they had undergone for exactly this reason. Had they not been drilled into stupefaction, there would be no way to organize a battle, much less a war.

Give the men some credit, he chastised himself. They were all good, bold lads. They would stand when lesser men would break the line. One only had to see the chaos within the ranks of the Portuguese to know the difference between good soldiers led well, and green soldiers with questionable leaders.

"No, I must insist." The sound of Major Letchfeld's voice drifted to Thomas as he approached with Lieutenant Mason, fresh and neat, having had a lovely night's sleep well billeted. All the details of the major's uniform were attended to—his jacket was brushed, his epaulettes dusted, his boots gleamed with fresh blacking. Marching their way over the broad expanse of the major's gut were freshly polished brass buttons. They were begging to be filched by Elise's sticky fingers, thought Thomas with a smile. And his hair, like Richard's, was freshly powdered. Thomas would have given anything to turn and look at the expression on Richard's face. It seemed Lady Letchfeld's powers of influence were strong.

"Pardon me for saying so," the lieutenant was saying to his superior, "but I cannot see the wisdom in ordering Mr. Russell to follow the flag. Who would replace him should the unthinkable happen?"

"The medical officers always follow the colors into battle. It's always been done," Letchfeld sputtered. He seemed surprised to be challenged on protocol.

"But these are modern times, sir, and modern times calls for modern warfare. Normal military tradition should not apply here."

Letchfeld attempted to draw himself higher, but there was really no point—he outranked Lieutenant Mason, who was being quite bold. He merely had to bark an order and that would be the end of it. "Modern war? *Modern war?* What is modern about leaving our wounded men on the battlefield without help? Is the indignity of being dragged from the field to a hospital a modern innovation? If that is modern, then may I say that I am proud to be old fashioned."

"Sir, I merely ask that you consider the loss of morale should our battalion lose its only surgeon. He cannot care for the men if he is dead, sir."

"Don't be ridiculous. The men don't give a damn whether they've a surgeon. They march with honor, without thought for their own lives. They fight for God and King, sir. *For God and King.* You would do well to look to your own men for your inspiration. I begin to question your mettle."

"You there!" the major turned sharply on his heel to address Cox, who shrank from the attention. "What do you think of this modern nonsense? Surely you'd rather Mr. Russell was with you on the battlefield?"

"Well, sir, I should like. . .that is to say. . ."

"Russell's predecessor would have never stood for it," Letchfeld continued, ignoring Cox's stuttered reply. "Did you know Mr. Williams, lieutenant? No? Of course not, but I can tell you Mr. Williams would never have stood for it. Now *he* was a great surgeon. He died a soldier's death, on the green with the lads, honorably, bravely, without a word of protest. He never would have stood for watching the action from the safety of a hospital."

"Did not Williams die instantly?" enquired Lieutenant Mason. "I believe a cannon ball ricocheted off the green and took his head clean off his shoulders."

"Just so," agreed Letchfeld. "God rest his brave soul. Never a word of complaint. Ah, devil take the French. There go the cannons now, there'll be action soon. Fetch Mr. Russell, if you please, lieutenant. At the double."

The rest of the army wasn't going to wait. Word of the advance came quickly and Letchfeld was brought his horse. Bill's drum began to roll along with the drums of other lads in other companies. Fifes began to trill. It was a heady sound, and put fire in the belly. The music compelled the feet to lift and move the body forward even when the mind doubted the wisdom of it all.

It was a slow march, and after twenty feet or so, they were called to volley rounds into the hillside. The English artillery sent cannon balls whizzing overhead and caused trees to explode into splinters. It was a terrific noise, but the French had the better position on top of the hill, and no soldier shooting upwards into trees could possibly do any damage to an enemy line. No matter how many times the stock of Thomas's musket slammed against his shoulder, it was still for nothing. He was more certain than ever that the goal was to make enough noise to keep the enemy's eyes on the center line, giving the flanking troops time to close the circle.

The enemy, however, situated on higher ground, was hitting targets with much more accuracy, and they weren't shy about firing back. Thomas couldn't see through the smoke, but the dread that fell over him made it clear men were dying. Skirmishers hidden behind the trees were picking them off, one by one. Every time he had to step to the right or left, he knew it was to close the gaps created when a man had fallen. Thomas blanched as the first cannon fire hit the line further east of where he was standing. The screams cut through him and the line jostled broadly as the men adjusted. He wondered if Mr. Russell was nearby. Perhaps Letchfeld was right—it did make him feel better to know he was there. It also made him feel terribly selfish to think such a thing.

It was midmorning when the French cannons stopped. Thomas's mouth was so dry he licked his lips, hoping to drink the sweat that ran in rivulets down his face. Instead he tasted blood on his cracked lips. His eyes burned from gun smoke. His ears rang. His arms and shoulders ached. Lack of sleep and lack of food made it difficult for his legs to hold him steady. But, thus far, he was still alive.

"Hold your fire!" cried Sergeant Taylor. The valley echoed with the same orders made by other sergeants all down the line. The French had not been fooled by Wellesley's trick. They'd fallen back, slipping out of the closing circle, and now the British were advancing once again through a field of boulders and into a thick expanse of trees. "Stay together," Sergeant Taylor called as they marched forward.

Thomas broke file to walk around a three-foot tall block of granite. Sometimes, it just wasn't practical to follow orders.

"Out of the question," Russell said to Elise, hand up, eyes closed to argument. "Absolutely not. You will stay here and await the first casualties." She watched him trot away with Jenkins and Lieutenant Mason and waited until they were twenty paces ahead before leaving the safety of the farmhouse to follow into the already raging battle.

As she ran, the occasional spent musket ball fell out of the sky to bounce off her chest. The first one made her stumble in fear, the second one made her feel invincible, and the third made her realize how foolish it was to be running towards the front line where last she saw Russell before he was cloaked from view by clouds of gun smoke.

She saw him again when a small breeze stirred the smoke. He was setting up his station near the standard-bearer, which, Elise realized with a start, was the precursor of a red-cross banner of first aid. Next to the standard bearer, Bill kept up a rolling drumbeat. Elise could see his stiff back, and her heart ached as he stood banging away on his drum, exposed and vulnerable. Although the colors weren't being flown for the sake of the surgeons, it still worked well as a marker for finding help, and the wounded were already stumbling towards it.

The shattering noise of the battlefield filled Elise's head and squeezed her chest, making her gasp for each breath as she approached Russell. She threw herself to the ground under the rain of another volley of musket fire, one hand on her pack, one hand pressing the emerald against her sternum, and struggled to adjust to the crashing cannonade. The trill of the fifes playing "Hey Johnnie Cope," over and over drilled through her skull. Smoke burned her eyes and throat. It wasn't until she saw a wounded soldier stumbling towards her that she was able to pull herself together. She army-crawled towards a boulder where she could hunker down and work safe from being shot.

With protection at her back, she could start to concentrate again. She watched the line for men to fall out, allowing her time to mentally prepare for what was coming as soldiers dragged their broken bodies towards her. She formed a small team with Russell and Jenkins, working separately but close enough that equipment could be shared, tossed back and forth as needed. Elise was terrified something might happen to either of them—there were thousands of soldiers and so few medical personnel.

Her patient was weeping in pain as he stumbled away, making room for the next man. There hadn't been anything she could do but tie a sling around his shattered arm. How long would it take for someone to circle back and care for the soldier properly? Too long, she thought, knowing there would be no possibility to save the limb.

The morning lasted years. The battle seemed endless. It was an all-consuming ocean with no edges. When the cannons finally stopped, it took a while for Elise's bones to stop shaking in sympathetic resonance. Tears rolled silently down her cheeks in relief, but she didn't have the luxury of taking a breath. She was too busy pushing her probing finger into a hole in someone's flesh to feel for a musket ball. She stole a quick look at the troops, and was puzzled by their restlessness. As she drove her forceps into the hole, she prayed the battle was over. "Easy, honey," Elise soothed as she pulled out the ball. His lips peeled away from his gritted teeth in silent pain and he bucked against his mates who held him pinned down on his back.

Suddenly the drums began a different rhythm. The earth vibrated as the men began marching again, pushing forward. Elise's heart sunk. It wasn't over.

What started out as an organized advancement quickly turned messy as the men were forced to move around obstacles in the field. The lines fell apart. Through the smoke, one man drew her attention as he stopped to adjust his pack. He was the only one with enough self-possession to resist the forward thrust of the mob and just stand alone like a stone in a stream for the simple pleasure of taking the time to remove his hat and run his hand through his hair. Although dressed like the others, he remained singular, unique. For the length of a breath, there were no others in the world but that one man.

She wasn't the only one to have noticed Thomas. Running perpendicular to the army from the direction of the trees, a French skirmisher was headed straight towards him with his saber drawn. Forty feet away, he crouched stealthily and circled to approach Thomas from behind. Elise knew Thomas could lay the Frenchman flat in seconds, but only if he saw him. Turn around, she begged him in her thoughts.

She didn't hear the musket rounds whizzing past her ears. She didn't feel the scarab, tucked between her breasts, pulse red heat to her arms and legs. She was already running when she made the decision to run. She was reaching for her knife before she remembered she was carrying it. Her mind was five steps behind her body.

Just as Elise leaped on Frenchman's back, Thomas pivoted. His blue eyes were vividly framed by the black gun smoke that smeared his cheeks. His lips drew away from his teeth in a wolfish snarl as he ducked under the wide and wild swing of the skirmisher's saber. Over the man's shoulder, Elise saw Thomas's blade flash as he stepped inside to punch his bayonet up through his opponent's gut. Her own knife came down into the skirmisher's neck.

It was almost too late when he saw her. Thomas just barely succeeded in shifting his bayonet six inches to the side; his forward momentum sent him crashing into the Frenchman. The three of them tumbled to the ground.

Instinct made Thomas jump up and reach for his weapon before reaching to check his anger. "Bloody hell, woman. What are you playing at? I could have speared you both!"

"Get him off me!" Elise struggled to get out from under the skirmisher's weight. Her arm was pinned. She couldn't breathe. Thomas lifted the body and tossed it aside with no more effort than he would give to sweeping a cat off the kitchen table.

"Get the hell back to camp." Thomas pushed her roughly as she struggled to get to her feet and she fell back to the ground. "Go on with you!"

"I couldn't let him kill you!"

"So you thought you'd save me? I can take care of myself!"

Her knife. She needed her knife back. She crawled over to the body and saw the skirmisher's face for the first time. His eyes were open in death, clear brown orbs in the middle of a dimpled face. "He's just a kid." She touched his cheek, barely old enough for stubble.

Thomas kicked the body out from under her hand, making her recoil in shock. "Never look in their faces when you kill them," he said, pulling Elise's knife from the boy's neck. The squelching noise made her feel sick. "They'll haunt your dreams if you do."

"Jesus," she breathed. "How many people have you killed?"

"I've no regrets for any of them. I made London a better place."

He wiped the knife off in the grass and offered it back to Elise. She reached to take it and saw her hand was caked in blood; the blood of the men she'd patched was now mingled with the blood of the boy she just killed. Her stomach clenched violently, her shoulders heaved.

"I don't have time for this," Thomas snapped. "Don't go soft on me now. Take the knife." He shook it impatiently at her. "Take it!" Suddenly he grabbed her arm and dragged her behind a boulder as shots rang out again from the trees. A ball ricocheted off the rock just as they huddled down together to wait for the smattering of musket fire to pass.

"How 'bout a smoke?" Elise squeaked, a weak joke. She touched his breast pocket, feeling for the clay pipe she knew was there.

Thomas ignored her question. He lifted her skirt and sheathed her knife against her leg.

"He was going to kill you. I couldn't let you die," Elise said again.

"Because you really wanted a nice, long smoke."

"That's right." Elise attempted a smile but was distracted by the blood on her hands. She tried to wipe them off on the grass. "He was just a boy," she whispered, looking at the body. It jerked as rounds sunk into it.

"It was a boy's foolishness to think he could sneak up on me, but he still would have cut me down like a man if he'd caught me. There's not a thing to feel badly about. If you hadn't killed him, I would have."

"Where are you going?" Elise clutched his coat when he stood, alarmed that he would leave the shelter of the boulder.

He peeled off her hand and quickly stepped to the body to pull off the boy's boots. "These should fit you," he said, returning. "You should check his pack. There might be something you could use."

Reluctantly, Elise reached for the boots but ended up heaving a second time. The emerald seared painfully against her sternum as her bile rose.

"Don't do that; don't lose your iron," Thomas urged gently. "You're always going on about needing shoes. Now you've got them. What did you expect, Elise? That we'd all be murdering each other with warm smiles? Stay steady, do you hear me? It's not over yet. The French have withdrawn to a better position and it's going to be harder to roust them out. If the officers don't get it right, we'll be cut down."

Elise looked at him, alarmed. His words weren't helping to reassure her.

"Go back to that farmhouse. That's where you belong. I need to know you'll be safe so I can rejoin the company."

"I can't go back."

"You'll do as I say."

"I can't let you die, Thomas."

He pushed his hair back. A smile played under the scar on his cheek. "So, now you're the one looking out for me?" he asked gently. "Go back and wait until the fighting's done, then come find me."

"That's not—"

"A dead healer's no good to anyone. That fool Letchfeld shouldn't have sent the surgeon to march with the colors. It's damned short-sighted. If the lads can't make it to the farmhouse, they're needing the sweet arms of their maker, not a healer." He stopped Elise with a fierce look as she took a breath to argue. "I mean what I say. Wait until the fighting's done, then come find me. You can help me pull the wounded back down the hill."

Thomas touched her open palm, then lifted her hand into his own to squeeze just for a second before dropping it and bashfully shoving his fist into his trouser pocket. "You'll come looking for me?" His voice was pleading. His blue eyes pierced her.

"I'll find you," she whispered.

He nodded and sucked in a deep breath. Then rolled his shoulders under the weight of his pack and readjusted the straps. "They'll think me a bloody coward if I don't get to the front," he mumbled. Elise felt a wrenching ache as Thomas fell in with the other soldiers.

Hiding In the Bushes

The second Thomas left Elise's side, the world came crashing back. She was almost surprised to see soldiers rushing past the boulder where she sheltered, on their way to make a second stand. The enemy fire had let off as the French rear guard had fallen back. She rose into a half crouch to look over her boulder and scanned the field for Jenkins and Russell, her promise to return to the farmhouse already forgotten.

"Where in the hell have you been?" Russell demanded when she jogged up to where she'd set up her medical station. "Jenkins has already started advancing with the color guard. Let's go."

Elise couldn't wait for everyone to stop yelling at her and start thanking her. She shoved ribbons of bandages back into her pack and shrugged it on.

As the army advanced, wounded men dropped and were stepped around and left behind. Trotting from fallen man to fallen man, Elise stayed well behind the front line while Jenkins followed the flag and Russell split the difference between them.

To Elise, the men didn't look like "England's finest" in their boiled red wool, despite their pride of uniform. They just looked hot and haggard. The late morning sun shone brutally down on black felted shakos, boiling everyone's brains which might have explained why the soldiers still carried their packs, despite being actively engaged in combat. As a matter of principle, Elise pulled the red coats off every man who could walk to her for help, and cut the coats off those who were carried and dropped at her feet, no matter where their wound was located. Every single one of the them begged for her to leave their jackets alone, but only after they first begged for a drink. She closed her ears to their pleas. The two canteens she'd filled that morning were empty, and wearing wool in the summer was just plain stupid.

Despite the conditions, the English were winning. The French retreated not once, but twice, both times reaching better positions on hilltops. By late afternoon, the enemy was outnumbered, outmaneuvered, and full-on running, leaving behind their cannons and anything else they couldn't drag along quickly.

But for the small medical team, the job continued. Elise looked up into the ascending trees as she finished wrapping a bandage around the large forehead of a short man who was explaining the advantages of accepting his marriage proposal—mostly the enticing promise of a hovel full of children. "I'm already married," she muttered, too preoccupied to give her patient much attention. Thomas was somewhere in the thick woods above her. Her stomach was clenched with anxiety. She would have left immediately to go find him, but was too busy bandaging the head of a man already brainless.

"If you find your husband has not survived the day, please think of me," requested the soldier.

Elise's head whipped back around to look into his earnest face. The guy had balls. "You're all set. You can rejoin your company now."

He squeezed her thigh meaningfully. "I'll not forget your kindness this day. Was your husband in Colonel Lake's division? If so, there's very little likelihood that he has survived. If you've not heard, the fool charged his men up the hill prematurely, nearly costing Wellesley the entire battle. They were all killed or taken prisoner. Lake himself, God rest his soul, didn't make it through the day."

Elise felt her stomach twist more tightly. It was one thing to see the wounded and work actively to patch them up. It was entirely different to hear a story and be left wondering the truth of it. The hand on her thigh tightened like a shackle. "I can see you're concerned. There's no need for worry. You'll be a good wife to me, I can tell."

"Do you want to keep your hand?" Elise asked with a smile.

He blinked at her in confusion, then let go of her thigh when he noticed she was brandishing a scalpel over his wrist. When it finally registered he'd been rejected, his mouth twisted in anger. "You've made a big mistake. I was taking pity on you, nothing more. You're hideous— nothing but sinew and bones. And your nose is much too big. Pity your poor husband. I'm sure he wishes he were dead, even if he weren't."

Elise watched him stalk away, the end of his bandage trailing from his head like a white flag. Much of what he'd said, with the exception of the insult about her nose, was true. She was nothing but skin and bones, especially after all the marching they'd done. Richard was definitely pitiable, given the loss of his business and pride. What's more, Richard could be dead. Her entire company could be dead, for all she knew. She looked back up into the trees. She had to go find Thomas.

"Where are you going, Mrs. Ferrington?" Russell called from fifteen feet away. It was now impossible to tell the freckles that dotted his nose from the splattered blood across his face.

"I'm. . . MacEwan. . ." she pointed up the hill, too tired to form a sentence.

"Private MacEwan just passed by not two minutes ago. He looked straight at you. Didn't you see him? He was headed to the hospital with wounded. You might as well go there yourself. I'll be along shortly."

Thomas looked right at her and didn't stop. Elise sighed. She rummaged in her pack and found, buried under rolls of bandages and rattling spools of thread, a small vial of her rainy-day rum. It was, officially, a rainy day.

It had taken seven hours for the army to advance to the base of the third hill, but only fifteen minutes to return to the hospital where Elise had started the day. Even so, she was confronted with the results of the war before she even reached the converted farmhouse. There were so many wounded being carried off the battlefield that the hospital couldn't take them all inside. Instead, they were placed under the shade of trees to wait their turn. Piles of them huddled together, many dying slowly.

Elise stood on the edge of the farmyard, trying to steady her breathing as she surveyed the carnage. No one was separating the wounded by those who most urgently needed help. Soldiers who'd been assigned the job of aiding the surgeons would appear in the open doorway, toss a leg or an arm onto the pile that was growing near the front steps, and haul inside another wounded man to take the place of whoever just lost a limb. Whichever man was closest to the door won the prize of a second chance at life. It was as simple as that.

A heavy hand squeezed her shoulder, making her jump. "Steady-on, Mrs. Ferrington." George Russel looked at her in concern. It hadn't taken long for him to catch up to her. Despite the grueling day, his jaw was set for the next stage of tending to the troops. "You should take a rest. No one will fault you if you don't go inside. It's no place for a woman."

"Have you heard of triage?"

He shook his head.

"It's where someone separates the wounded so that those closest to death are served first to save their life, whereas those without life-threatening issues, a broken finger or a twisted ankle or whatever, get served last."

"That seems reasonable. Did Bill Stanton make it through? You go rest and send Bill along to do triage."

"It takes someone with medical knowledge to triage. Otherwise mistakes get made. Some things you have to know to look for, blood pressure, heart rate, that kind of thing. If you miss a sign, people can die. Let me stay out here and sort the wounded, but tell everyone inside they have to take whoever I tell them to take."

"I merely ask that you allow us to rest by occasionally sending in a man with insignificant ailments after every third mortal wound." He threw up his hand as Elise drew a breath to argue. "If you queue up all the difficult cases, you'll exhaust the surgeons."

Elise reluctantly agreed to throw in something straightforward after every five hard cases.

"Good. Then I'll tell the others. 'Triage' did you say? Sounds French. I wonder if Napoleon knows of this."

"I think he does," Elise said with a slow smile, suddenly remembering a bit of nursing trivia she learned in school.

As soon as Russell disappeared through the farmhouse door, Elise began the heartbreaking work of organizing the wounded into categories. She started calling the lawn the "waiting room," and pulled other able-bodied men into helping her move those who couldn't move themselves. It renewed her spirit to do something she was trained to do without being second-guessed by the stifling culture or hindered by inconveniences. By the time the sun was setting, most of the men had been pulled off the battlefield and placed into three categories of gore: those likely to live no matter what, those unlikely to live no matter what, and those who straddled the middle and needed immediate care.

No one noticed as she stepped through the door to the make-shift hospital, which was as it should be. The medical staff was too preoccupied with saving lives to see that a ragged woman in French skirmisher's boots was taking in the scene. From the doorway, Elise could see that the first floor had just two large rooms. One of the rooms had a few scattered chairs. The other held a kitchen table, solid and wide, reminding her of the deeply scored table in the kitchen of the Quiet Woman. Spread out on the table was a soldier, pinned to the wooden slats by Thomas's powerful hands. Thomas was listening, along with two other gentlemen, to a senior surgeon who was gesturing with a hacksaw while delivering a lecture. Scattered in all the corners of the room, other surgeons made repairs to bleeding men while keeping one ear open to the man pontificating at the table. Blood stood in puddles everywhere.

"There you are," Russell smiled, tying the last knot for a patient who grimaced behind a leather strap held between his teeth. "What do you say? Four hundred? Five hundred wounded?"

"About that," replied Elise.

"Did you hear that?" he called to the other medical personnel. "Only four or five hundred wounded!" A loud cheer went up.

"Damn that Colonel Lake," grumbled an older man as he splinted a broken arm. "It'd be half that if it hadn't been for his stupidity."

They worked deep into the night, and when the last man's wound was dressed, they worked longer to bed them all down comfortably. Elise tried to maintain a semblance of cleanliness, pulling water from the well outside and mopping the floor with a rag tied to a broom, organizing supplies, and helping wherever she was called to help. Later, she made herself available as the patients tried to sleep, giving water to the thirsty, checking bandages, calling over doctors when wounds that had been missed were discovered.

As morning light started to creep in through the windows, visitors arrived. Men wanted to see that their fallen companions had survived the night. Usually, they didn't stay long, leaving broken-hearted even when finding their friends alive—if the men had spent the night in the hospital, prospects weren't great. Just as the morning started to clang with noise from the camp, Richard came in, dragging a feverish Collins. Elise immediately removed him from Richard's supporting arms and bedded him down outside, behind the house and well away from the other soldiers.

Soon after Richard had left, Lady Letchfeld stepped inside with a large basket artfully hung over her arm. Elise's head jerked up to see the elegant woman, clear-eyed and well rested, lift her silk skirts over the mess of bloody gauze that kept accumulating on the floor. She passed out salted beef and sips of water to a few of the men, tucked them into their blankets, then swept out again, leaving behind a sweet scent of rosewater and a haughty grimace directed towards Elise. For the surgeons, she left wineskins and fresh loaves of bread.

"What an angel," called a soldier breathlessly from the corner. "A beautiful angel of mercy. An angel of light, she is."

Tears pricked Elise's eyes. She didn't do her job for the praise, but to have it directed towards the undeserving felt like a slap in the face. Her dress was stiff with men's blood; her hair was crusted with the salt of sweat; her mind was shadowed by images she'd never be able to erase. But Betsy Letchfeld, fresh as a lily, was the one the men gushed over. It was too much. Elise threw down her mop, causing heads to swing around to look at her. "I've been slaving away for twenty hours straight," she shouted, pointing at the hapless soldier. "What did she do for you? Nothing! She comes in here and breezes around a little, and suddenly she's the one you call an 'angel of light?' She's your Florence

Nightingale? I fucking saved your life!"

"Mrs. Ferrington," George Russell shouted. "Apologize at once."

"Who's Florence?" asked the soldier.

Elise laughed in disbelief. "Apologize for what? For pointing out injustice? If you're going to be doling out praise all willy-nilly, how about sending some over here. I mean, look at me. Look at this," she waved her arms in a wild gesture to encompass the entire world. "This is going to give me nightmares for the rest of my life. And it's Lady Letchfeld who—"

"She's the major's wife!" croaked the indignant soldier in the corner. "A right gentlewoman, unlike you."

"Well then, fiiiineee. I apologize for besmirching the name of a woman who was lucky enough to be born wealthy." She bent over in an exaggerated curtsy. Movement in her peripheral vision caused her to whirl around. Thomas was approaching her with the same kind of care she'd seen him take countless other times at the bar when a patron had had too much to drink. "I'm warning you: do not check me." He froze. Was he trying not to smile?

"Let her be," sighed Russell. "She's earned the right to grouse. Get on with you, Mrs. Ferrington. Go take a rest. You too, Thomas."

Elise tried to slam a roll of muslin down in anger, but it floated lightly to the ground, unraveling in a pretty coil and making her angrier.

"Such a coarse woman," she heard someone say in a loud whisper as she stormed away.

"Indeed. Shocking."

Her bath was a cold bucket of well water and a stiff curry brush she found in the barn behind the house—a far cry from the long soak in a hot tub that she longed for. She wanted to burn her clothes, but settled with scrubbing her dress the best she could with it still on. Her apron had taken most of the gore, she was happy to note, sparing her dress the worst of it. She doused her apron in the bucket and wrung red water out. Diluted blood pooled between her feet as she sweated to get clean. Behind her, the queue of soldiers that had formed for their turn at the well were beginning to make noises for her to hurry up.

There were sweaty men everywhere, thousands of them dotting the landscape like zits on a teenager. Elise pulled off her boots and scrubbed her feet and legs, feeling self-conscious. She hadn't thought about Quidico since Collins had chased him away, but she knew he was there, hidden somewhere, looking at her. It was strange to think that she'd be back in Tucson soon. She'd be able to use real shampoo and shave her legs. She'd get a pedicure. She'd go to the grocery store and buy pasteurized milk and a box of fruity-ohs while wearing nothing but shorts and a tank top. She'd eat bowl after bowl of the cereal in the bathtub.

Dropping the horse's brush into the bucket, she kicked it to the next man in line and walked across the camp to find someplace quiet to take a nap. Not far from the farmhouse rose an enormous oak, its base surrounded by a stand of deep green rhododendrons. Elise threw her boots and pack over the densely crowded bushes and pushed her way under. The roots of the tree created a small clearing, nearly as big as a king sized bed. The ground was soft with moss and sheltered from the sun. Finally, she had her privacy. She pulled her dress off and hung it and her soaked apron over bushes to dry in the sun, then stretched out in her chemise, bone weary.

Just as she was about to descend into the sweet oblivion of sleep, the sound of feet scraping to a stop outside the rhododendrons made her jerk alert. She caught her breath and peered under the greenery. Although they were the same army-issue shoe that every infantryman in the British Army wore, she recognized the feet as they walked to the other side of the tree. The gait was light, slightly splay-footed, with a surprisingly short stride for a tall man, as though ready to change direction at a moment's notice. The toes turned to point towards her.

"Elise? I know you're in there. Why are you hiding in the bloody bushes?"

"Because I'm tired of people looking at me."

"I told you to go back to the farmhouse."

"I did, after I finished my job. I was going to come find you. Why didn't you wait for me?"

"You were busy making eyes at that soldier."

Elise sighed, remembering the marriage proposal she rejected. "Come in here, you idiot. I'm not talking to you through a bush."

"Bloody hell." His curse was the gruff equivalent of a shoulder shrug.

"This way." Elise reached her hand under the bush so he could see where the entrance was. Grunting, Thomas lowered his chest to the dirt and poked his head through, eyeballing the narrow passageway with skepticism. Seeing his glowering face framed under the greenery made Elise snort.

"You must take me to be a fool. There's no room for me in there."

"There's plenty of room. You'll see."

He pushed his pack in first, then passed a skin of wine under the bush.

"You've been drinking? You never drink."

"I'm not drinking," was his gruff, embarrassed lie. "Help me in." His hand reached for her and she pulled while he kicked and squirmed through the opening. Suddenly, the little clearing around the base of the oak seemed much smaller. Thomas brushed dust and broken twigs from the front of his shirt and sat cross-legged next to her, looking around and nodding in approval. "Quiet little spot," he said. "Leave it to the rabbit to find a safe hole."

"I'm not a rabbit."

His blue eyes swept her up and down, assessing. "You're right. More like a porcupine, I reckon." Thomas rearranged his pack to give them more space and scooted himself backwards to sit behind her, leaning against the trunk of the tree. "Care for a smoke?"

"Oh, hell *yes*," Elise said.

The silence that rose between them felt comfortable as she watched him pull his pipe out and fill it with three pinches of tobacco, the first gentle, the second more firm, and the last a deep squeeze into the bowl. "Damn, I've no flame," Thomas said suddenly. "Wait here, I'll be right back." He had some trouble wiggling out of the clearing on his own, but once he was back on his feet he growled through the bush, "do not touch my wine whilst I'm gone."

Elise froze with the wine skin already at her lips, then went ahead and took a deep gulp. "There wasn't much left!" she called, and smiled at the curse she got in response.

It didn't take long for him to return with a lit pipe, a second skin of wine, and a loaf of bread. "Where did you get all this?" Elise sighed in wonder at the bounty.

"I stole it."

She couldn't tell if he was kidding, and decided not to press.

Thomas again leaned back against the oak and spread his legs to either side of where Elise sat cross-legged. They passed the pipe back and forth and the smoke rose prettily up into the canopy of leaves. The wine was cool and sweet. It opened her pores and flushed her skin. The bread was warm and aromatic. Not five hours ago, she'd taken a leg and thrown it out the front door of a farmhouse, but now the softness of the moment was blurring the edges of the memory.

"Where is Richard?" Thomas asked, breaking the spell. "He should be here. It's not for me to be sitting with you like this, in the bushes no less. You're not even decently dressed."

Elise blew smoke over Thomas's scowling face. "Come on, we were having a nice time. Don't ruin it." Thomas knew full well where Richard was—he was sneaking off somewhere with his Lady Letchfeld and making reckless plans. Later, it wouldn't be his violin he would be fiddling.

"He should treat you with more respect," Thomas grumbled.

"I think you've had enough," Elise laughed, taking back the wine. "He does treat me with respect. He's never tried to kill me for the emerald. I'd call that pretty respectful."

"How do you know he hasn't asked me to do it for him?"

Elise sputtered on a badly timed swallow. "Did he? When?"

In response, Thomas twisted a fold of her chemise into his fist and pulled her towards him to cage her between his legs. His other hand clamped around her neck. His palm was warm against her throat, his fingers pressed along either side of her spine. She looked into his eyes as he squeezed gently, a caress.

"You're not frightened?"

"Of you? No."

Thomas's mouth turned up at one corner, stretching the white scar bisecting his lip. "I'll kill you and Richard both and keep the emerald for myself. Don't think I won't." His hand squeezed tighter. Elise felt the pressure on her larynx and had a flash of doubt. Then he let go to steal the wine back. "To hell with you, you hateful wretch," he said affectionately, taking a long sip. "How dare you not fear me?"

Elise leaned against his thigh and sucked air through the stem of his pipe. "It's cashed," she said, and knocked the ashes out on a root.

His hand slid under her hair to pull a lock of it forward and let it slide through his fingers. "Where did you get such a lion's mane?" he murmured.

His scent was like smudged sage. Elise took a deep breath and the emerald pressed hot against her breastbone.

"You don't want it?" The jewel appeared in her hand, although she hadn't thought to pull it from her breast and didn't remember doing so. It glowed eerily in the shadow of the oak.

"No, I'll not touch that devilish stone. It's brought nothing but pain to all of us. Why would I want it?"

"Money."

"Look at it move. It's alive."

"That's just the pulse in my hand."

"Think what you will, but I'll believe it's living and breathing. Put it away."

Elise studied Thomas's features. As usual, he was unreadable. "Maybe Richard's just hoping I die on my own," she said tucking the emerald back into her corset. "That's a pretty good gamble, I suppose."

Thomas shrugged.

"I don't want another day like today. I feel like I've been battered. I don't think I can do this again."

He pulled another of her curls forward just to see it rebound when he let go. His eyes crinkled in a smile. "It's not today anymore. It's tomorrow."

"No wonder I'm so tired."

Thomas nodded in agreement and settled his broad shoulders against the trunk of the tree. "Are you sure you don't want to join the others? Mrs. Gillihan will be wanting to see you." He tugged off his red jacket and rolled his sleeves up over his strong arms. The buttons of his shirt strained across his chest as he filled his lungs with a long, exhausted yawn, and his black hair fell into his eyes. "It's beginning to warm up, isn't it?"

"Oi!" Thomas cried out in surprise, rubbing the back of his head after it had cracked against the tree. His blue eyes flashed angrily. "What do you mean by lunging at me like that?"

"Oh God, I'm sorry. I didn't mean—"

"Have you gone completely mad? I've already a knot on my head from a week ago."

Elise hid her face in her hands, muffling her apology and feeling ridiculous. Through her fingers she could see him glaring at her. Slowly, his initial shock melted from his features as understanding bloomed. "Were you meaning to. . ." His eyes narrowed with suspicion. He took her wrists and gently tugged her hands from her face. "You *were*. You were aiming for a kiss, weren't you?"

His long black lashes shaded the emotion that shone in his eyes. That, and the mop of hair he constantly struggled against. Elise would have brushed away his forelock for him but he held tightly to her wrists. Instead, she leaned forward, uncertain how she'd be received a second time, but determined to find out.

His mouth was surprisingly soft, but unresponsive. He dropped her wrists like he'd been burned.

Elise placed her hands on his shoulders and breathed his name in his ear like a question. She tried to meet his evasive eyes. His shoulders trembled. His hands balled into self-resistant fists. "I'll not be drawn in," he whispered. "You're a married woman."

"Richard doesn't love me," she reminded him. "He's never loved me." She slid her fingertips along his jaw, tilting his chin so that he would look at her. "But you do. I know you do."

Elise gasped as Thomas suddenly crushed her to him and buried himself in the crook of her neck, breathing in the scent of her. He raked his hands through her hair, then slid them over her arms and up her back, as though he couldn't get enough but didn't know where to start. Her name was strangled deep in his throat, a hoarse mangling of vowels that ended in expelled breath. Then he placed his palms against the sides of her face and kissed her.

It burned. It dissolved her into particles then rebuilt her, airless and gutless, empty of everything but rushing blood and flesh. Tasting his kiss was like tasting smoke curling over her tongue, flavored with clove, leather, and gunpowder. The kiss made her eyes close and her fingers spread open. It made her arch her back and thrust her hips. When he left her lips, she clutched at him for balance as he painted her skin with his mouth and tugged at her chemise.

She pulled herself back just enough to help him. There were ribbons and knots and stays, all complicated notions that made it impossible to undress quickly. But he, at least, had buttons. She could manage buttons.

She pushed away his shirt and was confronted with the history of his violence. A long scar crossed against his hard stomach, another parted the black fur along his breastbone. The third floated over his ribcage, white and thin like the silk thread that had once tied him together. But here along his flank was the last place she'd touched him, weeks ago. She'd reticently kept her hands right here, sewing his skin together along the gaping knife wound he'd earned saving her life. Now the stitches were gone, but shadows of them remained as tiny dots where she had pierced his flesh with a needle. She ran a finger along each suture line, and he sucked in a long breath. She was piercing his flesh, even now.

Thomas flipped her underneath him and the earth rose up to meet her. He reached down to pull her skirt higher as her burning spine sunk into the cool moss. Elise wrapped her legs around his waist and set the rhythm, encouraging him with her thighs and hips. She led until her vision blurred and her breath exploded. Then, when his mouth covered hers again, she gave herself to his pleasure.

THE NEW MOON

Thomas and Elise didn't get much sleep.

It was three, maybe four hours before the call came to march again. They dressed quickly, heads reeling with the wine, with their thoughts, with the scent of each other. He was the first to crawl underneath the bushes and back into the world so he could rush to line up for inspection. Elise paused to breathe before pulling her damp dress over her head and crawling out, knowing she'd be heading to the hospital where her own needs would be set aside for hours.

She found George Russell in the same place she'd left him, making her wonder if he'd allowed himself some rest. He was busy prepping patients to travel with the moving army. His eyes were bloodshot and his face was pale, but his energy hadn't flagged. "I know you'd like to stay with your husband," he said, smiling at her as she walked towards him, "but you'll be traveling with us instead. I hope you've already said your goodbyes."

The recent memory of her long goodbye crashed over her, sending zinging currents of electricity down her arms and into her hands. She took a deep breath. "Aren't we all going to Lisbon?"

"No longer. We're heading back to the beach. We've word that more ships are arriving and Wellesley wishes to protect the disembarkation of the new forces and send these wounded men home. The army will be moving quickly, too quickly for us, burdened as we are." He waved an arm encompassing the soldiers who could no longer walk.

"I want to be with my husband," Elise said quietly, knowing it was a lie. It was Thomas she wanted to be near.

"I appreciate your loyalty, but your husband will be marching overnight without stopping. Even if you wished to see him, there would not be time."

Elise turned and took two wistful steps towards the troops as they lined up.

"It's no use," Russell said gently. "They're already as good as gone."

Elise sighed in resignation and went to find Jenkins, who would help refill her pack so she'd have the necessary supplies for nursing along the road. That was it, she thought, that's all she'd get. That moment she just had with Thomas was her sweet goodbye. There wouldn't be time to see him again before the new moon and if the spell worked, she'd be gone forever.

If the spell didn't work, she would leave the army and head to Lisbon on her own. There, she'd sell the emerald and buy passage to the States. Either way, there wouldn't be a second time with Thomas. She might as well get used to it.

She should have been excited to be so near the end of her nightmare, so close to returning to her old life, but instead she felt rocks in her stomach as she helped bed the men down in mule carts. She should have been planning for what was coming, but her thoughts constantly returned to the sun dappled afternoon. Each flash of memory churned her, flushed open her capillaries and flooded her mouth. As the carts rolled out and the miles along dusty trail began to slip behind her, the sensation caused by recreating scenes in her mind from that afternoon with Thomas became an addiction. She hated herself for going back to it, over and over.

While the infantry continued through the night, the men and women following them camped in the fields after traveling miles of gently rolling hills. Elise bunched a blanket under her head and tried to make herself comfortable in the dirt. The night air was warm, full of the scent of wild rosemary and sage, and hinted at the ocean nearby. The gnarled trunks of small plots of tied grapevines, standing like crippled soldiers in formation, were eerily silhouetted by the thinly slivered moon. While everyone slept under the stars, Elise stared at the sky.

A dark shadow passed in front of the stars making the sky flicker like a disruption in the electrical current. Elise sat up in alarm, her heart pounding. "Who's there?" she hissed, straining to see in the darkness.

No one.

Cautiously, she laid back down. Her heartbeat slowed. Her eyes became heavy again. A log fell in a nearby campfire and the sound of sparks drew from her a sighing yawn. Exhaustion draped across her like a veil of brightly colored scarves caught on a breeze. Long black hair tickled her arms. A hand caressed her cheek. She opened her eyes again. Quidico smiled and held out his hand for her to see the green beetle in his palm.

"This night," he whispered, "I swallow my grandmother so that tomorrow night, when you swallow me, we will all live as one for eternity." He placed the metallic beetle in his mouth. His golden eyes locked with Elise's green eyes. His Adam's apple bobbed unpleasantly. "Come to us tomorrow night. We will await you. Follow the sound of our music."

Elise woke up in the early morning with a painful kink in her shoulder and a low-grade tension headache. Her midnight encounter with Quidico, if it had truly been an encounter and not just a nightmare, haunted her. Quidico was like the blister women endured for a new pair of snakeskin heels. The horrible thought of what she'd promised to do with him to gain her freedom from the nineteenth century weighed on her as she walked the final miles.

It was late in the afternoon when they finally reached the beach. Despite having been anxious to leave the shore just days earlier, Elise was relieved to see the ocean again. Ships were anchored just off shore, and along the beach teemed fifteen thousand souls all worked to prepare for them to disembark. No one noticed when Elise and the medical team quietly began their own operations for returning the wounded to England.

Elise wanted nothing more than to find her company, and by extension, Thomas, but there was no time. Four more wounded had died during their march, and others were in bad shape after the bone-jarring journey in mule carts. She'd insisted on being the only one to care for Peter Collins, confident that she was vaccinated against whatever it was he had. And now George Russell was ordering her to be the personal nurse of some hoity-toity who was too sick to come to shore, making any free moments she may have had to say her goodbyes impossible."

"I can't go," Elise said, flatly refusing.

"What do you mean? Why ever not?"

"I've got other plans."

It was a dumb excuse, but his demand had taken her by surprise. Plus, her headache had grown, making it difficult to think of a plausible lie.

"What plans could you have possibly made that can't be cancelled or delayed? A cutter from HMS *Brazen* is already waiting for you on the beach. You're to leave immediately."

"Now?"

"Yes, Mrs. Ferrington. Now."

"The thing is, I really do have this super-awful headache and—"

"To the devil with your headache and all your other excuses!" Russell exploded. "For once, do as I ask. Sir Arthur Wellesley himself asked me for my best nurse. Your reputation has preceded you, and I cannot be made a fool."

"My reputation?" Elise was taken aback by the notion that she now had a reputation. Russell's exasperated expression confirmed it. "Fine. But I'll have to come back to shore to sleep here at night."

"You are to stay on the *Brazen* and tend your patient. I have lauded your excellent behavior and knowledge, to the point where your services were asked for as a personal favor for Wellesley himself. You would be supporting a special friend of General Dalrymple. Please, Mrs. Ferrington. Do not embarrass me. Do not make me a liar!"

"General who?"

"Sir Hew Dalrymple, General Dalrymple. He's preparing to take over this entire expedition. You must go," Russell pleaded. "I've promised Wellesley you'd help the general's friend and if you behave well and demonstrate your superior knowledge, it would reflect well upon me and might even lead to advancements in my career."

Elise's eyes narrowed. He hadn't mentioned if she would stand to gain anything in this deal, implying she should be swayed to be some wealthy invalid's personal nurse by the advantage it would bring to *his* career. "Do you think the general will let me call him Hew? Pewie Hewie?"

Russell glared.

"Fine. General Pimpled Dalrymple it is, then." Elise turned to leave. She'd go help the general's ailing friend for a few hours, she decided. The surgeon wasn't a bad kid, and why shouldn't she help him out before returning to Tucson? She'd sneak away during a quiet moment when her patient was sleeping. The nights were warm enough that she'd welcome a swim to shore.

She felt a sudden pang of guilt and swallowed hard, remembering how Mrs. Gillihan had helped her get dry the last time she'd been swimming. She'd wonder what had happened; she deserved an explanation for her disappearance.

This was not her time, Elise told herself. This was not her war. It was a blip, a kink in her timeline. None of them mattered, not Mrs. Gillihan, not Richard, not Collins, not even Thomas. She gathered her things and walked towards the beach where the cutter was waiting to take her to the ship, feeling like a traitor.

The trip to the *Brazen* was agonizingly slow. The sailor's oars went in and the little boat bucked over a wave. The oars pulled out. They went in again. The boat bucked. The oars came out. Thrust, pull, buck, thrust, pull, buck. Elise clenched the bench in her fists, fighting a wave of nausea. She pushed Quidico from her mind as her hips moved with the rhythm.

Her headache still throbbed. Elise opened the drawstring kitbag of herbs she carried everywhere and rummaged for willow bark. She suspected that chewing wood and getting splinters in her gums merely changed the focus of her pain, but it was better than nothing. She stared blurrily at a point on the horizon, waiting for it all to stop. The oarsmen continued pumping.

When the cutter finally drew up alongside the massive hull of the anchored *Brazen,* a chair was lowered down from the weather deck for her convenience. Ropes were attached to the chair at four points, but nothing prevented it from flipping backwards and dumping her out should the men above pull the ropes at different speeds. As soon as she was hauled into the air, she clung to the arms of the chair as desperately as she'd clung to the cutter's bench, thinking how much easier it would have been for her to just take the ladder. This, so men couldn't see up her skirt, she thought gloomily.

Elise was met on deck by a third mate, who shooed away an old, and distinctly odiferous sailor who carried a set of knitting needles. The third mate directed her to the chief steward, who introduced her to General Dalrymple's valet, who apologized for the inconvenience and thanked her for her time. Even though she'd met three people in the space of fifteen minutes, she'd only actually moved about ten feet closer to her patient.

"Just direct me to the general's friend," drawled Elise. "Also, I'll need boiled water, soap and towels."

The general's valet nodded. "Right away, madam. Will that be all?"

"Just one more thing: General Dalrymple said I should be given a bottle of his finest." Elise didn't specify a liquor, not wanting to limit the choices.

He narrowed his eyes, too polite to challenge her lie. "Yes, madam."

"Actually, two bottles. The general wanted me to have two bottles."

An attending sailor looked askance at the valet and was sent off with a nod and a flick of the hand. "Right this way," said the valet.

He led her aft of the mainmast towards the officers' cabins. Despite the quarterdeck being reserved for the more senior members of the crew and their guests, the rooms were still tiny, the doors to each cabin placed so closely together that it seemed there couldn't be space for anything inside. By the time they'd reached the general's cabin, Elise's headache throbbed painfully in her temples and burned behind her eyes. She had cheeked the willow bark pulp, but now she started chewing it again in desperation and pressed her eyes with the heels of her hands. The valet rapped sharply on a door. The sound was like a jackhammer.

"*Oui? Entrez-vous,*" came a high voice from the other side of the door.

"Mrs. Ferrington, are you well?" The valet looked at Elise in concern as she squeezed her skull between her palms. "Perhaps we should find another nurse?"

Elise took a bracing breath. She thought of the faith George Russell had placed in her. "No, it's okay. . . I mean, I'm well." She'd gotten this far; she'd see it through.

"Before I let you in, I need your solemn vow that you will not breathe a word to anyone that the general's friend is French."

Elise raised her eyebrow and nodded. "Not one word," the valet reiterated. The door opened slowly. "Miss?" he called into the room while demurely looking at the wall rather than the bed. "I've a nurse here to help you, miss."

From deep inside an adult-sized wooden cradle that swung by ropes from the rafters came a questioning grunt, "*Hien?*" Four fingers curled over the wall of the bed and the round face of a black haired woman floated to the top of a pile of blankets. She craned her neck away from her pillows to look at who had arrived at the door. Her brown eyes were clear and cunning, widened in shock at seeing Elise. "*Ciel!*" the patient exclaimed, suddenly sitting straight up. "*C'est vous!*" The bed swung violently from its ropes. "Eet eez YOU!"

Elise reeled backwards with what felt like a ten-piece mariachi band screaming behind her eyes. She gasped in fear and recognition. From the woman's head, two segmented antennae unfolded from underneath her hair as her brown eyes split into four, then eight, then split again and again until she blinked over compound orbs. It was the black beetle of her dreams, the one responsible for pulling her through time.

"Have you two met?" the valet asked, alarmed by the sudden and violent reaction of the two women.

The beetle composed herself immediately. "*Euhhh. . .*" she said, sucking in a breath, "eet eez you, zat 'as come to me for zee nursing, *non?*" She batted her insect eyelashes at Elise, which was very disconcerting, but the message was still clear: de-escalate the situation. Pretend everything is normal. It wouldn't do to have anyone know their history.

"Mademoiselle Bonnediseuse, may I present Mrs. Richard Ferrington. I'm sure the two of you will get along handsomely." The valet smiled. "Ah, and here's the hot water. Perfect timing."

The valet's assistant suddenly appeared with a bucket of water and two wine bottles tucked in each of his armpits. Elise snatched a bottle, pulled out the stopper and tipped it past her teeth.

"Ugh. What is this?" she gasped, nearly spitting out the cloying, woody liquid.

"The Dowager Whitefoord's award-winning elderberry wine. She's the general's great-aunt, I believe, and is well loved. The general finds it to be a reparative tonic." The corner of the valet's lips curled. "It's 'his best' although it may have turned a bit. It's been a long voyage for all of us."

Elise took another long pull of the vile wine. It burned slightly as it went down, and made the joints of her jaw ache with its acridity, but, inexplicably, it also soothed her head.

The valet bowed deep as he exited the room. "Enjoy," he drawled.

When the door shut, Elise looked at the black beetle with unrestrained wonder. "You're not really sick, are you, you big faker."

"Big fakaire?" Bonnediseuse's antennas waved with confusion.

"Liar. Not. Sick."

She blew a breath through pooched mandibles and rolled her shoulders in the enduring French gesture of, "if you say so," also interpreted to mean, "can't be helped," and "not my fault." She brought four legs over the side of the bed to push herself further up and turned her compound eyes on Elise.

Every bit of Elise was taken in by a kaleidoscope of pupils. She was reflected upside down on hundreds of retinas. Her own vision blackened around the periphery in a narrowing field of view. Elise backed away to the door and fumbled for the latch. "What do you want from me?" she demanded. The bug didn't answer. A shimmering thread between them grew ever more substantial, like a golden tether, as Elise's sight narrowed. She felt herself being pulled along by the thread—a familiar sensation. All doubt as to how she'd been pulled away from Tucson was now gone as the two of them floated in a dark space as substantial as a lucid dream.

You did this to me! Elise screamed. *Why!*

Hush, you're hurting my head with your angry cries.

Your head? What about my head? It's killing me!

Ah? Interesting. Perhaps you would feel better if you were to stop fighting our connection? I brought you forth because I needed your assistance. I suppose I should have known you would be alarmed to meet me, but I admit I am a little disappointed. I had hoped to be greeted as a mother.

What the hell are you talking about?

Can you not understand me? Her antenna circled in consternation, as if trying to find better reception. *I thought all persons in the between could understand each other. Perhaps it's something to do with being a golem?*

I understand that you are a bug. I understand that you dragged me away from my job and my friends. Send me back. Send me back to Tucson right this instant.

You see worshipers of the Goddess Isis as scarab beetles. Do not be frightened, it is a common vision for initiates. Concentrate a little harder and you will see me in my true form. She smiled as Elise squinted in concentration.

Slowly, Bonnediseuse's thorax returned to being a chest and shoulders rising above a demure black dress. Her antenna receded back into her black hair that fell loose around her round face. But her eyes were still large, like puddles of mud. *I'm waiting,* Elise said.

Waiting? Waiting for what?

Send me back!

I created you from nothing, so there's nothing to send you back to.

How dare you tell me I had nothing. I had everything: a great job, friends, a kick-ass apartment. I even had an IRA and my car was paid for. Now? Now I've got nothing. I mean, look at me! Look at my boots! I had to literally kill someone for these, and they're not even cute! And it's all because you pulled me off my timeline.

Adelaide frowned. *I don't understand. What is a car? What timeline?*

I'm from the future, stupid!

The sound of cackling laughter startled both of them. From deep in the void, a proud woman floated towards them. Her hair was wrapped in a colorful scarf, as was her waist. She held the hem of her red skirt to her waist and her underskirts tumbled over her legs like a waterfall.

Avó! exclaimed Elise. *What are you doing here?*

You've reneged on your promise to me, Elise Dubois.

No, I didn't! I was going to come later.

I don't believe you. You and Mademoiselle Lenormand are plotting against me.

Who? Elise looked in surprise at the woman in the bed. *I thought your name was Bonnediseuse?*

The woman gave another of those irritating Gaulish shrugs.

I was totally going to meet you, Avó. There's still plenty of time. We wait for the new moon, right? When does it come out?

Avó and Adelaide looked puzzled, and it slowly dawned on Elise why they'd be unable to answer her question.

Enough, Avó snaped. *Since you refuse to carry my great grandchild, I will take the emerald. You have not the strength to control it in any case.*

Adelaide gasped at the audacity of the Romani leader. *You would deprive all of womanhood for your own greed? The emerald is for all of us. It was never meant for one person alone. It must be returned to Mademoiselle DuBette so that our voices will one day be heard.*

Yes, DuBette told me of her plan. How absurd. You don't honestly believe she wishes to share one gemstone with all the women in the world? The cunning woman has you fooled. She will sell it and keep the money for herself.

She would never do that. The scarab is the key to the Thoth tablets.

The Thoth tablets are a myth created to justify the existence of divination cards.

Adelaide gasped at the affront and clutched at her chest.

There's no magic in cards, laughed Avó. *Any powers you may have, and I don't doubt that you have powers, lies within you. You might as well dump those cards you carry into the ocean. You've forgotten which items are props, and which are real.*

Mademoiselle DuBette told me that la Société has an ancient copy of the Thoth tablets. That emerald will unlock the alchemical formula and give economic power to womankind. We would finally have a voice, now, and for generations of women to come.

Avó spat derisively into the void below her feet. *Women already have power: the power to perpetuate humanity. The only power that scarab will give its possessor will come from its worth on the black market. You know it to be true, otherwise you wouldn't have given up your chase to become the general's mistress. What has the old man promised you, Lenormand? An apartment in London? How are your English lessons coming? Does he like your pretty accent and pet you like a lapdog when you speak? Nothing changes for us in the future—ask the golem, she will tell you there are still wars. There are still those that go hungry.* She gave a disgusted sniff and suddenly disappeared.

Elise and Adelaide stared in shock at the place where Avó had just been floating. *What did you mean by saying the scarab is the key?* Elise demanded.

Adelaide studied Elise thoughtfully. *Are there many golems like you in the future?* Before Elise could answer she brightened, *if you're from the future, perhaps you can give me hope? One of our sisters, was Olympe de Gouges. Have you heard her name? Does the world still speak of her?*

Never heard of her.

A sad look fell over Adelaide's face. *Tell me: are the voices of women equal to men's?*

As Elise weighed how to answer the question she felt dread slide over her like a shadow. *I think she's here.*

Who? Adelaide looked around. *I see no one. Senhora Ineriqué de Laroque is gone.*

Avó's here! Send me back to my body! Now!

Oh! You mean here, there. Why didn't you say so?

The second Elise dropped back to her body, she opened her eyes and slapped a hand over her breast where she kept the emerald. Avó was leaning in towards her through the open cabin door with eyes fixated on her cleavage.

"Hands off! It's mine!" Elise cried out, leaning back. "How did you get here?"

"What do you mean, how? I'm *una bruja*. Witches get things done."

"You flew?" Elise's eyes grew wide in wonder.

"No, *idiota*. Quidico rowed me here. He's tied up next to the ship where no one will see him and awaits our return." She pointed a rheumatoid finger at Elise. "You hurt him."

"Oh, please."

"You did, you heartless woman. He saw you leaving shore and came running to his Avó for solace. But you will do things to him to quickly make him forget. Eh? I've a feeling about you—you are not so innocent." Her eyes sparkled with meaning. "Enough talk. Let's go."

"I've changed my mind." Elise slowly backed out of the door.

"Then you do not want to return home?"

Elise's head was whirling with conflicting thoughts. None of it made any sense. "Of course I do."

"Then let us go now. There's no time to waste. Quidico awaits."

The woman cornered Elise in the narrow passageway and grabbed her upper arm with her claw-like hand. Back in the cabin, Adelaide was struggling to get out of her swinging bed and was dumped onto the floor.

"I need time to think," Elise said, twisting out of Avó's grip.

"Didn't I already tell you? Time is elusive. It doesn't exist in the way you think. It exists in circles, not lines."

"I don't know what that means," Elise said as she sidestepped down the passage. "You're just trying to confuse me. You're making things up. I don't believe you can send me into the future." She turned and ran out to the weather deck and straight to the rail.

The ocean reflected the late evening sky in dark grays and calming pale pinks. The regular rhythm of the surf rising and falling against the side of the ship's hull soothed. Time existed in the ocean, metronomic, eternal, and definitely not in circles. Elise gazed out towards the shoreline. It wasn't that far. She could make it, but did she want to? What if Avó was telling the truth? Her mind spun in confusion. There were no good choices. When nothing was normal, when nature refuses to work the way you expect it to, how do you decide which foot to put forward?

"*Attention*, Elise!"

Elise heard Adelaide's warning and whirled around just as Avó flung the contents of a glass vial at her. It splattered against her neck and chest and dripped onto her stomach. Without thinking, she touched the white viscous liquid. "Ugh. What *is* this?"

Avó tucked the vial back into a pouch at her waist and stretched her arms to the sky in prayer. "Goddess, I call upon you to bless this woman." Behind her, sailors began to turn towards the commotion, scratching their heads.

"Oh my God. Is this what I think it is?"

"Plant this fertile valley with the seeds of my family."

Elise felt sick. She tried to wipe the worst of it off her neck with the cuff of her sleeve.

Suddenly the old lady lunged. "Get off me!" screamed Elise, fighting to keep the woman's fingers from worming their way down her bodice towards the gemstone.

Adelaide rushed to help and grabbed a handful of Avó's hair. The old woman howled in pain, her back arching dangerously as Adelaide pulled her chignon towards the deck. Out flicked Avó's hand from deep inside Elise's cleavage, popping the emerald from Elise's breasts and into the air like a round shot from a cannon. Six eyes followed the jewel's trajectory into the sky, then six hands desperately reached for it over the rail.

Plouf

They stared at the exact place the emerald dropped into the ocean. After an initial silent pause to swallow the loss, the witches began speaking in a flurry of heated French. Although unable to understand the exact meaning of the conversation, Elise could interpret the general tone well enough, given the sharp gesticulations and unfriendly facial expressions. When Avó's hand cracked across Mademoiselle Lenormand's face, Elise decided she'd had enough.

Kersplash

The sudden silence was welcome relief from the high pitched noise coming from the fighting women. As the weight of her dive carried her towards the ocean floor, bubbles from her nose tickled her ears. Her eyes burned as she strained to see in the distance. The deeper she went, the more the pressure increased in her ears and lungs; the more the pressure increased, the less she wanted to swim. Just as she was about to turn around, she saw a green reflection.

She kicked and the ocean's floor came into view, strewn with rocks and seaweed in dizzyingly divergent forms. The emerald was here, somewhere underneath the mass of undulating flora. Elise slid her hand over a boulder and the mucilage of the plant-life left a silver shimmer on her palm.

Suddenly instinct pressed her to turn around. The ache in her lungs became an urgent howl in her mind. Faster. "God, help me swim faster," she thought. Her boots had filled with water, weighing her down. Frantically, she pulled them off. She broke the surface, gasping for air as she treaded water.

The loss of her boots hit her hard. As she circled her arms and kicked her legs to stay afloat, the waterlogged wool of her dress creaked uselessly. Her skirts tangled around her legs, frustrating her attempts to keep her head above water. Suddenly, Elise's garments enraged her, a symbol for all that she had endured—all the self-doubts and supplicant behaviors, the simpering, the slitty-eyed scheming, the shirking, everything. *Everything* was now due to the dress.

She tore off the apron and it got caught on a wave, becoming nearly indistinguishable from the ocean foam in the fading evening light. Next to go was an underskirt, set free with a violent kick. The dress sank straight to the ocean floor, and good riddance.

The corset was from the devil and had a tight grip. Elise tore at its ribbons and they knotted in her hands. She scraped at its bones and they left long red welts along her ribcage. Her chest flared red-hot against the indignity of the irritating garment. She twisted and pulled. She pushed and wiggled. Finally, she pulled her knife from its sheath and used it like a letter opener to slice her corset from top to bottom. It drifted away like a manta ray, trailing pink ribbons for its tail.

Her one comfortable garment—her only protection against the scratchy wool of her dress and the tight boning of the corset—was her chemise. Elise pulled that off last, and with a small pang, let the ocean pull it from her hands. No longer encapsulated, she stretched wide. Her breasts floated and bobbed independently from each other with the shifting waves.

Above her, Adelaide and Avó were still yelling. Elise looked up to see them pointing in her direction as sailors squinted down from the ship, looking for her bobbing head. A knotted rope was tossed from the rail and missed her by ten feet. Elise ignored it. Instead she dove back down, striving once again to retrieve the emerald.

Now free from the burden of her clothes, she moved with more skill, undulating at the waist, scooping water with her hands and kicking her feet. The ocean was growing darker as the sun fell further towards the horizon. The waves had caused her to move from her position directly over where she thought she'd seen the emerald, and disrobing worsened her orientation. The ship had moved as well, drifting on the current, so she couldn't use it to mark the position where the emerald had dropped. The area of ocean floor she needed to scan for a single, small gemstone was now much larger.

Her lungs burned. She kicked hard for life, for breath, and broke through to the surface again.

"There she is! No! There! THERE! She's right there!" screamed a voice. The women were speaking English now, trying to engage the sailors.

"What's she doing? Does she have it?"

"I cannot tell. Don't just stand there, man. *Do* something."

"Madam, please. . ." a masculine voice interjected.

"I'll send Quidico in his boat."

"No, wait! I think she has it!"

"Madam. . .madam, please stop pushing me."

"There! She's right there! Throw the rope again! Throw the rope!"

Elise filled her lungs again. She was about to dive when she saw a figure walking towards her from the beach. She released her breath and treaded water, squinting into the distance. It looked like whoever it was, was holding a white flag in one hand. A flag of truce?

It didn't matter. She didn't care. As she kicked up to dive under, a familiar sound cut across the water—a hiccupping cry, a kitten's mewling. A baby.

Elise's head whipped around to look at the shoreline once again, sputtering as a wave broke over her face. The man had gotten closer, now knee deep in the water, and was shadowed in pinks and grays from the setting sun. Even from her distance, she knew of only one person who could remain dignified even while kicking though the surf. For a moment she watched as he approached, until she realized it wasn't a flag he was waving, it was her corset.

Down she dove. As her search became frantic, the wailing baby echoed in her ears, causing a suffocating guilt. It wasn't just her underwear Thomas was carrying. That had to be Edwina tucked against his side.

She swam on instinct, the deepening evening increasing the murk and making it impossible to see the ocean floor clearly. Her heart sent her forward. Her body pulled her towards the gemstone and by some miracle she was able to make out a tiny gleam. She kicked hard, striving towards it as it winked at her teasingly. The tips of her fingers nearly grazed it, just three more inches, that's all she needed to touch it. Five more inches and she would be able to scoop it into her palm. She was eight inches too far away.

Too late. Her lungs strained, her instincts turned her around.

Back on the surface she pulled in a long breath and let it out again in an angry explosion of curses as she slapped at the water in frustration.

"Elise!" she heard Thomas's frantic call. Edwina's cries echoed his urgency.

"I'm busy!" She treaded water, torn and irritated. She wanted to make one more try, but it seemed useless. The emerald was just too deep, the tide was high, and night was coming on.

Thomas pushed further into the ocean and her heart tightened in fear for his safety. A large wave hit him in the chest and knocked him backwards. Spray haloed his head as he wildly wind-milled her corset and danced on one foot before finding his balance again.

Behind her, the *Brazen* had drifted even further away and was now at the end of her anchor rope. Avó and Adelaide had fallen into a defeated silence. Quidico had circled around to investigate his grandmother's screams and his little rowboat had been noticed by the sailors. He was now pretending his purpose, all along, was to trade his wares. A line of people all stood at the rail, squinting into the evening light as he offered up a rainbow of silk scarves and straw hats.

Elise dove one last time. Her eyes burned as she strained to see in the gloom. She could almost feel her pupils dilating as she fiercely willed them to take in more light, but it was futile. She could barely even see her hand as it reached towards the rocks below. Night was falling upon Portugal. The emerald was gone.

She swam towards the shore and, with the cresting of a wave, emerged from the ocean directly in front of Thomas. He greeted her with a choked syllable of surprise and joy, a throaty grunt that meant either, "you-fucking-idiot-you-scared-me-to-death" or "oh-thank-God-you're-alive."

"That's the sweetest thing anyone's ever said to me." Her smile twisted as the sincerity of his response made her throat ache and her eyes prick.

"I saw you diving off the ship. I thought. . ." He squeezed his eyes shut and crushed her against him in a one-armed embrace, tucking her head under his chin. His body was hot in comparison with the cool ocean water. She could have lingered longer against his chest, but he pushed her away to look into her eyes, stirring another kind of heat. Then, impulsively, he kissed her.

A large wave broke against them. "Watch out for the baby," Elise laughed as their kiss became a sputtering, wet mess. Elise tried to dry Edwina's howling face. "Why are you holding her? Is Amanda back with the company?"

Thomas's expression clouded. "The Collinses," he paused as he hunted for the right words. "They wanted you to have her in the event that they. . .They thought you were the best one for it. . ." he paused, looking into the baby's face with a mixture of wonder and sadness. "She's yours now. Yours and Richard's, that is." He readjusted Edwina in his left arm, bouncing her expertly to quiet her.

Another wave hit Elise's back and lifted her off her feet. She treaded water while trying to wrap her head around this news. She couldn't help but think of Avó's spell, cut short. "I can't take Edwina," she whispered.

"I'm so sorry," Thomas said awkwardly. "They say Amanda died peacefully. Collins will join her soon, I'm afraid. Death will take whomever he wants, good people and bad."

"I don't know anything about being a mother."

"Don't be daft. Of course you do. All women do." He cooed at Edwina's little pink face and his features softened, even as the baby screamed harder.

Elise sighed as she remembered Mademoiselle Lenormand's words about generations of women struggling to be heard. She didn't want to argue. She didn't have the strength for it anymore. "That's my corset."

Thomas seemed surprised that it was still balled in his hand. "Would you like it back?"

Her feet found the sandy bottom of the ocean and she stood. "No thanks."

Thomas's eyes grazed her body. "Venus rises," he whispered, letting the corset float away. He drew two fingers from the tip of Elise's chin and down her neck, stopping at her breasts and sending a shiver of electricity through every nerve. "What's this?"

"What's what?" Elise glanced down and gasped in surprise.

Like a charm suspended on a long necklace, the gossamer wings of an insect hung between her breasts, burned onto her flesh in angry, red lines. Imprinted on her sternum was the scarab's body. Hieroglyphs were clearly visible.

À Suivre

ABOUT THE AUTHOR

With a French father and a mother from New Orleans, Anne Gross's interest in the Napoleonic era was inevitable. Currently, she lives in San Francisco with her husband and beloved chihuahua, where she's working on the continued adventures of her recalcitrant heroine.

CPSIA information can be obtained
at www.ICGtesting.com
Printed in the USA
LVOW03s2135020418
572056LV00003B/11/P